Sex

AND THE

CYBORG GODDESS

by

Alexis Rafael

CONTENTS

ACKNOWLEDGMENTS

This novel would not have been possible without the guidance and inspiration of Siew Hwa Beh, Satene Cat, Eric Edson, Caroline Fitzgerald, Kristin Glover, Mary Halawani, Harriet Harvey, Estelle Kirsh, Navin Kumar, Reseda Mickey, Bobbi Owens, Rabbi Jonathan Omer-Man, Dr. Mikio Sankey, Nancy Spero and Lenore Weitzman. I am grateful to Michelle Lang, Shelley Powsner, Dr. John Schultheiss, and to Ann and Preston Browning of Wellspring House for the time and space to work. I thank the following individuals for their editorial suggestions: Miriam Cantor, Judy Card, Anita Frankel, Jill Ganon, Mollie Gregory, Amy Halpern, Allison Lewis, Marlene McCurtis, Mark Mars, Brooke Mason, Kathleen Meier, Deena Metzger, Cheryll Roberts, Norma Sepulveda, Sabrina Simmons, Julia Stein, Arlene Stone, Louise Wolfe, Terry Wolverton and Mary Yost.

For my sisters:
Jessica and Margaret, alive and safe;
Fareba and Nbila, alive in spirit.

PART ONE

Pillow Book of a Yale Co-Ed

CHAPTER ONE

Wolf's Bones

To hell with my day! I much prefer your night.
— Colette

A na Olivia Fried crossed the Yale courtyard, an old raccoon coat draped casually on one arm with the guitar over her shoulder. She was a far cry from being a scholarship student, but she wanted to look like product of elite prep schools she never attended. A bearded guy in a flannel shirt, loaded down with a satchel of books, glared at her as his sandals clip-clopped over the flagstones beyond a banner welcoming the "Guys & Dolls of '73." This guy probably thought she was part of a female invasion. After all, they'd never let female undergraduates into Yale before. She threw him a half-smile, making mental notes as a natural blonde young woman in a tan John Meyer jacket strolled by with a rattan basket of chrysanthemums, followed by an equally fashionable mother in pearls and a trench coat. Ana's long, black hair and her long, thin legs—in purple tights, to hide the scars—sailed past the backdrop of neo-Gothic, ivy-covered walls.

Anna Fried had been a nervous wreck throughout the application process to Yale. The odds against her even getting in were almost a hundred to one. But ever since she'd skipped eighth grade, she'd counted the months until she would apply to college. Forty-three months exactly. She had it all planned out. Cum laude in English and then a career at *The New York Review of Books,* where she'd meet either a famous author to nurture or someone rich enough to support her reinvention of herself.

She knew she had talent as a writer. She had long ago withdrawn into her van Gogh yellow room, where she lived in her canopied bed reading and writing in a froth. There was no need for her to huddle with the teenage girls in the parking lot, primping their bee-hive hairdos while waiting for the school buses to take them home through the deepening shadows of the late afternoon. She had already raced home on her bicycle, where the Bronte sisters awaited her. *Wuthering Heights* offered much deeper love than any she could find in a high school hop.

She read everything by Dostoevsky and Tolstoy, and identified with Anna Karenina. She also read Flaubert, Fitzgerald, Joyce and Colette. Hemingway was important: he didn't waste words. She flew on the wings of Shelley and Blake, and hoped someday to write as well as Plath without committing suicide. She hung Franz Kafka's portrait on her cork bulletin board, hoping for a change in her insipid teenage life on the scale of *Metamorphoses*.

She wanted to write as wildly as Kerouac, and was sure that she only lacked the life experiences to make that goal. Clacking away at a novel on her portable typewriter, sometimes till dawn, she managed to create a conflicted protagonist somewhat like herself. So far, this protagonist had only begun to hitchhike across America, but those 95 pages helped make her Editor-in-Chief of the Scarsdale High School literary magazine. If only her mother hadn't read the novel just when Ana had settled on a plot. Hiding the manuscript under the bed hadn't done her any good; her mother had discovered it while vacuuming. Madelyn Fried resented being an antagonist.

Ana had just come home from band practice, and stood in the vestibule with her piccolo case and her book bag. "It's insensitive stereotyping your mother," said Madelyn, slamming the door behind her. Ana was too shocked to take off her wet shoes. Her mother tossed dozens of pages of her novel across the living room's thick, yellow carpet, which matched her dyed blonde hair.

"You cannot describe me as a housewife twirling a paint brush. It's denigrating, it's one-dimensional," Madelyn shouted, an Abstract Expressionist brimming with outrage and self-pity. "You didn't even acknowledge the mother handing her daughter the torch of creativity. And, oh boy, the sacrifices you left out."

"But it's my book," Ana lamely protested, scrambling to pick up the pages.

"I want you to edit out all the negative parts," Madelyn said firmly. "If this were one of my paintings, I'd scrape that portrait right off the damned canvas and start over."

That's when Ana decided to work day and night—anything to get into someplace other than Sarah Lawrence, the small women's college only six miles away from Scarsdale, that town full of scars. She had to get away from her mother, and not just out of an urgent need for privacy and personal justice. She sensed the '60's would explode on a far bigger scale at someplace like Yale. It was time to be part of a bigger picture.

Ana raced ahead across the courtyard, trying to disassociate herself from her family. Her mother lugged a Samsonite suitcase while pulling Ana's six-year-old brother along the path. All Timmy wanted was to pet a poodle connected by leash to some professor's wife. As for her sister, Vickie was caught up in a world of her own.

"Vickie, come on, snap out of it," her father barked, spilling books out of one of several milk crates in front of the entranceway. Ana and Vickie sometimes thought of Marty Fried as a cross between a Doberman pinscher and a Chow. He tried his best to keep his attacks in courtrooms or on tennis courts. He was beginning to grow bald; he took out his handkerchief and mopped the sweat from the bald spot on top of his head.

Marty was disappointed that Ana had chosen Yale over a girls' school. The high school guidance counselor had recommended

Mt. Holyoke for Miss Fried, whom James McKay referred to as the Princess.

"Oh, you're a swell dog, Mr. McKay. You're OK," decreed Marty. He was worried that his daughter would be lost, intellectually, at an Ivy League School like Yale. He was also jealous; he had worked his way through City College, then N.Y.U. Law, by alternating semesters with full-time jobs at Rexall's, then at a chemical corporation. While he ruminated on his past, his wife had scraped the N.Y.U. sticker off the windshield of their BMW and replaced it with a new blue and white one from Yale.

"Hurry, cutie," Madelyn urged Timmy, while Vickie, fourteen, sulked in a shadowy corner of the courtyard outside Vanderbilt Hall. "First we gotta get rid of your sister's stuff. Then we're going to the bookstore to buy you a Yale tee-shirt," she said, ruffling his red hair and touching up her lipstick in a ceramic compact mirror. "Won't that be nice?"

Ana put down her coat and portable typewriter just inside the entranceway to her new dorm and straightened her miniskirt around her legs. Marty and Madelyn Fried had bought her the coat from a second-hand shop on the Lower East Side, driving all the way down from Westchester to teach her about her roots.

"I had my Bar Mitzvah on the next block," her father said.

Her mother had mixed feelings about being Jewish. Katz' Delicatessen with its intoxicating smell of pastrami was one thing, but life would be so much better as a goy. Before she met Marty Fried she had landed a job as a secretary to the editor of a budding new review, *Greenwich Village Arts*. Harrison Mandell had promised to publish one of her illustrations, but that was before he pressed her body against his office door, and would have taken it further if he hadn't been happily married. At a cocktail party in honor of *Greenwich Village Arts'* exclusive interview with the painter Robert Motherwell, Madelyn met the wife from Vassar, who was dressed in demure lilac silk. It was only a brief encounter, but long enough for Madelyn to assess where she stood as a woman and an artist.

After she was married herself, she did everything she could to push her husband into moving away from Brooklyn, as if that would legitimize her to the rarefied society of the art world, or at least give her the privacy to paint away from the constant judgment of their meddling relatives. She did win a prize or two for her watercolors on Cape Cod, but then came the baby—Ana Fried.

The shopkeeper had given her parents a substantial discount on the coat, leering at Ana. He raised his nicotine-stained fingers to pat her on the head, then furtively stroked her shiny black hair before busily cutting off the price tag. The raccoon coat had a few holes in it—after all, it was almost fifty years old. It looked extravagant enough—something out of *The Great Gatsby*. But it was nothing like the chocolate mink that Marty had surprised her mother with in the aftermath of one of their fights.

Timmy had to go to the bathroom and Marty trotted off with him.

"Ana, don't go frittering away your time," her mother said in the privacy of Ana's new dorm room. "Be sure you enroll in the courses that have the most interesting men."

"You mean the ones with money," Ana said wryly.

"Do you think *I* went to college?" Madelyn demanded. "I had to go to secretarial school. Don't get smart with me." Madelyn Fried believed that when Ana fell in love at Yale, this would be the turning point, not to mention her personal triumph. Almost everyone at Yale was rich and successful, and her daughter's marriage to a Yale man would compensate for Madelyn's sacrifices: all her driving around the suburbs in an endless loop, giving her daughter every after-school advantage. All those clothes she'd bought her thrown in a corner, while she herself had to make do with last years' stains and styles. And with four long years of tuition payment ahead of them, forget any more summer vacations in Europe.

She pulled Ana's collection of Russian novels out of a milk crate and hoisted them onto a shelf with an angry thwack. "And whatever you do, don't go losing your virginity. Save it for marriage. Otherwise, you might as well kill yourself."

Ana had been expecting a different speech from her mother. Something like how proud she was of Ana embarking on an Ivy League education. Ana looked out the leaded glass window in a dull rage. So why had her mother bothered to buy her half a dozen miniskirts and padded bras? To turn her into a more attractive commodity? Ana already wanted to give up, except that her mother had already started unpacking the Samsonsite luggage with gusto, stuffing the piles of underpants, stockings, tights and padded bras into the dresser. Ana bent down in front of her mother, awkwardly adjusting her mini-skirt, and slowly picked up one of the books on the floor.

"Don't act too smart. You'll never catch a man that way," said Madelyn, pulling back her blond hair with a rubber band, so that the roots showed. "And take off those awful purple tights. You could use a more flattering color."

Ana knew better than to talk back. She took them off, wadded them into a little ball and stood there, pulling her miniskirt around her long white legs. She was waiting for her mother to hand over the bright red ones.

No high school boy would have been caught dead dancing at a hop with a nerd like Ana, with those plain flat shoes and little white socks her mother made her wear. But her long, folksinger hair and tall, thin figure had to count for something, even if her breasts were on the small side. She'd been too bookish in high school to date, but she'd spent months reading articles on sexual freedom. And then there was the music, Bob Dylan crooning "Lay Lady Lay," while she dreamed of lying across his big bed. Any doubts about wanting, needing and pursuing sex had been vanquished by Aretha Franklin's "Respect".

As soon as you drive off this campus, I'm getting on the Pill, she swore to herself—just not out loud. The Pill was the new invention liberating women's lives across the country. Why not hers, too? Meanwhile, Ana could hear her sister pounding away on the piano downstairs practicing a Dvorak concerto, the weird melody of its *poco andante* echoing up the Vanderbilt stairwell. It was so embarrassing the way Vickie always tried to show off; Ana wished her parents could shut her up. Regardless, she made her way downstairs to say good-bye to her sister, carrying the guitar, its neck hitting the banister. Vickie didn't even look up, focusing on her fingerwork.

"Hey, Vick, I have a present for you," Ana stated nervously, holding out the guitar. "Here."

Vickie stopped playing. She took the guitar and gruffly turned it over. "What? Another hand-me-down?" she asked, dismissive of the worn-out frets. Ana looked at her sister, whose uncombed bangs half-covered her luminous eyes, which had drifted up to some sheet music—Yale pep tunes which had been abandoned on the music rack of the piano. Her figure wasn't so bad, thought Ana, assessing the hemmed-up tartan skirt and the somewhat faded red sweater. If it just weren't for her posture and her nose.

Ana tinkled a piano key, unsure what to say. She didn't want to sound patronizing. "Just be sure to write some terrific songs while I'm gone. OK?"

Vickie strummed a chord or two, testing out the guitar. She began to sing "Blowin' in the Wind." Ana joined in, though slightly out of tune. They might have gotten past the second chorus, but Madelyn had to round up Timmy and Vickie and pack them into the BMW. Marty kept the engine running through the perfunctory hugs good-bye, a *New York Times* draped over the steering wheel.

"Bye, Mom," called Ana gaily from the third floor window, ignoring the squabble which had already started in the car over how much time it would take to find the store where Timmy was going to get his Yale shirt. "Don't worry, I'll write!" But once the car turned the corner, she collapsed on the narrow bed, beset by terror and stifling tears. She set the alarm clock but it was impossible to sleep, even though she'd been up since dawn. They'd left her alone in such a prestigious place that she couldn't measure up. If she failed now, how could she face going home? What was the point of life if she couldn't finish her novel?

Ana wanted to make progress with Chapter Four, fleshing out her rebellious character and deleting whatever was overly sentimental, but she was also eager to make new friends—especially with men. While she was trying to decide which she wanted more, she sat picking at a tiny blackhead near the end of her nose, hunched over a compact mirror. Her mother had offered her a nose job, but what was wrong with being herself? She felt she had nothing to hide except this little blemish on her nose took so much of her attention that she hadn't finished unpacking her books, and her novel was at the bottom of the box.

Maybe the best thing about going away to college was escaping her mother's critical eye, always seeing the possibilities of Ana as someone else—another Princess Grace, a new Madame Curie, another Katharine Hepburn, Joan of Arc Fried and Miss America all rolled into one—if she only got a nose job. Maybe now she finally had a chance to free herself from all the distractions of her over-achieving high school life. She hoped she wouldn't be lumped together with the other 230 co-eds. She hoped she could make some friends.

As if by magic, Joyce Takahashi appeared on the threshold of the dorm room in a pink matched sweater set. Her petite, porcelain looks would probably be a heart-stopper to half the men on campus.

"Hello," said Joyce, smiling shyly, and twirling a strand of her pageboy. "Ana Fried, right? I guess we're roommates." Ana quickly hid the compact mirror under the blanket and bumbled up to make her hellos. It only took a minute to find out that Joyce was from the West Coast, and wanted to be a heart surgeon. Impressive!

Then there was Tammi Bradley, a tall redhead from Chicago who managed to pull her heavy trunk up to the third floor by herself.

"Hey, let us help you with that!" said Joyce. Tammi plunged onto the couch in the living room they would be sharing all year and kicked off her stiletto pumps.

"Gee, I just can't believe we're here! I mean, even in my wildest dreams, can you imagine it?" Tammi asked, full of high-strung enthusiasm.

"And this is just the beginning," Ana added boisterously. "I mean, with Sexual Liberation and…" she broke off, faltering, as Tammi looked up at her politely. No one seemed to want to be the first to ask if the others had already had sex.

Finally Joyce broke through the awkward silence. "You can get a free prescription for the Pill at University Health Services," she stated matter-of-factly. "No questions asked."

But they were brimming with questions for each other, and decided to probe further over a pizza. When it arrived they lunged into their dreams of love and marriage, with the Rolling Stones blaring in the background. They all planned to fall in love appropriately as soon as Tammi and Joyce had biochemistry down and Ana's first novel got published. Out of a thousand young men in each class—a number which Yale had sworn to uphold, despite the female incursion—there had to be a Mr. Right for a significant percentage of the co-eds.

"Of course, getting married is a given," said Tammi, and Joyce and Ana hastily agreed. Ana had already picked out her children's names—Jeremiah, Sarah and Catherine. And the color of the bridesmaids' dresses—either lavender or orchid, even if her mother preferred yellow.

"I'm all for lavender," said Joyce. They looked at each other self-consciously, wondering if they would one day be each other's bridesmaids. As for whom to marry, was it inappropriate to admit that money counted in such matters?

"Almost any ordinary Joe will do as long as he has an advanced degree and smokes a pipe," claimed Ana. She didn't want a lawyer like her dad, always looking for the logic of any given situation, usually to prove her wrong. Besides, her father practiced divorce and family law. That had to stack the deck against prospective suitors.

By the time the last slices of pizza disappeared, certain truths began to emerge. Joyce wasn't sure if she wanted a boyfriend or a husband if it would keep her from becoming a doctor. Ana didn't want to repeat her mother's mistakes. Tammi had already slept with her boyfriend, who couldn't move to New Haven to continue the relationship. All three needed birth control.

Howard (pre-law) and Silvio (pre-law) and Steve (pre-Supreme Court Justice) had been knocking on the door of Ana, Joyce and Tammi's freshman suite for almost an entire week since classes started. If only they would go away, thought Ana, already chickening out on losing her virginity. She felt so inadequate—she wouldn't know what to say or do. Instead she was hiding out in her monk-like cell and feverishly working on a chapter of her novel in which Kathy steals a motorcycle, escaping over the Rocky Mountains. That way, if she did get distracted, at least she would have made progress on something other than the research for some academic papers. Joyce was already ensconced in her bunk bed to a night of reading about cellular respiration, and someone had to answer the door.

"I'll get it," said Tammi, who didn't seem to mind being interrupted. Tammi recognized Howard from her "Introduction to 20th Century Poetry" class, which she was taking for fun to balance CHEM 125. He was very tall, though not athletic-looking enough to be a basketball player. Howard was pretty cool with his long Ringo Starr moustache, thought Ana, as the guys proceeded sheepishly into the room. As for Silvio, with his black, stringy hair and darting eyes, he seemed somewhat uncool in his tweed jacket, and

Steve looked like a drip, with his vacant grin like Buddy Willard's from *The Bell Jar*. She might as well start acting free sooner or later, Ana thought. And Joyce was an agreeable type, so it was easy for Tammi to convince both her roommates to step out for twenty minutes: the semester had barely begun.

"Oh! We love you, Howie!" squealed Tammi. He seemed a bit startled by her bubbliness. "Oh, Howard, you poor thing!," continued Tammi in her high IQ, high-pitched voice. "You don't understand romance, do you?"

Were they all supposed to kiss him to make him understand? Ana hesitated, having never been kissed, other than that one stage kiss in a high school play. But he laughed it off and drove the girls around the Old Campus in Steve's VW van through the teeming rain. A lost Afghan hound panted by their car dripping wet. He was wagging his tail so he must have been happy, the guys decided. "Oh! We are *all* so happy!" sighed Tammi, who had just discovered the art of combining White Russians and marijuana in the back seat of the van.

Ana took her first puff of marijuana. She had never actually smoked anything before, and it left her choking and gasping for air. But she had read about pot; she really wanted to be a hippie, and Silvio was so encouraging the way he was rubbing her shoulders. She marveled at the bright neon colors streaking by them on the rainy streets as they drove around the block. Listening to Howard and Tammi singing like frogs in springtime, she realized that life was not a course to be aced. It was not an extra-curricular activity.

Steve was worrying about the police when everybody decided that the word *bullshit* was only a fad. This was a big relief to Ana, who had been worrying about the use of language all evening. "Words like *asshole* or *bullshit* will no longer be big deals by next year," Howard affirmed. He filled his lungs with marijuana, held it for dramatic emphasis, and then exhaled. "Words like that don't horrify anybody anymore, really." He passed the joint to Joyce, who politely declined.

Ana wondered what was expected of her, then said, "Yeah, and I was gonna call my novel *Life's a Bitch!*" They broke into laughter. Joyce got out of the van to walk back and get in some studying, using the campus newspaper for an umbrella to keep her pageboy hairdo dry. Steve was so disgusted by the sweet stench of marijuana that he walked off in the opposite direction to thoroughly dissociate himself from everyone. There went one possibility for a relationship, but Ana didn't care if they never saw him again—he wasn't really hip enough.

Tammi threw her arms around Howard Birnbaum, because it was so adorable the way he stopped at two green lights by mistake. His thick, brown moustache gave her a glowing feeling, and he steered over to his off-campus house, and Tammi's high heels got full of water crossing the street, but it didn't matter, as long as they acted charming.

Tammi and Ana waltzed into the room, shivering in their mini-skirts. Chauncey Fitzhugh (pre-med) was on the bed asleep, covered with an army surplus blanket. His dark blond hair was tousled, one arm hung down from the blanket, rippling with muscles attained from varsity crew, and his face was stubbled but attractive. They woke him up with "Oh, Chauncey? Now we're going to kiss you!"

"What's this bullshit?" he said. "Watch out, I'm sleeping in the raw."

Tammi closed the door. "What are you doing?" stammered Ana, staggering backwards in embarrassment at Chauncey's naked body. She almost saw his penis. Tammi went ahead and helped Chauncey get dressed. The most important thing, Ana realized, was to try to act sophisticated and existential. Howard looked at his watch. It was extremely late, and he led everybody back to the van where Silvio was double-parked, listening to the news on local radio.

"You should have heard the body count," said Silvio. He was fervent about protesting the Vietnam war. He had just joined the Moratorium Committee to organize a demonstration at the university.

"Hey, let's not ruin the evening by rattling off statistics," said Howard. He and Silvio were going to stay in the van so one of them could butter Ana up while Tammi took Chauncey to the doughnut stand across the street, but Chauncey refused to budge in the pouring rain.

"Hey, Tammi, you're the only one with an umbrella. Go buy us a baker's dozen, will ya?" asked Silvio, putting his arm on her shoulder. Pushing him off with a defiant giggle, she opened a blue and white umbrella that looked positively patriotic against her wet, red hair, and scooted out of the van to cross the street.

"When Chauncey says *bullshit*, he doesn't mean it," insisted Ana, still fixed on how embarrassed she'd felt. "Right, Howard? He just says it not to betray his real self." She had just discovered the "real self" in her psychology text, and felt that this might be a good place to show it off.

Howard said, "I've roomed with Chauncey for over a year now, before this campus went co-ed. If he calls you a piece of shit, he means you're a piece of shit."

"Me or Tammi?" Ana fumed, overly sensitive and taking everything personally. Tammi crawled back into the back seat with a bag full of warm, sugary doughnuts. She tore off bits of doughnuts and tried feeding them to Chauncey in between nibbling his ears. When he brushed her off, she recited e.e. cummings: "i like to feel the spine of your body and its bones, and the trembling—firm—smoothness and which i will again and again and again kiss, i like kissing this and that of you, i like..."

"Poetry's bullshit!" scoffed Chauncey, smearing jelly doughnut on his moustache.

"Oh, you just don't understand," said Tammi, still trying to placate him. "Chauncey, we love you." Love? How could she love anyone she'd just met, thought Ana. But maybe Tammi was just saying that to sound cute.

"You girls want to go anywhere else?" demanded Howard. "We've been at it for over an hour, and I have a physics quiz tomorrow."

Silvio dropped them off at Vanderbilt Hall, and drove off to return Steve's van. Chauncey said goodbye and promised to return Tammi's umbrella. The girls left their soggy shoes in the co-ed bathroom, and Howard fell asleep in their living room. Ana and Tammi fell into their bunk beds, with Ana remembering to set the alarm clock. Like a firing squad, its seconds would explode one after the other, sending them to the doom of morning classes in which she might not excel. But for now, the important thing was to get some sleep, while Joyce continued reading biology for the rest of the night.

The phone rang early the next morning.

"Ana Fried?"

"Yes, this is she." Dammit. She had slept through her psychology class. Where was Tammi?

"This is Lawrence Stimpson, the treasurer of Wolf's Bones. I'm calling because—I don't know if I should mention this, uh—you probably know about our secret societies..."

"Is your secret society tapping me because of my good looks, or because word has gotten out that I'm fast?"

He laughed. "No, not at all! That is—We usually look for potential leaders of America."

"You mean like the assholes who are bombing Vietnam?" she retorted, thinking of what Silvio had been trying to tell them in the van.

There was a momentary pause. "Why don't you just come to our get-acquainted meeting this evening? Then we can decide if this is a good idea or not." She faltered: *They* would decide—together? In other words, *she* wouldn't decide, whether out of curiosity or not, whether to attend the meeting in the first place? She struggled with this logic, unable to come up with a fast enough rejoinder a second time.

Lawrence picked her up in his black sports car with the top down, his sad gray eyes offsetting the brutality of his square jaw. Compared to St. Paul's School, with its cross-country skiing, Yale thus far was somewhat boring. He figured that the three cases of Coors in the trunk of his sports car would perk up their first meeting. Ana looked attractive enough with her miniskirt and pearls; he wondered about the other girl, Gillian Carmichael, whom he'd sent Oates Pitzer to pick up and deliver to Wolf's Bones.

The room was full of medieval furniture and eager young men in jackets and ties. Ana recognized a Glenn Somebody from her seminar on *La Divina Commedia*. He gave her a watery grin.

They were taking off their shoes in preparation for a get-acquainted exercise. The first round of beers had been passed around the gargoyle-studded room, and now Glenn, who introduced himself as Glenn Cox III, started mentioning his great-grandfather, who was once the ambassador to Madrid, and the powerful connections this opportunity would afford them, until someone politely interrupted and suggested that this was going to be a non-verbal exercise and that everyone should hold hands. Oates was reaching out to her and Gillian when Ana suddenly leapt to her silk-stockinged feet, remembering something she'd read in an underground newspaper on a bus in Lower Manhattan.

"Secret societies are no more than breeding grounds for the C.I.A.!" she announced, grabbing her shoes and storming out of Wolf's Bones along with the only other woman, a diminutive blonde in beige.

Gillian Carmichael turned to Ana in the hallway. "Wow, that was gutsy!" she said, as they put their patent leather pumps back on. "You certainly know how to confront those guys! We should really discuss this—maybe over at the Elizabethan Club, over tea?"

But Ana brushed her off, striding past the gray stone statuary outside the building.

Inside, after a brief debate, Lawrence Stimpson was appointed the task of asking the co-eds if they had been offended by any introductory remarks. Ana was walking across the Old Campus in a light drizzle when he caught up with her.

"Just think how we're outnumbered, Larry! The whole situation could have deteriorated into a gang bang. I mean, with all that beer."

"You're paranoid, but cute," he declared. He had already apologized to Gillian—the blonde—and thought his work was done for the day. He looked Ana up and down. Would she like to go to the Friday Night Classics with him? To have a date—any date—spelled progress to her. If they hurried, they could catch a flick by François Truffaut in Linsly-Chittenden 101.

Ana was intensely moved by the indignities suffered on screen by Antoine Doinel, the poor, neglected French boy of *The 400 Blows*. His parents reminded her of her own, always fighting about their marriage, even if Marty and Madelyn Fried had a lot more money, enough to send her off to college. And her mother was just as cold and calculating as the one in Truffaut's film, bribing her to get more and more "A"s, telling her to wipe the smirk off her face. By the time Antoine was dragged off through the dark Parisian streets in a police van, Lawrence's arms were wrapped around her thin, quavering shoulders. She had completely forgotten herself. She was sobbing softly, losing herself in Lawrence's masterful hugs—hugs her mother could have given her when she was small, but didn't.

Lawrence continued to hug her as they walked out of the sweaty classroom-turned-cinematheque. In the shadows of the entryway to his dorm, she wiped her eyes, red and swollen from crying in hard contacts. She excused herself to use the bathroom, so she could take them out. Should she take off her silk stockings before meeting him back in his room, or wait?

"Can you still see?" he asked her as she felt her way towards his inner sanctum in the dim light. He had put on Joni Mitchell's new album. Fortunately for him, his roommates were out late.

"Well, nothing has sharp edges anymore. You don't look like such a Hawk," she said. "Just a WASP." She hoped he liked her wit.

She let him press her against his J. Press suit. On the dark red leather couch, he took off his jacket. She might as well surrender to *something*, she thought. She didn't want to have gotten on the Pill for *nothing*.

When he pulled off his undershirt, revealing an appendix scar, it looked like a millipede crawling in soft focus over his abdomen. It completely turned her off. Then she caught a glimpse of his purple, swollen penis, but she couldn't pull herself away in time. He had a brisk way of thrusting his penis in and out of her that wasn't what she imagined losing her virginity would be like, and when he thrust it in too deeply, it hurt.

"No, stop!" she cried. "Ow! Lawrence, no!" Despite her pleas, he wouldn't stop. His mechanical hammering got faster and faster. She closed her eyes and tried to listen to Joni—anything to avoid her own feelings, or his look of brute determination.

"Did you put in your diaphragm?" he whispered belatedly. There was already something squishy inside her.

"My diaphragm?" she asked.

"You silly goose," said Lawrence, already getting dressed. "Don't you know? Free birth control's part of the co-ed experience!"

She lay there, wondering whether he would be more hurt than relieved if he found out she was already on the Pill. The very first morning after being dropped off in New Haven, she'd visited University Health Services for her free prescription. But he probably thought she was waiting to get on the Pill just for someone like him. Lawrence somehow managed to look formal in his boxer shorts, his nakedness above the waist offset by a posture that beckoned from a comfortable future when he'd be meeting with heads of states. She gave him an enigmatic smile while he finished getting dressed, unwilling to admit how much he had hurt her. It seemed to take him forever to adjust his tie in the mirror. She felt cold and goose-pimply as he glanced back at her nakedness under the open window.

By the time she got dressed, she was angry. If she hadn't gotten on the Pill in time, she would probably already be pregnant. She would probably be getting an abortion or getting expelled and committing suicide before finishing her freshman year. Not that Lawrence cared.

The first time she took acid with Howard and Chauncey, she somehow let it slip out that she had made love to Lawrence, the secret society guy allegedly tapped by the CIA. Chauncey and Howard looked at each other, trying to determine whose turn was next; Larry and Chauncey had gone to prep school together. But Ana had started to cry, remembering her terrible experience with Lawrence. She felt that she had chosen poorly in her effort to be "liberated", on top of which her mother would label her a whore. If you agreed to take off your clothes, was it rape, or just bad sex? What if the Pill didn't work? Could Yale expel you if you got pregnant? She wasn't sure what the rules were. Where would you get an abortion if you needed one? For someone so smart, how come you didn't know the answers?

Besieged with shame and guilt, Ana held onto all six foot two of Howard, desperately sobbing. Howard was somewhat perturbed by this. He had been biding his time, and now he was consoling Ana instead of fucking her.

"There, there," he said, rubbing his fingers along her wet strands of dark hair. "You're only having a bad trip."

CHAPTER TWO

Dudes in the Good Life

If he went on pretending that nothing was amiss,
then even worse things might lie ahead.
— Murasaki Shikibu, *The Tale of Genji*

The communication groove was the really *significant* part of the new Yale, so nobody really had to go to classes. "Talking's cool; books are passé," stated Chauncey.

When she did go to class, Professor Gilroy would invariably call on her to explain a line of Dante's *Inferno*. He would look at her dumbfounded and tease, "Miss Fried, I had no idea that a young lady could sound so brilliant!" She resented being a guinea pig in the experiment of mixing women's bodies and brains. It was bad enough for her mother to have instructed her not to appear too intellectual or she would never find herself in a relationship.

Back in Vanderbilt Hall, Howard pulled out a little clay pipe. He filled it with hashish and lit it adroitly, passing it to Chauncey, who inhaled deeply. Chauncey passed it around the room to Silvio, Tammi and Ana. They observed the glow of the pipe, and sat around smoking it.

After two months, getting stoned was becoming routine. They justified it, quoting Rimbaud's "pleasure of escaping from modern suffering." Silvio Chiodoni pulled out a set of master keys that could take them through the maze of underground tunnels connecting the entire campus. "I have the keys to higher learning right here," he smirked. They all laughed hysterically in agreement. It was said that Silvio's dad was a locksmith with connections to the Mob. Any concept they could play with to avoid the inevitability of corporate success would do. Most of their dads worked for corporations, and they felt doomed.

Silvio's "Open Sesame!" echoed into the labyrinth beneath the campus. It was 4 AM when they made their way through the dark tunnels, their dulled minds turned to a Bunsen burner high. Chauncey and Tammi raced ahead, their footsteps and shrill cries echoing down the long dark tunnels while Ana and Silvio embraced under a warm blanket of underground steam. Then Ana did a series of demi-pliés and grand jetés to show off her figure.

"Hey, dudes, you made it!" Chauncey crowed when the others caught up to them. They shuddered in the dark, imposing tomb of Sterling Library. It was completely deserted. There were no guards in sight. Howard christened an eighteenth century globe with Chauncey's French champagne.

"It's the good life!" yelled Chauncey, chasing Ana down a row of study carrels.

Silvio kneeled on the floor, momentarily morose. "They're bombing Vietnam—how can we celebrate anything?" Tammi was busy making confetti out of some historical papers of John C. Calhoun.

"Why don't you knock it off, Tammi?" asked Silvio. "You think we brought you girls down here to destroy historical documents?"

"Everybody should know Calhoun was a racist pig: he once owned slaves. How could Yale ever dare to name a college after him?" she retorted, throwing the bright bits over Chauncey, Ana and Silvio, and crying, "Power to the People! Power to the People!" They watched the little bits of yellow, crumbly paper shooting up to the ceiling and falling on their hair in a light snowfall.

Chauncey jumped on top of a table and decreed, "We're no longer just Yalies. We're the Dudes in the Good Life!"

"Dudes in the Good Life?" smirked Howard.

But Chauncey insisted. "The rest is bullshit, man. This is the perfect nomenclature to describe our ascent to consciousness."

That was five minutes before he passed out, and had to be carried through the steam tunnels back to the couch in Ana and Tammi's dorm. He woke up snorting with laughter in time for breakfast, and Joyce could barely put up with her roommates' attitudes.

It seemed like it was all one big joke that they had forgotten about their studies, lying around wearing blue jeans with holes in them, with a boy in their room, while Joyce hurried to clasp her little pearl necklace, spray on some Shalimar and rush off to Molecular Biology. By now, Ana and Tammi felt there was absolutely no point in grooming oneself for the upper classes, since there was going to be a revolution. They might as well try to forget any residual guilt about class issues like the thousands of dollars it was costing their parents for an Ivy League degree.

"The simple fact is that most of the planet can be incinerated within less than a day..." Howard paused to inhale... "should the war get out of hand. If it doesn't happen over North Vietnam..."

"Where do you stand on the draft?" asked Silvio, thoughtfully fingering his light stubble.

"Well, I'm safe," said Howard. "But that's beside the point."

"I'm scared shitless, myself," said Chauncey. "My number is five, man. They could call me any time. I'd freak leaving college and everybody." But this was rhetorical: most students could get their doctors to write notes declaring them unfit for battle. They didn't even have to burn their draft cards.

Ana had taken to meeting Silvio alone in the late afternoons, after the classes that she attended intermittently, to discuss the Peace Movement. It was dreamy, she felt, holding hands through the steam tunnels, listening to Silvio's views on violent vs. non-violent protest. He told her about the students who had been clubbed and tear-gassed at the University of Wisconsin and in the burning barricades in Paris the previous year. At first she felt repulsion at his smoke-stained fingers, but then she let herself go. He was probably going to become a leader of SDS: Students for a Democratic Society. It sounded so dangerous and romantic, though safer by far than the Weather Underground, which believed in bombing the Establishment.

He turned to her in her favorite section of the dark tunnels under a blanket of steam and tweaked a lock of her black hair over her ear. "You know, Ana, just last year, SDS called for the liberation of women as a conscious part of our struggle," he said.

"Oh, really?" she asked with a bright, false smile. She had known about Women's Lib as far back as high school, even if they hadn't discussed it. Still, it was good of Silvio to make conciliatory gestures. Maybe they could talk about it upstairs. She gave him a little hug and played with his moustache.

It would be great to have a working class lover to spite her mother. Madelyn's ideas about sex, love and social class were embarrassingly reactionary. Not that Ana was in love, exactly. She was more in love with the idea of love. But after they started pulling off each other's clothes in her room, he criticized her petit-bourgeois date outfit and pale pink lipstick. She'd worn the Kelly green dress from Lord & Taylor's, silk stockings, patent leather pumps and her grandmother's pearls especially for disrobing for him. Now that they'd undressed, how could she answer that his tweed jacket looked worn-out and sleazy?

She muffled her hurt feelings against his hairy black chest. He sweated against her breasts until she was crying in confusion and need. Just when she was about to have an orgasm, he withdrew without ejaculating. She was on the Pill: what did it matter if he came inside her? But he was not a bad lay—definitely not a one-night stand. Maybe a two-night stand, she hoped, as he lay there smoking cigarette after cigarette, talking about the Cuban friends he'd met on the Venceremos Brigade.

He took her to the antiwar Moratorium on the New Haven Green. She'd made sure to wear hiking boots to the demonstration although the newness of the heavy expensive leather was chafing her ankles. Silvio looked so handsome in his red wool scarf, waving Mao's little red book in the air—and his breath smelled like Gauloises. She wished she had brought a camera to photograph him. He seemed to be in his element among the 15,000 demonstrators... even heroic, shouting "Solidarity!" together.

Then he let go of her hand. He had begun flirting with a braless girl gyrating on the Green in a see-through gypsy skirt. Ana figured she must be turning him off with her bourgeois clothes and make-up, but they had just finished making love that morning.

She braced herself for a cold brisk walk back to the dorms in her aching boots. He didn't even notice when she left: He was too busy defining brotherhood and oppression.

"What did you expect?" he asked later. "Monogamy?" She didn't want to admit how belittled she felt at becoming two-night stand material or how embarrassed she felt for being possessive. "What did you think of the demonstration, anyway?" he asked. She still couldn't talk. She nervously checked to see if her bangs were covering her forehead and adjusted her lipstick. Silvio lit another cigarette impatiently, then scornfully remarked, "You're just a fur coat and a fancy education your parents paid for, aren't you?"

He was too busy to wait for her to defend herself; he had to rush off to organize the next demonstration. One of the dining hall workers had been fired for protesting the speed-up of workers on campus by throwing a glass of juice at her supervisor—and sixty students were taking over the University Personnel Offices in Wright Hall to win back her job.

The students succeeded in achieving their political objective, but after a closed hearing, forty-five of them were suspended. One of them was Silvio Chiodoni. He used the rest of his tuition money on a new Harley-Davidson and set off for the open road. Her mother would have been happy that the possibility of this turning into a fling was over: Silvio no longer belonged to Yale.

The remaining Dudes in the Good Life continued to meet as if nothing had happened, sprawled out on the floor in Pierson College debating whether it was better to drop out and join the demonstration in Washington, or to get a degree as an organizational tactic. Ana wanted to interrupt their bull sessions to talk about the Women's Movement, which was the next big thing on the horizon—just as important as Vietnam, if not more so.

"You're so politically naive. Really, Ana," Howard complained.

Tammi shrugged her shoulders. She was pouring Kahlua into the coffee. "If you talk Women's Lib, you know they'll just call you a man-hater," she whispered to Ana. But this felt vaguely unfair. She had read a thing or two about consciousness-raising groups, where women sat around in a circle exchanging private views to overcome sexism. They weren't necessarily indicting men.

A consciousness group was forming somewhere on the other side of campus, and there was some sort of lecture series on sex over in Battell Chapel. Ever since that night with Lawrence, she didn't know how she felt. Which would be better for her future as a writer? A stable marriage that would allow her to focus, or free sex, without responsibilities? But talking about sex in a chapel seemed counterproductive. Maybe if she studied politics she could catch up with these other women, thought Ana, feeling too insecure about the issues to show up untutored to one of their meetings. She had to make some kind of progress, take some kind of stand, try something bold and important that no woman had ever done before, or she'd end up as just another secretary. So she signed up for a course in Poli Sci.

The problem with this class was, Jonathan (pre-Pulitzer Prize) sat in front of her. Jonathan Scholz had given her her first real orgasm as well as the clap. Instead of taking notes on Marx and Marcuse, she doodled the outline of Jonathan's Jewish Afro and his leather jacket, doing her best to stop herself from crying into her flimsy spiral notebook. Now that he wouldn't sleep with her any more, she had flip-flopped back from believing in one-night stands to wanting a relationship. Fortunately, the professor ignored her completely. He only called on male students. Perhaps it wasn't too late to drop the course.

She'd taken to chronicling her one-night stands in the margins of her notebook. She was proud of the variety of orgasms she had achieved. There was Jimmy Aikens, Class of '70, a soccer player and a gentleman, who brought her a box of chocolates and asked if he needed to use a condom. His finger had been enough to make her come. Elgar had a nice, sensitive cock, despite his spindly legs that turned her off somewhat. But when he sucked on her earlobe like a cat and entered her from behind, she roared with excitement. Afterwards, he played the viola.

Later that week was the pillow fight with Danny from Comparative Lit, feathers falling in slow motion like sad, cold snow over their naked bodies. She had goose bumps after she came: he threw his old army jacket over her torso and sucked at her clitoris to make her come a second time, then a third, calling, "Oh, Danny! Oh, Danny!", uncertain whether to ask him to stop or beseech him for more.

The mere fact that she could experience pleasure was one of the major achievements of her lifetime. She felt that this was so important, someone should be giving her an award as one of the first women to legitimize what it meant to be a sexual pioneer. Not just setting the stage, like Margaret Sanger through the promotion of birth control, but actually trying to live a life of sexual emancipation.

The theory was that women on the Pill could have one-night stands as easily as men. It was indeed a splendid theory, as long as she could keep it from her mother. It was her mother who had encouraged her to make Yale men her educational priority. Her mother should be proud of her for her ability to attract men.

Now that Silvio was gone and Howard and Chauncey were ignoring her, she gave a great sigh and pulled out the notebook to write. "Bill Grigsby, Tuesday. Senior class - future computer scientist. Massachusetts. Adjusts the condom over his bright pink cock the way he might adjust his tortoise shell eyeglasses after blowing his bright pink nose, determined to plod onwards when studying with a cold." It was just a one-night stand. Still, she remembered a strenuous orgasm.

There was Harold Slater, Scholar of the House. Stripped to his underwear for a one-hour study break with Ana, he methodically set himself to stroking her pubic hair as if she were a Persian cat. He seemed incapable of recognizing her clitoris, let alone rubbing it. Ana grabbed his hand and guided it into the right spot; he quickly returned to stroking her intently, although he couldn't succeed in making her purr. Who the hell was he to come all over her sheets, smiling with a smug little quiver of satisfaction?

Then there was Ed Talbot, Jr., who also hailed from Westchester County. She tugged at his long penis with a few hard jolts, as if pulling the cord on an electric lawn mower. Once he got it going, he seemed content to whir away at Ana's body and spit out her feelings like cut grass.

There was Juan Bocanegra, whose first and only prior experience was with a girl he met down in New Orleans when she jumped out of a giant cake. He'd been too drunk to remember the details, but with Ana he remained sober, determined to keep track of every detail from how many seconds it took to unhinge her bra to how many thrusts it took to get her to moan. "He wanted to devour me to the last crumb," she wrote.

Jerry McCall was a blue-eyed, blue-bearded thing with an acoustic guitar, a prelude to the pickaxe of the second act. Count Bluebeard with a black heart, picking the heartstrings of women to hang on his college wall like stereo speakers. And Ana and the others just kept writing and writing, pulling his beard into their bloody inkwells, their papers due the next morning. Life was not a fairy tale, and maybe grades counted.

In Comparative Lit, they were reading just enough of *The Tale of Genji* for Ana to start researching the women of the ancient Japanese court, who had taken notes on their sexual escapades a thousand years earlier. Sometimes they turned these notes into fiction, sometimes they turned them into "pillow books," diaries of musings and observations kept under their pillows. She could imagine herself ripping off layer after layer of pink, red, maroon and pale yellow silk along with the layers of centuries.

Surely what she was doing had some historical significance— she hadn't been sleeping around for nothing.

Maybe in a prior lifetime, Ana was Sei Shônagon, author of *The Pillow Book*, whose flotsam and jetsam of likes and dislikes inspired her loose-leaf ramblings, enabling her to run away from her immediate past. She thought of Shônagon's musings about the court as she evaluated the young men wallowing above the Yale courtyards. Some of them would be more interesting as raw material for spy thrillers than a chronicle of sexual experience, tucked under one's pillow. Greg Fischer hadn't taken much time in fucking her after an evening with the Russian Chorus. Was he practicing for a secret Cold War mission? Oates Pitzer's penis was short and rather stocky: just as inelegant as his behavior, mountain climbing up her breasts. Then there was Howard, whose moustache had tickled and smelled of her cunt for hours after cunnilingus, now huddled over a game of chess with Chauncey. Neither Dude was as good in bed as Jonathan Scholz, despite his giving her the clap, then dropping her. As soon as she had recovered from Jonathan, there was Behram Sinha, whose soulful eyes were an incantation to a glorious night of tantric sex in the back of a Volkswagen bus.

Behram was a sexual connoisseur, exploring every corner of her body with his black moustache and gentle, puppy-like tongue. He sighed in between each of her screams. He was patient. It was probably unfair to reduce him to a sex object in a pillow book.

Maybe it was wrong to compare the intrigues of the Imperial Palace and its men to the secret societies and trysts of Yale, especially from the eyes of a second-rate writer like Shônagon. When she researched ancient Japanese texts, she came across the papers of Chogen, a monk known for laying the foundations for perpetually reciting the name of Buddha. Surely Ana's research and chronicles wouldn't only result in lovers' scandals and despair. Yet, looking back at the pages she had written about Silvio, she recalled that her lips had been cracked from too much lipstick and too long a blow job. He seemed to have left her more muddled than enlightened. The important lesson was he left her.

Was it possible—could she even dare to imagine herself as Murasaki Shikibu, the greatest author of the Heian era? Ana was writing in fragments, just like Shikibu—"When we finally arrived, the moon was so bright that I was embarrassed to be seen and knew not where to hide." "My future rose up before me like a dream and I began to think unwanted thoughts…" —and she could describe one mixer after another, just like Shikibu's parties full of hot princes and princesses enjoying the koto music and poetry, with you-know-what delicately obscured in mist. "…I shall never forget the sight of them without their clothes." She could take it one step further, using Shikibu's diary as an opportunity for writing midrash, filling in the blanks with shards of her own, frank sexual expression.

Then there was the novel, all thousand-plus pages of *The Tale of Genji* by Shikibu. Agonizing about her series of lovers, Ana took to reading one hundred pages further into the book each time she slept with someone else. The extent of Ana's sexual exploits could never measure up to Prince Genji's, who seemed to have hidden beautiful courtesans in every corner of each of his palaces, each one of them drenching the corners of her kimono with more and more tears. Yet none of the men she'd slept with seemed half as heroic as the Shining Prince.

The Tale of Genji seemed to be lacking any structure, without any real suspense until the last chapter, well after the main protagonist had already died—not that Murasaki Shikibu had indicated how or when he died. And the ending was so abrupt, leaving it up in the air whether or not the girl who'd tried to drown herself would be dragged back to the general, or be left a nun, hidden away from the floating world. At least it had an ending. Her own novel had gotten stuck in Denver.

She closed Shikibu's book and stared at a floating world of neo-Gothic architecture. Its gargoyles leered back at her.

Yes, she could write a pillow book of her own, just as full of genitalia as the original Japanese concubines', and teeming with passionate poems. She could almost feel herself stifling in layer after layer of kimono like Ono no Komachi, languishing behind a curtain, unable to wait any longer for the perfect man, when any man would do, just as long as he was at the court.

She'd start with the "morning-after" poem which she'd written as a thank you note to Danny from Comparative Lit:

My purple-penised love!
My slow-gyration,
nation-of-snow-born love!

My oh yeah
bubble gum balled
yo-yo neo-love!

My kitchen garden
circumcision love!
My snap decision love!

When she got back to her own dorm room, she would illustrate it using brush-stroke calligraphy with gold ink on dark blue paper. Maybe later on she would add some abstract photos of male body parts, stamping the front cover with a red seal of menstrual blood. Her 20th century pillow book would surpass the sexual posturings of Henry Miller and his sexist gang. In a cloud of smoke, she congratulated herself on her chutzpah and eroticism, until a wave of nausea hit her, imagining her mother sitting at the desk in her dorm room, turning every page.

"Hey, Ana, are you detaching yourself from the group?" asked Howard, looking up from the chessboard in his living room in Pierson College.

"We're the Dudes in the Good Life, remember?" said Chauncey. Sensing a flicker of doubt on her face, he slowly rubbed her back. So she got even more stoned and agreed that everything was once more hilarious, although in between joints, she began to read Marx, which confused her.

Ana just figured if things didn't go well with one Yale lover, "Well, I can always screw another of the Thousand Male Leaders." Howard and Chauncey looked at each other, and agreed that this was wise.

CHAPTER THREE

Morning-After Poems

Burning in secret,
my feelings will consume me.
And how sad to think
that even the smoke of my fire
will end as an aimless cloud.
— Fujiwara no Shunzei (1171-1241)

When the Black Panther Strike came to Yale, the first to leave were the Dudes in the Good Life, eager for an excuse to carry on with their good lives away from the campus for the rest of spring semester. Chauncey Fitzhugh's parents sent him on a European tour to London, Paris and Berlin, and Tammi went snorkeling with Howard in Hawaii.

But Ana decided that if the university was going to blow up in smoke, she should see it with her own eyes through her brand-new Nikon camera. After trading in her old Canon for a Nikon, she had just enough Hanukah-Christmas money left to cover the balance and pay for some black and white film. She had already broken in her hiking boots. All of her cultural demi-gods and goddesses would be in New Haven for May Day: Susan Sontag, her favorite critic from *The New York Review of Books*; LeRoi Jones, who had changed his name to Amiri Baraka; the French playwright, Jean Genet; and Allen Ginsberg, who would probably bring his harmonium and lead the chanting. A million protesters were expected, and Ana was eager to be among them. Maybe she could even sell her photos.

The Green was already teeming with thousands of students and outside agitators along with the National Guard. The tension was palpable as Ana scanned the faces looking for the perfect shot. Her concentration was broken momentarily as a young Black Panther supporter handed her a pamphlet that read "All Power to the People!" She stuffed it into her camera bag and hurried through the maze of mostly white bodies towards the podium.

But before she could get any closer to the action, she bumped into an incredibly cool-looking white dude with fawn-colored, uncombed hair hanging almost down to his waist. He was carrying a scraggly backpack and a sleeping bag.

"Hi, um, I'm Octavio Bell. My friends and I are with the San Francisco Mime Troupe." He gestured at three more backpackers with sleeping bags. "We're looking for a crash pad—you know, just for tonight."

"Oh sure," Ana replied, trying her best to act casual, but thrilled to participate in anything so radical. It would have been even more hip, though, had they been black.

She took Octavio, Raymundo, Shiro and Maureen up to her room. Then she called home to tell her parents not to worry, but they were in Block Island. Her sister picked up the phone instead: Vickie was home recuperating from a nose job.

"Everybody's expecting the worst trouble, Vick—it's so exciting!" enthused Ana. "Nobody thinks the Panthers are going to get a fair trial!"

"Yeah, but isn't it, um, dangerous?" asked Vickie in a nasal voice. "You know Mom and Dad are gonna worry, aren't they?"

"Fuck them," chortled Ana, reveling in her right to free speech. "Those liberal clowns! They're just paranoid that commuters will be shot on the trains from Westchester County on their way through Harlem. Vickie, you should see the barricades and soup kitchens going up around here!"

"Oh yeah?" Vickie sighed. "How come?"

"I'm not clear what the racist charges are. But there's going to be a giant protest. It has something to do with this Black Panther dude, Bobby Seale."

"The Panthers. Didn't I read about them or something?"

"It's all over the news. Bobby Seale either killed a police informant, or else it has to do with why police are assassinating Panthers all over the country, I forget which," she replied breathlessly. "Anyway, the San Francisco Mime Troupe's crashing in my room for the demonstration. Isn't that incredible?"

"Wow," said Vickie, who sounded depressed. Ana could hear a soap opera playing in the background. "What's the San Francisco Mime Troupe, anyway?"

"You know, guerrilla theater," said Ana impatiently. "They invited me to see a street performance of 'The Independent Female.' I mean, they wander all over the world, giving people free bread, giving people food for thought and spreading the revolution. You'd really like the protest songs."

"Do you hear this funny beep over the phone?" her sister asked. Ana couldn't hear it. "I think we're being recorded."

"Hey, Vick! You ought to come up here and visit—it's so amazing! They've promised to let me join them if I drop out!"

"Cool! Listen, I gotta go," said Vickie, then hung up. It was just like Vickie to be jealous when something exciting happened to her sister.

Back in the room, Octavio and Shiro were opening up a bandanna full of peyote mushrooms, while Raymundo helped Maureen hang the collective's laundry over the windowsill. It was Ana's first time taking mushrooms, and the room began to melt.

The telephone was ringing like an avalanche. It was her sister Vick calling her back, this time from on top of a glacier, trying to tell Ana about some sleeping pills she'd taken. But Ana was too busy hugging Shiro to listen to her.

Shiro had just finished explaining the conspiracy charges that Bobby Seale faced in connection with the Democratic National Convention in Chicago, where five to ten thousand young people had been beaten and tear-gassed for protesting the war—an important fact of political history that Ana had somehow missed when dating Silvio.

"The Black Panther trial is only the tip of the iceberg," said Shiro, who was wearing such a cute tee-shirt, silk-screened with Chairman Mao.

"That's why it's so important not to riot," added Octavio. Then tear gas started pouring through the college courtyard up to the room. They put a wet towel under the door, but the tear gas was coming through anyway: Maureen was crying and wheezing with asthma. Shiro tried to protect her from the tear gas by covering her with his sleeping bag, but she couldn't breathe. She started beating at him with her fists. "Those pigs, those assholes," she struggled to say, "They're tear-gassing us for nothing!"

Ana was going blind behind her contact lenses. She took them out, dropping them on the carpet in her frenzy to escape the pain in her eyes. Someone had called the New Haven Police Department on the phone. "What the fuck is going on here?" demanded Octavio, who seemed to be the leader. "We were minding our own business in the privacy of our own room. Now we are being tear-gassed? Why are you doing this to us?"

Ana went out looking for rioting crowds to photograph, but she couldn't find any. All she could see were students flailing around on the floor of the college cafeteria. Her eyes were burning too much to take pictures, and she was clutching her throat. One of the students got up from the floor and took her to the People's First Aid Station. Out on the Old Campus, student activists and Panthers were serving thousands of demonstrators salad and brown rice, in between the music and the chanting. She was filled with hope as she took her 35mm Nikon out of the case and started shooting.

The next morning's newspapers were full of lies. They reported how the college administration, together with the National Guard and the local police, had done an outstanding job at keeping the peace. What an injustice. The whole thing was so disillusioning, especially for someone who now fervently believed a new generation was radicalizing America. She felt she needed to talk to someone about it. But Vickie wasn't answering the phone.

There was one black student in her photography class: Diane Campbell, medium tall—the same height as her sister—with a short Afro, an Irish fisherman's sweater, and eyes that seemed to melt right through you. Diane had already packed up her Minolta and lenses and was off to a meeting of the BSAY.

"Right on," chirped Ana, trying to tag along. "Does 'BSAY' mean 'Black Student Alliance' or 'Black Students At Yale'?"

"It means that I'm about fifteen minutes late." She buttoned her sweater over her linen beige skirt.

Ana sympathized. She knew all about lateness. "Oh, yeah," Ana said blithely. "You mean like Island Time?"

"C.U.N.C.R.," quipped Diane, refusing to feel devalued.

"What does that mean?" asked Ana.

"See You In..."

"Consciousness-raising!" finished Ana. "Right on!"

"Do you even know what I'm talking about?"

Ana smiled bleakly.

"You don't even know about the rally? A whole group of us are organizing to take over the Student Union."

"Oh! Why?" asked Ana.

"More women in the curriculum, women professors, career counseling, campus day care. We need to demand full co-education."

"Like, no more token women?"

"You should join us. Women and Men for a Better Yale, the Sisterhood... Haven't you heard of any of these groups? The Sisterhood would probably do you a world of good."

"Yeah, Sister! Right on!" said Ana. But Diane just looked her up and down and left.

Ana refused to give up. The next time she saw Diane, she tried another approach.

"You're minoring in anthro, right?" asked Ana.

"Who told you?"

"I read this really neat book, *The Pale Fox*?" said Ana. "It's all about Dogon initiation rites of West Africa. Like, *giri so* means the word at face value, and *bolo so* means the word from behind, and um, there are like four stages of initiation altogether, and initiation means *sacrifice*."

"'The Pale *What?*'" said Diane.

Ana was rather breathless. "And, and all these different ways of exploring meaning for these people, they just mean for the *men*, and, um, the women surely have their own initiation rites, only the anthropologists only interviewed men, those sexist motherfuckers."

"What?" said Diane, mildly.

"I was just thinking, you know, about the sacrifices that the Black Panthers were making, and..."

"This isn't where my head is at," said Diane. "I minor in paleontology, I major in economics, and I don't concern myself about the Panthers." She smoothed her hands over her linen skirt.

"Well, I just thought," said Ana, unable to acknowledge anything other than her own thoughts, "that the Panthers have done so much to reinvent politics—you know, holding the pigs accountable and all that. And as women, we can learn from that, especially in our right to reinvent love."

"Reinventing love?" asked Diane. "Reinventing *love*? You're asking us to join a group of *love* inventors? Just find me a boyfriend I can stand behind on this campus. Don't give me your pseudo-anthro sexual initiation rap." But even if Ana felt subject to attackability, even if Diane insisted on her right to be a moderate, at least one cloud had lifted: they were talking.

Ana was halfway across campus on her way to attend her first consciousness-raising session in Davenport College, when she realized she'd forgotten to take the Pill that morning, and had left the container of pills back in Vanderbilt. She ran breathlessly back to her suite, only to realize she'd been carrying the little round plastic container in her purse all along.

By the time she arrived at the meeting, bangs glued to her forehead with sweat, she was twenty minutes late. She took off her pink wool scarf and her raccoon coat, apologizing profusely. What she really meant with "I'm sorry, I'm so sorry," had nothing to do with being late. Ever since May Day, she was sorry to have been born white, for belonging to the upper middle class, for screwing around with the wrong people, and for choosing to attend an elitist institution like Yale, where demonstrations didn't go far enough and where none of the students had been shot dead that week by the National Guard like at Kent State. She was sorry that she was so behind in understanding how to connect the dots between any of this, and hopeful that the young women sitting cross-legged on the carpet could provide some answers.

Introductions having already been made without her, she didn't have the courage to say any of this. She recognized Tammi, Joyce and Diane with her short Afro among the dozen young women. They were already passing around a hat, putting in little slips of paper scrawled with their names to determine who would lead that evening's session.

"One Thousand Male Leaders be damned," one of them was saying as she passed the hat to the next young woman.

"The administration is fucked. Five hundred male leaders and five hundred female leaders would be more like it, instead of a few token co-eds in each dorm," said Tammi.

"This isn't a policy session," said Diane. "It's our time for consciousness-raising."

The name of Jennifer Grinnan, an American Studies major with a blonde pixie cut and a great tan, was chosen out of the hat. A hush descended on the group as Jennifer assumed a serious expression, spelling out the rules for C.R.: everyone participates, keep it personal, confidentiality, no interruptions, no attacks. The group agreed on the topics for their first month: career expectations, sex, and issues of self-esteem.

Diane Campbell nodded a greeting to Ana, who came in from her tentative perch in the doorway and took a place in the circle of women on the floor. "We've bought into the idea that we have to be the men our mothers wanted," began Diane.

"Or the men our mothers wanted us to marry," broke in Tammi.

"My mother worked fifteen, sixteen hours a day cooking and ironing clothes for the rich folks in Memphis to supplement my financial aid at this high-class school up North," Diane said. "She's been wanting me to get an MBA since I was ten."

"Is that what you really want to do?" asked Joyce, softly.

"To run a bank?" scoffed Diane. "Hell, no. I want to make movies."

"Me too!" yelled Ana, and clapped her hand over her mouth.

"Are we talking about career goals, here, or sex, or what?"

"Why don't we just combine the two topics and deal with sleeping one's way to the top?" cracked Sue Hinton, a stout girl from Cincinnati. The women groaned—surely with a Yale degree, a woman wouldn't need to do that.

Tammi cleared her throat and volunteered the first story. She seemed much more serious in a room full of women than she had been in the pizza parlor with two roommates. "My parents threatened to disown me the day I lost my virginity," Tammi began. "They're staunch Catholics who love their church. You know, big family reunions every year in Deer Park? At least that's how it appears," she added dryly. "When I was in junior high, I met Jefferson Goodlett. We were in the same math class. After awhile we started doing homework together in the gazebo beyond our rhododendron bushes. My parents were always busy playing golf at the country club or taking the boat out on Lake Michigan.

"One afternoon, we had just finished trigonometry. We got carried away inside during a thunderstorm. I don't know, before we knew it, we were into orgasms instead of trig." Tammi blushed under her freckles and her long red hair.

The word "orgasm" brought murmurs all around. "Did you come, too?" someone asked.

"At my first sexual experience?" There were several sympathetic laughs, including Ana's.

"We didn't hear my parents coming home early. I guess they got rained out," continued Tammi. "We pulled apart really fast, and I tried to hide Jefferson in the closet. But my father had already heard us, and when he opened the closet door, there was this teenage boy standing there, stark naked—and he was black. You should have seen my father's reaction.

"We were too young to drop out of school and get married. My parents helped me get my first abortion despite their religious beliefs. They told me they wouldn't disown me if I came here," finished Tammi. She gestured at the dorm room full of women, adding softly, "I'm glad we're among friends."

Ana was still reluctant to share her fragile sense of sexual liberation with the group, let alone her embryonic thoughts about race, wealth and politics. Everyone seemed sympathetic to Tammi's interracial story, unless they were being polite. But what if Ana was the only one among them who believed in free love?

"It's harder for women to make friends here, let alone keep them," said Joyce. "There's so much pressure to study, or to find Mr. Right."

"What if you're studying sociology, and Mr. Right turns out to be a myth?" Sue scoffed good-naturedly. "It's even harder if you're looking for a woman to love," she added. The room grew silent.

Were they talking about eradicating the male power structure? Or about sex and marriage? Ana remembered her mother's words about sex on her first day at Yale—the ridiculous double message about virginity, wrapped in a half dozen mini-skirts. It was so annoyingly ludicrous to expect anyone in the room to understand how out-of-date her mother was. What other mother would ever tell a daughter to commit suicide over a hymen? All she could do was to burst into laughter.

"I'm sorry," she said, "but I have to leave a little early." She threw her pink wool scarf over the shoulder of her raccoon coat, and walked out.

Her feelings festering inside her, she began to take her writing more seriously. She took out her pillow book every night to write another poem, until the notebook was half full. She even experimented with traditional calligraphy, turning the best of the poems into short scrolls of rice paper. Hoping to find someone who would acknowledge her efforts, she tucked a few of them into her backpack and took them to her creative writing seminar headed by Tod Mulholland. His fifth book had just won the Pulitzer, and he was rumored to be the upcoming judge for the Yale Younger Poets series. He looked her over as she approached the lectern. She was wearing an Army surplus khaki shirt which hid most of her figure. His blue eyes glared with impatience above his lion's mane of a beard. With trembling hands, she proceeded to read the poem she had written for Silvio the morning after he'd left for Chicago, in order not to feel so abandoned:

SLIDING UNDER SILVIO

Already my body feels heavier
by the ton
like a boat crossing the Indiana line
laden with ore
and your penis,
so metallic when we make love,
and your lips,
molten like steel

and your will as invincible,
as I sink
under your love.

She held it up high for everyone to see. The letters of the poem were painted in India ink over a silver-plated city skyline. But nobody had any comments. The room was full of empty stares.

The hip bard spoke. "Women poets are great. I love them—in bed." The class responded in an uproar of adoration—the guys hooting, the small handful of girls giggling or silent. Ana glanced nervously at the poet, whose turquoise-studded silver belt held up his faded jeans.

"Don't expect much from your writing," he said casually. But she had already begun to abandon whatever remained of her literary aspirations, unable to recognize herself in the all-male pantheon of poets: Shelley, Blake, Yeats, Wordsworth and Donne.

He grabbed another one of her hand-painted poems. With a casual wave of his hand, he took out a cigarette lighter. Its silver plating gleamed for a moment; then the flimsy paper burned in front of the entire class. Ana tried to smile, as if it were a joke, ready to run back to her freshman suite to incinerate the rest of them herself. Pretty soon it was reduced to a few specks of ash, which faltered in the open doorway as the students left the classroom, then flew out to mix with the rest of the soot high above the New Haven Green.

CHAPTER FOUR

A Portrait of the Artist as a Young Woman

Instead of taking up her existence, she contemplates in the clouds the pure Idea of her destiny; instead of acting, she sets up her own image in the realm of the imagination; that is, instead of reasoning, she dreams.

— Simone de Beauvoir, *The Second Sex*

Instead of torching the rest of her writing, she had buried it at the back of the closet under a collection of old sneakers. She didn't write another thing for the rest of freshman year other than academic papers that had nothing to do with Heian literature. Fed up with roommates, she holed herself up in a single room in Ezra Stiles and brooded. The next fall, she made a half-hearted attempt to rejoin the consciousness-raising group, hoping that the women would rally around her, but instead they seemed to resent her barging into an intimate discussion of an all-campus women's conference that she had somehow missed. Jennifer, Joyce, Tammi and Diane had all become serious students, leaving Ana floating in their wake.

By the middle of her sophomore year, she was thirsting to create something that would validate her. But she had flitted into art history as a major instead of art, poetry or fiction. It was more expedient to look at paintings for a degree. Professor Everett P. Landau rubbed his hands briskly as if he'd just gotten off a ski lift, his eyes feverish with enthusiasm. He handed out his syllabus and bibliography with a yellow-toothed smile and a few cursory remarks which elicited smug yawns from the class, along with toadying smiles. Then he proceeded to lecture on modern sculptors.

"Giacometti: tender in his treatment of the human body. The feminine becomes worked upon by some outward force, passive and pathetic," she wrote dutifully into her notebook. Brancusi, Picasso, Lipchitz, Gabo—the names of all these men sped by so fast, there wasn't any time to question them, but Ana had merely detached, writing next to "Giacometti" in French, "*Je regrette. Je regrette toute ma folie.*"

She began to doodle on the back of the syllabus. It might be interesting to make 16 millimeter film loops of the sculptures to project in class instead of slides, to honor their three-dimensionality. Not that Landau would be interested in a woman's idea. The only woman artist his syllabus even mentioned was Georgia O'Keeffe, whom he had described as "a real bitch" when introducing the course, as in: "Stieglitz had a wife who was a painter—a real bitch." Was nobody else going to complain? There had to be a few more women artists renowned enough for a survey course called "Twentieth Century Art." They couldn't all be as mean as Georgia O'Keeffe, or amateurs.

She confronted him after class, but he rebuffed her, saying with a smirk, "If you find any, let me know."

She dutifully looked for any other female names in the history of art that she could find. (Was Camille Corot a woman or a man?) There were several articles on Helen Frankenthaler, the Abstract Expressionist whose style her mother had been trying to emulate. What particularly impressed her in the interviews with Frankenthaler was her absolute priority of art-making over any friendships or relationships. No one could interrupt Frankenthaler in her studio, period. But then, Frankenthaler had never had children. According to the painter, a traditional husband and family took up too much time and space. She gave it all to her color field canvases, stained with paint mixed with turpentine.

Ana turned to the collection of rare, original photographs of Georgia O'Keeffe that had been taken by Alfred Stieglitz, the husband whom she had left in order to paint in the desert. Yale's Beinecke Library owned the entire collection, each one covered by its own layer of acid-free archival paper like a holy veil. Ana stared at one photograph in particular: the gray, angular face held Ana in thrall in a steady mocking gaze. She traced the outline of Georgia O'Keeffe's famous face with her finger when the guard wasn't looking. The husband and wife must have been thinking of each other—Alfred through his viewfinder, fighting her perhaps with the defiance of his half-closed eyes; Georgia from beyond the two-dimensional frame, seeking recognition as a woman beyond the power of her art. At closing time, Ana relinquished the boxes of black and white photographs, thinking, "With the right man, I could match her."

She peered out the door of Sterling Library at the cold dark night. She wished some gentleman would hold the door open for her or keep her from the uncertainty of walking alone. She braced herself for the short walk back to Ezra Stiles, entering the black oblivion of night as if sliding into an ancient Greek vase painted with satyrs struggling with a nymph. She needed someone who appreciated art. Someone who could support her in her art-making. And with that man, she might no longer feel so lost. She might feel that she actually belonged.

She realized then how tired she was. But on the next block she bumped into someone from SDS. Silvio had introduced them before he got suspended. Don? Dan? He was some kind of community activist, although she couldn't remember his name. He was certainly no Silvio, although his beard was rather intriguing.

"Will you picket with us in an hour?"

"Why?"

"Don't you know the dining hall workers are striking again? Yalies are so goddamn apathetic!" he cried in exasperation, walking hurriedly away from her.

Ana let out a big sigh. She would have liked to get more involved with something if he hadn't rushed off. But papers were due, and taking any more time off for politics or art just seemed irresponsible.

No sooner had she closed the door to her room than someone named Dan called, asking if she would volunteer to help make banners and signs. He said they needed someone with artistic skills. They were getting ready for a big weekend in Washington. She really couldn't be bothered at the moment: she was twelve pages behind on her term paper on the Parthenon and teetering on the edge of depression. But Ancient Greek art was boring and keeping her from the future. There were only a dozen pages between her and another adventure. Marching on Washington might be fun.

Three hours later she rushed breathlessly to the bus in her hiking boots, just as it was about to pull away from the curb. The driver motioned her on board: protesters filled every seat in the front. She recognized Dan, Silvio's friend. He was wearing a leather jacket, and didn't look half bad.

"Am I too late?"

"Yeah, we finished all the banners. Where were you?"

"I'm so sorry. I had a really important paper."

"More important than ending the war?"

She retreated up the aisle to sit in the back of the bus and nurse her wounded feelings. Everyone else talked and sang "Turn! Turn! Turn!": their voices grated on her nerves. She allowed herself to fall asleep, exhausted from an all-nighter with a dead civilization.

But once in Washington, D.C., she joined the throng of a half-million protesters, chanting as loudly as she could muster. She marched for over a mile before treating herself to some lemonade and a tab of acid. Then she danced about a reflection pool in a gauzy skirt, her small breasts bouncing above the water in a see-through blouse, while several others from her bus were beaten, gassed and arrested for crossing police barriers with the banners and the signs.

By her junior year, the safest, most effective way for her to deal with art was by initiating a course on the sociology of women artists. It was a field of study that had previously never existed, but which Dean Stocker of the School of Art conceded might have experimental value. The dean arranged an individual tutorial for her, since she couldn't find anyone else interested in a course in women artists. Max Aaronson, a tenured professor whom she had never met, would teach it in name, while a young, untenured sociology instructor named Phyllis Weinberg would do the work.

Meeting a woman instructor for the first time was a letdown. None of her other professors were female; she had expected someone exceptionally brilliant. Phyllis Weinberg was so young and soft-spoken, how could her ideas be of any possible significance? And her shirtwaist dress looked so middle-class.

"I'm really excited about this course, so let's get organized," Phyllis Weinberg said, assessing Ana, who seemed a bit restless. "Don't feel that you're the only feminist in the world challenging the art world," she continued. "We have to resist letting Yale Syndrome dominate our thinking on such matters. For example, the West Coast women artists have proposed an Affirmative Action plan of establishing hiring quotas in Studio Art at UCLA, Davis, Irvine and Berkeley. And they want women's art hung in every show. You can research that, can't you?" she asked gently, but in a nasal, high-pitched voice. "You might want to contrast that to the situation at Cal Arts, where there's already a Feminist Art Program in place."

That was all the way in California. Hitchhiking there might be fun, but then why not drop out like Silvio, if she was going to hit the road? She slept through her second scheduled tutorial locked in the muscular arms of Bruce Duff, a long-haired freshman.

"Mrs. Weinberg is too mousy to be a good teacher," she explained to Bruce, who grunted, putting his arm around her again as she turned off the alarm.

Phyllis Weinberg was gently persistent. She called Ana half an hour after the class should have begun.

"Who? Oh, Mrs. Weinberg!" Ana exclaimed, pulling herself away from Bruce to untangle the telephone cord. "Oh yeah, I just finished underlining half of *The Second Sex*!"

"It's *Ms.* Weinberg. Ana, can we make up this class next Monday at 4 PM?"

"Oh, sure. Thanks!" said Ana.

"Bring a three-page outline of your paper: a summary of the reading in *The Second Sex* and how it applies to your hypothesis, a list of women artists you're planning to interview, and a final section on managing the feminine role," said Ms. Weinberg. "Don't forget to include your own view of how you envision the future of women in the arts."

"Let me get a pencil. I'm feeling overwhelmed," said Ana. She reached over Bruce's body for the desk, wondering where she was going to find any women artists to interview. And what did Weinberg mean, "managing the feminine role"?

"Since you missed today," Ms. Weinberg continued gently, "I want you to write up some of the recent changes in women's relationship to work in general, in comparison to women artists in a male art world."

"Excuse me?" She put her hand over the receiver. "It's too much work," she muttered to Bruce, who was much more interested in her legs than her brain.

"What a bitch!" said Bruce, and rolled over.

"Some of this you can do from personal observations. Just jot them down in your diary," said Ms. Weinberg. "The rest will have to be researched over the weekend: women artists' access to galleries, museums, reviews, monographs, retrospectives... You know, that kind of thing. See you Monday."

Ana hung up in a daze. A diary? After what had happened with her pillow book, she had sworn to stop writing anything personal—forever.

Ana descended the stairs to her residential college dining hall for a late lunch, wearing her ballet slippers and a clingy skirt over her leotard. She smiled demurely at the smorgasbord of Male Yale, hoping that no one would ever call *her* a bitch.

"Hi, Ana," said a young man with a blond moustache and gray, gleaming eyes. He tipped his black, broad-brimmed Amish hat. She paused with her tray of salad and lime jello.

"I'm Phil. Philip Westover. You're Ana Fried—I know. I'm in your film class." He cleared his throat. "Actually, I missed the first two classes," he added, a bit embarrassed. "I was down in Pennsylvania, photographing the Amish." That explained the hat. He seemed to be looking her up and down, all the way from her long black hair to her ballet slippers. He cleared his throat a second time. "I hear you're quite a creative chick."

She had stopped listening to him. She was concentrating on the green color of her jello. The way it wiggled would have been perfect in 48 frames per second, she thought as she devoured it. Thirty-two frames per second was better for filming dance movements than jello.

She prided herself for mastering the technology of filmmaking so quickly in class. At first the 16mm Arri camera had felt like a machine gun, with its dull black metal casing and its long, heavy lens. But when Prof. Malenek showed her how to load it, she had raced to be the first on his list to use it, filming the audience watching *Breathless*. The footage came out perfectly exposed—she had pushed it two stops in the right direction, from f5.6 to f2.8.

She organized a movie happening the following weekend, lugging a heavy projector down to one of the squash courts and filling it ankle-deep with popcorn. Now, because of her hand-painted posters, the small space was mobbed. Movie audiences were clapping wildly from all four directions at the actual spectators, who seemed to understand minimalist concepts of time and space, and that, in a happening, anything goes: clothes were coming off, and two New Englanders had begun to fondle one another with tentative gestures under their matching button-down shirts. A fat guy sat by himself, eating popcorn from a corner of the floor and watching.

Four squash players suddenly arrived. After a brief debate about the violation of their space, they ended up hitting kernels of popcorn back and forth with their racquets, mostly over the heads of the spectators, though occasionally hitting someone. So far the fighting was under control.

Each 16mm movie loop was slightly different in length: four movie audiences clapping at different intervals was a bit disorienting, especially when one of the loops broke and spun wildly around the projector with a thwacking sound. With four projectors running simultaneously, the fuse blew, plunging the squash court into darkness. Ana had to remain demure, as if these were part of the happening, looking artsy in her purple tights and Mexican silver bracelets. Philip Westover was nudging her through the salty waves of popcorn. "You're fantastic," he was murmuring. "You probably know that."

"You like this?" she asked, scrunching up her nose. Her career wasn't exactly going to come to a halt if no one found the fuse box. Happenings were merely alternative stratagems towards achieving notoriety, in case she couldn't find a more suitable medium by the time she turned twenty-one. Still, he had appealed to her sense of ego. In the semi-darkness, backlit by a shaft of light coming through the entrance of the squash court, his profile was sort of cute.

He took her to the Yale Cinema Series to see what was playing. It was the immortal classic, *Jules and Jim*. Unlike Lawrence, who had set himself to work hugging her at the first possible opportunity, Philip was getting up every half hour or so, running to the projection booth to change reels.

"I make money to pay for books and stuff by projecting," Philip whispered in the dark, trying to hold Ana's hand while he had a chance.

"What?" she said, lulled by his physical warmth. But she wasn't focusing on Philip; her eyes were glued to *Jules and Jim*. It was the second film she'd ever seen by François Truffaut, and even more extraordinary than the first.

"May I see the last slide again?" Jim had asked, referring to a certain ancient statue with a mysterious smile.

"I made a close-up of it, too," the other man had said. Jules and Jim could see that the statue was an icon of love. They rushed off to an island in the Mediterranean in search of the actual statue, vowing that they would follow that colossal smile anywhere if they ever saw it on a woman. And then they met Catherine, whose twelve foot tall lips flooded the screen with light.

Her impetuous freedom ignited Ana's blood. She vowed to see the world of free love through Catherine's eyes, without the tragic ending. She would record the inner world of women, only without the distortion of all the male chauvinists quoted in the film like Swinburne and Baudelaire, calling Woman "monster, assassin of the arts, little fool, little slut." As she stared at the freeze frames of Catherine, Philip murmured to her in the semi-darkness, "You're unique, Ana. You're a beautiful, creative chick." She didn't want to tell him how much the word *chick* annoyed her, and how it was ruining the moment.

When the lights went back on, she turned towards him. His long blond hair covered his eyes. Could she get him to smile a young man's version of Catherine's smile, or was it more important to call him on his sexist name-calling?

"Would you like to go back to my dorm and take photographs with me?" she asked.

"Cool!" he said.

She posed him in the shower for Professional Ektachrome slides. She took two or three with the hat, then another four without it, focusing on his blond moustache and upturned nose at f2 with a 50mm lens. The 35mm still camera wasn't half as intimidating as the 16mm camera in "Introduction to Film Production."

It was easy enough to convince him to take off his clothes. She took two full figure nudes. What a thrill, turning a man into an art object! She approached him to rearrange his arms and torso, à la Stieglitz. Then she turned on the cold water, and he laughed.

"Just what do you think you're doing?" he asked, but he didn't stop her from clicking away.

I wonder what you're thinking, smirked Ana to herself. You probably think you're one of those sensitive male artists: you're just longing to identify with us out of mournful loneliness, is that it? Or do you expect me to help you achieve creative immortality?

"Don't get my Nikon wet!" she protested as he reached towards her to pull her into the gushing shower.

"Hey, what frame are you on? Is it 36A yet?" he asked, teasing her. "When do I get to take some?"

She dropped her camera lightly onto his pile of clothes, and turned the water to warm. He began to pull her long dark hair through the water and to massage her breasts.

She took off her silver bracelets and reached for his penis, surrounded in a yellow square of sunshine by a blond halo of pubic hair. What a fascinating photo, she thought, an instant before he pulled her towards him. Now the water and his own warmth were surrounding her instead. While they made love, the round lens of her camera faced the ceiling as if photographing heaven.

CHAPTER FIVE

The Proposals

*As the history of patriarchal culture and the
representations of herself within all levels of its cultural
media, past and present, have a devastating effect upon her
self image, she is customarily deprived of any but the most
trivial sources of dignity or self-respect.*

— Kate Millett, *Sexual Politics*

Monday
*Ms. Weinberg is actually giving me college credit
just for keeping a diary of whatever happens to me that's
gender-related!*

But first she had to come up with a list of conditions necessary
to the creation of art:

- having the freedom to reflect, to wait, and to experiment;
- not having your work idolized, categorized, or ignored;
- not being concerned with moral weight;
- not having critics waiting to get you;
- not having patrons, producers, publishers or dealers expecting something;
- not being censored;
- not getting pregnant.

"Not a bad start," said Ms. Weinberg. "But what about skill-training? You realize, for example, that traditionally, American women were never allowed to study from live nude models, don't you?"

Tuesday
Ana Fried, Woman Artist?

"Sure, you should be an artist, just so you're not too good at it," Philip joked, when he came over to study for midterms.

"Will you teach me how to load film this afternoon?" asked Ana. "It's so much cheaper than buying individual rolls."

"Yeah, yeah," he said, grabbing her behind. The whole day passed in making love.

When Philip was asleep, Ana sought answers in his sleeping body. Contemplating the image of his tanned thigh muscles at rest through her camera interested her much more than finishing her required reading for the week: Linda Nochlin's *Why Have There Been No Great Women Artists?* She watched the sun moving over Philip's blond chest, picking up the brilliance of a few manly hairs. She touched his blond moustache—he shivered in his sleep. Silently she slid beside him, watching his chest rise and lower as he breathed. She listened to him snoring, hard, then soft, then hard. His flesh was soft and sleepy; the sunlight spreading over his penis, the afternoon shadows deepening on his legs. She took another photo; he moved in his sleep, covering his face with his elbow. She said, "Philip?" Philip didn't say anything, just rolled over their books, awake and erect, ready to start again.

After sex, he opened up his book to a scenario by the great Russian poet Mayakovsky in which a girl is kidnapped from a movie set by an artist who lands her in "real life." Ana looked at it with suspicion: Philip seemed all too eager to kidnap her creativity to help him fulfill his own filmic aspirations. She felt drained, listening to Philip's ideas, which mimicked her own.

The only woman she had heard of making films was Maya Deren, whose *Meshes of the Afternoon* had screened at the Museum of Modern Art during her last summer vacation. Maybe she could be the one woman filmmaker of her generation, the way Maya Deren had been in hers—unless there were already others out there, about to be discovered. Maybe the door to filmmaking was really never going to open to women, and she ought to try something else. If not film, painting, if not painting, poetry, she thought to herself, floundering for a medium. "I can almost see the poem…Can I really go back to writing poems?" she wondered.

The film class was watching Luis Buñuel's first film, *Un Chien Andalou*. She hunched over in her seat and scribbled down some notes for what might become a poem:

> Slicing the eye of the moon
> without guilt
> all it sees now is the dream of choice
> between suicide
> and sexual conquest
> your desires as heavy as pianos
> weighing down carcasses of my breasts.
> It's just a game to you
> You who once closed all textbooks
> you who denied me
> until I watched
> your corpse fade out
> like a moth against the night
> with no words except
> the gestures of the wind
> —the whispering of the ocean—
> to let me know
> it was time
> to start again,
> and…

The class had ended; everyone went rushing out.

At her next session, Ms. Weinberg took her to task. "Don't be so facile with your investigations," she warned her. "Look at other institutions which have conspired to thwart the achievements of women. Museums that show almost exclusively male artists, for example. Aren't the women's groups protesting?"

But if there were any protests, she hadn't read about them. They certainly weren't in the art history books. Rather than focus on the politics and contact the activists as Weinberg suggested, she would explore the visual power of art itself, the kind of art in which she was indoctrinated. Why emulate some unknown woman artist, when she could study the brush strokes of the so-called masters?

If some of the greatest Renaissance artists—da Vinci, Michelangelo, Raphael and Fra Angelico—had learned by studying Masaccio's frescoes, so could she. She bought several gallons of wall paint in primary colors. She wanted to emulate Masaccio, too, by applying his revolution in perspective to her own tumultuous times. She wasn't about to let her pretensions stop her.

On Thursday, she set to work in blue, green, yellow and red, mimicking Masaccio's frescoes of the Brancacci Chapel on the scale of her single room. She did not pray to Jesus for inspiration like Fra Angelico had prayed before he painted each cell of his monastery. She merely outlined the biblical figures using a ballpoint pen. Nor did she tell the administration about defacing Yale property in her residential college. Instead she focused on reenacting the 15th century artistic discovery of emotion in the rendering of Adam and Eve's expulsion from the wall next to her closet; she overlaid Freudian sexuality onto St. Peter's pulling of the tribute money from the glistening, squirming body of the fish; and, like Masaccio himself, she snuck in her self-portrait among the many bodies interwoven in red, yellow and green in hasty brush strokes along the bedroom wall. The only thing left was to film it.

Thursday

    I have finally realized that film is an amalgamation of all of the arts that I have previously studied. I no longer have to be a flibbertigibbet about my artistic identity. It is only natural for me to be a film director. If necessary, I will appropriate the best of male directors' mise-en-scènes. In a few years, with any luck, my first feature will be screened at Cannes. I have finally found someone to help me. Philip Westover says that when he graduates, he's going to inherit a major Connecticut estate and use it to produce my films. We're going to start production right away, even before his trust fund kicks in: a short film called "Body Painting Movie." My storyboard intersects the dance movements of actors' bodies with the composition of the Brancacci Chapel. Philip is going to do my camerawork the way Maya Deren's husband shot her 16mm masterpiece, "Meshes of the Afternoon."

On Sunday afternoon, Ana and Bruce painted their naked bodies in primal colors, using wide brushes, then their hands: his penis red, her breasts green, yellow on his abdomen, always in syncopation with the yellow, green and red of the walls behind—garishly lit with 2,000 watts of light—leaving blue to provide contrast along the length of their arms from their shoulders to their fingertips. Philip watched Ana and Bruce through the wide angle lens until the film ran out. He threaded it in backwards by mistake—half-blind with jealous rage—instead of using the second roll of film, until it too ran out. Then he ran out of the room, slamming the door behind him. And it came out unfocused and double-exposed, looking like a nuclear explosion.

Tuesday

    Philip said he was sorry for how my film turned out, though he can't pay me back for the film stock. It felt so good

*making love to him, I ended up forgiving him. But I should
have been putting together a proposal for my senior project
today, whether or not he still wants to produce it.*

Her new project was going to be a documentary about the
New York art world, portraying the top artists as overblown ego-
maniacs if the Senior Projects Committee would accept it. "The
history of art has reached a point of moral dilemma," her proposal
proclaimed. Her film would explore how artists are hindered or
encouraged by the political scene, economic considerations, and
artistic trends. Why should the elite few win all the media attention, while thousands of obscure artists struggle in poverty? Her
plan was to expose the art world's hypocrisy.

She got the idea from the pamphlets that the Panthers had
handed out on May Day. All Power to the People's Art! She would
blow the whistle on the decadence of the artists, the elitist stance
of the gallery owners, the corruption of the modern critics, and the
racist and sexist practices of the museums. The art world needed
a revolution.

Prof. Everett Landau, who served as the advisor to all projects
pertaining to modern art, would have preferred that she write
about the apolitical Camille Corot, as punishment for her having
confused the name of a Greta Garbo movie with one of the fore-
most 19th century pre-Impressionists—and naturally, a male. And
wasn't there a rule that precluded the production of undergraduate
theses on anything but paper? But Ms. Weinberg intervened on
her behalf, alluding to President Brewster's quest to modernize the
academic requirements for God, for Country and for Yale.

She was ready to put her theories—such as they were—into
practice. She began to commute weekly between New Haven and
New York with a 16mm camera, a tripod and a light meter. Her
growing strength in handling the equipment and her increasing
ability to express herself through a camera lens exhilarated her.

Her interview questions focused on the innate ugliness below the surface of successful artists and their world. Her artistic style would parody their paintings: For Roy Lichtenstein, she would film a dot matrix in high contrast film stock and turn the interview into a comic strip, which projected onto a large screen, would surpass the size of his largest paintings, like the eight by ten-foot "Temple of Apollo" whose background was entirely made of dots. She was sure she could make her film a work of art.

Face to face with famous artists, however, she felt like a groupie.

"How do you communicate as an artist?" she asked, nervously adjusting her bangs.

"There's a great deal of subjectivity that I don't think you can identify," said Jasper Johns. This struck her as profound. Although the greatness of Johns as an artist was debatable—and if she weren't so tongue-tied, she would have debated it—she found his greatness as a philosopher of art indisputable.

Jill Barrington was the only woman artist Ana interviewed. Other women artists weren't famous enough for what Ana wanted to achieve. Frankenthaler had a name, and of course, O'Keeffe—but they were unreachable. Without name recognition, her film might not be treated seriously. Jill was a third-choice token woman.

"It's very weird sitting here being photographed like this," said Jill, "talking into a microphone in my studio. It's like a one-dimensional..."

Ana interrupted. "Could you say that again?"

"Again? One-dimensional *what*?"

"Start from the beginning, only move your shoulders sideways while you're talking."

Jill laughed. "It is very weird, talking into a microphone in my studio like this. It's like being a one-dimensional creature."

"Why?" Ana asked. "Can't you present your views as an artist?"

Jill turned impatiently and pointed at the huge, black canvases stacked against the wall behind them. "Art is the art that you make, not what you say about it, and not who you are or what your personality is like."

Sometimes, after a particularly long, in-depth interview, she'd miss the last train. She tried sleeping on the floor of an artist's studio, or hanging around Grand Central Station until dawn; once, she slept with one of the artists, just to remind herself that she was liberated. She didn't get much sleep, and he failed to give her much of an orgasm. There was no point in digging out the pillow book from the back of her closet. It felt like an artifact from another century, and she no longer wanted to shock Philip with a trail of other lovers.

"What are you looking at?" she asked him irritably, coughing at the smoke that had permeated her dorm room in her absence. Philip was sprawled out on the foam mattress getting stoned. He hadn't shot a roll of film in over a month.

"An oak tree, an oak with brown leaves," he replied. "A couple of angels hovering in the sky. Soldiers on top of the buildings pouring molten lead on the students below." He was probably thinking up an anti-Vietnam film—animated and experimental.

She took a puff of marijuana and used the buzz to explore her own mind.

"Are you going home for Thanksgiving?" he was asking.

Her breasts were floating on the surface of his eyes, one by one like paper boats on a clear pool. "Are you?"

"I'm going down to Pennsylvania to do some more shooting on my Amish film. Wanna come with me?"

Just then there was a phone call. It was Ana's parents, ten minutes away from the campus. They had driven up to New Haven especially to congratulate her on having her art world thesis topic approved.

Philip quickly folded over the foam mattress, stashing his belongings in a cardboard box towards the back of the closet. After all, her parents were paying for her room and board, not his. Ana ran frantically back and forth. What if Philip found her pillow book in the closet? And what would he think of her mother?

"What is that stench?" said Madelyn, as Ana opened the door.

"It's incense, Mom."

"Incense?"

"Sandalwood incense, imported from India," said Ana. Her parents pushed their way into the room, taking off their coats.

"Oh, my God! What have you done to the walls?" gasped her mother, surveying the gaudy frescoes.

"Interior decorating," said Martin drily.

"Yes, but the *colors*," Madelyn said in shock. "Who's going to pay to repaint this?" Philip pretended to study.

"I can't even cover the costs of the film. You know that, Dad," Ana said.

"He paid your full tuition," said her mother. "Isn't that enough? Do you know how hard he works for this?"

"Madelyn, please," said her father.

"I've gone without a new winter outfit for two years," said Madelyn. "She's oblivious of the sacrifices we make. Oblivious."

"Thanks for the dress, Mom," said Ana. "I'm sorry I forgot to call you."

"Oh, *now* she thanks us," said Madelyn. "I thought Saks forgot to ship it out. And what do we have to show for it, you..."

"*Please, Ma, don't use 'You ungrateful bitch' in front of Philip*," Ana was praying. "*Please, I'll do anything. I'll get off the Pill and give you a baby to torture.*"

"What do we have to show for it except this shifty-eyed boyfriend," Madelyn continued, "and don't tell me you're not living together!"

"Actually, Mrs. Fried, I was just leaving," said Philip, hiding under his long blond bangs. "*Oh no you don't, you coward!*" Ana was screaming at Phil, inside herself. "*You can't leave yet! You haven't married me, the way my parents are expecting! You haven't given me a diamond ring with enough carats to prove I'm marrying up!*

You can't leave yet! You haven't even produced my movie, and you're making me into a failure!"

"Nice to have met you," said Marty, affably.

"Yeah, um, Ana and I are going down to Pennsylvania to film the Amish in a couple of weeks. Any chance we can borrow your Volkswagen?" Philip said.

"I don't see why not," said Marty, eyeing Madelyn. Ana was frozen solid. "I only use it to get down to the train station. Actually, I could use the exercise."

"For God's sake, Marty, all that exercise—you'll get a hernia," said Madelyn. But then, as if the spell had been broken, a breeze wafted strangely in through the open window, picking up two of Philip's photographs of an Amish wheat field, and keeping them suspended waist-high like a hula hoop in slow motion. Madelyn Fried agreed to lend them the car, and she and Marty put their coats back on and receded through the door as if they were phantoms.

Ana had a splitting headache over what had and hadn't been said.

"You can't let it worry you," said Philip. "Anyway, Kent's on his way down from Harvard. We roomed together at Hotchkiss. I'm sure I told you about him."

"Oh, I guess…" she replied morosely.

"We're going to The Game. Maybe it'll cheer you up." She huddled against him, trying to forget the rest of the social world in a strong embrace. But Philip restrained her with a couple of light kisses while he thought it over.

"Shh, not now," he said, extricating himself from Ana and pulling on his Army jacket. "You don't know Alloway. He'd probably come while we were screwing around. It would take him all weekend to get over it."

Two hours later, Kent Alloway arrived in his long dark coat and crimson scarf, the spitting image of a Massachusetts senator. Consequently, Philip and Ana did not make love before the

Harvard-Yale game. Ana, Philip and Kent sat on the Harvard side, blinded by the sun and drowning in hoarse college cheers that celebrated a series of touchdowns by Harvard. Ana sweltered as the sun beat down on the second-hand raccoon coat. Her birth-control pills were making her bloated and fueling her headache.

Philip was getting exasperated that she wasn't being enthusiastic enough about Yale's need to score. Instead of booing, she concentrated on pulling some lint off her pink wool scarf, trying to decide whether to take it off and spoil her conservative image. Kent was examining a hot dog that was excessively dripping in mustard. Tall and brooding, he would probably look down at his constituents the same way someday.

"Hey, how much did you have to pay for these tickets, anyway?" Philip asked him, as Harvard scored again.

"Oh, never mind," said Ken. "I got a discount up in Cambridge."

"No, seriously. I'd like to pay you back. I'm making a pantload of money now—shooting pictures for the *Yalie Daily*. Five bucks per photograph—I'm on the staff."

Ken flipped through the program for the game. The Yale side was cheering, and he politely read an article while Philip leapt up on the bench.

"Hit 'em back, hit 'em back, way back!!! Right on! Come on, Ana. It's a lot of fun if you don't take it so seriously." She had unbuttoned her raccoon coat and was fanning herself with her copy of the program. If only they could have made love while there was still time. Philip turned to Kent and elbowed him. "We're going to smash your team yet!"

The cheering died down. Philip looked over Kent's shoulder as Kent turned the page to a series of pictures in the program in which a smiling girl dressed in nothing but a referee's shirt demonstrates the positions for the touchdown, the missed down and interference.

"This is incredible," Kent marveled, turning to Ana. "Your women's lib group ought to do something about this. It's blatant sexism! Yale's co-ed—it should know better! Philip, would you look at that?"

Ana surveyed the crowds urging on the team in orgiastic frenzy. The smell of old popcorn was making her feel nauseous. The final score of 35 to 16 favored Harvard, but with Philip's lack of attention on anything other than the field, Ana wallowed in personal defeat as if she were only a pebble under the football that had been kicked around.

Neither she nor Philip could whip up much enthusiasm about tailgating parties though Kent had driven his Alfa Romeo down especially for the occasion. On the brisk, cold walk back to the parking lot, their shadows elongated along the cracked sidewalk in the late afternoon, Philip and Kent ensconced themselves in a serious conversation about the massacre of Vietnamese civilians at My Lai.

"My feet are killing me," Ana complained.

"OK, honey, you go off and fix yourself up now," said Philip, pointing indulgently at the shuttle bus. "We'll meet you over at Branford. I've decided to introduce you to my parents, so look good. They'll probably drop by."

Ana arrived at the reception in the Branford College Library in a demure black dress and pearls, her hair brushed viciously back in a bun and held together with a black silk bow. All the chairs had been pushed away and noisy couples leaned over punch bowls of liquor and juice. Professor Sidney Brubacher, who taught Italian Renaissance Art, stood in one corner with his docile wife, two children in miniature suits tugging at the sleeves of her Hungarian embroidered peasant blouse: they wanted their mother to get them some more punch, and off she went on her mission, looking like an older version of a co-ed.

Some Branford residents whom Ana only vaguely recognized were debating whether Lukacs was a Marxist or an anti-Marxist. The fight stopped in mid-air, acknowledging Ana's presence.

Prof. Brubacher cleared his throat. "How pretty our English majorette looks this evening!"

"I'm specializing in Art History, Professor Brubacher," Ana replied," grabbing a miniature pig in a blanket as a plate of them sailed by.

"Of course… Did you go to The Game today?"

On the word *Game*, the Whiffenpoofs congregated on the balcony and commenced singing a capella.

"We're poor little lambs who have lost our way:
Baa! Baa! Baa!
We're little black sheep who have gone astray:
Baa! Baa! Baa!

Ana scanned the library, wondering if Philip had arrived. Mrs. Brubacher had returned with the juice cups, spilling little if any on her peasant blouse.

"Have you seen Philip Westover anywhere, or his parents?" asked Ana.

"I can't say I've ever met them, honey," replied the professor's wife, looking around for napkins.

"But…"

"For Christ's sake, Annie. We're trying to listen to some music," said one of the Branford students, shushing them.

Kent Alloway appeared at the crowded entrance, taking off his crimson scarf. He and Ana stared at each other in embarrassment, each surprised that Philip was not with the other. She thought of sleeping with someone—maybe even Kent—in retaliation for Philip not showing her off to his parents. But then again, there was always that chance of Philip's good intentions, and that he was spending the evening with his parents discussing his future with her, and that he'd decided it was OK to marry a Jew, and nothing could stop him.

Just two days before Thanksgiving weekend, Ana decided that getting in another interview before going *anywhere* with her boyfriend was mandatory. If Philip planned on proposing in Pennsylvania, she wanted to have first accomplished something major with her career. So she rushed down to New York with her camera in tow, headed for the studio of Robert Rauschenberg.

She wanted to dismiss Rauschenberg as an alcoholic has-been. It had been over a decade since he'd pinned up nudies beside the *Birth of Venus*. Instead she found her camera dueling with his visual brilliance, moving the camera in syncopation to his moves around the canvas, gluing and shellacking cardboard boxes that he'd found on the street.

Afterwards, the head of the Whitney Museum took her out to lunch.

"You do know," he began, "that Clement Greenberg, Barbara Rose, and in fact all of the critics with whom we're acquainted in New York are excited by a film about the New York art scene."

"Wow, scary feeling!" said Ana, acting small and feminine. She didn't want him to know that for the climax of her documentary, she was going to plant a realistic bomb sculpture that would "blow up" the art world, creating a nuclear maelstrom of concrete and shredded canvases.

"I don't even know where to stay in New York City, when I come down to shoot the interviews, Mr. Halstrom," she said demurely.

"Can you cook?" he asked, aware of her allure. He coughed politely when she didn't answer. "Are you good with kids?"

She was pretending to be part of the linen tablecloth.

"The art critic for *Mademoiselle* is looking for a babysitter," he said casually. "I'll get you her number after lunch."

But Ana was thinking as she glanced up at the tall, elegant Roger Hallstrom, that *Mademoiselle* was beneath her. "*Just get me YOUR number. Just let me call you later. Just break off your engagement. Let's just us rule the art world.*"

But she was her own worst enemy. "Mr. Halstrom," she began, sipping her Chablis with a nervous little cough. "Don't you know that galleries for modern art have been created at the very moment in art history when art can no longer be hung on museum walls? Art critics and museums are going to be redundant."

He smiled indulgently at her and put his hand on her knee. It was becoming increasingly difficult for Ana to focus on the art of revolution.

"By the way," he said to her kindly, "I've heard about your photos. Word gets around when you're at Yale. Why don't you give Henry Riccoli a call? I'm sure Henry'll be happy to take a look at Ana Fried's portfolio."

Ana was sure that it was Philip's jealousy of her incipient success that made him call off their filmmaking trip to Lancaster, Pennsylvania, even though she had written some of his script. Or maybe it was her bickering about whether it was fair that she should have to pay for all her birth control pills.

He drove down to Pennsylvania with his new friend, Paul J. Smith. Paul had acquired a Ford van with a sunroof *and* a brand new 16mm sync-sound Eclair NPR. The camera equipment has nothing to do with it, thought Ana. He's only trying to make me feel abandoned and worthless.

Well, she'd show him! She'd spend the night in the editing room. She could work on her own film without any help from anyone! The long Thanksgiving weekend had begun: there would probably be nobody left on campus while she edited her footage of Johns and Rauschenberg in peace and quiet.

She luxuriated in an all-nighter working at the Moviola without distractions of any kind other than the clickety-clacking of the 16mm film jumping through the gate as she synced up the image to the sound. In the morning, she trudged to the train station, juggling her Samsonite suitcase and a small Styrofoam cup of coffee. There was no escaping Scarsdale. She finished Simone de Beauvoir's *The Second Sex* en route, underlining significant quotes: "Her life is passed in washing pots and pans, and it is a glittering novel; man's vassal, she thinks she is his idol; carnally humiliated, she is all for Love." In view of the passages underlined in ballpoint pen, she reexamined her enthusiasm for Roger Hallstrom. Perhaps she wasn't capable of being his idol. He certainly wasn't hers, especially if he was only planning to seduce her. She wanted to spend her life making art, not just...

...she almost missed Scarsdale.

By the time she got to the big, white Neo-Colonial called home, everyone was already seated around the dining room table: her parents, Vickie, Timmy, and Guadalupe Ramirez—who had once spent two weeks with the Fried family courtesy of the Fresh Air Fund's program for underprivileged youth from the slums of Harlem. Guadalupe's two-year-old son struggled on her lap. Her husband apparently had not been invited.

"Is there anything I can do?" asked Ana.

"Never mind. It's done. Sit down."

"OK, OK." She sat down at the table setting next to Vickie, under the dark, watery green of Madelyn's abstract that was trying hard to be a Frankenthaler.

"Look at you with the rings under your eyes. What have you been doing all night, I wonder?"

"I..." *Maybe if I'd been a better girlfriend, he might have wanted me with him, helping him make his movie, thought Ana. I could be over a hundred miles away from you and your insults. What right do you have to criticize me, anyway? If you spent half the time in your studio that I spent in the editing room last night, your abstracts might look more like true expressions of the soul. And instead, you think I was out whoring: Don't bother to say it.* She glowered in silence.

"Forget it," said her mother. "You're a bad enough influence on your sister as it is."

Vickie was wearing a low-cut black sweater, revealing too much of her brand new breasts. She couldn't smell or taste anything because of her botched nose job, and her face was blotchy from drinking. *I didn't tell her what to wear. I didn't tell her to mutilate herself. I didn't get her drunk. You're the one who abandoned her for your pseudo-art. So how can you blame me?* thought Ana.

"I don't know why we're even celebrating. It's not like we didn't steal the land from the Indians," said Vickie, swirling the dark wine in her fragile wine glass.

Their visitor eyed the approaching storm with a nervous grin. The baby was squirming in her lap; she put him down on the floor with a plastic spoon to keep him occupied away from the grown-ups.

Madelyn began to carve the turkey, assaulting the dark meat with an electric knife. Marty took out a heavy flash camera to com-memorate the event, aiming first at Guadalupe, who smiled at the camera just as the flash lit up the room. Then he backed off into a corner to capture his entire family, but his wife was glowering into the lens. "Just a goddam minute. Girls, spit on your bangs, and sit closer to Timmy." Ana threw a look of apology at Guadalupe for being left out of the picture. Then the Frieds said "Cheese!".

"Where's the baby?" beamed Marty. He spotted Jose on the floor.

"Lupe, pick up the baby. It's disgusting the way you let it crawl under the table," stated Madelyn, pointing the electric knife at its antique splay legs for emphasis. Marty pointed his camera and shot. The blinding flash made the baby's eyes look like a wounded deer's.

Guadalupe picked up Jose and went into Vickie's room to change him.

"I can't smell a thing," said Vickie, her words oozing like gravy.

Madelyn glared at Vickie and Ana, who were avoiding each other's gaze. "Guadalupe's baby is the closest I'm ever going to get to having a grandchild, isn't it?"

"Can't we just enjoy the turkey?" Marty complained.

"What about grace?" asked Timmy.

"Well, in this house, it's enough to thank your mother," said Marty diplomatically. "Look at this turkey! Honey, we all thank you for your wonderful cooking and cleaning this week." *Thank you, Mother, for your cooking and scrubbing and screaming and slapping us all through childhood*, thought Ana.

Madelyn doled out huge globs of sweet potato soufflé onto everybody's plates except Vickie's.

"Where's mine?" Vickie shot out.

"You're fat enough," said Madelyn, perfunctorily. Ana felt like throwing up. Maybe it was the birth control pills.

Vickie ran out of the room in tears, pushing past Guadalupe Ramirez, who stood in the doorway holding her son in her arms. He started to cry in the suffocating heat from the kitchen. "I'm sorry, Mrs. Fried, we have to go. My husband's waiting in the city," she said. "But thank you. Thank you so much for everything you done for us."

"See?" said Madelyn, gesturing to Ana and Timmy. "At least someone has manners around here." She walked Guadalupe to the front door, giving her an extravagant hug and a Neiman Marcus bag of hand-me-downs. "Vickie, please wrap up a turkey leg in tinfoil for Mr. Ramirez while you're in the kitchen, would you, dear?"

Madelyn was hugging the baby good-bye and closing the door for Guadalupe.

"She's always putting on a show," muttered Ana.

"Shh!" said Marty, trying to second-guess his wife's emotional state.

"Why the hell aren't the pies on the table already?" complained Madelyn. She had spent the entire day cooking with no one to help.

Ana fled to the kitchen carrying her and her sister's half-eaten plates, while Timmy continued to mush up his food at the table. Madelyn beat her to it, returning with a crème de pumpkin pie in one hand and a chocolate pecan pie in the other. Marty got double wedges of both, while Ana voted for the pecan. Timmy only wanted pumpkin crème for something more to mush.

"If there's anyone to thank, it should be your father and all his litigation work, without which there'd be no silverware or crystal on this table, let alone food," said Madelyn drily, doling out the ice cream.

Rather than talk back, Ana sat there, trying to meditate. She did her best to concentrate on each chakra, from the base of the spine all the way up to her crown chakra, hoping to calm down. She could almost imagine her crown chakra emerging from her mother's womb. Birth was such a miracle. She wanted to come up with a poem, but she couldn't find a way for the "ess" of *emptiness* to rhyme with *bliss*, which was stuck in her imagination.

Marty and Timmy retreated upstairs to watch TV, leaving the females to do the dishes under the supervision of their mother.

"Take that Baccarat out of the dishwasher," barked Madelyn. Ana and Vickie numbly washed and towel-dried each wine glass, while Madelyn made sure they had added a little salt to the dishwater so that there would be no water spots. They were too fragile for the dishwasher.

Then, with her daughters gone, Madelyn got on her hands and knees and scrubbed the turkey juice that had dripped onto the floor of the kitchen.

It was Ana's last afternoon at home. She had finished Simone de Beauvoir on the train before she arrived and had some free time.

"Hey, Vick! Whatcha doing?"

"Nothing." Vickie stuffed the rest of the Snickers left over from Halloween under the pillow and turned off the record player. Her room looked like a collage of 33 rpm records and dirty socks. She didn't look too overweight, just a bit down in the dumps from the nose job.

"Wanna hypnotize each other and study our past lives?"

"Are you kidding? Since when do you believe in reincarnation?"

"I don't. It's just a game," said Ana blithely, pushing aside some of Vickie's wrinkled plaid slacks so that she could sit down on the pink chenille bedspread. "Well, wanna help me practice my interviewing?"

"Uh," said Vickie. "Okay. I don't have to practice piano 'til later."

"Great! Here's what you do: Pretend you're a famous woman artist, and I'm interviewing you. I want to include more women in my film. Okay?" Ana opened up her loose-leaf notebook.

"Stop patronizing me," said Vickie, in her new nasal voice.

"It's a school project. Now here's the first question," said Ana, taking out a pen. "What influence has married life had on your work?"

Vickie smirked. "None."

"How did you choose this particular field of art?"

"I thought it was funny."

"Come on, Vickie. Just pretend you're a painter instead of a wannabe pianist, that's all. Please? Next question: Why do most of your peers feel that they cannot paint if you can?"

Vickie thought for a moment, pretending she was a painter in front of an empty canvas. "They don't have my talent, ambition and self-confidence?"

"Wow, Vickie, that's great," said Ana indulgently. "Where do you get these traits from?"

Vickie laughed. "That's easy. From Mom."

"How do you plan to support yourself as an artist?"

"I don't know," said Vickie. "Prostitution?" They both laughed.

"Have they encouraged your brother to be an artist too?"

"No way."

"Why not?"

"Because boys are destined to succeed at whatever they do, with or without their parents' help," said Vickie. She thought for a moment. "*I* don't really believe that boys are destined to succeed, but our parents sure do."

"How did you arrive at this conclusion?" asked Ana, trying not to laugh.

"Well, it's obvious what Mommy thinks," said Vickie, "and Daddy just goes along with it."

"In what way is it obvious?"

"Well, who do you think gets all the attention? They're over at the school watching Timmy's soccer game right now."

"I thought they were dropping him at the babysitter's. Aren't they going to Las Vegas for the week?"

Vickie was losing her patience. "I don't want you to write all this junk down," she said.

"All right," her sister said. "What do you want me to ask you?"

"You could ask about my music," suggested Vickie.

"Bo-o-oring."

"So ask me about my sex life."

"Tell me about your sex life," said Ana.

"Boy, is this dumb! I don't have one yet," croaked Vickie. "Other than fantasies," she added.

"OK, OK. No one's interested in your adolescent fantasies. What do you hope to achieve through painting?" She picked up her pen, focused on the sociology of art.

"Nothing. I already told you, I wanna be a songwriter," said Vickie, prodding the guitar at the foot of the bed with her brightly painted toes. "Go ask Nevelson why she always works with the same junk."

"Louise Nevelson? How do you know about her?"

"Just because I'm stuck here practicing piano most of the time doesn't mean I never go to the Museum of Modern Art!"

"OK, I get the point," said Ana, embarrassed that she'd forgotten to include Nevelson in her art world project. "Give me one of your Snickers bars."

"I don't have any," said Vickie quickly.

"Yes, you do. They're under your pillow," said Ana.

But before they could start a pillow fight, their mother called upstairs.

"Where are you?" Madelyn demanded. "We've been ready to leave for the airport for the past ten minutes. If you get into the car immediately, we can still drop you girls off in the city."

Ana rushed to get her book bag and her camera case together, then climbed into the black BMW behind her sister and their parents.

"Look at your hair," said Madelyn to Vickie. "Couldn't one of you have combed your hair, at least? It's much too long—you both look like derelicts. And what's the idea of wearing your miniskirts into New York City? You look like whores!" But they were going to miss their flight; there was no time to change. Vickie ate the rest of the bag of Snickers bars as Marty and Madelyn drove down the Saw Mill River Parkway, while Ana tried to study in the back seat by flashlight. Unable to focus on her books, she watched the shadows from the streetlights on the shiny leather upholstery.

Vickie and Ana got out of the car on the Lower East Side. Madelyn slammed the door shut, then rolled down the window as an afterthought. "We'll call you from Nevada."

Marty stepped on the gas and pulled away from the curb, but Vickie had left the guitar in the trunk. She started gesticulating wildly. Her father saw her in the rear view mirror and circled back to 14th Street and 1st Avenue, yelling at Madelyn to keep quiet.

The BMW screeched to a halt in front of Vickie. Madelyn got out in her new mink coat and opened the trunk. "You inconsiderate jerk, leaving it in our car. Your brain's disintegrating with all the drugs you've taken!" Ana knew better than to stand up for her sister. Instead she pulled at one of her cuticles till it bled.

The car sped down the street as Madelyn cursed her daughters in her looking glass of the rear-view mirror. Vickie's guitar and yellow parka were already a blur in the gray streets. She was running off to a Frank Zappa concert, where she was hoping to score some acid.

Ana felt deserted by both her parents and her sister. Her camera case and knapsack full of books were much too heavy to lug for more than a block or two. She had been planning to film the Empire State Building lit up at night. But as a symbol of the phallic power of the New York art world, it seemed too obvious. Besides, her sling-back heels were too tight: she'd never make the twenty blocks to 34th Street. She took off the shoes, stuffed them into her knapsack, and ran down into the subway, fraying her tights on the dirty metal steps.

After an hour and a half in Grand Central, trying to study in between bites of a bagel, she got on a train headed north. She kept opening up her knapsack of books, trying to study before the train could reach New Haven, but her mother's insults reverberated in her ears, multiplied by the hellish echoes of the train screeching along the tracks.

At Yale, Philip took her to the midnight screening of a new film, *Ramparts of Clay*, about a woman who supports a strike in a North African village by refusing to perpetuate old rituals. The villagers try to drive out her demon by throwing chicken blood in her face. The demon looked like Ana's mother, telling her that she was an insensitive jerk and a whore, who would never have children. Ana struggled to read the subtitles through her tears, then turned around and faced the raw light of the projector. Philip tried to be gentle. He took her back to her dorm room, but she couldn't breathe. She closed her eyes. She couldn't erase the image of chicken blood from her mind, only it wasn't in black and white like the film—it was red, red like a bucket of paint, or her mother's lipstick, smudged on a paper napkin.

She made an appointment at the Department of University Health with the first available shrink the next morning. But when she entered Dr. William Goldstein's office, all she could think of was the way that his wife had decorated it. Each of the three windows was tastefully adorned with white, pressed chintz curtains. Prim bouquets of dried flowers hung between each window to distract from the view of red brick walls beyond the office itself. Ana felt like the pale beige walls were closing in on her. The campus psychiatrist's Persian carpets were starting to levitate; soon they would smash her body against the ceiling. She wanted to puke on his floor. At least she could throw a bucket of paint against the jeering windowpanes. A bucket of red paint from the bodypainting film, which was such a disaster.

He waited patiently for her to come out of her shell while she continued to take in the decor. Then she looked at Dr. Goldstein out of the wounds that were her eyes. She began to talk about her unachievable expectations about Yale, and about the film of the woman polluted with blood. But the session was already over.

"Let's do some thinking about childhood before your next session, shall we?" he said, gently ushering her out of the office.

CHAPTER SIX

Valium and Voicelessness

Ana wrote in her diary:

One to Three Years Old

  Mommy didn't have room in her womb for me, but she regained her figure soon after the birth.

  Mommy leaves me in the house alone. Then she goes shopping. She spanks me for crying. Where Daddy? When Daddy coming home?

Six to Twelve

  Mommy says the boys threw snowballs with rocks inside at me because they like me. Mommy gives me candy every day. Mommy makes me practice saying "little lonesome lollipop." Mommy pays me fifty cents to finish reading "Little Women."

  Mommy tells people I'm a genius when I skip a grade. Mommy makes me curtsey in front of the dinner guests. Mommy tells me to stand up straight. Mommy makes me spit on my bangs so she can photograph me. Mommy loves me more than Vickie. Mommy hacks away at tree branches in the back yard. Mommy threatens us with knives when she cooks. Mommy tells me she'll kill us if we make noise when she and Daddy take naps. Mommy makes a dentist cut my tongue till it bleeds. He tells me my annunciation of "little lonesome lollipop" will improve, and gives me two red lollipops to prove it.

"You're making a lot of progress," Dr. Goldstein began, encouragingly.

"But we still haven't dealt with why I'm here," said Ana, twisting the small beige pillow's silk fringe around her fingers. She thought she had fooled him with her expressions of anger, but she felt betrayed, as if she had betrayed herself.

"Can you reiterate for me what you see as your main problem?" He looked down at her and waited, but her words had evaporated. He sat patiently.

"It's this university," she said. "Everything here is so male—not just the athletes and the professors, but the poets, even the stuffed leather chairs."

She couldn't release her painful thoughts. She was stuck in a hazy intellectuality where gender was everything. Dr. Goldstein said that nothing she had said made any sense to him and that she should try to communicate for him more. She attempted to say that ever since she arrived in New Haven, she'd felt trapped. Trapped in Bluebeard's castle. That every co-ed was destined to hang on a meat hook, like Bluebeard's trophy wives. (*Mommy! Mommy! Read me a story!*) But she couldn't say any of this. Instead she smiled nervously, thinking to herself that the only escape was to flunk out.

She cleared her throat. "I feel like I'm drowning in masculine culture," she said slowly. "The sexism here is so entrenched."

He looked through her file. "You have excellent grades," he said, looking up past his horn-rimmed reading glasses, "and you're such an attractive young woman. I really don't see how organizations like Yale could cause anxiety in themselves," he said in a gentle, soothing voice that belied the brutality of his judgment.

"I feel like I'm a guinea pig," she said.

But according to Dr. Goldstein, the real problem was probably that her mother had failed to connect with her when she was a child, and had forced her to grow up without existing in her true self. It was by now obvious to Ana that Dr. Goldstein knew absolutely nothing about how hard it was to be considered a super-woman, let alone how intensely anxious it felt to be a token woman in male-dominated fields like filmmaking or art.

"My wife is an artist. *She* doesn't feel any undue anxiety about that," said Dr. Goldstein, pointing proudly at the oil painting that was mounted on the wall behind him. "And as for women's lib," he added, "that won't get you anywhere in terms of lessening psychological anxiety." But Ana had stopped listening to him. She was staring at the painting of the Maine coast in summer that his wife had painted in angry dabs of Mars black and moldy green. He'd probably use my art like interior decorating, too, she thought as she stood up blinded with tears, making her way to the door. Dr. Goldstein rose to his feet, looking concerned for the first time—even alarmed. He suggested a prescription for Valium, but marijuana was enough for her. She slammed his door on the way out and refused to make a follow-up appointment.

"Ana," said Ms. Weinberg, "your paper on the sociology of women artists is very interesting."

"Well, yeah, but…" Ana began, then stopped herself. She had to get over these self-deprecating habits.

"This part that answers Linda Nochlin's question, 'Why Are There No Great Women Artists?' in particular," said Ms. Weinberg, rifling through the pages, cutting Ana off by speaking hurriedly. "You're entering into a dialogue with the world at large with your in-sights. If you cut it down to thirty pages, you might get it published."

They sat down and went over each of the fifty-five pages. No one had ever paid this kind of attention to her writing before.

"And especially this part, with Frankenthaler and this other woman artist, saying, 'We were friends, but not connected, since we competed for the same prize—honorable mention.' This explains a lot about why women haven't valued their friendships with other women in the art world. I'd move it up. It's important."

She thought about what Ms. Weinberg said when Diane Campbell approached her in the Common Room the next day with an application form for the First Annual Morehouse Ivy League Student Film Competition. She glanced down at the first few pages. First place was $10,000.

"Shall we co-apply?" asked Diane, willing to gamble that she had found a creative counterpart in Ana.

"Film is the universal language that transcends the voicelessness of women and can liberate the oppressed!" declaimed Ana, eager to value a female friendship. She imagined their great-great-great-grandmothers linking arms across the globe, having survived a Russian Tsar and a plantation owner down in Mississippi. She wanted to hug her, but Diane just looked at her.

"Let's not be too flighty," said Diane, opening up the budget section of the sixteen-page application form and laying it out over the stuffed leather couch. "I really need this support," she said. "My family isn't rich enough to back my films."

"My family doesn't back my films either. That's because they don't believe in them," replied Ana. "And I'm not financially qualified for scholarships." Inwardly she was frustrated at her inability to find a Yale partner rich enough to simply write a big check.

Diane wasn't going to get into a personal discussion. The grant included money for salaries. Even if they split it, it would enable them to make a film without having to scrounge for outside, sell-out work.

The competition was organized in such a way that each university—Harvard, Yale, Princeton, Columbia, etc.—would choose one project to recommend to the Steering Committee. So far, no one at Yale had come forward to apply other than the two young women.

Ana and Diane agreed that it was best to sacrifice their individual projects in the name of solidarity. "Women in Cinema" would deal with the images of women disseminated globally through mass media—something that no one anywhere had ever taken on, as far as they knew. They might be the first female filmmakers of the '70's taking apart—through the use of film clips—a media that treated women as sex objects. They would seek to document women's contributions in history. They would call for an end to the trivialization of girls and the abasement of older women. They would call for an end to gratuitous on-screen violence against women.

"Let's just remember that we're dealing with real women here," said Diane. "Womanhood is not an abstraction."

They wrote, revised, typed, proofread with Wite-Out, and hole-punched the proposal, placing it in a three-ring binder to deliver in person to Professor James Morganthau, the Chair of Yale's pre-selection committee. They hoped he and his committee would agree that their proposal was not only worthy of support, but that it topped the rest of the applicants'.

Prof. Morganthau was straightening up his office. He seemed to be about sixty, with a shock of white hair and deep, honest wrinkles. He seemed delighted at their arrival. He greeted them with a firm, rugby-player's handshake, and offered them tea. Ana was dressed in a red pantsuit and pearls; Diana's miniskirt was short but tasteful, matching her pale yellow blouse. "We had no idea such a pretty girl would apply for the Morehouse Competition," he said to Ana, opening up a tin of Danish cookies and describing the history of intercollegiate grants. He left the black girl out of the conversation. Ana and Diane looked at each other, their bright smiles fading.

The determination was to be made the following week, in the conference room in Trumbull College. All Yale applicants were to bring in five copies of their treatments, budgets and supporting materials for consideration. This time, Diane and Ana showed up in slacks and button-down shirts. The room was empty. Calling the contact number for the First Annual Morehouse Ivy League

Student Film Competition Steering Committee up in Cambridge, they were told that no one had bothered to apply from Yale.

"You mean our paperwork wasn't even processed?" asked Diane.

"What they mean is, no *men* applied from Yale," said Ana, seething. "No white men." Ana and Diane had no lawyers, mentors or advisors who would fight for them. "This is exactly what my paper was trying to say," said Ana, pacing back and forth. "Institutions make it impossible for women to excel."

"Let's not intellectualize," said Diane, with a sigh.

"Well, why not?" asked Ana, agitated. She walked towards the door, then turned in the doorway. "All right, I see your point. We've got to be practical, right? We've got to find secretarial jobs or something, fast. Anything to pay for some 16mm film and processing." After all, her mother had gone to secretarial school.

"Ana." Diane, who was already applying for a Rhodes Scholarship and a Fulbright, looked her straight in the face. "We are not going to be secretaries. We are going to learn the fine art of persistence."

CHAPTER SEVEN

Ordinary Rape

"Speaking of woman as the devil," Nick McDermott began under his breath, as Ana strode up to the projection booth in Linsly-Chittenden Hall, ready to switch reels that very minute if it meant a paycheck.

It never occurred to her that there simply weren't any openings for a projectionist. She looked at his taut, muscular body, hoisting film cans onto the rewind bench, and loading them up with reels. She politely informed him that the Yale Cinema Series was discriminating against women and minorities. Nick glanced up at the screen, where Marlene Dietrich was larger than life. Then he got down to business. "We aren't discriminating against you as a woman," he said, "because, if you haven't already noticed, there's been a girl projecting for the Yale Cinema Series for the past three months." He slammed the film can shut.

"Yes, but she's your girlfriend!" said Ana.

That made him reconsider. "Well, if Philip wants to give up part of his job to you, we really don't care."

She skipped jubilantly up to her dorm to share the news with Philip, but Philip wasn't at all happy with the idea. He flopped down onto the foam mattress and groaned. "What part of my job are you talking about?" he asked.

"Half?"

"I still don't get what the problem is with typing jobs," he said, casually reopening Arnheim's book on film as art.

"I want to be a projectionist, like you," she said, snuggling up to him under her grandmother's old quilt. With luck, she'd have the money to bring her footage to the lab the following Monday.

"Look, I'll give you some of my hours, okay? Just don't get better at it than me," he said gloomily, turning back to his book.

"This is just a stepping stone. I'm planning on becoming a director, and you know it," she retorted.

In a conciliatory moment, they both claimed that competition was an outmoded trait of the military-industrial complex. After sex, their competition escalated. At first, Philip had been willing to be a production assistant on her art film. He carried her tripod and lights for her through the Museum of Modern Art, so that she could film half a second of each painting in the permanent collection, three minutes per set-up. No one had ever been allowed such privileged access before. But now he was sinking deeper and deeper into stony silence, studying furiously in between flitting from one off-campus project to another.

He had left his Amish project unfinished, unsure whether it was compelling enough for a Senior Project. He convinced his parents to back a documentary about lobster fishermen, and then used the money to start shooting the history of soccer. None of these projects had been edited, and he blamed her. She was busy printing and mounting half a dozen of her photographs of male nudes for a gallery exhibit in New York—some of them of his own body, and some of them of Bruce's. She could have been in the editing room, helping him, instead of sequestering herself in a darkroom. He was jealous enough of the movie she was making about the art world with money she made from the projectionist job he got her. To top it off, there were her "A's". No matter how many stabs he made at studying, Ana's grades were always higher.

The first time Philip had threatened to leave was during Warhol's opening at the Whitney, mobbed with celebrities and fans. She had already loaded the Arri 16BL with 16mm Ektachrome in the back seat of the black Cadillac which Philip's family had lent him for the event. Andy Warhol himself had consented to the filming, flanked by his superstars—Candy Darling and Ultra-Violet, who preened before her camera in front of the multiple silk-screened portraits of Marilyn Monroe. Ana did her best to make them look decadent and ludicrous, zooming in while Warhol fondled his Polaroid camera like a pet dog. The glamour and excitement died down as she finished the last roll of film. She took the heavy camera off her shoulder for her boyfriend to hold while she put on her raccoon coat.

But Philip thrust the camera aside. "Ms. Superwoman!" he jeered. "You can do it all." She put the Arri 16BL on the floor and struggled to pull the coat on by herself. It seemed like everyone was watching and could see the holes in the lining.

"What are you going to do, marry some cute little nobody?" she taunted at him. "Don't you know I'm going to be a great film-maker some day, influencing the world of cinema? We should be working together!"

"Damn it all, Ana! Nick's right when he calls you a castrating bitch."

"Poor babies," she jeered. "Why don't you and Nicky tell Dr. Goldstein all about it? He'll probably recommend Thorazine to you both."

"You're a bitch!" he repeated. "You sound like Valerie Solanas!"

"I shot Warhol with a camera, not a gun! You were there!"

"I shouldn't have been anywhere near you."

"Society's sick! Not me!" she shouted, and ran out to the parking lot, lugging the heavy camera herself. Philip followed at a safe distance behind.

"You'd get plenty of support if you'd settle for art teacher and wife. It's crazy trying to be a girl director," he said in the car.

"*Girl* director?" She didn't have the strength to go on fighting with him all the way up the thruway. She had to save her energy to unload the 16mm film from the camera, once they got back to the campus. "You don't understand me or my work," she said finally, trudging up the stairs to her room with the camera case, sweating under the heavy fur coat.

"I understand one thing, Ana. You're cozy with the head of the Whitney Museum!" smirked Philip, locking the door to her room behind them. She backed up, trying to avoid his approach, as the phone started to ring.

"That's ridiculous! He's gay! Besides, you're the only one I've fucked for an entire year!" she screamed at Philip, her hand muffling the receiver.

"I thought you believed in free love," scoffed Philip.

"I do! I do! But…"

Ana could hear Vickie crying on the phone. "Please talk to me, Ana!" she was begging.

"I can't talk now," replied Ana, sotto voce. Her sister started mumbling a semi-incoherent soliloquy about some rock band try-out where they'd made her take off all her clothes.

"What a bummer," said Ana quickly. "But I know you'll get over it. Or you can go see a shrink or something, can't you?"

Philip watched her hang up. "You're just a selfish neurotic, aren't you?" he continued. "Your mother's right."

When she tried to slap him, he held her hands. She broke loose like a furious mare and swung open the door to the hall. He grabbed her, trying to hold her, trying to calm her down, but she swung at his face, clawing at empty air as he ducked. He ran after her down the hallway, their footsteps hollow echoes as he reached for her. But as he reached, she shrank back and fell, hurtling down a flight of stone stairs.

Ana lay on the landing, her arms and legs akimbo. It looked like he had pushed her. "Leave me alone!" she was screaming, in between loud, heaving sobs. "Everybody leave me alone, or I'll kill you! I'll kill you!"

By now she was certain he had pushed her. She raised her head and turned her face towards his portrait of dismay. But he couldn't have really pushed her down a staircase, could he? Surely he loved her too much for something like that. Philip put on his black Amish hat and backed down the stairs, avoiding her eyes: He was planning on leaving for Maine in the morning to film another lobster fisherman and maybe moving out.

Ana was sobbing quietly on the landing and examining her bruises. Her arms had hit the stone steps, and her silver bracelets had cut against one of her wrists. Joe from upstairs peered down from the landing above her. "Hey, you need help? An ambulance or something?"

She took herself to an emergency room, and later that night, tried to call Diane. She dialed painfully, her right arm in a sling. She was certain that Diane would listen, that Diane could talk some sense into her. But Diane's phone had been disconnected, and nobody had seen her in class for days.

Sunday

Dear Diane, she wrote, *Why haven't you called? I'm really sorry that I kept insisting on talking about the Panthers. I didn't know what else to say after those bourgeois motherfuckers turned us down for that grant. I was really naive, I guess. Now I realize that I shouldn't have assumed you wanted to talk about Black America with me. Since it's the very first time that women and Blacks have had a chance to climb the ladder of success, I wanted you to know that I really hope you get to fulfill your dreams. As for me, I don't have any dreams—not after yesterday. I don't know if I believe in any ladders of success. What's the point of studying for exams? I don't know if I should tell you this, but I think my boyfriend threw me down the staircase in the dorm.*

Maybe Philip didn't really push me down the stairs. Maybe I just made it up, like he says. Maybe I just fell. But...

Philip had come back to the room to finish packing, and insisted on reading over Ana's shoulder as she struggled to keep writing, despite her aching wrist. She covered the paper with her sling, and he went back to prepping for his film as if nothing had happened.

> *Philip holds me on his lap, rocking me back and forth like a baby, saying, "Oh you baby, why are you so sad? Is it because I'm leaving?" and I just say, "I'm sad because of this and because of that," not wanting him to know that you and I met in the Sisterhood. The Sisterhood's a complete joke around here. I don't believe in organizations anyway, do you? Philip keeps saying, "Come on, Ana, tell me what's the matter," so I tell him something like, "It's not enough that Bobby Seale's been released," and he just says, "You know that's not what's eating you." So I say, "You always tell me I exaggerate. That I shouldn't be so emotional." Then I swallow my tears, and then, and then, I just can't think of any other way to be.*
>
> *I wish you'd call, Diane. You could tell me what to say.*

Philip had called off his shoot. His duffel bag lay near the door. He had decided to move into Paul's dorm at least until Ana calmed down, but he wanted to wait until after his final exam. He was lying on the mattress, reviewing his notes on *The Birth of a Nation*.

She stood up and brushed herself off, then shut the door without saying goodbye. She had already taken her first exam on Tuesday: she had aced it.

A light fog had started to envelope the campus: she was grateful for its anonymity as she made her way down Elm Street with her arm in a sling. Arriving at the screening room a half hour early, she locked herself into the solitude of the projection booth. She had seen Truffaut's *Jules and Jim* before, and remembered Catherine's exuberant freedom as played by Jeanne Moreau. Her own exuberance had vanished. When it was time to change reels, she found herself lost in a daydream about marrying a dull and untalented man. But an equally dull pain pushed her awake. She was clumsy with her arm in the sling: the second reel clattered to the floor of the projection booth. It was difficult enough to pick it up, let alone thread it through a projector. By now she was alert enough to pay attention to the second reel. Jules was quoting Baudelaire: "'I wonder why women are allowed to enter churches—what could they hope to say to God?'"

Ana thought, "What's the use of sacrificing my intellect and talent to marry a talented intellectual with views like that!" She really had to break up with Philip. Good thing he was moving out. She'd be able to stop analyzing whether or not he had pushed her. She busied herself with rewinding the previous reel.

"You're a pair of fools," retorted Catherine.

"I don't approve of what Jules says at two in the morning," said Jim.

"Then protest."

"I protest!" said Jim, but that was not good enough for Catherine, in a dazzling performance by Moreau, who pushed back her veil, took off her hat, and jumped into the Seine.

But even that was not good enough for Ana. What if she jiggled the projector so that the film ran backwards? Instead of beginning to drown, Catherine would rise from the water like Venus in her shell. She would not need Jules or Jim to save her, nor would she die in Reel Three.

She glanced outside the booth. The auditorium was filled to overflowing with mostly male students looking for release from the pressure of final exams. Catherine's eroticism was upstaging the point she was trying to make. But Ana identified with her maverick protest, taking a leap for womankind. She hit the rewind button and carefully adjusted the loop as the film proceeded to run backwards.

The male audience reacted immediately, booing. Some threw candy bars and pencils. As the lights went on, Nick McDermott was running up the aisle, preparing to drag her out of the projection booth.

"What is this, some kind of a protest?" Nick demanded, careful to avoid her sling.

"Right on!" declaimed Ana, grabbing one of the rewinds with her left hand as he approached her.

She was holding on as hard as she could when Nick and three other members of the Yale Cinema Series pulled her down from the flimsy wooden structure at the back of the auditorium. They fired her on the spot, then forced her to march down the aisle full of hooting, jeering young men, some of them throwing spitballs.

They could take their lowly job and shove it: Did they think she was going to perpetuate the sexism of their media forever? The Male Cinema Series would be down on its knees some day, begging for a chance to screen her work.

She got back to the dorm just as Philip finished moving out. By now her head was throbbing with the loud rock music coming from downstairs, and her arm was aching. It was impossible to sleep, so she decided to pull on a day-glo lime green mini-dress that had been hanging in her closet and catch the tail end of the Yale-Columbia mixer that was spilling out into the courtyard.

A medical student from Columbia University named Leonard asked her to dance: "I Can't Get No Satisfaction" was her favorite song. Leonard had thick black-rimmed glasses, and she didn't quite get his last name, but his smile was demure and his black leather jacket was refreshing. She had left her sling upstairs, and looked relatively graceful although she could barely stand up. He could hardly keep his hands off her, eager to spend the night with her and pushing her upstairs. After the quickie, he offered her a ride into New York City. She accepted: if she got her footage of Andy Warhol processed, she could edit it into her film in time for graduation.

Ciné-Art Labs opened shortly after dawn. She counted out seventy-eight hard-earned dollars and gave it to Vince, the lab owner, in return for the 16mm original and workprint of Warhol's opening. They screened the workprint in a dark corner: his silk-screen paintings and superstars were perfectly exposed.

"That's some outfit you have on," said Vince, staring at her thighs in the semi-darkness. She was still in the mini-dress that she'd put on for the mixer the night before. "Don't forget—all the free developing you need, and I mean, we can develop something special right here like you wouldn't believe." She sent him a charming little laugh of denial as he rewound Ana's workprint onto a yellow core. He tossed the tightly wound 16mm workprint along with the original footage into a 35mm tin can, and pushed it snugly into her backpack. "You and your work are so hot, babe, I'll throw in an air conditioner. Brand new," he joked.

She smirked good-naturedly and walked out the front door.

"Baby, you're gonna need it this summer," he called out after her. "Remember, it's gonna get hotter."

A few blocks west was the gas station from which Ana had hitchhiked twice before, saving money for *The New York Art World*. She covered her bare shoulders with the jacket that the medical student had given her to keep warm after the mixer, rubbing her still-aching arm. She squinted down the street, overly aware of her long white legs. The glare of big new cars pulling into the gas station and the smell of their gas and the dust their wheels raised were feeding her headache. Men's hot glances fell against her breasts like bird droppings as she hurriedly glanced down at the paperwork from Ciné Arts. She crumpled up the receipt: a wood-paneled station wagon had screeched to a halt, its driver leaning out the window.

"How far are you going?" Ana asked.

"Depends how far you want to go." She gave him the finger; he pushed on the accelerator, watching the curve of her legs in his rear view mirror.

Another car stopped, a white Mustang. The guy driving was a blond-haired hippie. "I'm heading up 95," he said.

"OK!" said Ana, climbing in. He was kind of cute, although his car stank of cigarettes. His New England looks almost matched Philip's. She tossed her backpack into the back seat.

"Where're you heading?"

"New Haven."

"Right on," he said. "I'm headed for West Haven, myself. Ever been there?"

"No, not really," she replied. He pulled a beer can out of a paper bag, guzzled it, and offered her some.

"How old are you?" he asked.

"Why?"

"Just wondering, sort of," he said. "My name's Joe."

Ana looked out the window. "I'm Marianne," she lied. It was stuffy in his car.

"I used to go down with my pals to New Haven, crash those Yale mixers, you know?" Joe said. "You sneak into the colleges and you can drink all the free beer you want to."

"Oh, I used to go to those mixers!" said Ana brightly, taking off Leonard's jacket. "What cattle shows!"

Joe looked at her bare shoulders and stepped on the gas. "We'd try to get into girls like you, but you were all a bunch of snobs."

"They're just cattle shows," repeated Ana insistently in her lime-green party dress.

"I can't fight these big trucks," said Joe. "Got into a fucking mess last spring. Totaled the car."

Ana wasn't sure she'd heard him correctly in the din of morning traffic. "The whole thing is fucked up. The country's the only place to live, I guess." The cigarette smell was getting to her. If only the window on her side weren't stuck.

"Can you lay off?" he said. "Can you just lay the fuck off?!"

"I don't have to listen to you swearing at me like that!" said Ana indignantly. "I'd rather get out and get another ride."

"Slow down, will ya, Marianne? I just can't listen to you bitching anymore, so take it easy." Joe turned on the radio. It was the

Staple Singers. He reached for something under the seat. Then he said, "Why don't you put your head on my lap?"

Ana thought he was kidding until she saw the gun pointed at her head. "Look," he said, "I don't like using this, so why don't you do what I say? Here," he said, maneuvering the gun to his other hand without losing his grip on the steering wheel, "put your head down, like this." He pulled Ana's head to his faded jeans with his free right hand.

Her head was pressed against him. "Look, you're making a mistake. I have VD."

"Undo your dress."

"Listen, the minute I got in the car I thought you were a cute guy. You don't have to be doing this with a gun. Why don't you put that thing away?"

"Come on," said Joe. "Pull your underpants down."

"Look, I think you're cute. You don't have to be doing it this way."

"Pull your pants down."

"What?"

"Your underpants."

"Why don't you give me your phone number instead of going through this hassle and we can get together later, when my period is gone?"

Joe was getting upset. "Are they down? Come on! Answer me!"

"Yes." He felt Ana up, manipulating both girl and car through traffic, his hand in her vagina, listening to the music.

"That's fine. Go-o-o-d. That's what I like to see," he said, adding softly, "It's been so long since I had a broad."

"Listen, you're making a mistake," she tried to say. It shocked her that her brains were unable to protect her body.

"You lying bitch!" snarled Joe. "You don't really have your period, do you?"

Ana struggled to get up, her sore elbow hitting the steering wheel.

"Bitch!" Jumbled flashes of a gas station and tollbooths churned past. He slapped her down with the muzzle of the gun.

"But I'm a human being, too," she tried to say. "You can feel my breasts. You can even *feel* that I'm a human being."

She lay passively as he drove through the automatic tollbooth in Greenwich, the gun pressed against her head. Approaching the Cos Cob exit ramp, he said, "I'm going to get off so we can find some woods. OK?"

In a state of panic, Ana thrust herself out of Joe's car as it slowed down briefly. But she couldn't grab her backpack with her Senior Project footage before he raced off. She jumped wildly at the navy blue sedan in the next lane, screaming, "Help—this guy's driving off with all my film in his car! He tried to rape me!" Her whole body shook as she opened the door of the car.

"You look like a hooker," said the woman in the driver's seat, eyeing the hysterical girl in a torn mini-dress. Ana had jumped into the car and slammed the door shut, begging for help from a middle-aged woman wearing plaid slacks with a circle pin on her navy blue jacket over a pink cotton blouse. The woman hesitated for an instant, then hit the gas. They careened after the white Mustang, racing the wrong way down a one-way, tree-lined street. They found themselves skidding over the athletic field of the private school where Philip's sister had once played lacrosse, and caught up with Joe as his car crashed into the bleachers.

The woman got out of her blue sedan. She went over to Joe, who was unhurt, though his car was totaled. Ana started to rush away down the sidewalk. The footage in his back seat seemed worthless compared to her life and reputation.

"Hey you, don't run off!" called the lady, opening her navy blue jacket and exposing a police badge.

"I didn't do anything!" Ana replied hastily, cringing with guilt.

"Sure you didn't," said the lady police officer. "I'm Officer Healy. Are you sure you two didn't know each other before this happened?"

"I never saw him before in my life!" cried Ana. What would her mother do to her now?

Officer Healy asked the two of them—Ana and Joe—to get in the vehicle.

"You're lucky I just went off duty. I never handled this stuff before," said Healy, placing Ana's backpack in the trunk. She was going to take them down to the station.

Joe pleaded his innocence in the back seat. "I swear I never did *nothing* wrong before this. I swear I didn't. I just wanted to help, officer. I don't know what got into me."

Three male police officers escorted Ana Fried through the Greenwich Police Station. Crossing the sterile waxed gray floor, she felt as though her body were on trial. Philip's parents lived in Connecticut—they might read about her in the newspaper. Now she would never get to meet them.

"I don't want to press charges," she said.

"We're simply trying to establish what happened. Don't worry," said the detective. "We won't be giving out any information to the news."

"Things like this happen all the time," said the police chief.

"What do you want me to say? He had a gun which he held against my head," said Ana. "He used his hands to feel me up—and he was planning to rape me."

"Specifically, what was he doing?" asked the police detective.

"How many gory details do you need?" she asked. "He was working his finger up my vagina!"

The policemen looked at each other, then led her to a small, ordinary room. A policewoman with pink plastic eyeglasses smiled at Ana from her gray Formica desk.

"Mrs. Rogers will help you file a formal report," one of the male officers explained, "if you'd like to sit down over here for a few minutes. Miss Ana Fried—spelled F-r-i-e-d, not F-r-e-e-d—alleges to have run into some trouble with a white male, age approximately twenty years, from who she accepted a ride."

"He was trying to rape me!" Ana interrupted. Joan Healy had returned from the ladies' room, eyeing her colleagues apprehensively over a cup of coffee. She stirred some creamer into her coffee and left the room.

"Can't get these women libs anymore!" the male officer muttered, then turned to Ana Fried. "Dear, you don't seem to understand the legal aspect of this. You're maybe a smart girl. But Connecticut law states that if there is no penetration by the male genital organ, there is no rape. Unless we can establish a clear case of intent, the charge will have to be assault with sexual mischief, no matter what you *think* he intended."

"He was carrying a gun," she said.

The detective interrupted. "You're a lucky girl. This officer saved your life, even though she was off-duty." Mrs. Rogers nodded sagely. She seemed sympathetic. "Hey, tell Joan we're going to fix her up a citation," he said sarcastically to an officer bringing in more coffee.

"He was planning to rape me," she repeated. "He was getting off the highway to find some woods so he could do it." Mrs. Rogers busied herself taking notes.

"But isn't this conjecture on your part?" He looked at her dayglo lime-green mini-dress.

"What should I have done? Let him do it so you'd have proof?"

The police chief tossed his colleagues a "just-another-hysteric" expression, and tossed Ana her backpack. "Fine...I think we have enough," he said to Ana. "We'll let you write it up now, Mrs. Rogers."

The policemen left the room; Mrs. Rogers offered Ana a cigarette. They watched through the glass pane as Ana shook her head "No". One of the officers drove her to the railroad station. She was longing to get some sleep on the train. But as the train jerked from side to side, she continued to stare straight ahead, her body erect, listening to the film rattling against the tin can inside her backpack. She pulled her backpack up from the floor between her legs, and held it in her lap.

Hours later, she found herself outside Philip's suite in Silliman, the residential college he had moved into with Paul. A bit of a jock, Paul had just walked out from the shower with a towel wrapped around his waist, whistling "Monday, Monday."

"Hi!" he said. "Your boyfriend's in there, all right. Keep knocking." Embarrassed, he walked quickly to his room and disappeared inside.

Philip opened the door, buttoning his pants and yawning. He was surprised to see Ana standing there.

"I've been up all night," said Ana, in monotone. "I missed the train."

"I know you better than that. You were screwing around with someone else," he said, noticing the torn, short dress. "Serves you right—sex addict." But recognizing the anxiety in her face, he took a deep breath and tried to draw her towards him.

"Seriously, what's wrong?" Philip asked gently, taking her backpack off her shoulders and putting it on the floor.

"Someone pulled a gun on me."

Philip pulled her into the room, turned off the rock music, and held her in his arms, his moustache grazing the top of her head. "He didn't do anything to you, did he?" he asked. "You know what I mean."

"He was going to rape me," said Ana, beseechingly, "but a policewoman saved me."

Philip let go as Paul came through the room in a cheerleader's uniform, smelling of after-shave. "Hey, Paulie! Guess what happened to Ana," said Philip. "Some guy almost raped her!"

"Gee, that's too bad," said Paul.

"What a bastard!" said Philip.

Paul turned sharply in the doorway, punching his fists in the air as he disappeared into the hallway. He called back, "You ever need me for protection, just yell."

Phil had already started kissing Ana out of solace.

"He just seemed like an ordinary guy," said Ana. "He didn't look like a rapist." She huddled against him.

"Don't let it worry you," he said, finally, and looked at his watch apologetically. "You know how it is. My psych final's tomorrow and I've really got to cram."

He convinced her to leave, but she'd only gotten as far as the laundry room of Philip's dorm. She tried to call him on a pay phone to discuss their relationship. There was no answer. She was so fixated on calling him that she hadn't noticed Lawrence Stimpson walk in and close the door until he was standing right in front of her. He had just come back from Mory's, his breath reeking of gin and vermouth. "I saw you at that French flick the other night. What was it called? *Jules et Jim.* You were making that mam'selle they shared go backwards." He was swaying back and forth. "You must be pretty liberated, huh, to pull a stunt like that?"

Ana laughed a bit too nervously. "I guess you could say that."

He reached out and stroked her dark, Jewish hair. "So, you still believe in free love?"

"Do I believe in free love? That's a funny question." She opened the door to a dryer that had stopped spinning and checked them for dampness, as if the wet clothes belonged to her.

"You do or you don't?" Lawrence asked, looking her over.

Ana was unnerved. Somehow she should have changed out of the torn dress before showing up at Philip's dorm, but she was so confused. "Why don't you ask my boyfriend... You know, Philip Westover?"

"I'm asking you."

"Of course. I mean, yes. But not with you."

He leaned over her, pressing her against the dryer. "Oh? And why not, may I ask?"

"Your sexual style is strictly possess and destroy."

"Aw, come on—it was great last time. Admit it."

"I've fucked all your friends, from Mockery to Disrespect, but that's not my idea of free love."

Her wit was charming the pants off him. "You mean you've started charging?" He started unzipping his fly. "Don't worry, I can pay. What, fifty bucks?"

She wanted to slap him, but he had her pinned against the dryer, its clothes spinning rapidly again. Suddenly she noticed Paul, standing in the doorway. He looked embarrassed to see his roommate's girl with another man.

"Paul!" she yelled, as he grabbed his clean clothes from another dryer and backed out of the room. "Paul!" she shouted in agony, counting on him to protect her. But he had already closed the door, and no one could hear her over the din of the washing machines.

Lawrence had unzipped his pants. She could already see the appendix scar crawling across his abdomen. He was trying to lower her underwear while keeping her pinned down. Then he vomited in front of her, splashing her dress.

"Aw, gee! Please excuse me, Ana. I'm so sorry!"

He had taken a white linen handkerchief out of his breast pocket. He meant to clean her off as a gesture of gentlemanly behavior, but she had escaped in the lime green dress.

She was running up the courtyard steps to Philip's room. She needed the security of his love and his understanding more than ever. "Phil? Let me in! Let me in!" She shook the door handle. "Damn it! Let me in!"

"Leave me alone," called Philip feebly, through the door.

"I want to talk to you!" screamed Ana.

"Not now. Go away."

"I don't care. I need to talk to you now. I have something I want to talk to you about."

No answer.

"I know you're with someone. I don't care! Open the door!"

The door opened cautiously. It was Paul Smith, not Phil. Ana threw herself at him. "Bastard!"

Paul tried his best to calm her. "Annie, what's this going to accomplish?" He noticed a peculiar smell.

"Let me in!" Ana was crying furiously. "All of you are bastards! Cowards! I want to see him!"

"He's busy. He's not going to see you."

"Yes, he is!" she cried hysterically. "Yes, he is!"

"Maybe you should see a shrink." Ana smacked him. "Jesus fucking cunt!" said Paul, and slammed the door.

Ana ran out into the courtyard. Stumbling through the grass, she took off her shoes and ran up to the building, barefooted. Philip's second-story window was shut. "Open up, you motherfucker!" She threw a shoe at the window, but it missed. "Talk to me! Phil! Philip!" She threw the other shoe. This time it bounced against the tinted glass with a thwack.

At the window appeared the blinking face of Jennifer Grinnan, the American Studies' major with the pixie cut from the consciousness-raising group four years earlier. A shirtless Philip quickly moved into the window frame and put his arm around Jennifer, who was beginning to look concerned. "We're trying to study for an exam up here. What do you want?" he asked, shocked.

"I need an abortion!" screamed Ana, although by now she was bleeding and in need of a tampon. She was screaming from menstrual rage and every other kind of rage, including a murderous rage at Jennifer Grinnan for sleeping with her boyfriend.

But her screaming couldn't induce him to come downstairs. He would never see through her screaming enough to love her again. She was done for. She wasn't good enough, or pure enough. No one would ever love her again. Not even her mother, she sobbed to herself, closing herself into the telephone booth outside of his dorm to call home.

"I was hitchhiking from the city yesterday, and this blond-haired hippie pulled a gun on me! He... And everybody thinks that..." She was wracked with sobs; her mother could barely make out whatever Ana was trying to tell her.

"Where are you?" she demanded.

"I'm back at Yale. I had to go to the police station, and..."

"The police! For god's sake, why of all things did you have to be hitchhiking?"

"You never give me an allowance. I'm trying to make a movie in New York City," she spurted out, in between sobs.

"Forget the movie. What did he do to you?"

"I can't forget the movie." She started sobbing again. "Without the movie, I can't graduate."

"Was he black?"

"No, he wasn't black. He was blond. He was blond like Philip. Please, Mom, can you just come up here and get me?" She was so delirious, she didn't even know whether she was talking about the guy with the gun, or Lawrence.

"What? At this time of night?" Madelyn shouted for Marty to come upstairs. He put down the newspaper and padded to the hall.

"Ana," her mother said. "Calm down. What do you want us to do?" She covered the phone and filled Ana's father in on the details. "Take a warm bath, Ana. He didn't shoot you, did he? You'll get over it. Just don't ruin our vacation plans."

Ana held the phone tightly, like a rubber toy. "Aren't you coming to my graduation?"

"No, Ana, we'll be in the Bahamas." Ana had scrunched the phone against her cheek, sobbing silently. "And another thing," said Madelyn. "Don't tell Vickie—you'll set a bad example."

"I love this draft," Ms. Weinberg said. "Before you send it out for publication, I'd just add Dr. Matina Horner's quote: 'If she fails, she is not living up to her own standards of performance; if she succeeds she is not living up to societal expectations about the female role.'

Of course, you're getting an 'A' for the paper," she added quickly.

Ms. Weinberg apologized that this would be their last meeting, since Wellesley had offered her a tenure-track position which Yale wouldn't match. She was moving to Massachusetts, and she had to pack.

Ms. Weinberg seemed too busy for Ana to tell her that she was the first, last, and only teacher who was ever in tune with what Ana needed. She was the only teacher who had ever tried to understand her. Instead Ana mumbled something about not knowing which publications should be sent her manuscript.

"Oh, and by the way, you can leave your gender journal in my box anytime this week. Would you like me to mail it to your home address when I'm finished grading?" asked Ms. Weinberg in her gentle, mousy voice. Ana nodded. She hadn't finished writing it.

Her last journal entries had been a series of hysterical and pretentious fragments centering on her victimhood and berating herself for having associated with Tammy, Howard, Chauncey and Philip in the first place. She recognized her immaturity as a writer—how she skirted around the problems of trying to liberate herself, unsure of the stakes and unwilling to face the responsibilities of inner truths she had barely begun to recognize. And yet, reassured by the knowledge that no one except Ms. Weinberg would ever read it, she buckled down to complete her journal for "The Sociology of Women Artists" in time to pass that final course, pulling another all-nighter in the process.

Some of it was incoherent. The effort itself left her so drained and exhausted that she debated whether or not to attend her graduation ceremonies. At the last minute she decided that she owed it to the dining hall workers to participate. She would help them in their organizing efforts by protesting the graduation from within, even if it meant getting a piece of paper that was her own ticket into the elite—a guarantee that she would never wait on tables or type for a boss. Graduating from Yale was no longer a selfless cause to please her mother. It had become a selfless cause to please the masses, she rationalized. She would stand there among the thousand men and women of her class and protest.

Twenty-one

I'm leaving Yale without a single lover or even a friend. Fuck Tammi, Fuck Howard, Fuck Chauncey and Fuck Joyce and their disapproving glares. They SWORE they'd protest the farce of our graduation, but none of THEM carried "Support the Workers" signs except me and a handful of people that we sort of knew. What convinced me to wear these workmen's overalls in the first place? Fuck Howard and Chauncey in their long, black, sweaty graduation gowns, and Fuck Tammi and Joyce in their bright skirts and blouses. Their parents must have talked them into their stupid attire at the last minute, while mine were busy snorkeling with some client "friends" who have a yacht. The hell with Lawrence Stimpson, Jr. and his parents. I was completely invisible to them. And the nerve of Philip showing up with a conventional date who probably doesn't even go to Yale.

Not that I really care. I'll always remember the gun of the sick bastard in the Mustang better than my graduation. Tammi Bradley gave me this phony, super-concerned expression, saying, "Call me if you need me."

As for Diane, she's disappeared. The rumor is that she was sexually assaulted in the co-ed bathroom, and she's dropped out. Maybe a couple of Skin and Bones boys did it, but no charges have been made. I always figured there was something sick about secret societies: no one's held accountable. If I had a grenade, I would have thrown it into the crowd. I'm thinking of joining the Weather Underground to bomb whatever family, God and Yale represent.

CHAPTER EIGHT

Failures of Success

Good morning, Heartache, here we go again.
— Billie Holiday

S he didn't feel that she could go home in the shape that she was in. Besides, her film was premiering the following Tuesday in New York. It was the only thing she could feel good about. So she took the train into the city, rocking back and forth with her suitcase on her lap, wondering if she should open it and get out the tequila before the train pulled into the station.

After wandering down to Greenwich Village, she ran into someone from her French Lit seminar at Yale outside the Village Vanguard, but she couldn't remember his name. He had a handlebar moustache, and had become a linguist. He had planned to specialize in sub-Saharan languages at grad school—anything to avoid the draft, but the draft had ended in January, leaving him adrift.

"It's still 'Make Love, Not War,' right?" he asked, grinning at her.

"Right on!" she said, trying to sound blithe.

"Greg Fischer, remember?" He reached out and tweaked her hair, ever so gently. "Greg from Silliman. Russian Chorus."

She took a deep breath and tried to smile, putting her feelings on automatic pilot when he suggested his East Village apartment as a crash pad. Anything to avoid the battleground that was her family, even if the East Village was filled with the fossilized remains of hippies who had lost out to junk. She would have preferred to be fighting it out with Philip, but Philip had made it perfectly clear that he was through with her, and there was no longer any reason for her to believe in marriages or families. Ms. Weinberg had encouraged her to think independently, but Ms. Weinberg was no longer there to encourage her, and she wasn't ready to think things through independently on her own quite yet.

Greg carried her suitcase all the way to Avenue B and up six flights of stairs. It weighed a ton with the bottle of tequila and the 16mm film inside, mounted on a steel reel.

She paused momentarily on the fifth floor landing, having tripped on a used syringe, while Greg continued to trudge up the dank, dimly-lit stairs with her luggage. "I'm dying of thirst, aren't you?" she cried gaily up to him. He put the suitcase down, panting, whole-heartedly agreeing.

His roommates flung open the door at the commotion in the hall. Greg wasted no time in introducing Ana to the guys: Alan Beimann, a botanist specializing in hemp; and Jeff Katz, a budding artist with waist-length black hair. They helped him open a bottle of Portuguese wine to toast their independence from their alma mater, though Jeff had graduated from Yale the year before, and Alan was a dropout from Brown. Just as they were about to raise their glasses, the doorbell rang. The more the merrier, thought Ana. They introduced her to Sara Zaslavsky, Greg's girlfriend, a senior from Columbia. She seemed a bit icy and claimed to just be stopping by to return a book. Ana had thought of offering the bottle of tequila; now she decided to hoard it.

"Miss Fried is thinking of moving in," said Greg, addressing his roommates. "With your approval, that is." Sarah apparently had no say in the matter but was fuming anyway. He hurried to light up a joint to ease the tension.

Alan glanced up at Ana as he poured the wine into some coffee mugs. "Hey, the place is desperately in need of a woman's touch.

Right, guys? Great to have you—rent's $120. If we split it four ways instead of the usual three, that's only thirty bucks each." But she'd never had to worry about paying rent before; she thought it was going to be a crash pad. Weren't crash pads supposed to be free?

Ana looked around the kitchen apprehensively. The kitchen had a bathtub in it. The stove looked like it had never seen a maid in its life. No wonder Sara hadn't already moved in. Cockroaches were cavorting among the dishes, and there was a mousetrap under the counter. Above the bathtub reeking of mildew was a faded, curling poster of Jefferson Airplane—left over from former tenants who were probably dead. At least she'd have the living room to herself; the guys had agreed to share the bedroom down the dark corridor that led to the toilet.

They were pouring another round to toast her upcoming screening. Jeff's long black hair quivered while he poured it out. "It's a competitive world, and it looks like you already made it," he said, impressed that her film was premiering at the Museum of Modern Art. Maybe he's a little bit jealous, thought Ana. His carefully drawn self-portrait hanging next to the refrigerator could never compete with Pop and Minimal Art.

None of them were going to the screening. Jeff Katz was busy cataloguing ninth century Carolingian art at the Met that week; Greg would be trekking up to Columbia University to discuss the possibility of a stipend; Alan had to make deliveries; and Sara was starting a summer job with the Dean of Students at Barnard. As for the artists featured in *The New York Art World*, Ana had forgotten to send out any invitations. She had no idea whether the museum had even thought to write a press release. She had barely gotten it together to mix the tracks and cut the 16mm negative in time for her final grade, though she had wanted to do much more.

Her screening was supposed to create a revolution in the arts. But when she arrived at the museum, wearing a red zip-up jumpsuit and matching sling-back pumps, there was already a commotion going on outside. There had to be at least two dozen women, picketing the museum, holding signs and chanting "Women Now!" Someone handed her a flyer, but she already knew from her Women Artists' course that MoMA had never had a one-artist show devoted to a woman painter. Her audience was probably going to be decimated, but the real question was whether or not she should cross the picket line for her Q&A. A film starring Andy Warhol and Robert Rauschenberg seemed to simply dovetail into the museum's policy of a hundred years of art by men. Who would know it was a protest film without actually seeing it?

She ran up to the woman who had given her the flyer, who was fashionably thin and seemed intelligent. Ana tried to explain that the museum was about to screen a film directed by a woman, and that she was that woman, and that *The New York Art World* was her first major achievement.

"Great timing, huh?" said the protester, trying to give her a hug of sympathy. But Women Artists in Revolution had already scheduled the demonstration. There was no backing down now, and besides, what could one woman's token film do to rectify the percentages biased so overwhelmingly towards men?

Ana jerked her shoulder away, feeling like a total failure. She was missing the premiere of her own film, and it was supposed to overthrow the art world. Instead she had let it be co-opted. She hadn't even interviewed any of the women now standing in front of her, chanting "Fifty Percent Women Artists Now!"

She shouldn't be crass enough to think of money at a time like this. But she'd counted on selling at least one 16mm print. Maybe there was a distributor at her screening, but how would she recognize him if he came out of the museum? She might as well not stand there any more, she thought, walking slowly away in her bright red pumps. Maybe Alan, Greg and Jeff would be patient with her share of the rent.

"I want to make a toast to three wonderful roommates," Ana began, slurring her speech. They had just consumed two joints and a six-pack and now she was ready to give them her tequila. Out of her line of vision, Greg was shooing Jeff and Alan out of the living room and quietly closing the door.

"Here's to the—the biggest erections in the Empire State," she was trying to say, though Greg was the only one left. "I'm abdicating feminism for, um...a few sensitive men." She held her tequila bottle on high, saluting her mother. Hadn't her mother always told her to go out with Yalies?

"To tell you the truth, Ana, you don't enunciate when you're stoned." Greg started unbuttoning her blouse with awkward fingers.

"So what? Do words matter here?" Her parents thought of her as a whore, so she might as well act like one. She laughed as his fingers began to tickle her, and helped him pull off her pants. He buried his moustache between her labia, scouting out her clitoris to suck. But it was only a damp sparkler orgasm that failed to heal her raw wounds.

Then Philip came back like a bounced-back tennis ball. Things hadn't worked out as planned on Jennifer's graduation trip to Barcelona. He had to call Ana's dad to find her East Village address. He put down his duffel bag and put himself to work, rolling a joint on the couch. He had shaved off his moustache and looked less like a hippie than ever before, despite his long hair. Greg was taking a bath in the kitchen, ready to call it a night. Ana closed her kimono tightly across her chest, and slammed the door between the living room and the kitchen to talk to Philip privately. How dare he play with her after all of his months of vague promises! He said he wanted them to come to some sort of an understanding of their break-up. Damned if she was going to discuss her Horatio Alger story gone bad.

Instead she let her fingers run up the fire escape of Philip's penis, using sex to obliterate her problems once again. By then his Mexican hash had gone to work, throwing her into the volcano of the fold-up couch like an Olmec offering.

Through the thin living room walls, Alan, Jeff and Greg could hear the loud sexual screams of her multiple orgasms, which had taken the place of intimacy. Afterwards, she put her kimono back on and trundled sheepishly into the still-neglected kitchen, where the three men watched her drink the dregs of the Portuguese wine from the previous weekend. She wanted to score her arm with a knife for every time some guy had tried to score with her on Avenue B.

"All Yale women are hopeless neurotics," said Greg, "excepting of course Miss Fried." He addressed the remark so directly at her genitals that her only reaction was to avoid looking at the three men standing there awkwardly. She certainly couldn't look at Alan, the macho cockroach smasher who'd convinced her to go to bed with him two nights ago.

Philip came into the kitchen for a glass of water and some Anacin, having already packed for Connecticut, where he'd given up toying with photography for Yale Law.

"How dare you leave now," she wanted to say. She walked him out to the stairwell. He hoisted his duffel bag onto his shoulder, then paused.

"I want to give you some money," he said.

"What for?"

"You can get a—you know, operation—for around a hundred dollars, can't you?" He looked so skinny in his Army jacket that for a moment she wondered how she could ever have loved him. Without his moustache, he seemed younger, almost naked.

"I don't really need an abortion," she said, sick of the ruse that had gotten his attention, and his lame, belated offer of help.

"Oh, well, in that case. I..." He turned away and started walking down the stairs, his long blond hair sailing behind him. Maybe she should stop him. If she just held on, maybe he would help her with the groceries and rent.

When she came back to the kitchen, nobody had anything to say to each other. They stood around shuffling from foot to foot, unable to discuss the uncomfortable situation. She obviously couldn't keep living with all of them and fantasizing about blood dripping down her arms. That's when she decided: "Well, I can always go to grad school, can't I?"

The day her parents returned from the Bahamas was the day that Ana had chosen to unpack her college trunk on the living room floor in Scarsdale. Clothes, papers, books were lying everywhere. Madelyn was aghast.

"Find a way to mollify your mother," said Marty, out in the hall, in his seersucker shorts and his tan. "She's ready to throw you out of the house."

Her mother still couldn't get over the fact that Ana had been careless enough to have hitchhiked, and it served her right that she was almost raped. Ana bore her mother's comments bravely. She concentrated on putting ice cubes in the water glasses and congratulating her sister, who had just been accepted into a local college. Vickie was too morose to respond. After lunch, Ana jumped up to clear her father's plate with its little pile of whitefish bones, and then she asked him to write a notarized letter for her, declaring her financial independence. That way she could apply to the American Film Institute, U.C.L.A., or Berkeley—any place three thousand miles away from her family.

"Can I be excused?" asked Vickie.

"Good idea, Fatso," said her mother. "The last thing you need is dessert. Take Timmy with you: make sure he washes his hands." She turned her attention to Ana. "This one'll be an old maid," she said to her husband. "She should be getting married, instead. Except she threw her virginity away..."

"Quiet, Mom. I need to talk to Dad."

Madelyn slammed a lattice-work apricot tart on the table. "Only old maids go to graduate school," she continued, dismissing her daughter's ideas. "Who is that woman lawyer in your office, Marty—the one who looks like a dyke?"

"Dad! I—I really need to discuss this letter! The National Scholarship Office needs it."

The glazed apricots gleamed against the setting sun, perfectly framed by the white chintz curtains. Madelyn took a knife and divvied up the tart.

"Here's the deal, Ana," her father said slowly. "Do whatever you want with your life—you're 21 years old. I don't need you on my tax forms any more. Though if you ask me, film school's a waste of time. Who's going to invest in a girl as a filmmaker?" He picked up his fork and took a bite of apricot tart. "And with the stock market the way it is now, well... As far as this fiscal year is concerned, I'm declaring you as a dependent. It's only appropriate to declare children as dependents while I'm paying their college tuition, right? Otherwise, you'd have to pay me the $100—the normal deduction."

"What do you mean, 'deduction'?" she said in alarm. "I didn't study economics like you. I only graduated in film."

Marty started a long, twisted explanation of the legal technicalities of income tax law and scholarships. He seemed to her largely uninformed, but then, she couldn't tell. He was always shoving his degrees down her throat.

"Where am I supposed to get the $100? I don't have a job, and you haven't given me a dime since graduation. I think you could legitimately call me independent without making me pay you for the privilege." He was reaching for the newspaper. He wasn't even listening. "You're my father," she shouted. "You're supposed to—I don't know—*invest* in me!"

"Isn't there a Philip in your life?"

They didn't even know that Philip had broken up with her. They could have hugged her like a child, or at least let her hide under the dining room table and cry. "Just what do you expect me to do, Dad? I failed to nab a rich husband, OK? Are you implying that I should sleep with someone for the money?"

Madelyn interrupted. "You're wasting your father's valuable time with the dramatics. Do you want some more pie, Marty?"

"Honey, it's delicious," he beamed, while Madelyn cut him another piece. If only she had stayed in New York with Alan, Jeff and Greg, instead of coming home to these sexist pigs.

"You didn't even answer me!" she exclaimed.

"What do you expect, with a ridiculous question like that?" Marty replied. "And also, Ana, what is this about a $200 bill to repaint your dorm room?" he added with an absurd whine. "Why'd you have to make it psychedelic?"

"Here she goes again with the surly expression," her mother said.

Ana ran upstairs to her room and slammed the door shut. She swore in exasperation. It wasn't only that they didn't want her to go to graduate school and seemed indifferent to her need for independence altogether. It was the rage she felt at the premiere of her film at the Museum of Modern Art, and her rage towards Philip. Her rage towards Lawrence Stimpson, Mr. CIA. Her rage towards the guy in the Mustang, pointing a gun at her head.

Her parents could hear her swearing through the ceiling as they cleaned up the kitchen, angry at Ana for not offering to help. "Please be quiet, Ana," her mother called upstairs. "Your father wants to take a nap before the dinner party starts."

Marty climbed the stairs to lie down. Ana walked out to the hallway and stared at his tired body lying on the cot in the next room. It was all her father's fault, and he owed it to her to help her for the rest of her life. Because he should have attended her Yale graduation, instead of sailing through the Bermuda Triangle. And now he was making it impossible for her to go to graduate school. He was probably right. Her whole education was a waste of money. He could have at least picked up the broken pieces of her life. Instead he was lying there in resignation.

"What do you want?" he asked.

"Nothing," she said. He probably wanted to be a good father. He just didn't know how.

Ana and Vickie put on new dresses from Saks Fifth Avenue, Size 10 and Size 14. "Gee, Ana, you look so skinny," said her sister wistfully, but Ana was light years away from acknowledging her sister's adoration.

"Are you girls ready to help serve?" called their mother in a singsong voice. Timmy planted himself in the master bedroom upstairs and watched cartoons.

"We're giving this little party tonight in honor of Ana," her mother gaily announced to the assembled guests while Marty poured martinis. "In case you don't know it, our daughter just graduated from Yale." She raised her martini glass, adding, "And our other daughter just got accepted by N.Y.U." She took a sip. "Of course, Marty had to pull some strings."

Vickie stood hunchbacked and mute, emptying an ashtray while Ana passed around the hors d'oeuvres and avoided getting pinched—torn between trying to be lady-like and taking the tough stance that her parents' guests were fools, mere liberals bored by Antigua and politics.

"Daddy should sue Dr. Mueller!" Vickie whispered to Ana when they were back in the kitchen. Vickie couldn't smell or taste the hors-d'oeuvres: cocktail franks that she was rolling up in bacon and stabbing with toothpicks.

"Why should he?" Ana was preoccupied, trying to take diamond-shaped pieces of toast out of the toaster oven without burning her fingers, then smearing them with caviar.

"My sense of smell is gone, that's why. He's a lawyer—he could do it if he wanted to."

"Oh, yeah?" said Ana, not really listening. "What are you gonna pay him with?"

But instead of saying something equally nasty, Vickie backed off.

"What's eating her?" Ana wondered, lost in her own pain, her finger under the cold water tap. Vickie retreated to an angry silence about her nose job while the horrible Dr. Mueller laughed raucously through the dinner of Vol-au-Vents.

"Oh come on, Vick. Look, I have a Carly Simon eight-track you can have, OK?" Vickie continued to sulk. "And I have a Velvet Underground album upstairs. You can have that too. I'll give them to you after the party."

"Forget it, Ana!" said her sister. "You just do these things out of guilt, that's all."

One of their mother's friends came into the kitchen while they were scraping the plates. "I was at your film premiere at the Museum of Modern Art, dear," said Mrs. Gottlieb to Ana. "How strikingly original! And such an interesting film, about such creative men! Warhol, Rauschenstein... But why didn't I see *you* at the screening, dear?" she asked Ana. Vickie turned on the garbage disposal.

"Oh, there was this bunch of women artists picketing the museum," said Ana over the din. "I didn't want to cross the picket line."

"But, I don't understand—it was your premiere!"

Ana rolled her eyes. There was no way Mrs. Gottlieb could understand the Women's Movement.

"Well, at any rate, I heard *The New York Art World* got wonderful reviews," continued Mrs. Gottlieb, "and I expect to see many more achievements out of both of you." She leaned over to peck the girls on the cheek, only by now Vickie had disappeared into the bathroom, trying not to cry at the attention Ana was getting.

"Mimi, get out of the kitchen. The girls can handle it," said Madelyn as she strode into the room. As soon as Mimi was out of earshot, she hissed at Ana, "Don't break anything!"

Ana felt the sharp sting of rejection as she mechanically placed the wine glasses upside down in the dishwasher. *You had some nice moments as a child*, her mother's rejection slip began. Her mother always had to have the last word, didn't she? *It is incumbent upon me to protect my own feelings of disappointment in life by refusing to empathize. We didn't send you to Yale to become a whore. We are returning your life to you, unused. Due to the volume of domestic responsibilities and present company, we are unable to personally...*

"Why couldn't you have opened your arms to me when I came home?" she blurted out. "Is your dinner party more important than my life?"

"You don't know the half of it," said Madelyn, hurriedly fixing her lipstick in the mirrory chrome of the waxed paper dispenser. "You want to know how I was raped by my stepfather in the basement? *That* was rape—what happened to you wasn't even *close* to what I went through." Ana was stunned, but her mother wasn't through. She held Ana by the elbows with her red manicured fingernails, talking through clenched teeth. "*My* mother tried to give me away to foster parents," said Madelyn, letting go of her. "My grandma went blind sewing every night in her kitchen for the shiksas. Did she ever complain? My great-grandma Rosa was also raped. By Cossacks. They killed her in front of her children. You think *your* life's so tough?"

PART TWO
In Black and White

CHAPTER NINE

Fallen Goddesses

I accustomed myself to pure hallucination.
— Rimbaud

The second-hand car was a birthday present from her father. It looked vaguely like the white Mustang in which a man pulled a gun on her a couple of months before her college graduation. Only it was a banged up Chevy, and smelled of cigars and cheap perfume mixed with the mold of the broken air conditioner. The car reached Topeka in a snowstorm the week before Christmas, needed another brake job somewhere in the Rocky Mountains, lingered tire-worn on the West Coast for a couple of years... somehow that Chevy made it to Memphis, where she died. Yet she started up again in the morning, after an hour on slow charge.

Off Main Street, a black man with a Ford truck waved the Chevy down. His hood was up: he said he only needed gas. Ana agreed to drive him to a gas station and he got into her car. But after having taken Valium when a producer in L.A. refused to hire her without fucking him first even though her college credentials should have been enough; after lying on the floor once the Valium wore off, unable to move, crying and crying for Philip, who was long since gone; after having looked in vain for a place to unpack her suitcase packed with her own ass and her two breasts, she wasn't about to look another man straight in the eyes.

This man wore a pink-striped undercoat, a black and white checked vest, and a checked coat on top of that. He said his name was "Retail". He held an open can of orange soda, sitting up beside her in the front seat of the Chevy, his breath reeking of bourbon. He asked for the name of her motel, but she wouldn't give it to him. He offered her a lid of grass, but she declined, afraid of getting arrested. Retail got out on the corner of Peabody and slammed the door shut in frustration. But it wouldn't shut all the way—the door was broken.

She took Diane Campbell's address out of the glove compartment. After all the shit they'd gone through in the world, it was terribly important for them to get together and try to do that C.R. thing again, she felt. The address was somewhere on the southwest part of the map, near Whitehaven. She drove through the middle-class streets, looking through her bug-festooned windshield for something she thought should resemble the tenements of Harlem.

It was only after graduation that Ana had thought to ask what had happened to Diane. There was a persistent rape rumor about the Skin and Bones boys circulating among the Sisterhood. Diane had stopped going to classes. She stopped eating, someone said. She had disconnected her phone, and nobody had seen her at graduation. Mrs. Campbell had carted her daughter back home to Memphis.

After Yale there was the parental derision at her graduate school applications. "Don't go blaming us again," said Madelyn. She forgot about graduate school over the next four years, but she hadn't forgotten about Diane.

She drove up to the cul-de-sac of a street of clapboard houses shaded by magnolia trees. A well-kept, two-story, light blue house stood at Diane's address, festooned with several lawn mowers and an old plastic wading pool. A fiftyish woman with straightened blue-black hair shellacked into place answered the door, and looked out from behind the black iron grating.

"Mrs. Campbell?" asked Ana.

"Yes, ma'am."

"Are you Diane's mom? I went to school with Diane, back up North."

"Oh, Diane. You missed that girl by a year or two, now." Mrs. Campbell looked at Ana suspiciously. "She's my niece."

"Well, what about her mother?"

"Lillian Campbell. She be up in Massachusetts a little more than...fifteen months now, I reckon."

"Gee, I - I wish Diane had told me all that. I mean, I know it must have been hard, really hard, leaving Yale and all that." Mrs. Campbell—Mattie Campbell—invited Ana into the living room to sit down on the plastic-covered settee. Mattie offered her a cup of coffee, but Ana's hands were already shaking from the four cups she'd had while waiting in the gas station to recharge the Chevy.

"It was rough at first," said Mattie. "Mm-hmm. But she went back to school."

"Oh, really. Where did she go?"

Mattie took a sip of coffee. "Harvard, up in Massachusetts." It figured.

"You wouldn't happen to have Diane's phone number, would you?" she asked the aunt.

"Well, I had it here somewhere, just the other day. Give me a minute to go see if I can locate it. You want some coffee now?"

Ana said no, and waited.

"I don't reckon I have her phone number handy," said Mattie Campbell after a spell, leaning on a cane. "But child, you being Diane's friend from Yale and all, why don't you come to my church this Sunday, and I'll give you the number then. It's the Pathway Church of Christ, over on the corner of Selma and Duane."

That Sunday morning, in a bright blue thrift store dress from Mississippi, Ana cautiously entered the Pathway Church of God in Christ. Mattie Campbell, wearing a nurse's white uniform, ushered her to a pew behind a row of bright-eyed children, all black. They turned around, smiling and giggling, to face the white lady during the gospel music.

Praise the Lord! Diane's aunt clasped her hand to Ana's, thrusting it in joyous paean towards the Christ on the wall, whose white face loomed over the congregation. The fat woman in the black and white tweed dress behind her writhed, possessed, and the little boy in front of Ana hid his face in the hood of his coat. A woman in a big-brimmed hat with a feather wrote down her telephone number for Ana with the stub of a pencil.

"Where's Johnny Lamar?" she asked her friend, named Rita Mae Jones.

"Johnny too hung over to play. Uh-huh!"

"Serves him right for mixing the blues with the Gospel," said Jessie Montgomery, pushing her way to the front of the church.

"Sister Jessie!" cried Mattie, with a huge grin that looked horse-like to Ana.

"Sister Mattie!" Jessie returned, crushing Mattie's white uniform in an all-out embrace. "Well, look at who you brung with you!" Jessie and Mattie and their old friend Rita Mae were hugging Ana Fried like a long-lost sister.

Behind them, everyone was singing about crossing the river towards the shore of freedom. The music was pounding in Ana's ears. She felt herself caught up in the electric current of the hymn. Then she began to drown.

Why wouldn't my own sister let me hug her like this? Could it really have been so painful for Vickie to be touched, after we found her, bruised and unconscious, that morning in the East Village? Why can't real sisters partake of hysteria and ecstasy, along with rest of the sisterhood of women?

A woman in a flowered housecoat was spinning in possession; her head fell back and several hands reached out to grab her. The music was pouring through Ana like dialysis. Its current was carrying her further and further from the abstract ripples of racial injustices towards the fathomless reaches of her own family's past.

Did her ancestors love their children, or were they too busy surviving? Did they boil soup before the pogroms, or let their children go hungry? Why was Vickie so unloved?

Someone tapped Ana on the shoulder. "Excuse me?" she exclaimed, jolted out of her reverie.

"Ma'am?" It was an old woman, staring at her like she was an exotic animal. "Ma'am, did you fill out your index card?"

"I'm sorry. What?" She could barely hear with the singing and shouting in the background.

"Ma'am, it's OK. Just fill out this index card with how many Christians and sinners there are in your household." But it wasn't OK. Not only were there zero Christians, there was no household.

The collection plate was passed around. Ana fished for a couple of quarters at the bottom of her knapsack, the same as her allowance as a kid.

It was always such a losing battle for Vickie to compete with her sister for anything. They came out of the same womb, but Ana was Number One. Even on vacation, Vickie was discriminated against. The water was too dangerous and Vickie was too young, they said, to tag along looking for sea glass. Ana stored the pieces of glass in the bottom of her baby blue princess jewelry box. Vickie couldn't go near it on pain of death. Night had fallen quickly, like a brown bottle that fell down the summer house's basement stairs, stinking of her father's beer. Ana re-examined her collection with a rusty flashlight under the bedspread, sorting the blue and green pieces on her pillow. They were even more beautiful than glass sapphire and emerald rings that dentists gave her for not crying when they drilled her teeth.

Mommy came upstairs, clicking her high heels on each step. She threw open her sister's door, screaming at Vickie for leaving the light on in the bathroom. All Vickie wanted was a hug; she was scared of the dark. But their parents were too busy fighting with each other. Mommy was packing a suitcase. On her way downstairs with it, she noticed the movement of the flashlight through the crack in Ana's door. Wham!—the light went on. Mommy grabbed the flashlight with a thwack. Then darkness. The glass on the pillow had fallen between the bed and the wall. Vickie kept up her crying in the next room. Ana got up and pushed the bed with all her might, getting on her hands and knees and feeling around on the dusty floor. Just then Vickie crept into her room, whimpering like a baby. Ana had to give her some of her sea glass to cheer her up, explaining how one of the pieces had once belonged to a mermaid.

But Vickie saw right through her. She knew Ana was keeping the best pieces for herself. Later, if Ana gave her sister any sort of gift, like a Rolling Stones poster, Vickie said that Ana was only doing it out of guilt, and she could buy her own damn self presents. She could have stuck up for her sister when their parents yelled at her for getting bad grades. At least she could have visited her in the hospital, when she O.D.'d. But Ana was too embarrassed to be connected to someone so broken and needy. There was probably a pay phone in the basement of the church. Maybe she should call Vickie and ask for forgiveness. *But fuck it*, she said to herself, *Vickie's probably given up on communicating with anyone, let alone me.*

Vickie tried to call her after slitting her wrists for the first time. But on that occasion, Ana was totally out of it. It was the second semester of being a Yale freshman, blurring the faces of Chauncey, Silvio and Lawrence into one monstrous egg shape, out of which was blazing the peyote star of a mocking Huichol Indian.

God knows Vickie kept trying to reach out for help. But Philip Westover could have been on the verge of proposing when Vickie called her collect from New York. Ana turned to the telephone receiver and muttered, "Gee, what a bummer. I hope things'll get better." The subtext read, "Just shut the fuck up. I can't deal with your pain."

The impotence she felt now about her sister was just like confronting racism as a white woman in an all-black church. Now that Ana needed a friend, she had no one to turn to. She didn't want to come across as patronizing. She stumbled out of the Pathway Church of God in Christ every bit a sinner, without any explanations or good-byes, and sped out of the parking lot wrapped in self-loathing.

In a small coffee shop on the other side of town, just beyond the airport, she masked her uncomfortable feelings with an over-abundance of food. Once nestled over the steamy warmth of her plate, with its slab of country ham, decorated with fresh, quivering yellow-eyed eggs, grits and fragrant, pale gravy and on the side as many biscuits as she could stand to eat, she could almost forget to feel sorry for herself. Karen's Kountry Kitchen had steamed over from the cold outside, making it impossible to see the cottonwood trees and traffic through the windows. This made it easier to concentrate. She pushed her half-eaten biscuits aside and took out a fresh, clean spiral notebook with a bright blue cover. Maybe she could start drafting an application to the National Endowment for the Arts for some blues project she'd thought of directing.

"Watcha writin'?" A tall, Southern white woman in a mink coat with gold hoop earrings and glamorously styled black hair was leaning against the lunch counter, putting out her cigarette.

"Oh, uh, nothing, it's just a treatment for a film." She'd reached the top of the second page and was nervously chewing on the Bic pen.

"Well, what do you know? Isn't that just something!" She sat down opposite Ana at once, taking off her blonde mink coat. The coffee that she'd transported with her across the lunchroom spilled all over Ana's spiral notebook as the coat sleeves hit the back of her chair. She scrambled to wipe it off, her cleavage showing. She quickly pulled out a cigarette case with the initials "JRH" mono-grammed in gold.

"Mind if I smoke?" She offered one to Ana, who was in a daze over the interruption. "You wouldn't happen to know a direc-tor that's interested in the blues?" she asked, her forty year old, blood-shot eyes boring into Ana's like black sapphires. Her name was Janyce Hardy—a hard-drivin', hard-drinkin' career woman with connections all over town, and she had just gotten a grant to produce a feature-length video on Beale Street, Blues Capitol of the World.

"Video or film?" asked Ana.

"Honey, we all know film's superior, but I can get quadruple the length of interviews on this project if I go to video, and man, oh man, these old blues fellows really have a lot to say." She exhaled a large cloud of smoke for emphasis. "You do know how to shoot video, don't you?"

"Well, I studied video along with film at Yale University," Ana replied in a self-deprecating mumble, trying to offset the elitism of her educational background.

"Yale? Well, how about that!" enthused the woman. "My father went to Yale. So'd my grandfather. Isn't that something, women going to Yale."

Janyce put out her cigarette and lit another. After Ana told her about the film she'd made at Yale which had screened at the Museum of Modern Art in New York, Janyce insisted that she reconsider video directing. After all, Ana didn't have another job in Memphis, did she? Not that non-profits paid all that well. But $350 a month was a start.

They were going to interview dozens of important blacks, beginning with B.B. King, who was a manual of the blues, fast women, dice and booze on Beale Street, the 125th Street of the South, home of its first black millionaire, the place where freed slaves would settle after leaving the plantation, where blues musicians got their style, and where Martin Luther King had marched. Only it had all been plowed down in the name of Urban Renewal, to keep the people from marching. Urban Renewal had signaled the death of Beale Street after Martin Luther King's assassination.

Her job was to resurrect it through Janyce Hardy, Inc.

On Wednesday, Ana moved into a loft in downtown Memphis that would only come to $200 a month. She bought a hotplate and had a phone installed. It was time to call someone to celebrate.

She decided on Tammi Bradley, whose number she'd been carrying around since college.

"I've finally landed a job!" said Ana, trying to impress her, although they hadn't talked in years. "I'm directing a feature, using the latest technology. It's a 3/4" videotape about the blues and black culture."

"That's nice," said Tammi, tentatively.

"Well, what about our so-called sisters at school? You know, the other women in our CR group."

"I don't know—law school mostly, I guess. Diane Campbell went back to school and got her MBA, just like her mother wanted her to," said Tammi.

"Funny you should mention it. I just drove down to Memphis, looking for her."

"You *what*?"

"Well, just on impulse. Nothing much was happening in New York City, not that she's here, or anything. So where'd *she* end up?"

"You mean after Harvard and the Wharton School of Economics? Working for Prudential up in Boston."

"God! What a sell-out," muttered Ana.

"Actually, she's the first black *or* female Vice President of Public Relations the company has ever had, and she's pushing forward a strong progressive agenda of Affirmative Action and minority investment programs," Tammi reported.

"Oh," said Ana dismissively, then paused. Her father would have liked her to have some corporate job, too. She'd already burned that bridge. "How're you doing, anyway?"

"Well, I'm seven months away from motherhood."

"Gee, Tammi, that's great!" said Ana, trying her best to enthuse. "Is there a lucky father, or what?"

"You knew I married Howard Birnbaum, didn't you? Howard will be finished with his internship at Cedars-Sinai exactly one month before the baby's due date."

"That'll be good for you," said Ana, vaguely remembering his name.

"Well, I've been offered a job as Assistant Professor of Medicine at UCLA's cardiovascular clinic," continued Tammi. "I'm thinking about it. I mean, medicine can be rewarding when you get to be with people at both the beginning of life and at the end of life. But you know, the first female doctors teaching at UCLA seem lonely as hell. And I'm the youngest one they've ever had. I don't know if I can take the pressure."

"I know what you mean. Being an artist can get pretty lonely, too," said Ana.

"Well, my husband's very supportive. I just have to make some choices," said Tammi.

Ana promised her she'd seriously consider going to L.A. for Tammi's baby's birth, then hung up. She rolled up her sleeping bag, patting it against the second-hand mattress like a pillow. She ate some tuna fish. She rinsed the tin can under the water tap, trying to remember whether she'd ever had a one-night stand with Howard Birnbaum. She seemed to recall a Harold—what was his last name? Then she put on the low-cut, satin dress her mother had bought her at Saks—or was it Bonwit's?—along with her Mexican silver bracelets.

Finally she made her foray into the world of blues, the world she had been waiting for, created by freedmen and ex-slaves, where tears were musical notes, and where it was OK to sing of heartaches. The pink and blue neon of the Club Paradise sign was pulsating as if it were beckoning her. A small crowd of raucously laughing people pulled her inside.

She sat twirling an empty cigarette box on the table. Johnny Lamar was going to begin a set in twenty minutes. She felt she was the only white person for miles around. Her mind began transposing Philip Westover's long blond hair shaking to the beat at one of her college mixers to the black bodies on the hot, pulsating dance floor. She yearned for Philip's body in her loneliness. Philip, who had ended up at Yale Law.

"*Hey, Mr. W!*" she called out in her mind, twirling the empty cigarette box, "*You should be down at the Club Paradise with me tonight, sitting at my table! You can start bidding for me the minute Johnny Lamar starts playing. 'Cause he's the boss man of the blues, and I'm going to be a smashing writer. My name's Jean Rhys, and I'm leaving Mr. Mackenzie. He was a real fucker! Lawrence, Chauncey, Horace: I left them all! All your faces turning towards me with your greedy eyes: I'm available. Step right up, I'll write about you, too.*" She started to write her own name onto a cocktail napkin, over and over in all its married variations from A-Z: Ana Aikens, Ana Fischer, Ana Westover. Then her drink spilled onto the napkin, smudging it. *Here, Mr. Westover, here's your chapter. Don't read too much into it, Phil. Don't ruin your eyes. Just let your imagination run away with itself. I'll run away, too! See me running, through your pink, pouting lips, into your smoke rings?*"

In her mind, she found herself swaying in time to a mournful blues, swinging a long, heavy chain around her naked body. Only her body was blue, and the chain was morphing into a necklace of human heads—the white, severed heads of a Thousand Male Leaders. But its heavy weight exhausted her; she needed to put such memories behind her.

She downed two more bourbons, trying to wipe out the futility of her thinking, yet trying to experience some sisterly bond by living out what her sister had experienced going to clubs like this in the Village. She was one of the few white people in this club; men seemed hesitant at first to ask her to dance. But the liquor made her more aggressive. After talking incoherently to Johnny Lamar during his next break, about starring in her blues video, she started fooling around with James Johnston, one of Club Paradise's stand-by musicians. He was sweating from the nearby stage lights, or perhaps it was an inner glow. His smile seemed so calm and observant compared to Ana's frenzy, and he was tall enough to lean on, which was a very important consideration, after so much bourbon. She thought that she might puke if she didn't have James to lean on.

She gave him the keys to her Chevy so that he could take her back to the loft. It was cold in the loft, but he slid the cream-colored condom that Ana gave him over his lustrous brown cock, and proceeded to warm her up. Many orgasms later, brewing a hefty dose of the crabs, she felt almost too sore to stand up. But James needed her to drive him home the next morning, where he showed her off to his ex-wife and kids.

They were living downtown in the Lorraine Motel, where Martin Luther King had been shot. His ex-wife wanted him to leave right away with his white whore. But he'd come all the way down to Memphis from Chicago just to see his kids for Easter. When would he ever see them again?

He was speechless with love when he held his son's head in his hands. "Are you on the road, too?" his son asked, looking up at the white lady. But Ana could not answer him; she was trying to be invisible. James extinguished the light in his daughter's eyes, telling her, "You look just like your mother." Their grandma knew how men are. James kissed his mother hello for the first time in years. He gave a hug to his big sister Dorothy, and his other sister. But he would not kiss or hug his wife after fucking a white girl named Ana all night.

After leaving James' wife's room, she stumbled across the parking lot to the empty pool of the Lorraine Motel. She considered jumping off the diving board below the balcony where King had been shot onto the blue-gray cement. Instead she sat down on the edge of the diving board and lit up the remains of a roach, pondering on some reasonable action that would take her out of the predicament she had created.

Maybe I should smash my car into the Mid-America Mall since I'm so smashed in the middle of the morning in the middle of America. She was a fool to think she could possibly solve the mystery of

King's death all by herself. What kind of an investigative journalist did she think she was? She squinted at the sun that was flaring at her over the roof of the building opposite the Lorraine Motel, and erupted into a raucous fit of laughing and coughing, coughing and giggling that didn't stop until the marijuana high wore off back on the worn-out mattress in her loft.

She got into her car and drove back to the Pathway Church of God in Christ the next morning, not bothering to search for Mattie Campbell in the crowded pews. Mrs. Campbell probably hadn't found her niece's number anyway, and Ana wanted to hear the gospel singing.

She'd walked in late, in the middle of the offering. The pews were brimming over with families, sweating and swaying, occasionally crying "Hallelujah!", and Johnny Lamar was at the organ. It was impossible to sit down although Ana was beginning to feel dizzy. She stood in the back of the church, feeling out of place. Yet because she was the sole white lady in the Pathway Church of God in Christ, all of these warm-hearted strangers were flocking around her. They shook her hands and hugged her the way her own parents never would have dreamed of doing.

A heavy-set, young girl with straightened hair and a glistening face swung up to the podium to sing "Let Me Convert Your Soul." Her throaty, majestic voice began to fill the room to the accompaniment of the organ, transforming it into a sea of swaying believers.

Ana thought of her sister, playing sonatinas for dinner guests. Their mother was constantly bragging about Victoria Fried's recitals and how she was destined for the Juilliard School of Music. After the filet mignon dinner, Madelyn would make Ana drag her six year old sister down the stairs.

"Vickie, come to Mommy and play something."

But Vickie hid under the dining room table, her big eyes peering through the immaculate lace table cloth. Then she reached up, digging her nails into Ana's bare arm.

"You spoiled brat!" Ana hissed. "All you have to do is play the stupid piano!"

Ana never recognized the pain shooting out of every black and white key when Vickie performed Vivaldi. But now, in a stoned state, Ana watched the keyboard of the church organ turn into the spine of the Black Goddess, who was bending over to suckle the wounded.

The girl at the podium stopped singing—she seemed to have forgotten the melody or the words to the hymn right in the middle of her solo. The choir was trying to cover for her despite the confusion. Someone was mouthing the words in the front pew, but the girl stood frozen in shame, unable to acknowledge her family through her tears. Maybe that's how Vickie botched her piano audition at Julliard. That time, Ana's excuse had been that she was out of town. But where was their mother? Where was their mother when Vickie needed help in the middle of the night in the throes of an acid trip? Had she never listened to Vickie's pain?

The girl's mother was wildly waving an offering of five dollar bills in the air. But Johnny Lamar stopped playing, abruptly ending any offerings. He got up from the organ and slowly made his way to the back of the church.

Johnny Lamar was standing right in front of Ana; the yellow light from the stained glass windows cast an unhealthy glow on the side of his face.

"What you know, girl? Didn't I see you over at the Club Paradise?" he asked, scratching his cheek.

"Maybe you did. Maybe you did," said Ana, agitated, wishing she could pass for black. She went out to the parking lot and sat in her beat-up Chevy with the windows rolled up tight, trying to calm herself down. If she looked hard enough down the identical rows of cars, she felt she would finally be able to identify the car of the bearded man who was really responsible for the death of Martin Luther King. (In her dreams, he had a beard.) It would have Arkansas plates and a peculiar dent. Somehow she would open the trunk of the car. In it she would find the gun that killed King. Perhaps this was the mission for which she had been sent to Memphis. At least that is what she now believed, when she was stoned.

In the glove compartment of her car, she found another joint. Her hands shook as she lit it and exhaled. Strange that she could find a joint, but not a gun. Served her right for playing detective and basing the evidence of a conspiracy on dreams.

In her mind's eye, she could see the gun that killed King. It had lain in the trunk of a car in a parking lot in Memphis. The white Mustang had sat there unnoticed, undriven, for months. *But now, like the sun emerging from a total eclipse, I've found the car! With Arkansas plates! It's grown so gigantic that I can barely handle the grotesque shadow it casts over the Mid-America Mall. I open the trunk effortlessly — mysteriously unlocked. There is the gun, at last. But is it the right gun? Its bullets drop into the palms of my hands, leaving me, tears falling, at the feet of Jehovah, Christ and Allah.*

By now the high was dying down. She forced herself to stop hallucinating. She managed to put on some pale pink lipstick in the rear-view mirror, then drove into work.

It was her first interview in Memphis with Rufus Thomas, the musician who had discovered B.B. King on Beale Street. Janyce had already set up the lights in the corner of the office, eager to start. Maybe Rufus Thomas thought that white folk had no business making this documentary? She had to keep it together—there was a lot at stake. She put her eye onto the rubber eyepiece and pressed "Record".

"There's nothing new under the sun," said Rufus, sweating under the hot lights. "Everything *was—is*. When Elvis came along, he wasn't taking ideas as such. He was taking the whole song. Bein' a white boy and shakin' his leg: Do you realize a black musician been doing that all his *life*?"

Ana zoomed out gingerly, praying that she could keep him in focus. She had to concentrate. "What's the relationship between blues and gospel?" Janyce was asking excitedly.

"Now, blues and gospel are just as close together as twins within their mother," Rufus responded. "Blues was related to hurt, pain, misery, rejection..."

She had to take the blues more seriously. She returned to the Club Paradise that night, intent on furthering her research. But by the time they finished frisking her at the door for weapons and drugs, the neon signs were pounding into her brain, and she needed a drink.

Standing at the bar was a hippie with translucent, blond-white hair. Haloed by an orange spotlight, he appeared rather god-like at 6'6". She giggled up at him nervously. The only obvious thing to do was to say hi: They were the only white people in the club.

"It's cool that we're here at the same time, huh? It's beautiful," he said. She noted his gentle voice. "I used to pass as albino, when white musicians weren't hired on Beale Street," he explained, while offering her a shot of tequila.

"What a coincidence! I mean, I want the blues to take me seriously, too," she said, smiling like a fool. She wondered if her thrift store dress was appropriate for a club like this. She added as an afterthought, "What instrument do you play?"

"You'll find out soon enough, babe," he replied. He ran his fingers through the platinum strands of hair that had covered his pale blue eyes and ran down below his shoulders, and winked. His break was over—he climbed up onto the stage to join the band, plugging in an enormous bass guitar. Definitely worth researching, she decided.

His name was Andy Riley. After endless sets of playing, he took her into the alley and bragged that B.B. King once signed the back of his guitar, the one that got stolen before he found his first electric bass. "Lemme tell you like it is. The customers, God damn them all, have no right, no right at all to say that white guys can't play blues."

He was drinking with bear-like bravura. "B.B. said I *could*, and he knows I could feel it, too. I'm telling you, girl, I can *feel* the blues." His fingers were going through the folds of her flimsy yellow dress. She was dizzy with tequila and desire.

By the end of the last set, Andy Riley was drenched in sweat and the recipient of standing ovations and howling applause. Maybe she had finally found a real artist, not some tepid jock with brains and culture. A well-educated man, he kills you slowly. He brings you a box shaped like the heart he's going to close up in it, and flowers that remind you of your funeral. But this man wasn't planning on giving her anything other than a blowjob. He was living in the moment, driving her in his '62 pick-up truck down to the Mississippi River. She could smell the intoxicating sweat at the back of his neck. She held her arms around him tightly as the truck bounced over a series of potholes on the levee.

When they reached the river, moths and mosquitoes danced like crazy in the yellow headlights. Ahead of them, the sand dunes gleamed in the moonlight like the gigantic, reclining thighs of a primeval god. Andy shut off his motor. They took their time getting down from the truck. In a reverent silence, they entered the church of nature.

Andy stretched out on a fallen log with his head in Ana's lap. He pulled some Indian algae out his tunic, along with a clay pipe from Oaxaca. A lizard with a blue tail darted onto a branch of a hollow tree that stood guard on the yellow sand beside them. Ana swatted mosquitoes while Andy lit up. Through the soft haze of smoke, they began to decipher hieroglyphics floating inside the tree trunk in the torpid light, telling them awkwardly of their destiny. From time to time, dune buggies roared into the silence, and mosquitoes buzzed; if they were quiet enough, they might hear the cry of a bobcat through the trees.

He took her in his arms, protecting her from the onslaught of mosquitoes. She wanted to be healed in the spiritual womb of his arms. He looked like a shaman in his alpaca poncho and his amber bead necklace. She was going to make it her business to research everything she could about him.

Andy Riley was the spaciest blues musician she could ever hope to meet. He would get so drunk his friends would have to carry him off his front porch to get to his gigs, but his body was so warm and bear-like they loved to do it. He'd once gotten so stoned smoking hashish oil and drinking absinthe that he had to be carried off the stage in a whorehouse in Tijuana. He'd divorced his wife 'cause he couldn't stay faithful though he lived with her anyway so he could watch the St. Louis Cardinals on Sunday afternoons on the living room couch with plenty of hot buttered popcorn; she gave him tender loving care and fed all six and half feet of him even though he was almost bankrupt. It was only when he stayed out all night long that she tried shooting him. His mother was the one who always forgave him. He was thinking of moving back to Missouri to live with his folks for awhile, but people kept coming over with one more lid of grass to sit on his porch and he'd forget to leave. By now he had taken off their clothes; they were so high that they had forgotten about the mosquitoes and chiggers. It was so comfortable in the sand, listening to the lapping of the river as he entered her with a little, loving sigh.

Hosanna!

Other than his occasional gig filling in at the Club Paradise, Andy had a regular band that played at a few local clubs around Memphis. The world hadn't recognized his talent yet, but someday she was certain he would be a great star. Meanwhile, he took her to meet his drummer Franco after getting stoned on hash.

Franco Spinella had taken five tabs of acid, a six-pack of beer and a Quaalude. Ana had worn her purple silk skirt. It wafted sensuously in the breeze. She was falling in love with his big black dog, Narky, who was busy chasing a turkey through a corn patch. Narky cornered that bird behind the shack that belonged to Franco and Pam, his long-haired Choctaw wife, whose eyes looked sad and bloodshot. She could smell freshly shucked corn and black beans with garlic simmering behind the screen door, where their yellow cat sat waiting for something to happen.

Franco and Pam's five-year-old Gary pounded on the electric organ while Franco played the drums, tapping the face of the moon awake. Andy had set up his bass, and was already playing jazz, eyes closed, his face moonlit. His bass had become an electric eel wrapped around the great wheel of fortune, its tail zapping the dice till they changed from black and white into neon pink and green. Then Ana played a riff on the flute long and loosely as a child, all the scales and arpeggios of childhood erupting from her lungs.

Hash blasted through her brain. Andy's father was a Hopi king. Ana had painted a paper bag yellow and brown on the dining room table, and cut eyes out to make a mask. She stood in front of Andy bouncing up and down in time to the music with her mask on her head and holding a half eaten corn cob in her hands, chanting, "I hope I'm hopping like a happy Hopi." She was ecstatic. She took off the mask, exposing her face to the moonlight streaming through the living room window. But a meteor took a swipe at her upturned face during a wrong note, and the eyelid of the moon clamped shut.

The electric light had exploded on top of the piano. Pam swept up the broken glass from the rug, muttering to herself as she looked for something to dispose of the pieces, then took it out to the garbage bin behind the house, thumping the screen door. She came back through the kitchen carrying a plate of Maui Waui brownies, still warm from the oven.

Gary went to stretch out on the rug, petting the yellow cat. His mother reclined beside him, propped up on one elbow and eating half a brownie, while his father ate the other half, still keeping time with one drumstick. The five-year-old looked up at Ana, his black eyes gleaming, while nestled beneath his mother's long, blue-black hair. Someday, Ana thought, this music would float around her like an angry wind through ancient ruins. In comparison, Beale Street was nothing but a home of lost souls. "Nothing but a home of lost souls," Ma Rainey had said.

Ana had begun interviewing some of the witnesses of Martin Luther King's last march. But she was having difficulty concentrating on politics or blues. Maybe the drugs were making her paranoid, but she had the nagging feeling that she was being tailed as she drove into work.

"People say that there was infiltration by some agency in America—without indicting any agency by name," one of the local ministers had said. "There was a heavy influx of out-of-town young troublemakers who were not part of the march, who broke all the windows in every pawn shop on Beale Street. I saw more police in one corner of a church on Sunday than I saw at the outset of the last march of Martin Luther King."

She was tired of Martin Luther King because she felt oppressed just thinking about oppression, doodling a poem in the margins of the transcript. But she was trying to keep keepin' on, for the sake of the world.

Andy played his bass as if he were embossing civilizations onto the wings of a butterfly.

"I was here the day the march took place, and I saw the very beginning of the march," said R.B. Hooks, the photographer, into the video camera. "In fact, they put a little sticker on my arm as a marshal. But into the hands of the very young blacks, they gave these tomato stakes—about four feet long, and they were supposed to have banners on them. Now, I remember suddenly these young kids from out of town started beating out windows, all up and down. Then a wave of people, police started shooting tear gas. I saw my son running with a camera; he was running blind, gas all in his eyes. You had some of your biggest people in town, your leading ministers, just running blind. They spirited Martin Luther King away in a car and took him on away." They would use archival footage of King, plus whatever she'd shot outside the Lorraine Motel until the police had stopped her, demanding to know what she was doing there with a camera at Butler and Mulberry. Then gospel music would fade up into a full choir, and cut to the blues: blues and gospel were twins.

Andy thought that whatever happened in Memphis happened simultaneously in ancient Egypt. Ana agreed: that night she wrote history with acupuncture pins on the skin of God's face, and by focusing her pin pens just right, she could see the double moon of Egypt and Memphis.

Ana imagined losing Andy's baby while in ancient Egypt, but he told her it was just a dream, and to put in her diaphragm.

"Don't you care?" she cried. "His lifetimes are pouring out of my eyes: Memphis, Egypt and Atlantis!"

He said, "You're all wrought up over nothin', baby," his fingers massaging her skull, playing the migration of monarch butterflies over her long strands of multi-colored hair. A lion's mane had set the Nile on fire. She clung to her stoned-out God, carried away by indigo and purple rivers until she melted at last into a blue pool of bliss. It was as if her lover had spilled starlight across the lake of the universe, and now he was writing her a song about it.

She was so happy with Andy that she no longer wanted to pick up a video camera. Yet seeing the world through eyes of love, she felt that she had never had such great potential as a video artist.

Everything was beautiful, until the arrest.

CHAPTER TEN

Blues Street

Ain't gonna let nobody turn me around,
turn me around, turn me around.
Keep on walkin', keep on talkin',
marchin' to the Freedom Land.
— Civil Rights song

His drummer Franco bailed him out. They were vague on the charges, but Ana figured it was drugs. She was ready to excuse him. Only a true artist could take life to its outer limits.

But Pamela disagreed. He'd been arrested in front of her and Gary's son. And it wasn't the first time for Andy. He'd violated parole: he'd been arrested a couple of times, and surely Ana knew how many women were in prison because of their boyfriends' drugs, and she should know because she'd spent six months in the penitentiary because of Gary already. This accounted for the sadness in Pamela's eyes, and Ana was thankful that she'd been warned before she became one of those thousands of women in jail whose boyfriends leave their stashes in their house. Before she would ever consider another date with the man who was ready to set her up, she vowed to forget how he had rubbed her feet at night and written her love songs.

She knew she'd be better off dedicating herself to work, not the funeral pyre of love. But Johnny Lamar fell sick with pneumonia, cancelling that week's interview. She agreed to go on one last date with Andy, to discuss their relationship. He drove her down to Mississippi, ostensibly for a picnic, for which there was no food other than beef jerky and some beer.

Sure enough, when they reached a deserted pasture, he jumped over the barbed wire fence and started inspecting every clump of bull shit in search of magic mushrooms. She couldn't stand the smell, and she couldn't stand him, but sixteen psilocybin mushrooms soon sat between them on Andy's Mexican straw mat. Dark gray clouds moved in swiftly, sending out shafts of light from the setting sun, and threatening darkness if not rain. This man was supposed to be her protector, and she felt betrayed. Andy was too obsessed by the mushrooms in front of him to listen to her complaints. "Let's start eating those mushrooms now," said Andy in his gentle voice, putting his arm around her. She reluctantly said OK, curious about tripping this way.

The light in the woods became eerily metallic as Andy meditated on his half of the mat. She could feel herself pulled into the force of his prayers, her body magnetized by his praying hands, the red and orange of her eyelids pulsating. The sun began to be eclipsed by the moon, filling Andy with power of a magnitude beyond the comprehensible.

Suddenly rain began falling from a solitary tree in the clearing before them although beyond it, the sky was still clear. They drank the manna from the sky. They felt their bodies trembling, merging into a single sphere of light. Voices all around them were calling out how good it was to be in this place like in ancient times, holding one another. Surely they had fulfilled a prophecy and had reached a holy place.

"While knowledge comes from books," she was furiously writing on her side of the mat, "wisdom falls directly from the trees like manna. So much for the rain forest, so much for acid rain, so much for wood pulp, so much for corroded pages upon pages, rotting in libraries..."

"Stop writing," Andy said.

"This is how it starts," she thought. "Woman understands life through love of a man and then his artistic power destroys her." She tried to go back to her notebook.

"Be here," he said. "Be here for me." The dark clouds had obliterated the eclipse, and it had begun to rain. Andy laughed at the rain gods. He announced that he was leaving for Mexico in the morning; he just wanted one more sweet moment under the umbrella.

"Why didn't you tell me this before?" said Ana, her face turned ashen pale. She and Andy had been like the branches of two intertwined trees, but hers had just been struck by lightning.

He wanted Ana to leave for Mexico with him that very night. Why not go to Mexico with him? It was better than having him abandon her in Memphis where nothing much was happening. With Beale Street plowed under and paved over, the video documentary was just an assortment of talking heads. Maybe she could have a Carlos Castaneda-type of experience somewhere in Mexico, something transcendent.

She showed up at Janyce Hardy, Inc. just before closing. Surely Janyce could lend her the fifty dollars for bus fare to whatever obscure part of Mexico Andy's shamans resided. Andy and Ana had it all planned out. Of course, she hadn't mentioned his arrest at work. Janyce invited her to the bar around the corner to discuss it.

"Before you go off trekking through Mexico with your albino space cadet, you need to follow through with Johnny Lamar," Janyce argued. "Do you run away from all your projects?"

Ana took offense along with another gulp of Southern Comfort. This wasn't the kind of support she had in mind at the moment. She really needed the fifty dollars. The peyote wasn't going to be free. "Look, Janyce, I've worked my ass off on this puny, regional project, with almost nothing to show for it. Forty hours of video, that's nothing! You know what the networks use?"

"Well, I know damn well what the networks have at their disposal. Millions of dollars, that's what!"

"I'm just going to Palenque while Johnny Lamar recuperates. Besides, didn't you tell me the grant money for *Blues Street* ran out?"

Janyce glowered over her drink. "Where's your sense of dedication, Ana? I thought you had committed yourself to editing video sequences with me for the rest of the week. Listen, honey, we've got a great project. A great project, full of stories. How the local Black leader, Rev. Long was run out of town for standing up to Boss Crump, the white mayor; how Martin Luther King marched on Beale Street, and was shot... Hell, you know these stories by now! And when B.B. King sings, 'These memories shouldn't be left to die,' well, we just need Johnny's story to end it. He'll be out of the hospital next month."

"So we'll use the B.B. King footage instead. The guy is world-famous, Janyce. What's the problem?"

"Problem is I paid for this entire project and I want it done right. When B.B. says, 'It's so much that I owe to Beale Street,' you can't save that to the end. That's the beginning of the whole show!" She ordered another Jack Daniels. Ana didn't want one.

"I don't know. I have a boyfriend now," Ana said trying an honest approach, while carefully avoiding debating the structure of the video. "He really wants me to go to Mexico with him, and really, the timing couldn't be more perfect, I mean, while we're waiting for funding. Actually, I was kind of hoping you'd lend me fifty dollars towards the trip."

Janyce smoothed out her dress and put out her cigarette. "'Scuse me while I go powder my nose," she said.

When she came back, she was singing a different tune. "Ana, I want you to stay here in Memphis and be my partner. It's a lucrative proposition, so hear me out." Ana stopped squirming. "Did you know we're sitting in the music capital of the United States?" asked Janyce, lighting another cigarette for emphasis. "Beale Street is just the beginning. Rhythm and blues, country, jazz, rock, gospel: this city has 'em all. Memphis is the music capital of the world. And guess who's gonna videotape it all? You an' me."

The bar was too noisy and crowded. This was important. Maybe they should have met in Jim's Grill, which was quieter.

"And after we finish *Blues Street*," continued Janyce, leaning towards Ana confidentially, "I'm gonna concoct all sorts of projects for us. Not just in video, either. 16mm, maybe even 35mm! What are you interested in, exactly?"

"I don't know, environmental issues, maybe?"

"Great! The Mississippi River is right down thataways." Janyce waved her gold-bangled arm in the air. "Yours for the asking." She ordered another White Russian for Ana. "I'm talking Hollywood pictures. Imagine what kind of revenue a couple of million dollar productions would bring to this location. We could renovate the Orpheum Theater, where Duke Ellington and Cab Calloway used to play; we could even build a Music Museum."

But Ana wasn't necessarily enthusiastic. The liberal in her agreed with Nat D. Williams, the black emcee they'd interviewed, saying, "You got a better educated Negro now. He would go down there and resent the idea of being exploited as a lodestone to make somebody some money." On the other hand, just how much money was Janyce offering her if they became partners? She didn't have the vaguest idea of what the going rates for co-producers were. She didn't want to appear unknowledgeable. What about creative control? Or Janyce's drinking? In her embarrassment, she said nothing.

"Well?" Janyce was staring at Ana with angry, bloodshot eyes.

"I don't know, Janyce. It's great of you to ask. But maybe I need to sleep on it. I mean, would it really hurt for me to take a few days off?" Janyce was looking at her in disbelief, but Ana really didn't want to be trapped in Tennessee making videos at a crummy little company with its fake oak paneling forever.

She started thinking of their black and white interview with Hays Riley, one of Beale Street's gamblers, that had come out a little overexposed. They had asked him about Holy Joe Boyle breaking up the prostitution, the numbers racket and the gambling houses, and Hays had replied, "I had my bags packed and everything, and when he told me I had 24 hours to leave town...I was a little smart and cocky during that time, and I said, 'Well, you can have 18 of them back.' I got in my car and went right out 51 and into Chicago."

Maybe Ana would never have the guts to talk like that, but by then the bar was closing. To become a film director, you have to relocate to Los Angeles. If not L.A., at least she'd have to reconsider New York. All these possibilities lay before her; meanwhile, Janyce had peeled off in her dark green Corvette. Otherwise, what was the point of working so hard on her first film back in New York? If she couldn't hit up Janyce for an immediate loan, she could at least be free to follow her heart. And her heart was not inclined to pour its blood into another film. Her heart was saying it was all for Love when she called Andy from a pay phone to pick her up. He was running twenty minutes late.

Ana had already packed her bags, and now she took a snort of Andy's cocaine for the road, shivering in an icy breeze that shot up from the Mississippi. "I've got one pyramid for when I'm tired of living, and two more we're going to ransack," the cocaine pushed her into singing.

"I've got Tut's phone number in my get-away car,
and ray-guns on my dancing hips.
Modern America! Don't leave without me!
Do it, 3,000 A.D.!"

She liked her words so much, she wrote them on a paper napkin, pressed it against her lipstick, and folded it into her flight bag to give to her lover for Christmas.

Here came Andy in a brand-new, bright red pick-up truck. She threw her suitcase in the back and jumped into the front with her flight bag, eager for a quick kiss. He seemed intent on running over houses of sleeping people like a demented Santa Claus escaping to the airport, only there were no reindeer and he was calling himself

Quetzalcoatl. She needed him to reassure her that everything was normal. If he would only pay attention to her and hold her instead of the steering wheel, flying the truck all the way to Mexico City. Instead he dumped it outside the Memphis airport, making her realize that he had probably stolen it. They argued about it during the bumpy flight, quietly, so as not to attract undue attention from the flight attendants. She sipped her ginger ale and willed herself to gallop from cloud to cloud until the soda spilled into her lap. In Mexico City, her suitcase failed to arrive. She couldn't remember having checked it. She wanted a hand-embroidered cotton dress to replace her sticky wool pantsuit now that it felt like a hundred degrees outside the terminal. But Andy was too nervous to wait until the next bus to Villahermosa. He gave her one of his extra large t-shirts and baggy cotton draw-string pants that he used for meditating and made her put them on. She felt like a clown.

"Girl, it doesn't matter what you look like, as long as you're with me," he said, as they rested on a park bench under the palm trees of La Venta Park. He rubbed his hot, sweaty body against hers, but she found his attempt to reassure her unbearable in Villahermosa's tropical heat. She pushed him away and stood up feeling twice as ugly.

"Look, just let me find this Olmec altar, OK?" she muttered, trying to focus on the Mexican guidebook despite the acrid smell of his draw-string pants.

"I'm kinda in a piña colada mood," said Andy.

"All I want is ten minutes with an ancient altar or throne. Is that too much to ask?" He insisted on walking with her along the dirt path, pointing out monkeys half-hidden in the jungle palms and shooing mosquitoes like a brave warrior. Finally, he wandered off in search of turquoise, green and purple shawls and alcohol.

She found Altar No. 4 half-covered with palm fronds and leaves. She leaned against the side of the large, cool stone, imagining the bloody sacrifices that must have been made there. On the front of it, an Olmec ruler was sitting at the entrance to the underworld under a bas relief of fangs. She pulled her camera out of her flight bag and tried to take a photograph.

"Baby, I got you a soda," said Andy. He touched the ice-cold can to her arm, causing her to jerk the camera.

"Forget it, I'm not thirsty," she said, taking out her frustration on both of them. She should have stayed in Memphis. She could have been doing professional camerawork.

He pulled out a small, multi-colored blanket he'd bought and smoothed it out in front of the altar. There wasn't enough room for Ana to sit beside him and meditate. At least there didn't seem to be any people or monkeys watching them in this section of the park as far as she could tell. She took off Andy's sweaty clothes and used them to cover the sharp stones. For a moment, she let the breeze assuage her feeling of shame as she laid her buttocks on his shirt. She tried to suck his towering pink cock as if it could let down milk to pacify her in this strange place of staring statues. But he couldn't keep his erection, and on their way out of La Venta, hurrying to catch the bus to Chiapas, he sprained his ankle.

Somewhere in Chiapas she lost her cash while Andy lay sprawled out in a blue Mayan hammock, recuperating and growing a beard. The blond-white stubble gave him a degenerate expression, but also excited her when he murmured the words of a new song against her smooth, tanned cheek.

"Baby, I want you to stop worrying. I still have two twenty dollar travelers's cheques."

"That's all?!" Now she really had something to worry about.

"It's enough to get us to the Mayan pyramids. As soon as I can walk again..." She panicked. "Baby, just wait, I'm telling you like it is. This Mayan stuff is inspirational." He closed his eyes, fluttering his blond-white eyelashes. "These pyramids, they just give me this... this kind of intuition, like maybe we've already been there in another lifetime. Maybe we're already there! I'm gonna write the best song you've ever heard, anywhere."

She stood in a long line at the bank, worrying about getting the runs, with the drawstrings of Andy's pants pressing tightly against her stomach. Her money pouch covered her breasts like a poorly fitting breast implant. She felt like the entire line of people was staring at her. Maybe it was just paranoia, brought on by the marijuana she'd smoked for breakfast. She looked down at her guidebook, trying to memorize conversational Spanish phrases: "¿Se habla ingles aquí?" ¿Dónde está el baño?" "Estoy perdido."

By the time she had reached the head of the line, the bank was almost out of pesos. She realized she had better cash her last fifty dollars' worth of cheques along with his forty if they were going into the jungle. Who knows when they'd have another chance? However, hers were only cashable at one bank, and Andy's at another. The second bank was about to close, and she had to find a restroom.

Andy hobbled out to a souvenir shop and bought a huge sombrero with his remaining cash, putting it on to make some shade. "¿Donde está mi sombrero?" he drawled in his Southern accent to a laughing busload of Texan tourists while she rushed back to the first bank with her credit card. That bank didn't give cash advances, but they told her where she could call her credit card company, in a telephone center just a few dusty blocks away.

It should have been easy. On the reverse side of the card was the "call-collect" number. But the telephone operator seemed unwilling to help her with the Mexican dialing system. The hot sun beat down on her through the windows, aggravating her PMS. Maybe if she didn't appear so frustrated speaking Spanish. She tried to smile at the operator, despite his bemused disdain. She gathered that she should have known what city code "904" stood for, and it would have helped if a turista like her were wearing something more presentable. The operator looked at her as if she were an idiot and pointed to a pile of telephone books. She waded through the books until she determined that "904" meant Jacksonville, Florida, then dialed and got disconnected. She walked back to the operator and planted her feet firmly in front of him. Wasn't it his job to help her with the call even if she was almost out of pesos?

El operador used halting English and sign language to suggest that she give him a blow job. Then he'd place her call. Ana gave him the finger and hurried out, in urgent need of a restroom.

Juggling the last roll of toilet paper over the dirt floor of the only restroom she could find, it fell into the toilet and she had to pull it out, with no hot water to take out the stench. There was cold water back at the hotel: it ran twice a day. But Ana had missed her chances to shower for days, waiting on existentialist bank lines which had so far netted her fifty bucks. What the hell was she supposed to do without money? Ask the operator to help her call her father for a loan? If she had taken Janyce up on her business offer at least she'd be making a decent living.

Andy played his bass in return for free meals and some drugs for his uptight bitch in the hotel cantina. She sniffed at the beans on the buffet and went back to languish in the hotel room. She couldn't sleep under the mosquito netting full of holes because of the smell of rotten papaya in the sink which had no water, and a dead lizard mixed in with the rubbish left on the cracked floor. Nor could she fall back on reading. The hotel was busy remodeling: a light bulb had recently been installed, but there was no electricity after dark. Not that there was anything worth reading in English.

When they finally reached the Mayan pyramids, the inspiration of the trip had been marred by arguing with Andy about who was going to clean up the dead lizard. It hurt him that she wasn't spiritually liberated enough to marvel at their ancient splendor. He climbed out of her reach until he re-sprained his ankle in the tomb of Pakal and had to be carried out by tour guides.

Andy hobbled back after a late night gig and crawled into the comfort of the blue Mayan hammock. He'd been eyeing señoritas at the bar in the way the way he had looked her up and down when they first met. Ana was pacing back and forth, unable to decide what to do about Janyce's offer and wondering whether it was still available. She was unwilling to suffocate any longer under the mosquito netting. She had been up all night, doing lines of cocaine and twirling her hula hoops of negative karma while waiting for Andy. Now that he was back, she had to go up to the roof to breathe.

The constellations had shifted from their normal places. A certain transcendence came from staying up till almost dawn, especially while high. Staring at Orion made her imagine the fall of the world. Stupid world, cutting down its rainforests like cutting into the lungs of the world, deflating it like a giant balloon. Didn't the Mayans know how bad their timing was, cutting down their jungles in their greed to grow corn? Then came a devastating drought while the jackals writhed and moaned. So ended the grandeur of that ancient empire; and now a global empire was crashing all around her, destroying the earth as it fell under a sky without falling stars, without celestial warnings of any kind.

That was it! The documentary that she would make to save the planet! She had to tell Janyce! She grabbed her bags and left Andy in Palenque, sleeping alone in his hammock as the sun rose. With any luck, she could catch a night flight back to the United States.

It took several hours to get through customs with her sleepless, manic expression. The customs inspectors were intent on finding her stash. She'd picked up a green and magenta straw bag in a tourist shop at the airport which would finally take her credit card. But she hadn't hidden anything in it: not even their dog could find a trace of drugs. They were simply etched on her face.

She made her way to downtown Memphis, feeling like a pile of bricks, catching her breath in the shadow of a pawn shop. If she could make it to Walker Avenue, maybe she could score some cocaine. But on second thought, she was trying to get off drugs—besides which, she had no cash. She resolved to pull herself together.

Finally she strutted into Janyce Hardy, Inc., wearing Andy's huge sombrero.

"Well, lookee who's here!" crowed Janyce. After a few laughs and a recommitment to their friendship over a few drinks, they buckled down to editing video sequences: the bulldozing of Beale Street, B.B. King, the Church family, Boss Crump. Janyce specialized in the music while Ana focused on the politics and tried to lose herself in her work. Janyce said nothing more about the partnership, and Ana failed to mention her Mayan vision of saving the world.

A month later, Johnny Lamar had recuperated enough from the winter's pneumonia to resume his interview for *Blues Street*. They followed him with the Sony camera and the 35 lb. JVC deck from the Club Paradise to the Pathway Church of God in Christ, explaining his connection to the blues. This was the last interview they needed to call it a wrap.

"Let's go celebrate," said Janyce, thumping her on the back. "Meet me at Overton Square!"

They met at T.G.I.F.'s. Ana was wearing the most business-like outfit she had—a purple worsted suit from Peck & Peck that she'd found in the Sacred Heart Thrift Store in Walls, Mississippi.

"Well, aren't you looking spiffy," said Janyce sarcastically, and turned to order drinks for the two of them. Ana waited expectantly.

"So, now that we're almost finished with our first documentary, let's decide on the second. What'll it be?" asked Janyce.

This was the opportunity Ana had been waiting for. They could apply to the National Endowment of the Humanities for a major series comparing the Mayan and Spanish Empires to American Imperialism. And if Janyce wasn't ready to think in terms of such magnitude, Ana would go it alone. Meanwhile the two Southern Comforts had arrived. Ana put her fingers around the glass nearest her. Her hand was shaking as she thought of what to say.

"What about, um... What about a one-hour Special on W.C. Handy?" she offered in a meek voice. "Or B.B. King? Or Elvis Presley?" It's not that she wanted to sell out to Janyce's way of thinking.

It's just that she needed a job. She could always make documentaries that would change the world for the better later on.

"Why just *male* voices?" thundered Janyce. "Women are an integral part of this community!" She splashed down her drink. "You think their suffering isn't just as serious as the blacks experienced down on Beale? The Women's Movement hasn't eradicated all the pain. Not by a long shot. Now lookit here, I'm just as serious about women's blues," she said, lighting up another cigarette. "Ma Rainey, Alberta Hunter, Bessie Smith, Little Laura Duke! Now, those women could *sing*! But they had to fight a music industry that did almost nothing except exploit 'em. They had to fight the goddam lechers in the audience and probably the men back home jeering at 'em. Plus the goddam racism on the road."

"That's right," said Ana, torn between the moral discomfort that Janyce hadn't thought to offer this directing gig to a black woman filmmaker and the fact that she needed a job. She reached for a salted peanut.

"I'm concerned about people who won't give expression to the beauty and wonder stillborn within them. Waiter, get me another! I'm serious about women, about their unwanted babies, and welfare, and incest, and harassment, and their blues—especially their blues. I'm just as serious about women's blues, and I refuse to give up on women!" Janyce declared triumphantly.

"You an' me, we're gonna do a series," she continued, pulling out a cigarette. "All about women. And I'm kind of thinking that a film on prostitution would do rather nicely for openers. The men'll go wild over it, naturally," she guffawed, "and it's a feminist topic. And I am a feminist!"

"Prostitution's an interesting topic," Ana hastily agreed, although a bit morosely. Look what had happened to her proposal back at Yale.

"You bet your sweet life it is!" said Janyce. "Bein' sorry to have been born a girl is serious. Now as far as the oppression of the blacks, we're dealing with that, just by making *Blues Street*. And as far as you bein' a Jew, you can't tell me about the oppression of the Jews. I've been to Eastern Europe—seen Auschwitz with my own eyes. But the suffering of *women*, that's what I'm talking about!" She downed another Southern Comfort. "The orgasms of wives—faked orgasms, the prostitutes their men run off to—that's serious. The facelifts, straightened hair and silicone are serious, too: there's big money in the business of self-hatred. Big money! The sky's the limit!"

Ana excused herself to go to the ladies' room, but Janyce grabbed her arm. "We can start with a documentary, to show 'em we're serious, Ana. And that's just the beginning!" Her hair was getting frizzy in the moist atmosphere of the packed bar. Ana could barely understand; Janyce kept slurring her words. When Ana came back, Janyce kept raising her glass to her, saying, "The sky's the limit!"

Only one thing. Ana was pregnant.

Pregnancy was like a sleeping pill. The fetus was telling her to forget the pain, to put down the broken pieces of glass, to massage her wrists, to not take life so seriously, and to laugh. But Janyce was telling her to go deeper into Martin Luther King's assassination and to reveal the truth through their black and white, reel to reel interviews with those who had witnessed his last march.

"You can't trust the lies of mainstream media," Janyce insisted. "You've got to follow your instincts."

There had to be a pattern between Rev. Long, who had been harassed and threatened and run out of town years before, and Rev. King. J.B. Martin had also been run out of town. Lieutenant Lee was beaten up. And what about Malcolm X in New York? And other black leaders in cities across America? No, Amerika! She began to see the connection between torching black communities like Tulsa's in the Red Summer of 1919 and the razing of black communities like Memphis' in the 1960s. Could *Blues Street* connect these dots of history?

Just because the police had searched her car outside of Jim's Grill that week, did she really think that made her an authority on black history? There had to be a black filmmaker somewhere capable of collaborating with her, ready to serve black people and their history. But she failed to make those connections.

It was already after midnight. She should have gone home hours earlier to nurture the baby within her with food and sleep. Instead, she was working around the clock to complete something of her own before the baby's birth. Except it wasn't her own; it was something that belonged to the black community, whose story she was barely capable of telling. She was just reaching for another videotape when she tripped over the extension cord between the two tungsten lamps left over from the interview with Johnny Lamar. As she fell, she knocked over a pile of photographs shot on Beale Street in its early heyday: beautiful mulatto couples sporting diamonds and ostrich feathers, pausing on their way to the Midnight Ramble to pose for Fess Hulbert's box camera.

Ana clutched at a handful of photos as a sharp pain pulled at her abdomen and left her writhing on the floor. She cried out for Janyce. But Janyce was out on the town, drinking somewhere with her husband. She cried out for help from anybody—a janitor, perhaps. But nothing responded except for a heavy silence.

She listened to the heartbeat and the blood flowing within her in horror. Its heartbeat was out of sync with her own—it just couldn't be! The blood was already coming out of her. She stared at the red splotch like it was some kind of foreign flag. She thought routine thoughts of getting up to wash out the blood, and yet she felt so heavy as if some man were still on top of her, weighing her down with his stench mixed with anti-perspirant until she vomited. She looked down at the Abstract Expressionist mixture of vomit and blood, and thought of stirring it up together like Italian marbled paper in a rare book of poetry. Then she blacked out.

The blood continued to ooze out of her for days as she waxed and waned in and out of other lifetimes. Her thoughts dredged along the side of her womb for whoever had drowned there. Sullen barges now floated downstream in her direction. They were laden with cone-headed blacks egged on by Orisha gods and goddesses. They were laughing at her for falling off her pedestal and for the naive, racist patterns of her life. An indigo priest stood at the helm of one of the barges, flies encircling his contorted face, leading a chorus of taunts for having miscarried.

She lay in bed for days, eating nothing, calling no one, staring at the flies on the ceiling. Then one day she crawled out of bed and went back to work on *Blues Street*, forging each cut out of her own, inner blues. *Blues Street* was going to be the tribute to the baby that would never be born. Its spirit would cross the great waters to Africa, to suckle at the breasts of Yemanja, goddess of the oceans. What might have been her baby would float up the rivers of the generations as a kind of tithe to the kings and princes of the Mali Empire, the brothers and sisters of the Akan, and the Yoruba elders.

Ana wandered in the desert of her empty womb, unprotected by her great-great-grandmother Rosa, slain by Cossacks. It didn't occur to her to get in touch with Andy. He couldn't protect her from anything other than a bad acid trip. And somewhere in her wandering, Ana's childhood was wrenched from her, like a baby from an auction block.

CHAPTER ELEVEN

The Third Degree

It don't take too much high IQ
To see what you're doin' to me.
— Aretha Franklin

"Where are you? Are you in trouble?" her mother had wanted to know.

"I'm...I'm in Memphis. Mom, I need to ask you..."

"In Mexico?"

"No, Memphis, Tennessee!"

"Tennessee? What the hell are you doing there?"

"I'm getting my life together, Mom." Ana paused. "Isn't that terrific?"

"Oh," said Madelyn. She sounded feeble. "You're going to miss your sister's funeral," she said, but Ana didn't hear her.

"You want my Memphis phone number? OK, got a pencil?"

"Her funeral! Dammit, her funeral!" her mother kept trying to say, but the connection was terrible.

"Look, I'm sorry I haven't called more often," Ana said, trying to butter up her mother to ask for $500 for the back rent until another Beale Street grant kicked in to pay for the rest of the *Blues Street* editing. She couldn't understand why her mother was crying. "I know I've been a bad daughter..."

"Why aren't you coming to Vickie's funeral?"

"Vickie? She died?"

"It was so terrible, I can't even talk about it. Just take the next flight to New York!"

"Mom, I—I can't. I'm sorry Vickie died, but I have a job—sort of. It's the first good job in my life."

"How could it possibly be important at a time like this?"

"It's a video—and I'm directing."

"Get on the plane or I'll disown you."

Tim Fried picked up his sister at the airport. He was six inches taller than when she'd left New York, and his face had sprouted pimples. With his red hair cropped in an English style, he looked almost old enough to be collegiate. She knew there was something wrong when she found out he had driven to the airport in the family's new silver BMW on a learner's permit.

"Let me drive," said Ana.

"Are you kidding? You know what Mom and Dad say about women drivers," he said smugly.

An eight-track was playing an old, slow song by Neil Diamond which Tim was trying hard to ignore, drumming a fast-paced rhythm on the dashboard. "I'm sorry," said Ana, "I know Mom and Dad forced you into this."

Midway to the Bronx River Parkway, Ana turned off the music. "How did Vickie really die?" she asked, attempting another conversation.

"Why do *you* care, Ana? You weren't around. You didn't even take care of the dog you got in high school." Ana took a deep breath. "The last thing I remember before they carted me off to prep school was you fighting with her," said Tim. "Didn't she chewing-gum your *Seventeen*'s together or something?"

Ana was watching the road split up ahead. "She's still my sister. I'm just curious about how she died."

"You knew she committed suicide, didn't you?" he said, his hands gripped on the steering wheel.

"No, I didn't know," Ana said slowly.

"They found her corpse on the floor of Mom's studio, soaking in blood."

"Are you kidding? We were never allowed in there."

"She cut off her hands." He paused. "First one, and then the other."

"That's impossible to do." Her brother was a shitty little liar.

He paused. "What do you think?"

Ana didn't know what to think. Maybe she cut her wrists, but not her hands. They were for playing the grand piano in the living room.

"Blood's everywhere. They still haven't cleaned up the mess. She used your Girl Scout knife."

Her arms shivered with pain. They swept past the rolling hills and budding trees of Westchester. "Oh, Jesus," she said, shutting her eyes tightly. She was flashing back to her mother, hacking away at overgrown willow branches in the back yard.

Ana opened her eyes. Her brother was driving with one hand on the steering wheel and the other in a bag of roasted peanuts: the BMW was beginning to swerve across the parkway.

"What do you think you're doing?" she asked.

"Trying to make it home in time for the funeral," said Tim.

She offered to take him to McDonald's for breakfast if he'd stop driving.

"Sometimes—Well, I sometimes think of killing myself too," she told her brother as she slid behind the wheel in front of the drive-up window. She sounded calm and casual, but she wasn't. "You know? Just for the thrill of it."

Even when they arrived in Scarsdale, Ana tried to avoid her mother. She used the excuse of vacuuming her brother's crumbs of hard-boiled egg and peanut shells from the floor of the BMW to buy herself another twenty minutes without a new set of problems.

Madelyn had baked while waiting for her prodigal daughter to be delivered from the airport. Two blueberry pies cooled off on the kitchen counter. She had poured pecans into a Karo syrup mixture, put the third pie in the oven, and set the timer. But she couldn't stand waiting any longer.

"Yoo-hoo! Hello? I'm over here in the kitchen!" her mother called out. Ana ran inside to use the bathroom. She had to throw up.

"Well, aren't you going to come kiss your mother, already?" called out Madelyn, but Ana wasn't listening. She didn't even notice the aroma of Southern pecan pie. "Ana?"

Madelyn turned to the ironing board, seething like the hot beads of steam that were cross-country skiing across Marty's white shorts.

On her way out of the bathroom, Ana stumbled into what had been her sister's bedroom. Her rock star posters had already been taken down to hang their mother's still lifes. Guest towels monogrammed "M.F." for "Madelyn Fried" lay on the pillows, proving that Vickie had never existed. Ana backed out of the room as if she had made a mistake.

She made her way downstairs: her mother peered over her bifocals at her. "What have you got on?" Madelyn asked. Ana was wearing a bright pink poodle skirt from the 1950's.

"This? It's from a thrift store in Mississippi," said Ana, opening and closing the refrigerator door. There was nothing appealing inside, but she had to avoid her mother's suspicious glare. She examined one of the blueberry pies on the counter—burnt around the edges. She failed to embrace her mother. If she touched her, Madelyn would know about the miscarriage.

"It's shocking," said Madelyn, looking down at the poodle skirt.

"Shock's mutual," Ana countered quickly. Madelyn had replaced her kitchen doors with green plastic bead curtains. She couldn't look her mother in the face. But maybe she could tell her mother what had happened. Maybe she would understand, the way women understand these things. God knows she needed a genuine hug.

"Take those clothes off immediately," Madelyn commanded. "You can't wear them to the funeral."

"Don't tell *me* what to do! I'm a grown woman! I just had a *miscarriage*," shouted Ana. "I just miscarried your *grandchild*! My fetus has just been spared your eat-all-the-vegetables torture, your sweep-the-kitchen torture, your practice-your-music torture, the multiple swirling faces at night, and the legacy of your hatred!"

"You just got here and look at the hysterics," said Madelyn, going back to ironing sheets. She smoothed a pale blue pillowcase over the ironing board. "I hear you're thinking of committing suicide now, of all stupid things."

"Oh, Vickie was stupid, too?"

"I say 'stupid' because why would anyone rather be dead than enjoy all the wonderful things in the world?"

"Name one."

"Art school, for example. I'm enrolling in the painting program over in White Plains. It's the only way I'm going to get my mind off such a terrible tragedy as a daughter's..." She stopped ironing, her voice on the verge of breaking, but only for a moment. "If you're saying this to get attention, don't bother. There are lots of wonderful things, if you put your mind to it, Ana. Like a husband, or a marvelous vacation, or some hobby—even a book!"

"Who told you I was going to commit suicide?"

"Timmy."

"It isn't true. I'm too busy making movies."

"Suit yourself," said her mother, "but you're stupid not to get married. You know, Vickie was engaged to a nice enough fellow. I'll give you his phone number—no use wasting him."

"Madelyn, be reasonable! Just try, for once, to relate to me as a person instead of as a daughter," begged Ana.

Her mother held up the iron, its hot side facing Ana. "Don't try calling me Madelyn, ever. I'll always, always be your mother. And I'd still be Vickie's if she hadn't had the nerve to do what she just did. Now get out of that god-awful skirt. By the way, you're sleeping in the guest room."

Ana jangled past the bead curtains and went upstairs to change her clothes. Madelyn came to the bottom of the landing. "That reminds me," she said. "I packed up Vickie's clothes in the attic. I labeled all her boxes. I want you to try some of them on now."

Ana climbed up to the attic like climbing up another Mayan tomb. It was an airless place which stank of mothballs, but it was the only place where her mother was unlikely to barge in on her. She had brought a knife up from the kitchen to cut open Vickie's boxes. That had to be better than slitting her own wrists. When she cut into the criss-cross of filament tape that had sealed one of the boxes shut, she saw her sister's doll lying underneath the flaps—a costly Madame Alexander dressed in a wedding gown of real silk. She carefully pulled the flaps open. Its white lace veil had been folded behind its black hair, exposing its face. The dead plastic eyes stared at her from the effigy of Vickie's corpse.

"Ana, I want you to throw away your wool cardigans," shouted her mother from the bottom of the attic stairs. "They're moth-eaten and scuzzy. You'll like Vickie's pastel-colored ones. They're real cashmere."

So it was her turn for hand-me-downs. The smells of worn deodorant and rancid cologne mingled with the mothballs layered between the pale blue, green and yellow sweaters. Vickie's musty scent was almost identical to her own. As she tried on one of Vickie's pale green sweaters, she began to weep. Who had given Vickie such a soft, beautiful sweater? She pulled the other cashmeres out of the box, one after the other, then took off the pale green one, so soft that it caressed her skin like Vickie's hugs when Vickie was a baby.

At the bottom of the box was Vickie's mink coat, lying like the corpse of a dead animal. It was a hand-me-down from their mother, who considered it a lavish gesture in return for Vickie's solemn vow to stop running wild. Once back from the furrier's, Madelyn made Vickie parade the mink in front of their father. Back and forth, back and forth in front of the couch Vickie walked, their father's distant eyes following her from behind his thick glasses, his newspaper perched temporarily on his lap, and Madelyn carefully appraising the alterations, avoiding her daughter's face.

Now Ana put on the coat, despite the suffocating heat. Scrunched in the bottom of one of the pockets was a joint. In the other was a matchbook. She thought she had quit for good, but that was before this thing with her sister had happened. She quickly lit it up the stale joint and took a series of short tokes. A couple of moths were hanging onto the mink collar, yet in Ana's mind, dozens of moths were soon balling away in luxury, some of them blown against a rich cloud of marijuana that only seemed to fertilize the deep brown fur. It was arching its back as they dug their way into the warm extravaganza, beating their wings in fury, until the minks sprang back to life and ran across the attic on their webbed feet. Poor little animals, that they should come to this! Why hadn't Vickie given the coat to charity, at least?

She looked at herself in the dusty attic mirror wearing her sister's coat, posing like a conventional model. Why the fuck was *she* the survivor? If it weren't for the smashed-up self-esteem from the fucked-up people in this cursed house, Vickie Fried could have just as easily made a name for herself playing concert piano. Ana Fried, the role model of smash-ups, should have OD'd down in Mexico, falling into the dark entrails of a Mayan pyramid. The gods must have screwed up which sister was which, she thought. Maybe it was not too late to change their minds!

She walked up close to the mirror to scrutinize herself, to somehow ascertain that it was she who was still alive. On her left leg was a scab that looked somewhat infected. It was just a mosquito bite left over from the night on the hotel roof in Palenque, but she pushed off the sweltering coat to get a better grip, and pulled off the dark crust of the scab to let it bleed.

Another cloud of marijuana poured into Ana's lungs. She seemed to have grown much younger, even younger than Vickie.

The sisters were seated on the dusty attic floor, their legs folded beneath smudged smock dresses. They were playing a game of jacks, surrounded by cardboard boxes carefully labeled by their mother. Whoever bounced the little red ball higher got to play Older Sister. Whoever lost would cry, "Unfair! You cheated!" The ball bounced into an open box, which was strictly against the rules of the game. Their faces became ugly snowballs mixed with soot, quickly melting on the floor along with their pee. They were too busy wiping it up to notice all the businessmen huddled around them, jostling for position with their ugly leers, leaning down to pick up the wet jacks, pocketing them with their fat fingers stained with nicotine and cum. And the white, plastic doll in the real silk wedding gown could do nothing to stop them.

At the funeral parlor, two dozen friends, relatives and former schoolmates of Vickie's were waiting for the ceremony to begin. Marty and Madelyn Fried had had their daughter cremated. There was no body; it was a secular ceremony, very tastefully done.

Ana slid into the pew, her black clothes rumpled and her hair a matted mess, lugging her loaded 16mm Bolex and a bag of lenses.

"How's your mom holding up?" asked one of the neighbors in a hushed voice of concern.

"Same as usual."

Madelyn was sobbing over her daughter's urn.

"I always admired your mom," said Mrs. Gottlieb. "She was such a strong-willed person, able to assert herself. And you look so much like her, dear." Ana said nothing, concentrating on screwing in a telephoto lens.

"Such a waste," Madelyn was saying, in between short gulps of air. "Piano lessons. Voice lessons. She was so talented. We went the whole nine yards for her!" Some cousins from Amagansett murmured their approval. Tim looked embarrassed. He turned his glassy, frightened gaze out the window of the funeral parlor at some boys playing catch across the street. Madelyn turned and faced the camera. Her tears shone under the lights, streaking the powder over her foundation into broad, leathery stripes.

Ana stared at her mother's perfect facelift through the eyepiece, thinking of her sister's botched nose job.

"You have to ruin the experience? You with that movie camera, making your own sister's death into a kind of docudrama! Do you have any idea what it's like to lose a child? Do you?"

Ana felt around the lens with her fingers, zooming in and out as her mother continued to upstage the funeral. It was as if her mother were squatting on her sister's corpse, gloating as she drank the blood from breasts that she had cut off with her kitchen knife and held high up above her head, like trophies.

"Will someone get that stupid camera out of my face?" cried Madelyn.

Her father rushed up to Ana, his face red with rage. "Stop filming! Do you hear me? If you use any of this in one of your so-called movies I'll disown you. And that's that!" Ana had never seen him quite like that—at least, not with such rage pointed in her direction. She didn't know what to do, other than smiling a little smile mixed with fear. Perhaps her father would grab her camera and smash it. She looked down at her Bolex in a moment of possessiveness, then realized that she hadn't checked the f-stop. Dammit, it was set at f32 instead of f2.8. All of the footage would come out black. She put the camera down on the pew and drowned out the secular blessing with her dark thoughts.

After the funeral, the remaining Frieds went to a Chinese restaurant and sat around a small, circular table, too numb to order any food. Marty was holding his wife's hand, looking tight-lipped and drawn.

"Mom and Dad want us to organize an anniversary party for them in this restaurant in February," said Tim in an attempt to break the ice.

"Vickie just died, and you already want to celebrate?" asked Ana. She was wearing a black cardigan that had formerly belonged to her sister.

The waiter came and suggested that they order Family Combination "B". Madelyn went back to the main topic. "Vickie ruined our last anniversary," she said, matter-of-factly.

Marty stared at his plate. He started dripping soy sauce over the edge of his plate as if counting the plagues of Egypt in drops of wine. As if he could have sacrificed a first-born son instead of a second-born daughter. Only it wasn't Passover.

"You wanna know how she ruined our anniversary?" asked Madelyn, lowering her voice. "It was those embarrassing songs..."

"Well, Ana gave her the guitar when she went away to college," ventured Tim.

"You stay out of this!" she said to her son. "I had no idea she was going to play 'Exodus' on the front porch for all the neighbors to hear. Did they have to think we were Jewish? And then, when she started playing those protest songs!"

"She was a good songwriter," protested Ana. "You didn't have to trash her talent."

"Those songs made me uncomfortable. They weren't what your father and I call music." They listened to the restaurant's Chinese Muzak, along with the clicking of chopsticks at the neighboring tables. "You were a bad influence on Vickie, and you know it."

At that, Ana stood up. "You called us whores before we even knew what it meant!" she exclaimed in a loud voice.

"Why, of all the..." Madelyn began, standing up across from Ana, a steaming tureen of egg-drop soup suddenly placed between them.

"Apologize to Mommy. She's upset enough as it is," said her father, but Ana didn't budge.

"I didn't raise you to be so unloving, you uncompassionate bitch! You should have offered me some comfort. You're so self-absorbed, you disgust me. You don't know even how to love!"

"But Vickie and I were mistakes. You only wanted a boy!"

Her brother started to protest, but Madelyn interrupted. "Congratulations on your miscarriage. Children eat you up, they consume you." With that statement, she left for the ladies' room, while Tim played a silent drum roll with his chopsticks on the table.

Madelyn returned from the ladies' room intent on maintaining composure. She poured herself some tea and asked Marty and Tim if anybody wanted an egg roll. Over dishes from Combination "B", the Frieds began to compete about the most unusual places where they had vacationed: Madelyn and Marty had houseboated in Kashmir in the middle of a war between the Moslems and Hindus. Madelyn had spent her forty-fifth birthday on camelback to the Pyramid of Giza. Marty had been to a commemoration at Auschwitz. But just to think about a concentration camp made Ana sick. She spat out her lychee nuts and ran to the ladies' room.

When she returned to the table, things had calmed down: there had been some discussion in her absence and everyone was opening their fortune cookies.

"You have to take care of Timmy this summer, so get it into your head. We're subletting the Gottliebs' place on Nantucket for the last week in August. We deserve some time alone, now that Vickie's dead," said her mother.

"Fine. He can help me edit my video," said Ana.

Marty cleared his throat. "There's another thing, Ana. Would you mind cleaning up the studio when we get back? Your mother doesn't have the heart to do it."

She found herself on her knees in her mother's studio. Powerful surges of grief and disgust overcame her as she scrubbed her sister's bloodstains from the floor. Grief for her sister, whose family never knew her, and guilt for never protecting her. Grief for the family who had lost her, and guilt for not knowing how to love.

Ana got up from her scrubbing to wipe away the sweat. Midway across the floor lay a Girl Scout knife. Maybe it was the one that killed her sister; maybe it was merely a look-alike, used for paring apples while waiting for acrylics to dry. She reached down and picked it up, studying its small blade of mottled gray and faint stains of dried blood. Madelyn must have tried to clean it off, then put it back in the studio, away from the shadow of their family life. Probably in the coffee can of palette knives and paintbrushes, lying on its side below the window ledge. Maybe she had kicked it across the floor. Ana folded up the knife, avoiding its sharp edge and pocketing it. Her heart pounded with guilt behind the closed door.

She hated her mother for always locking doors against them. They spent their childhood waiting for their mother to open the door and come out. She wanted to stab herself and join her sister. That's what she deserved. That's what Vickie wanted. Her body still ached with pain from the miscarriage. The floor stunk of Lysol and blood; she made half-hearted attempts to resume scrubbing away the big, angry blots of red. She could have mothered Vickie, at least. Then maybe this wouldn't have happened.

She looked up, sickened by the stench of blood. High above her in the corner was the painting of a miserable clown. It was the first painting in oils that Madelyn had undertaken, probably dating back to high school, long before her serious year at the Art Students' League. Its nose was bright Cadmium red, mocking the sullen blotches on the floor that had already turned to rust, and the dead unfeelingness of its eyes struck Ana with sudden pity for her mother. She pitied her for its triteness; she wept for her sister's pain; she mourned their lost art—her mother's, her sister's, and her own—and the miscarriages of all three of their lives, scrubbing back and forth at the red craters within them, until she sank on the floor, defeated from the fatigue of loss and sadness under the easel that still held an unfinished Abstract Expressionist painting next to a blood-stained mop.

PART THREE

The Talmud of Self-Hatred

I can laugh at the old false loves
and strike shame into those lying couples.
— Rimbaud

CHAPTER TWELVE

Baby Blues

the petals lift and scatter
like versions of myself I was on the verge
of becoming...
— Rachel Wetzsteon

A young German filmmaker watched Ana from the corner of his eye across the center seat. She was wearing a pale yellow sweater, but in the suffocating takeoff, sooner or later she would probably take it off. It was the first time that Karl Kirsch, 28, was traveling to the West Coast. German television had sent him to any number of foreign locales before, but never Hollywood. It annoyed him that the flight was late. Yet when the pilot announced in English over the loud speaker system another fifteen minute delay, Karl understood quite well that the soft mohair sweater of the tall, dark brunette was coming off. In her lithe, somewhat exotic body, wearing a black leotard and stretch pants, Karl found sufficient diversion from the sweltering cabin, the Hollywood trades and *Die Welt.*

It was her first flight West in years. Ana watched the moon spin like a nickel across the night sky out the plastic window of the 747. She had only taken a minute quantity of hashish, enough to take the edge off of grief and to tolerate flying in the opposite direction from Europe, where better adventures could have awaited her. One of her father's clients had offered her a job shooting video depositions in West Los Angeles. Her father expected her to be grateful. Now that she had a chance to think, she tried to convince herself that she really should be grateful. At least she wouldn't be stuck in a downward spiral like her sister; this would keep her out of trouble. Camerawork was giving her the opportunity to see some of the world while shutting most of it out.

The camera can be used as a critical tool to discount or to validate, to listen and to watch, to dissect, to distance oneself, to revere an object, or to meditate. You can force yourself upon a subject with a zoom in, or push away by zooming out.

"Excuse me, but are your night flights often so late?" Karl asked, interrupting her reverie.

Ana looked up at the polite young man, who seemed to be waiting for an answer of some kind. She wasn't sure she was ready for someone new. But then again, she was more than ready for something.

"I, well," she began in confusion. "Usually I just drive cross country and the hell with flying."

"Really?" he said.

"I'm not one of those fly-over people."

"Excuse me," said Karl, "I don't quite understand. I am from Germany. Can you say it again?"

She tried to sound a bit more blithe. "Like, New Yorkers think they're the center of the world. You know, like the Museum of Modern Art in New York City? It's our cultural mecca."

"Aha," said Karl, one svelte finger posed thoughtfully against his thin little nose.

"And then there's Hollywood. Everything in between the East Coast and the West Coast," she said, gesturing with her long, thin arms, "is just fly-over." *Oh God*, she thought, *not a real German. I was beginning to think he was attractive.* His long, blond sideburns made him look almost like Philip, except for the skinny tortoise shell glasses and trendy khaki pants.

Karl cleared his throat. "I fly very often. Like it is a routine."

"Oh," said Ana.

"Yes, just now I am going to cover the Academy Awards for German television. I am a producer."

"A what?"

"A producer."

"Aha," said Ana. Promising! At least Germany subsidized its filmmakers.

"Yes, last week I interviewed Golda Meir in Israel." He could tell that she was probably Jewish and that she wasn't the kind to get a nose job. Karl understood these things. It was important to demonstrate his lack of anti-Semitism casually to this girl.

Ana leaned forward against the tug of her seatbelt, worrying that the roar of the engine, let alone his accent, would preclude intelligent conversation. Karl interpreted her leaning forward in her black leotard as a come-on. For a moment, he enjoyed her cleavage. Then she blushed slightly and turned to peer out the window at the blue lights blossoming along the runway. They were taking off, and a breathless intoxication filled her as she saw her city slip away into lacy, intricate patterns like a computer chip.

"What's your name?" she said loudly, after checking her bangs in the reflection of the window. How lucky that she had the window seat.

"Karl," he said, "Karl Kirsch," and extended his hand, which was sweaty but warm and electrical.

"Karl Kirsch," she said, with a beguiling smile. "I'm Ana. Ana Fried." She smiled once more. He began to think of the possibilities.

"Kirsch—isn't that the German word for *cherry*?" she asked brightly. They had a good laugh over that one. She recited the lines she knew of Heinrich Heine, giggling at her mispronunciations, and talked about the film career of Riefenstahl.

"Ah, Leni Riefenstahl! An excellent woman filmmaker, despite her politics," said Karl. Ana was so thoroughly broad-minded, she was sure she could date a German without thinking of the death of six million Jews. For the time being, Ana's sister lay forgotten under the ground back on the East Coast. Karl and Ana were still talking in the Baggage Claim area while waiting for his camera equipment and her backpack to come tumbling down the conveyor belt. They held each other's business cards like valentines.

Karl went off in search of a luggage cart; in the meantime, Tammi Bradley-Birnbaum arrived at the airport to pick up her former college roommate. After quick hugs they rushed off in search of a bathroom for Tammi's son, Trevor. Tammi's long red hair, which she had always parted in the middle, had given way to a cropped, business-like cut. She and Ana reminisced about old times while darting in and out of the morning rush hour traffic on the Pacific Coast Highway. Trevor sat in the back seat, shooting oncoming cars with his plastic semi-automatic.

Finally, they arrived at their beach side duplex, where Ana could get some rest. She stretched out on the divan in the living room while Tammi put some coffee and croissants on a breakfast tray. Howard Bradley-Birnbaum ran in searching for his pack of tennis balls, stopping briefly to greet Ana. He no longer had a moustache, so Ana didn't recognize him at first. But Howie recognized Ana.

"We're so glad you could visit after all these years," he said. Tammi put her arms around her husband in a proprietary gesture. They went off into the kitchen to discuss something important.

"When are you going home?" asked Trevor, pointing his gun in Ana's face.

"Never," she said sleepily. "I'm going to stay here forever with you and your mom." She turned over to go back to sleep.

Trevor had another question. "How old are you?" he asked.

"28," said Ana, turning over. She sat up warily looking at him and his gun. "How about you?"

"I'm five," he said, adding impertinently, "When are you going to grow up?"

Ana explained that she was never, ever going to grow up. She had just got off the plane from Never Never Land the night before, and that's why she was so sleepy. That satisfied Trevor. He ran off to find the au pair.

Karl Kirsch had phoned her that evening, inviting her and her red-headed friend to the Café Figaro the next morning. Tammi was suffering from cabin fever and was more than willing to go along. "This producer could be your big break," she said to Ana, who was impatient with the traffic and ready to blast into West Hollywood. How exciting to be a filmmaking couple, traveling around the world!

They waited at a table in Figaro's. Ana was hell-bent on radicalizing Hollywood although her personal vision was somewhat vague. "You might have to pay your dues as a production assistant first," Tammi gently cautioned as the glasses of water arrived.

Karl found them in the remote corner of the café. "Please forgive me for being late," he said, "I had a telex." He ordered omelettes and cappuccinos for the three of them. "Your coffee is too weak for me in America," he said. He and Ana began to giggle even though they were really too old for that sort of thing. Through Tammi's eyes, Ana's prospective producer was not the impresario that Ana thought he was: a little wannabe, maybe. But she was willing to play along.

"Oh, you poor baby," Tammi crooned, wiping foam from the cappuccino off his blond, stubbled chin with a cocktail napkin. Tammi was not being very witty, thought Ana. Karl played them off against each other like castanets over their Spanish omelettes: Tammi, doctor and mother; Ana, artist and cunt.

"I wasn't a stay-at-home mom in the beginning," said Tammi, feeling the need to justify herself. "I spent the first two years of Trevor's life commuting from the Palms Springs Medical Center to Malibu." She took a sip of cappuccino. "Children can be the greatest challenge and the greatest joy."

Love love love! The biochemical high. The folds of Ana's omelette creased under the prongs of her fork, which resonated AM music. She felt her bottom whirlpool under Karl's blue eyes, half-hidden behind his tortoise shell glasses. The hot tub was overflowing with cappuccino and the conversation gathered like bubbles breaking in steamed milk.

Karl knew something of palmistry. "I can see by the side of your hands, Ana," he said, stroking them, "that you are much too sensuous to stay home with the Bradley-Birnbaums, eating chocolate chip cookies late at night."

"That's why I'm eating one right now, in the cafe!" cracked Ana, joining Tammi in awkward laughter as she split her cookie in three, and extended a piece across the table to Karl.

"Yes, you are unusually sensuous," said Karl, stroking her left hand, making her shudder. "Excuse me," he said, thinking deeply, "but I think you should develop unusual mores to go with it."

"Morays?"

"Like sting rays, only with a conscience," said Tammi, who had studied both species, one in Biology, one in Ethics.

"Hegel," explained Karl.

"Oh, yeah." Ana didn't remember any Hegel. We're going to fuck on the floor of this café, thought Ana, quickly converting to the cult of Karl Kirsch. A mushroom stuck out of her omelette like a wanton clitoris. She didn't know how much Karl wanted their eyes to meet, but his prick was unfolding under the ramp of the napkin as hummingbirds pushed oranges and lemons out of his mouth. "Go away, cats!" thought Ana, tittering like a sparrow at his gaze, as fragile as an egg shell. "Go away, bugs and owls, back into the night. Especially college chums named Bradley-Birnbaum." She didn't think to notice the musical notes from the jukebox, stuck like flypaper on the stucco ceiling:

> "I can't find the reason
> that my love won't disappear..."

Karl Kirsch turned out to be a small-time producer based in a West Hollywood motel. After covering the Academy Awards for Bavarian TV, he was lingering on for a half-hour show on the legacy of Chinese immigrants in America. He hired Ana for the camerawork when his Chinese-American cameraman quit at the last minute.

They flew to Sacramento together at dawn where they rented a small car that smelled of leftover smoke. He promised, if her work was good, he would take her to China. "But only if your work is good," he said. This seemed much more promising than Janyce Hardy. An international filmmaker!

In the small towns of Marysville and Oroville, just north of Yuba City, Ana filmed the nineteenth century Chinese temples: Buddhist, Confucianist, and Taoist. In between shots they went to Oroville Lake and picked blackberries, placing the rain-soaked berries in each other's mouths, ejaculating blackberry juice along with shrill laughter. Then they took the little car to the Bay Area, its windows wide open to get rid of the smell of stale smoke. He'd asked her to film close-ups of the temples with a telephoto lens from the window of the car as it bumped over the potholes in the roads. There was no way the footage would come out steady, but he was the boss.

He drove her to a hot tub establishment after work. They embraced naked in a private hot tub, which he had rented for an hour and a half from R.U. Wet, Inc. He seemed less sophisticated with his clothes off, splashing her, but she clung to him like a raft. Ana wanted it to become a working relationship. Only a partnership between two filmmakers could offer any real and lasting intimacy.

The night before his departure for the People's Republic of China, they agreed to sleep together in the West Hollywood motel. She told him that she hated her diaphragm, with its cloying smell like lemon custard. They decided to float the diaphragm in the bathtub for the yellow rubber duck to play with while they got stoned on marijuana buds.

Once his penis was inside her, his gentle pushing against her clitoris began to nourish her imagination. *A purple placenta enters the boxing ring like a heavyweight champion in a satin robe. Unborn babies are catapulting over umbilical jump ropes—getting ready for the next big match.*

The royal purple color of the placenta was beginning to overwhelm her. While he fucked her, she brushed away his damp blond bangs so she could see his eyes, which were pools of light reflecting the migration of her soul. She called him "Karli", laughing at her untranslatable, kitsch love as he came softly inside her.

In the morning he checked with the lab. The footage was unusable.

Such a sweet night for me with you that if the plane had crashed today I would not mind, he wrote her in a telex from Beijing. Ana was insulted that he'd left for China without her. Was she only good for sex, not camera work? Maybe she should turn to writing instead, eager to settle on something without continuing to flounder. His love was like new wine, filling her with hope and despair: hope that she might be able to love again, given his potential; despair that the summer would be spent without him.

She busied herself with new ideas for screenplays, poems and maybe a commercial novel in between videotaping depositions for a murder trial. She filmed corpses. She climbed up a tank truck for a wide-angle shot of the surrounding cars, stripped of their paint after a chemical spill. Soon she would have just enough cash for half of the deposit on an affordable place up in San Francisco. Karl was in the People's Republic of China, but this was temporary—in his next telex, he promised to move in with her if she would just find the right place. The Bay Area offered such potential for independent media, he said.

Accordingly, she signed a one-year lease on a one-room apartment near Ocean Beach in San Francisco, ready to decorate it with her credit card, if necessary. It had an extra little room in the back that was the perfect space for a professional writer though it was probably meant to be a laundry room, and might serve to house a bassinet.

She rented a car to pick him up from SFX the following Tuesday. As soon as Karl got off the plane from Beijing, she wanted to announce that she was ready to offer him American happiness and love. After her recent encounters with death, she was eager for life, and she wanted a baby. He was concerned about some missing video cables. "Not right now, Ana," he said crossly, filling out lost baggage forms. Ana meekly went to get the car.

Finally, they were in their cozy new apartment with its fresh white paint, watching Saturday morning cartoons together. He pulled off her underpants under a bright yellow quilted blanket which she had just bought in Macy's, along with the TV. As they started making love, Ana couldn't help thinking that, on some level, he must be sensitive enough to feel the memories implanted in her skin of other lovers. But his gentle, persistent fingering of her clitoris reassured her, and she was able to escape from thinking too much in a series of small orgasms.

After coming inside her, Karl simply murmured, "Will you marry me, Miss Rose?" He was repeating something from the kiddie show in front of them.

"Yes, Mr. Butterfly," said Ana, like a happy child. "My own butterfly."

Karl was jubilant. He got off her body and turned off the TV. He made espresso and laid out several maps across the kitchen table. "I think I start work researching our movie now," he said.

"I'm so happy, Karli," she said, pulling out some bubble gum. She had absolutely no idea what he meant by "our movie."

"I do not believe that happiness is all-important," said Karl. "Remember, happiness is only in the American constitution."

"Yeah?" She stopped chewing her gum. "I thought it was in the Declaration of Independence." She took out some little green curtains she was sewing for the bathroom windows.

He gave her an indulgent smile. "There are more important things than history," he said.

What Karl said about marriage while stoned didn't count. "I don't remember specifically talking about that," he said cautiously. "But I do love you." So he said. Then he went out in the middle of the night to check his telexes. She figured he was probably screwing someone else.

She picked up a *Cosmopolitan* in the local coffee house, riffling past the perfume-scented ads to "How to Tell Whether Your Love Is Real." There happened to be a pencil on the counter. She filled it out for lack of anything better to do, then went back to the apartment. Emboldened by the questionnaire, she confronted Karl as they sat on the bean bag chairs on either side of their new, fold away couch.

"Do you really want to marry me?" she asked.

"Without a Green Card, surely I will have to commit suicide," he admitted. He launched into negotiating.

"I thought we were going to marry for love," she said, and then paused. "$1,500 isn't nearly enough," she stated. "Besides, I consider it a form of prostitution to marry someone for a permanent residency fee."

This agitated Karl. "You have no understanding of how the State oppresses me!"

"But is that any reason to marry someone?" asked Ana, aching inside to get married all the same. Her mind kept going in circles. If he had no intention of giving her a baby, maybe she could use the wedding money for the final 3/4" master edit of *Blues Street*, which would enable it to get distributed.

Karl turned on the television to end the conversation with the Republican National Convention. Ana turned nonchalantly to her diary. *I hated Philip's snide, imposing self. He should have asked me what he could do for ME and MY film. Andy should have reassured*

me that it wasn't the end of the world that he had a criminal record,
she wrote.

She was ready to add Karl to the list, but she couldn't concentrate. She pretended that Ronald Reagan's speech at the Republican convention wasn't bothering her, and set another writing schedule in her calendar. This one allowed less time for writing, but thanks to Karl's influence, she was getting meticulously organized. She threw her calendar across the bed and ran out the front door, screaming, "I hate Ronald Reagan! Reagan and Ford are America's biggest assholes!"

Ana spent the next three hours sulking in the coffee house, huddled over yellow legal pads and notebooks until she couldn't stand thinking of another word. Besides, she had to do the laundry. But when she got home, the next door neighbor was lying on their couch in hot pink roller disco hot pants.

"What are you doing here?" demanded Ana.

Sandra had obviously been crying—she was wiping off mascara. "Um, I just wanted to use the phone?"

"The phone's in the kitchen," said Ana. Karl had ensconced himself behind the sink, where he was rinsing two wine glasses in a hurry. A half-empty bottle of Bordeaux stood on the counter. She looked at him, speechless.

"I'm sorry," said Sandra, embarrassed and upset, running her fingers through her yellow hair. "I just wanted to use the phone. It's like, I had this emergency, OK? Mario's condom broke. I need a morning-after pill. You only have 24 hours, you know? The Rape Crisis Center over on 18th Street gives out these pills, if you ever— you know, if you ever need one. I'm sorry…" She was putting her platform shoes back on, ready to leave.

"So are you fucking her, too?" asked Ana, closing the door without slamming it, trying not to go berserk. But Karl wasn't interested in fucking Sandra, despite the roller disco hot pants.

"Perhaps I have a—how do you say it?—crush," said Karl. "Not with Sandra. I develop a crush on my scuba diving instructor."

"Oskar Brock?"

"Yes, I think I would be interested in a homosexual fling," he said.

Karl came back alone after dining with Oskar and fucked her with a weird grin of distant thoughts. There was nothing she could do about anybody's sexual proclivities except scrape the shit off her middle finger, trying to second-guess Karl in his quest for satisfaction. "This is *it*," she thought to herself, howling with excitement, "He's going to come inside my body! Are you *ready*, baby?" But he didn't come.

"I was thinking perhaps it would interest me someday to have a family," he said, a philosophical expression etched on his tanned, handsome face, holding one finger up against his nose. She couldn't stand the anguish of time going by without a central purpose being fulfilled. Maybe he'd been hoping for passion to bring them together, for just one sperm to slip in, quietly but firmly, the way Karl himself was quiet but firm. They might have talked about it. She thought if she started to bleed again she would sob. But later that night, when she woke up with her period and almost unbearable cramps, she was relieved. She managed to get up and strip the bed of its blood-spotted yellow blanket and designer sheets, but scrub as she might, the stains were there to stay.

She tiptoed out to the back yard and hung the blood stained blanket on the line to dry, then went back in and lay back down on the bare mattress. Karl was in the next room with the door closed, making his night calls to Europe in a soft voice. Soon she was dreaming of Karl. He was clapping at her good little wife performance, frying human steaks and fries for him and Oskar Brock for breakfast. They wanted her to take photographs of the two of them swimming underwater alongside a shark after she cleaned up. She ran down the beach, dragging the camera equipment after her, afraid of somebody noticing how fat she had become before she could get in the water. Karl didn't know how to swim, and she began to wonder whether he was going to drown in the heavy surf. Soon his long blonde hair was bobbing in the water, entangled with strands of shit-colored seaweed. She slowed down, too exhausted to save him. Oskar surfaced on the horizon to pull his boyfriend— her boyfriend—to shore. She watched as Oskar gave him mouth-to-mouth. She wrote in the sand, *Dear Mom, Having a lovely time at the beach.* She wondered how long it would take for the tide to wash out her lying words and pull Karl's body back out to sea.

Ana remained faithful for an all-time record of 364 nights, hoping to snag Karl, if her diaphragm would only fail to work. It was the only part of her plan that she left to chance. Her sense of ethics wouldn't permit her to poke a hole in it. As for her baby, it was certain to inherit Karl's IQ. With a suitable nanny she'd be free to make movies with Karl.

They had separate calendars for the time Karl spent abroad. His was marked with pre-production dates; hers with the days of ovulation. Ana spent the nights that he was away in bed, re-reading Simone de Beauvoir's views on love. He did not resemble Jean Paul Sartre in the least—a major strike against him. Still, what Jean Paul and Simone and she and Karl had in common was none of them believed in getting married. She tried not to feel abandoned. Instead of debating philosophy with her like Sartre, Karl mostly kept paying her share of the rent and ranting about his broken Buick. She had been driving it around San Francisco, looking for work, having reached a hiatus in her career. It was a time of general cutbacks in national arts funding, when even filling in an application form to finish a book of poems or a video was a wasted effort as compared to, say, getting an oil change.

Any idiot could write a pillow book, she thought. The important thing was to perfect it and get it published or even self-published, once it was something more than a lewd list of sexual acts with an aesthetic veneer. She carried the manuscript with her to Benson's

Automotive to work on during the oil change. She'd been waiting to bump up the overall quality of a new erotic poem about Karl, but the awkward rhymes and metaphors for middleweight sex were even more distracting than the mechanical noises and fumes of the garage. What was the point of finishing it, if the other poems in the collection would only make Karl jealous?

"It's me, Karl," he said on the answering machine, "and I'm not sure if you need the $65 I have wired you to fix the water pump on the Buick, which, by the way, I wanted to thank you about, but basically I haven't had time—I'm pretty busy."

He came back at dawn with his heavy suitcase and took off his clothes that were reeking from his night flight. She thought, "Why should I run from sex, even fumbling sex?" But he'd gone off to check the hot water in the bathtub. Then he wanted a couple of Heinekens over brunch in a Mexican restaurant, despite his jet lag.

In Don Quixote's, he told her to think in terms of five-year plans. They reminded her of Khrushchev and the Cold War. "What happens at the end of five years other than finding a younger, still-fertile girlfriend?" she wondered.

She did the math in her head: One year for research, pregnancy and childbirth; one year for pre-production; six months for getting married and shooting the film. Six months for editing it; maybe another pregnancy; a year and a half for the film festival circuit; and another six months for television deals. She was not going to blow a real chance to make movies—movies that might mean something—with a promising producer who was sitting right in front of her drinking Heinekens. She had already blown one opportunity for a meaningful partnership, back in Memphis.

Finally Karl stopped toying with the taco chips and salsa. He cleared his throat—maybe he would propose, the first step to solidifying their partnership. As he opened his mouth to speak, she swore to herself never to take him for granted again.

"I have an appointment," he said. "I have to be at Paramount at five o'clock. So Ana, I want to ask you a favor."

She looked at him, her eyes brimming with expectancy.

"My tux," said Karl. "It needs picking up." He laughed nervously. "You know I can't stand wearing tuxedos. It's just a costume to me. You know how it is."

She looked away.

"I can't help it. It's a benefit," he said, and ate a chip.

She took a bite of cold chilaquiles. He looked at her with sympathy. "I can't say no to Randy. He's the executive producer."

"Can you ask him for an extra ticket?"

"Oh, come on, Ana. Don't be like that. Let's be rational about this."

If Ana would only pick up the dry-cleaning, the fairy godmother floating above the table would surely reward Ana by helping her pitch a film to Karl's executive producer when the time was right.

"It's a deal," she said. She looked down at her watch. It was only two o'clock. She gave him a small peck on the cheek and wondered how he would spend the rest of the afternoon, and with whom.

When Ana didn't get pregnant right away, she complained that she was lonely.

"I'll find you a kitten at the pound," said Karl, trying hard to cope with her maternal instincts.

While he was gone she tried to sandwich in some writing. It was high time she sold out, although it was difficult getting started. She often stared at his typewriter with longing and resentment when he was gone. He had made it off-limits: What if she broke it? His entire desk symbolized the abnormality of their relationship. Everything in its own quadrant, without any sharing: the typewriter, the Rolodex, the shredder, *Die Welt*. If she so much as touched it, it would all be over.

He came back with a six-toed tabby cat that looked even more insecure than she was. Ana named it Treblinka and fed it twice a day while Karl researched oil spills, the rings around Jupiter and the assassinations of presidents, methodically clipping out articles for possible documentaries and trimming them with cuticle scissors.

"Blinky!"

Treblinka liked to jump on the kitchen table while Ana was trying to write. She put her pen and notebook aside and puttered around the kitchen, then stood in front of the open refrigerator, munching away. She had discovered a bug-infested bag of oatmeal at the back of the cabinet while making Karl some breakfast, which had left a little trail on the floor. She might as well sweep the floor of their apartment and practice some German. She could hear her mother's voice echoing "Get that crumb! Get every crumb!" in between the German declensions.

She sat back down and tried to write in an indecipherable longhand which looked like Yiddish. In her dreams, they took away her writing. First the half-baked novel, whose blithe attempts at plot masked the silence and terror of her adolescence. Then the pillow book, with its laundry list of lovers. Then they took her body to Sheppard Pratt, the psychiatric hospital where F. Scott Fitzgerald had had his wife Zelda committed. This she knew from the feminist writing group in North Beach which Ana had started attending on alternate Sundays. By the time Zelda gave up writing to become a dancer, it was too late: Fitzgerald had already forged his literary style out of his wife's writing.

Now her handwriting was spinning around her like a baton while Karl Kitsch wrung her like a dishcloth. In her mind, her lover was the spitting image of Ted Hughes, the husband of the dead poet, Sylvia Plath, who had stuck her head in an oven. She was not striving for perfection. She would leave her films and novels and poems unfinished if only she could fully embrace life.

Karl was furiously typing to rescue whatever deal had been telexed to him the night before. It left him insanely hungry, but nothing was left in the refrigerator except moldy leftovers and sour milk. He asked her to stop writing so they could grab a bite at Don Quixote's.

They'd just eaten there five days before, already putting a hole in their budgets. She could barely look at the food. "Who's going to pay the bill?" she asked.

"What do you think is fair? I'm paying more than half the bill too often."

Ana made two little mounds of rice and beans, and flicked off the shredded cheese. She was by now fifteen pounds overweight and wanted to cut back. "I thought we were paying proportionate to our incomes," she said.

"Ha! You ought to make a bigger income." To him it was no big deal, but to her it was a major crisis. Her heart started pounding. The blanket, the TV, the fold away couch, the down payment on the apartment. She took out her credit card and flung it on the table.

She excused herself and lit up a joint in the ladies' room. When she came back, she promised to make lots of money. She had all kinds of ideas for screenplays and maybe even a novel. He wanted to know when they would be finished, optioned or produced. She still had a few hundred dollars or so before her credit card maxed out. So she merely teased him, calling him "Mr. Right Now."

"You know what I'm going to promise you?" he said, holding her around the waist after helping her with her coat. "I'm going to cut back on smoking marijuana, to maximize my sperm count." And they laughed together, happily arm-in-arm, walking out into the San Francisco fog.

CHAPTER THIRTEEN

The Slow Burn

"Poverty is the cause of many compromises."
— Jean Rhys

The following week began by dislodging a dried-out piece of cat food that was stuck between the washing machine and the sink. The day had already been translated into *der blaue Montag*. The minutiae of novels and poetry were giving her headaches. There was no point in resurrecting *Blues Street*, though she'd thought of doing so; with all the money spent on the apartment, there was nothing left over to duplicate tapes or ship them to whatever festivals still accepted work that was several years too old. What she really needed was to go to Europe and make a feature. People took women directors seriously over there. Sally Potter, Chantal Akerman, Agnès Varda and Susan Sontag were all over in Europe making features. If she wanted to catch up with the cine-feminist movement, she would have to get out of this relationship.

Karl had talked vaguely about producing a film about the Holocaust together before he flew off to Europe without her. She could surprise him by working at a temp agency for a few weeks and buy her own goddamn a ticket to Germany. But, she realized, she really ought to finish her screenplay first. That might save her from the demeaning fate of everyday employment.

She tried to practice affirmations instead of picking at her flea bites. She acknowledged that Karl Kirsch's car was merely a tool which did not have a personality of its own; she paid attention to the road and avoided accidents; she was able to get through another week without any money, without belittling herself in front of other people; and she remembered to feed Blinky, who remained blameless. If her father would just send her one more loan, she could recuperate from the anorectic curve of her financial situation. She could rent a typewriter, finish her screenplay in a couple more weeks, and be ready to send out query letters to dozens of agents.

She had already sketched out several scenes about alchemy and sex in a decaying mansion. In Act III, hundreds of plague-infested, menstruating rats would escape, and Kung Fu Geisha would fight against time to complete her mission of absolute power over men. Her writing group was very supportive.

Some of her best ideas came while weaving in and out of traffic after job interviews went badly. For example, Number One Geisha at the palace, addicted to cocaine by Freudian shrinks… Her gloves, strange concoctions of feathers and satin… her dreams, like haiku poems, passing from lover to lover. She called it *Geisha Girl Palace*, working late into each night that Karl was gone. She managed to find a coffee shop that would give her a cappuccino on credit. Back from the coffee shop, she picked out certain images from her old, frayed pillow book that she thought had commercial potential. She might as well put them to *some* use!

Karl returned from Europe at the end of the month. First he unpacked and poured himself a beer; then he read what Ana had achieved in his absence.

"Basically, you cannot write English well," he said.

"Oh, and you can't even understand half of the English!"

"Let's face it. It really belongs in the shredder."

"Vertig?" sneered Ana, and refused to fuck him. But late that night she picked up the pages, holding them in her arms like an errant child who won't stop crying. Then she inserted them into the shredder, destroying most of Acts I and II. Karl was right. Most of the women in her writing group were poets. What did they know about commercial screenplay structure?

It was not a good night for smoking sensimilla, but the total eclipse was too compelling. Karl walked softly into the bedroom in worn leather slippers, his blond hair backlit in the open window. He propped her up in his arms and dragged her off to the roof.

We are climbing a staircase of ragged, green scales of two dragons' tails. In her mind's eye, she could see them, entwined at one end. *Riding on the mystical knot of their tails is a woman holding the moon in her hands like a mirror. It is well within reach. I try to grab it from her so that I can see my own face. But the dragons start thrashing their tails. There is nothing for me to hold onto any longer. I'm in danger of falling into a vortex of deep space. The only way I can overcome my fear is by nursing at the breast that I've hidden in my brain.*

She doubted her ability to express herself any longer. Karl mocked her self-absorption. To him, the loss of creativity was no disaster. He drove off to film California's fault lines; earthquakes were the only real disaster.

"Don't destroy yourself while I'm gone," he quipped, looking at the bandaids that only half-covered the miniature volcanoes on Ana's legs. She had kept scratching open her fleabites.

"Don't worry," she retorted. "You know what one of the poets in my writing group says? `I'm not going to write a poem and slash my wrists, I'm going to write a poem and say it to someone.'"

That very night she scribbled a two-page poem in pencil. It began:

> "Blood sisters on Avenue B,
>> IUD
>> IOU
>> Unfold to the voodoo drums!
> We'll pound nails into the night

and pull thorns out of the eyes
of the men who could not cry,
    who jacked off to *Playboy*,
    who made us type their resumes,
    who told us to confide in them,
    who asked if we were lesbians,
    who called our dreams nightmares..."

She took it to an open reading in North Beach, where the audience politely applauded. They couldn't assuage her rage. She'd have to assuage it herself. She just had to figure out how.

Karl came back from the San Andreas fault driving a baby blue rental car with unlimited mileage. He was taking her to Palo Alto to celebrate Thanksgiving at a party hosted by German Television. The car had cruise control: he hoped it would take her mind off her problems.

"You don't know what Thanksgiving has even meant to me and my family," she fumed.

Karl parked and turned to her. She had never acted so sentimental about her family before. "I know a great deal about your Thanksgiving," he retorted. "So stop pretending I am a total ignoramus when it comes to American customs, OK?"

She glared at him as the blue car pulled into the driveway past an empty tennis court. Then he kissed her, attempting to demonstrate love and guilt.

"Poor Ana," he said, opening her car door. "I should have given you a plane ticket so you could see your mom, huh?"

"I don't know what I want," she said miserably. She wanted a boyfriend with insights. But they had arrived at the party.

Heinz Sovitzsky-Flemming, a charming, fiftyish man, greeted them at the door. "Ana Fried! I've heard so much about you, and your wonderful production," he said, giving her hand a warm squeeze.

"What production?" Ana asked.

"So modest!" murmured Heinz. "Karl tells me that you're thinking of directing a personal and historical perspective on the Holocaust for Bavarian TV. Excellent!"

Heinz was a man who kept his paunch in check through regularly scheduled tennis matches with Karl's ex-girlfriend Trudi Drescher. Trudi was part of a trio of blondes around the Thanksgiving barbecue pit, who were getting their doctorates at Stanford. Karl gave the blondes warm hugs of recognition. Ana ran up to a bedroom and flung herself over the overcoats. She punished herself for being fat by foregoing the barbecued turkey until hypoglycemia seized her like a whip.

"Karl Kirsch, the businessman!" she screamed in a jealous froth. He had finally come upstairs to get his coat. "Either you send me a plane ticket to meet you in Munich, or forget we ever met!"

He called her excitable and said it was a mistake to bring one's girlfriends to meet one's boss. She said polite good-byes to Heinz Sovitzsky-Flemming and the rest of the crew, including Trudi, Lori and Babette. Then she fumed against the ice blue vinyl rim of the rental car door, as far from the driver's side as she could tuck her body.

He doesn't need my jealousy; he doesn't need my anger, she silently recited as he sped out of the driveway.

She wanted her freedom. No, she wanted a baby.

He doesn't want my anger; he doesn't need confusion, she repeated to herself as they swerved onto the on-ramp.

He wants me to act like his mother, as long as he doesn't have to acknowledge it.

He turned the dial to talk radio and was darting in and out of traffic. She needed to direct a film, any film, before they crashed.

He wants a free, uncommitted relationship in which I pretend that I'm not free and act completely unfree and in fact, lose my freedom.

"You're going to leave me, aren't you?" she cried, addicted.

They made love in reconciliation back in their tiny apartment. He sighed and came. Ana laughed and said, "Who knows?" Karl said, "I certainly don't know," and went into the bathroom to wash himself. She sat on the toilet and dripped, hating his ambivalence.

"I love you," he said, when she finished dripping. She looked at him expectantly. "And, if you're a good girl, I'll take you to Germany for Christmas." Then he zipped up his khaki pants.

The next thing she knew, their forks were dueling with a piece of wiener schnitzel in a little restaurant off of Ossingerstrasse in Munich. They kissed each other across the table, a signal to the waiter that they were finished. She wanted to know when she was going to meet the Kirsches. He said he was neutral whether she met his mother or not.

"*I'm* not neutral! I've come all this way to meet her," she protested.

"Munich is a big city. Why can't you amuse yourself by sightseeing?"

"I want to meet both your parents," she answered flatly. "I'm not budging till I get their approval."

"My father—" Karl cleared his throat. "My father lost his mind fighting the Allies. Whether you meet him or not is immaterial."

"Quit stalling," she said, kicking him under the table.

"I would keep my marriage to a Jew a secret if we married. Mother has a cold heart," said Karl.

"Mother, schmuther," Ana retorted. *IF we married*? "You anti-Semites!"

"You have no right to accuse me," said Karl. "I am of a different generation entirely. Also, my father suffered more during World War II than your family did. We feel much more guilty about living on the backs of people who are poor, or about wasting electricity. I only talk about these things because you make me do it."

"Munchen is sehr schon, Munchen is sehr schon," she practiced on the autobahn, zipping by the black skeletons of trees.

Karl whispered a greeting to his mother at the door of their small apartment, letting his father continue to sleep. Frau Kirsch was a tall, angular woman with white-blonde hair and a permanent frown, who sat down on one of the two recliners after she had made her perfunctory greetings and started mending Karl's socks. Karl sat down on the other. They were talking too fast for her in German. Ana put up with it, waiting for the chance for her German lessons to pay off. It was never going to arrive.

"Home is where your love is," whispered Karl, holding her in his arms on the worn-out carpet of his apartment on Holzstrasse.

"What?" said Ana, preoccupied with the way the Persian carpet was itching against her naked thighs.

"Home is where your love is," he repeated, letting the English expression sink in with all its banality.

She listened to the pat pat pat of the rain as it hit against the dark windows, and looked over his shoulder at the velvet-covered walls. The dark red velvet was beginning to peel at the top. In the center of the large, stale room was a pale yellow ceramic stove used for heating the apartment. It looked like an oven for baking Hansels and Gretels. He was probably going to offer her cookies with red and green frosting and milk before they went to sleep, and they would sleep forever. He got up to put in a couple of logs, and climbed into the four-poster bed, smiling at her from under the eiderdown.

He patted the mattress beside him. "It's getting warm and cozy, nein?"

She put in her diaphragm with achy, shivering fingers, feeling displaced. She could have been one of the millions of Jews dying in the full fury of winter, marching towards the ovens of Bergen-Belsen, Buchenwald, Auschwitz or Dachau—but she could not imagine herself as an insignificant part of a pile of hair, gold fillings or bones. Maybe it was her destiny to rise above ordinary Jews, to commemorate them.

She stood at the foot of the bed. "I'm not ready to make love," she said. She was thinking to herself, *I'm not ready, period. I don't— I can't—I'm not ready to make a movie. I don't even have any photographs of my uncles who died in the ovens. I'm no Judaic scholar. I'm not making this film.* She pictured herself burning in the ovens under a blackened sky.

He drove her to the concentration camp through streets patched with ice instead of making love. He tried to be loving and compassionate, transcending sex. Ana would have nothing of it.

"Why didn't we get more film stock?" she asked impatiently. "Didn't you realize how important filming in Dachau is to me? How can I possibly know in advance whether color or black and white will impart the right emotional impact?"

"How is this film suddenly so important?" asked Karl. "You only flipped through a couple of books on the Holocaust before we left for Europe."

At Dachau, she set up the 16mm Arri camera on the tripod, and prepared to film the sign which read "Arbeit Macht Frei." For a moment she thought she could imagine the thousands of Jews who had trudged past the sign, too broken-hearted to read it. She was almost on the verge of weeping, but focused on which lens to use. Karl, meanwhile, was busy taking notes and signing location agreements.

Ana dragged the tripod across the gravel to film the Dachau ovens. The lining of her stomach felt ashen as she gazed at the ovens through the eyepiece, turning them into maudlin clichés. She had no spiritual eminence that might have qualified her to make a film like this, let alone the directorial competence she'd thought she had. The only real religion in her life was Film Art. If she had any spiritual sense, the Shekinah might have covered her with a shawl of stars when it got too dark to film. But she was spiritually dead.

Of course, Karl had forgotten to bring any lights to film the ovens. *He could have illuminated me*, she thought. In the dim light of the late afternoon, the ovens looked like the same brand that stood in the center of his living room, ready to bake children. She said nothing of her feelings to Karl—only that she was hungry and wasn't it freezing cold and threatening to rain again? Couldn't they wait until the next morning to film on Wienerstrasse, where her great-great-grandfather used to have a hat factory full of Jews?

In Karl's four-poster bed with its battlefield of goose-down pillows and comforters, Ana tried to think romantically about repopulating Munich. But *My Jewish Roots* was stuck in the birth canal of her imagination. Since PBS had heard about the film, she was treating her creation with great care. There was no room for his penis to impregnate her. She laughed a coarse, guttural laugh, thinking of how she was continuing to sleep with this son of an ex-Nazi in order to work on this all-important film of self-discovery even though she couldn't possibly continue to love him. He branded her with a French kiss, then suffocated her with a pillow for not complying,

"Filmmaker or woman! Choose!" She gasped as he shoved into her. Their lovemaking was like a little temper tantrum. Then the phone rang: he had to talk to somebody about ordering light stands for the next morning's shoot, and it was in Ana's best interests not to interrupt.

At the end of their production week, Karl drove her to the airport in his father's Mercedes. "I just don't buy these guilt feelings," he said. "I will never apologize for what happened before I was born."

On the line for the X-ray machine and the metal detector, she wiped the plastic smile off her face. She had barely begun to come to terms with her Jewish identity or her anger, and already she was leaving, without any further possibility of transformation.

Karl was drinking too much red wine, waiting with her in the Terminal Bar until it was time for the plane to load. He accused her of having taken him for granted, and she agreed, thinking to herself how wise she had been not to have signed any formal documents for him to produce *My Jewish Roots*.

"Fortunately, Karl came through with German television funding after all," Ana blithely remarked to her neighbors, an odd assortment of surfers and paralegals. Ana's thirtieth birthday party marked the Bay Area premiere of *My Jewish Roots*. Jeff Katz had flown in from the TV Gallery in New York that morning, and Karl had arrived from Tel Aviv that afternoon, after filming a mini-series in the Middle East called *Christians, Muslims and Jews for Peace*. He had brought her back a djellabah of sheer, purple silk, which she had put on for the party without a bra underneath.

Everybody sat on the floor around a borrowed crystal punch bowl of tortilla chips, watching *My Jewish Roots* with Ana and Karl. It seemed to be an intensely personal film about an assimilated family who had hidden their Jewishness from outsiders for three generations. When the lights went on, everybody discussed the Holocaust with its history of exile and imprisonment. Except Karl. He was drinking tequila.

"There's no money in showing *My Jewish Roots* on TV," Ana assured her guests—ever the victim. "PBS heard about the film in Europe, but they want *me* to come up with promotional funds— you know, radio spots, press packets, a commercial, even!"

"But it's going to show nationally?"

"Uh-huh."

"That's terrific!"

"Don't you think it's anti-Semitic that PBS is making me raise the money to air it, instead of paying me?"

"Oh, come off it. Lots of independents aren't being paid these days."

"Oh," she said with a slight air of disappointment, her persecution theory deflated.

"You're going to be hot," said Jeff Katz, hugging Ana's shoulder. "I can sense these things. You're going to have to let me give you that show in Soho."

She took his arm off her bare shoulder and studied his face. It was handsomely round, if a little puffy. A Nice Jewish Boy look. As for his baggy clothes, they were definitely first class. "How come I never seduced *you*?" she asked.

He gave her an embarrassed grin. "I guess I got engrossed in new hardware, or I would have gotten your number," he said. "But give me your number so we can talk about the show." She laughed a sophisticated sort of a laugh as close to Louise Brooks as she could manage.

I don't know where to go with my love, she thought. Karl was cornering the next door neighbor and kept plying her with drinks. *I don't know what to do with my love.*

Karl helped the neighbor to take off her hot pants and get in her hot tub. Sandra's terrier Jo-Jo barked at being splashed and returned to shake himself over the hors d'oeuvres. Ana, meanwhile, was telling the guests what it was like to film in her ancestral homeland, and how cooperative the German government had been. Karl wasn't making any progress in the hot tub: Sandra had taken too many drugs and was hallucinating.

He opened another bottle of tequila, leaving aside the salt and lime. The birthday cake that he had purchased for the occasion was brought out, and candles jabbed crookedly into its sides. Ana needled him about the cake. "Karl, you don't want me to blow these out, do you? This thing might catch on fire."

"There's nothing wrong with the cake," he said.

"It's lopsided," she insisted.

Some guests sang "Happy Birthday" to add decorum to the ritual. He watched the wax candles dripping onto the icing with remorse. Chocolate would have been better—at least it was a love chemical. Ana blew at the candles, but the marijuana had seized possession of her lungs, and she sputtered and coughed.

Finally the knife that was meant for her to cut the cake slashed at the balloon above her head. Its small explosive burp startled her out of her coughing and infuriated her.

"Karli! Stop ruining my birthday party!" Ana exclaimed in a high-pitched voice, laughing for the benefit of her guests. They caught on to the dispute when he pulled down a blue crepe paper streamer and hurled it over the cake, where it got stuck in the icing.

"You are the artist," he announced, "and you are taking me for granted." One of the guests bumped into the kitchen table, spilling tequila over the cake; the blue bled into the icing and made a little puddle the color of robin's eggs. Karl smashed the middle of the cake with his plastic cup. "This is what I think of your film that you use to make fun of me, my family, and my country! And as for your 'artistic' work, which nobody ever sees, and your screenplay, which you never finish writing…" he began, and stopped himself, remembering his role in the shredding of the first and second acts.

It was a carrot cake: some of the guests ate jagged pieces that they could cut out from the mess, and agreed that it tasted quite good. By now Ana was visualizing the oven that had baked it. Someone pulled out a cigarette lighter, but it was impossible to relight the sticky, melted candles. Leaving nothing but crumbs, they now departed for the sullen dawn.

Ana scowled her good-byes to no one in particular, other than the worm at the bottom of the tequila. She gathered the crumbs in the skirt of her purple djellabah and carried them a block away to the beach. She could vaguely recall tashlich, when one casts away one's sins into the sea. Picking through the folds of sheer silk, she looked for an offering to Karl, her omnipresent God. He was probably watching her through the broken window down the block.

She waded into the ocean past her thighs, hoisting her skirt higher; it billowed out in rage against the dull gray sky. The salt water lapped against the open sores on her legs.

She picked up a frosted shard of dull green sea glass. Poor little shard, spat out into indifferent tides. It wasn't sharp enough for cutting wrists. The ocean was wet enough without her blood. Dawn had drowned unwanted in the waves, and the sun pushed through the gray clouds like an afterbirth. She threw the last crumbs to the gulls, beset with trembling and fear. Was there no higher purpose to her life?

"I really don't want to be put into this position of covering your share of the rent indefinitely," he said over his morning espresso.

"So?" Ana brushed off some flour from her cheek and picked up the rolling pin. "Should I move out and get my own place? This was *my* place until you moved in!" She was making egg noodles from scratch, in homage of all her female ancestors who had martyred their lives slaving over hot stoves.

Karl gazed at her placatingly. "I think you should find a way to contribute more equally to our expenses," he said.

"You know I'm trying," said Ana. She turned on the stove and went back to rolling out the sticky dough. She no longer had her silver bracelets; she had pawned them.

"Can't your parents help?"

"You put it so delicately," she said, reaching for a knife. "I'd rather die." But after the ostentatious display of domesticity, whose only tangible results were long, uneven strips of goy-looking lokshen, she dialed New York.

"Hello?" Her mother answered. Worse luck—her mother had less economic sense than her father.

"Um, hi, Mom."

"Well, it's about time we heard from you," said Madelyn in her typical tone of disapproval.

"Mom, I'm coming home again in three months," Ana began. "It's for my retrospective."

"Oh, I should have guessed. You're not coming home to see us. You're always ignoring your parents. I had a painting in the Westchester Art Show last month, and you could care less!"

"It's a New York City retrospective, Mom. They're screening my Holocaust movie, my art world film, and even the Beale Street video, if I can just get the $150 reproduction fees together in time." Karl had put the noodles in the water—an egalitarian gesture.

"Oh, so it's about the money. What a waste," said Madelyn. "All you've been carrying around for far too long, instead of babies, are film cans."

"Film cans? Why on earth would I want to reproduce myself?" *Like you reproduced yourself in me*, she added bitterly to herself. She spit out her gum and took a deep breath.

"Gee, Mom," she managed to say without reacting any further. "I was hoping we could have a rational conversation." For a measly $150, she could start distributing her documentaries, which might have a worldwide impact. But she slammed down the receiver before ingratiating herself to her parents sufficiently to cover her debts. She wadded another stick of gum into her mouth, though chewing it made her teeth hurt. She could have gotten married to Mr. Green Card and cashed in the wedding presents to buy herself enough writing time to revise her work instead of feeding it into the shredder. And as for the noodles, they would probably end up in the garbage disposal.

But no, another interruption: Karl wanted her to take one of the secretarial jobs he had circled for her in Sunday's want ads.

"Oh, you're just obsessing about secretaries because you want to hire one that you can fuck," she groused.

"For the last time, Ana," he said, rolling over on the couch, his pale nakedness aglow in the sunlight, "let's ascertain that you are capable of bringing an income into the household." He glared at her disapprovingly.

"What is this, a test? I sold a print of my body painting movie to the National Gallery last April," she bragged.

"You know what I mean."

She glared at him, trying to stare down his ultimatum.

"You don't even have the money to go to your own retrospective," he said.

"They're paying my airfare, Karl!"

"What about advance publicity? Are they going to do a mailing? Can you even afford to xerox the invitations?"

"I don't know, I hadn't thought that far ahead," said Ana, peeved and preoccupied with draining Karl's noodles.

By Thursday, she had answered one of the ads at the downtown San Francisco branch of Morrison and Lymon, Inc. They hired her for her typing speed of 97 words a minute, which could have been used for taking dictation from the Muse. The job was merely another way for Karl Kirsch to become the creative one in the family, if there ever were to be one. He was excited by this new balance of power. In the morning, he sucked her clitoris before driving her to work downtown.

When she walked into Morrison and Lymon, a dozen other secretaries were sitting in judgment before their typewriters. She tucked her purse under her typewriter stand under the supervision of Arlene Mays, who had been dipped in a vat of Chanel No.5. The first task was to type the minutes for a stockholders' meeting written in longhand by Joseph Lyman, Jr.'s second assistant, which went on for several pages, but the correction tape kept getting twisted.

The air conditioning was soon lulling her into a deep sleep while Arlene and Gloria hypnotized themselves to the powerful voices of Albert Morrison and Joseph Lyman, Sr.. Occasionally Arlene would disappear into Al's office, or Gloria would take a two-hour lunch break with Joe. Ana was thankful not to be on a first-name basis with the bosses: one day she'd find her body parts mixed in with theirs in an unmarked desk drawer.

She seemed to have acquired the habit of sucking her teeth though she thought she was still in control: She planned to suck them until her dental benefits kicked in. But her teeth tumbled to her feet like a broken necklace while she was typing "y"'s for "t"'s and "b"'s for "n"'s. Then her tongue went to work, sucking blood out of the holes that were left, her calloused lips protesting when the tongue pushed past them. She'd run out of correction tape. She sucked on her teeth the way she wished Karl would suck on her clitoris again.

"What're you eating, Arlene?"

"Mmm! Delightful lemon yogurt!"

"Don't tell me," protested Gloria. "Mr. Lyman says I'll get fat."

"Oh, but you should try it. Two, three times a day—a few bites at a time. You won't get fat that way."

"Do I have to listen to this?" Gloria complained. "I can't stand it!" She popped her bubble gum.

"If you're on a diet, it's even better," said Arlene. She swooped up a quarterly report in a cloud of perfume, jetéeing and plieing past Ana's desk.

"Oh, did you take ballet lessons, too?" asked Gloria, wistfully.

"For just about a hundred years!" replied Arlene. Ana would be stuck listening to office soliloquies for over a century while her teeth ached. Arlene poked her head into her boss' office. "Look at these clunky shoes I have on now, though," she said, looking back at Gloria.

Mr. Morrison's aide Vance cleared the phlegm from his throat within the recesses of his cubicle. "Can I see you for a sec?" he asked Arlene. She tossed Ana and Gloria a goofy grin, checked her hair spray, and vanished into his cave.

Temporarily unsupervised, Ana tried to sneak in a few free xeroxes of her hand-drawn press release to her retrospective. Then she called Karl, who had driven her crazy driving her to work, feeling the meat of her thighs as they pressed against the clutch of his Volkswagen. But now all she got was the answering machine. Not only did she resent him for being unavailable, but for making her into a carbon copy of his ex-girlfriends—Trudi, Ilse and Luisa—all of whom had once worked part-time for Karl.

Ana nervously looked down the row of cubicles at the identical wisps of smoke rising from Gloria, Angelica, Debbie Ann and Suzie Q's cubicle dividers. She walked slowly past the cubicles, horrified by their identical smiles, one toothy smile after the other. She started making copies for Mr. Lymon's second assistant Vince. Like one ream of plain white paper, Morrison, Lymon, and Kirsch could have been one and the same body. She got job resentment so mixed up with boyfriend resentment that she couldn't remember what she was doing in the kitchen the next morning. Was she supposed to be making coffee for Vance, or warming up the copier for Vince? Finally she knew! Dancing like a Sugar Plum Fairy for Karl!

"Listen, you pompous stooge!" Ana screamed at Karl as if he were her boss. "I'm not doing any Zelda dancing for you unless it's to kick in your lying ass!"

"Zelda?" asked Karl. "I don't know any Zelda."

"Zelda! Ilse! Luisa! What difference does it make?" she screamed.

I can't xerox my anger. But I keep trying, she thought, as the first twenty copies rolled onto the tray at Morrison and Lymon. *I can't xerox my anger. But I keep trying. I can't xerox my anger. But I keep trying.*

She repeated the mantra in between sips of industrial coffee, even as the copier jammed: *I can't xerox my anger. I can't xerox my anger.*

She dreamed that rats were eating crumbs of an old Bundt cake she had baked. Worms were tunneling their way through holes in the cake, and crabgrass had overtaken the holes in the carpet. Dozens of condoms were strewn around the foot of the bed. Karl had enlisted as a soldier, killing prostitutes without remorse. Ana got up and typed his confession. She didn't know whether or not to betray him for getting her hooked on heroin.

She woke up afraid to write down her dreams. "Who's going to pay you to write the truth of your own life?" Karl said, and took out his cigarette lighter.

"Don't smoke too much grass," she cautioned him.

"And why not?" he asked, so close that she could smell his dragon breath.

"Because I am only a little ashtray, Sire."

"Say it as if you meant it!" he roared.

"I'm only a little ashtray," she said softly, and scuttled back to the bed stand where she belonged.

In San Francisco, life could not continue normally. She fell back into a deep sleep, dreaming that her mother had put her sister's shoulder into a meat grinder. Her father wanted to know whether the meat was going to be kosher.

Her parents sent Ana $500 for a one-way ticket home. She was relieved that they would come through for her in an emergency which she couldn't explain very clearly. But she set three clear goals for New York City. Number One, ask her parents to loan her the money to get back into filmmaking; if not her parents, anyone else would do. Number Two, get a write-up for her retrospective at the Museum of the New. And Number Three, forget Karl Kirsh ever existed.

What's-his-face hid at the desk behind *Die Welt* while she packed her clothes, her unfinished manuscripts, her heavy film cans, her video camera and her books in cardboard boxes. She sealed them with brown plastic tape and left them in the middle of the living room. Treblinka rubbed her tail against one of the boxes, waiting to be fed. But Ana had closed the door behind her.

CHAPTER FOURTEEN

Film Cans

O n the all-night flight, Ana finished outlining the speech she would give at the film screening and started plugging in some details. She asked the flight attendant for some ginger ale and tried not to spill it on her writing in the turbulence of the clouds. Perhaps the glory days of cinéfeminism had passed her by, she thought. She had to be more positive. She took a last sip of soda and smiled wryly, then pulled an air sickness bag out of the pouch in front of her. On it she scrawled, *And so I decided to abandon him.*

Only twelve people showed up at the Museum of the New. She paced back and forth in the lobby once the lights went out and the screening began. It was her own fault. She had xeroxed the press releases at Morrison and Lyman, but she had failed to bring them to a post office.

Face to face with her minyan of an audience, she decided to abandon her speech in favor of informal discussion. There were a few questions, followed by a few coughs and the scraping of chairs as a few couples got up to leave. The curator egged the rest of them on, congratulating Ana for her documentary film *My Jewish Roots.* All Ana could think about were the glitches and snow in the video work-in-progress that had just showed.

"Ana, we think you are marvelous for confronting the past head-on. What gave you the determination to maintain the legacy of your heritage?"

"Well, I just wanted to be a vehicle for some ideas I really cared about," she mumbled. "You know, like assimilation and, um, spiritual death." The curator beamed with her bright, beady eyes, encouraging her to continue. But she had never fully articulated any of her ideas, blaming boyfriends for having stifled her. Men liked intelligent women—but only to a degree. That Karl had failed to show up to her premiere was proof. "It's really great to see a New York museum screening work by women," said Ana, skirting the subject of spiritual death. "I mean, getting work by more than two or three women a year into museums like this one is practically impossible. And it's great when we can celebrate our survival. I mean, as well as the survival of our work..."

Her voice faltered, noticing her mother standing in the back in a sealskin coat, holding a bouquet of roses that had been dyed blue. The remaining people began to shuffle out. The projectionist had already rewound the prints and tapes. She waited for him to hand them back, then finally turned to her mother.

"Mom, what a surprise!"

"Ana, I'm sorry I was late. I really wanted to be here for you," said Madelyn, handing her the wilted, blue roses. "The train was late, and I couldn't catch a cab. All this rain. I only caught a few minutes of the last film..."

"That's OK!" said Ana, hugging her mom for having tried. Her mother reeked of Ylang Ylang.

"Your father wanted to be here, too. He really did. But you know, he's been working so late," her mother said, wistfully. She had never sounded so vulnerable.

"Yeah, he's always been a workaholic."

"I don't know if I should tell you this...I have a boyfriend," her mother blurted out.

"Oh, uh, that's nice, Mom," said Ana. "Where'd you meet him?"

"In Paris, at my figure drawing class last summer," said Madelyn. "But now he lives in New York."

"Oh." That explained the perfume and fur coat.

Madelyn had to leave in five minutes. "Do me a favor," said Madelyn. "Bring your boyfriend with you when you come up to Scarsdale. I want to meet him." Ana balked. "You're not going to skip Father's Day, are you?"

For once, Ana agreed with her mother: Father's Day was terribly important. What a great time to make Karl feel guilty that he was not yet a father. Madelyn was thrilled to see Ana being compliant for a change. She loaded the heavy metal film cans into some double shopping bags for her daughter, taking the lightest one with the videocassettes with her into the cab.

Ana wouldn't have met Karl's plane if her screening had been less of a failure. They had broken up the previous Thursday and had jointly decided for him not to interrupt her screening. But she had forgotten about their decision and resented him for his absence. He was coming to New York regardless as he had to be in Switzerland the following week, and she was a little frightened to be without either success or love. She staggered through the terminal carrying her shopping bags full of heavy film.

He arrived an hour and a half late. She could smell that something about him was wrong. It wasn't just the post-rain, ozone smell of the streets as they waited for a cab outside LaGuardia, or the damp, metallic stench of the paper bags.

In the Hoboken Holiday Inn, he began, "The human male is by nature not monogamous."

"Who says women have to be monogamous either?" She took out a condom.

"You want to make me your entire universe," he said. "It's stifling."

"No problem," she said, rolling the condom over his penis. "No one said you had to be monogamous. We broke up, right? So who are you fucking?"

"No one, yet," he lied. "And how about your ex-lover?"

"I have no idea to whom you are referring."

"The Southern boy." Whenever Ana began listing her lovers, it was torture for him.

Ana began to get defensive. "Oh, that one—Andy, you mean. He hasn't called for over a year. Who are you fucking?"

Karl was unsure about communicating with Ana after jet-lag and so little sleep. He got out of bed to make some instant coffee in the boil-it-yourself gadget on the bathroom counter, but Ana followed him into the bathroom, which was flooded with fluorescent light.

"There's this woman in the telex office. Teresa."

"Teresa? Oho!" She jiggled the light switch for dramatic effect. "So much for the double standard which you call 'the right thing,' you pompous jerk! 'Right stuff' up your ASS!"

It was scarcely two hours into their reconciliation meeting. The water had begun to boil.

"To hell with your lies about wanting to marry me! Oh, I see—you wanted your permanent residency. Take a permanent residency in hell!" she shouted. "Leave me alone, you bastard!!!"

"Ana, I just want to get some sleep." He poured the coffee down the sink. "Let's not be difficult—after all, this is my motel room."

Ana began to get dressed. After all, she could find some other place to go.

"What is 'difficult' about *me* is that my pain reminds you that truthful emotions are too difficult for you to relate to!" she pontificated, buttoning her blouse. "I hate you! Let me alone with your criticisms and 'caring' insults. I *hate* you! If I were pregnant I'd have an *abortion*!"

She ran out to the lobby and pulled out her address book. "New York City" was emblazoned across the cover in glitter nail polish, though the address section was a little frayed—half the letters of the alphabet were missing. She flipped through the pages, looking for someone who would let her crash in Manhattan. But all she reached were answering machines of former friends and by-gone casual fucks. She went back to Karl's room and knocked on the door.

He opened it, pressing his long, warm body against hers. She whispered, "Karl, do you want to go to Scarsdale with me for the weekend?"

"I don't see why not," said Karl.

"Good," Ana purred. They went back into the room and reconciled, and would have spent the whole next day at it in bed if Ana hadn't needed to see her father.

June Geisler looked up from her desk as Victoria Fried's surviving sister walked into Marty's law firm. "You just got a message," she said, pausing between spoonfuls of yogurt. "A Philip Somebody. He called to congratulate you on your screening."

Ana looked at June as if she were a Martian. She wasn't there to discuss old flames; she was there to have her father prepare a legal document. She wanted a rental agreement for the little apartment near the Pacific Ocean that she and Karl were planning to share in their new fresh start together. It was the next best thing to a prenuptial agreement although her father's paralegal thought it was half-baked. It was to be jointly signed by Ana O. Fried and Karl M. Kirsch as the landlord never bothered with formalities, stating that any rental monies donated by either party would not constitute barter for housework. Ana wouldn't allow Karl to move in without one: she was not about to waste another second on housework when she needed to make bigger strides in her career.

Karl seemed so compliant in Grand Central Station, helping her carry her heavy bags of film cans onto the train to Scarsdale, that Ana decided to wait till they returned to California to bring up the subject of domestic agreements, let alone prenups. The power of love would suffice. Meanwhile, she was planning to bury all her film cans and videotapes in her parents' attic behind the dozens of storage boxes from her father's legal practice and Vickie's life.

"Oh, by the way, it's Father's Day," she said gaily, trying to hide her raw emotions. "Just don't tell my parents about your dad going crazy—you know, fighting for the Nazis."

She rushed upstairs as soon as they arrived, leaving Karl alone in the entryway to introduce himself to her parents. Marty Fried had gotten off the earlier train: He was just opening up his briefcase when he remembered his manners.

"Um, care for a schnapps?"

"No, thank you, I rather have a headache," Karl replied. "Maybe you have some tea?" Mr. Fried excused himself and rushed out to the bannister in the hall, giving Karl the opportunity to admire the recessed display case full of antique china and Baccarat crystal figurines.

"Madelyn!" Marty was calling upstairs.

"What?" His wife was hurriedly taking the last curlers out of her hair to inspect the mess that Ana was making in the attic.

"Madelyn, can you come down and fix this young man some tea?"

"Just a minute, dear. Just a minute," she called downstairs, cursing under her breath.

Ana had snuck into her mother's room and was watching her mother brushing her hair, careful not to disturb her in her obvious bad mood. But Madelyn caught her eye in the edge of the mirror and hurried to give Ana a quick hug.

"What's with the hug, Ma?"

"Oh, I'm just so upset. I keep calling New York City, but there's never any answer."

"You mean that French guy you were painting with?"

"Shh! If your father hears you mention one word of this, you're finished," she said, with bobby pins between her teeth.

"Don't worry, Mom," said Ana. "I'm already finished."

"What, you told him already?"

"No, my career is finished," Ana said quietly, pausing to examine her mother's recent facelift in the mirror. They looked almost like sisters.

"I just want to be happy for a change," said Madelyn.

"Yeah, right," said Ana, bitterly. "Karl always says happiness is relatively unimportant." She put her hand on her mother's shoulder. Madelyn was surprised, but decided not to make a big deal out of it. She went back to brushing her hair, spraying it into place while Ana receded down the hall to blow her nose in the bathroom.

Karl, meanwhile, was buying time by looking at the ant traps under the coffee table and the blue ribbon stuck on a faux de Kooning over the grand piano. Marty Fried cleared his throat, and Karl looked up at him, feigning respect.

"I've supposed you've come up here to talk about the contract," Marty began.

"Contract?" asked Karl, politely bemused.

"Of course, I think the whole idea of a rental agreement stinks," said Marty jovially. "Communication, that's what you two need! Without communication, who's going to enforce any of the fine points?"

Madelyn had entered the room a little flustered, but pleased that Karl had been looking at her best painting. "Hi, Karl, I'm Madelyn Fried. I suppose you're into herbal tea?"

Karl stood up and shook her hand. "Actually, Mrs. Fried, I prefer regular tea."

"Oh, please. It's Madelyn. Marty, what am I interrupting?"

"We're talking law, Honey. Legal technicalities."

"Oh," said Madelyn vaguely. "Prenups?" She sauntered to the kitchen to fix herself a stiff drink and tea for Ana's newest lover. Ana bumped into her on her way out, rushing into the living room.

"Dad, I never did show him the agreement!" she burst out.

"You kids these days," said Marty, giving Ana a warm hug. "You kids are really something." Karl buried his head in the agreement that Marty had taken out of his jacket pocket and thrown onto the coffee table.

"'Any rent monies donated by either party will not constitute barter for housework?'" read Karl. "Why is this even necessary? Since when have you paid the rent, let alone the storage bills for your film materials?"

Marty laughed. "And the funny thing is that your girlfriend here wanted it to read, 'barter for sex or housework.' A pre-nuptial agreement—something to cover bequeathment and child custody, that I could arrange. I should know, after thirty-five years in divorce and family law. But this is filthy. It wouldn't hold up in court. And my paralegal, she wouldn't agree to typing it up either: she's a divorced woman with three children!"

"Look, Dad, I just don't want to be owned, OK?" Ana said.

"It's embarrassing. It really is," said Marty, downing a schnapps. "You and your mother! You ought to be moving in together—you're two immaculate women. Mr. Church here," he said, thrusting an arm around Karl's shoulder, "should live with me, so we can ignore housecleaning entirely. It's too silly!"

"It's not 'Church,' it's 'Kirsch,'" said Ana. "What are you drinking, Dad?"

"Karl Kirsch, I like the name," said her father. "I really do."

Karl tried not to say too much. He turned on the television with the pretext that he was analyzing American news for German television. Ana thought it impolite, but they were getting along without incident.

"Do you want to go swimming, Karl? We have a pool out back," said Marty affably over the din of the commercials. "I could lend you my trunks."

Karl announced that business necessities precluded the possibility of spending the rest of Father's Day in Scarsdale.

"Happy Father's Day," Ana mechanically muttered to her dad, avoiding his eyes. She resented Karl's cold feet, but perhaps he was only paying her the courtesy of avoiding having to explain his father's affiliation to the Nazis. They would never allow them to get married if they found out.

Just then the teapot boiled, and Madelyn came in with strong, black tea for Karl's headache. "Well, Karl," said Madelyn, standing back to appraise him, then placing two sugar cubes on the side of his saucer. "Just one thing. I want the wedding on the front lawn. Or I'll disown you. Is that perfectly clear?"

Ana was so embarrassed. Were they talking about caterers already? What about the nuclear power plant across the street? Her imagination was running wild.

"It's simply a problem of hors d'oeuvres," said Karl, stirring lumps of sugar into his tea. "I want white fish at my wedding. I really like white fish. I don't care for smoked salmon."

Time will remain frozen inside the Chuppah until Madelyn gets her way with the groom. Sitting next to Ana is a big fat woman with a scarf that stinks of furniture polish. They're waiting until the ceremony can begin. A little boy in a yarmulke rests his feet on Ana's lap, soiling her white lace dress.

Karl comes back in, wiping his feet on the porch. He leaves his machine gun in the umbrella stand in the front hall. It's camouflaged among the black umbrellas. Karl is amused but silently horrified by all of Ana's relatives. The fat aunt wants to shave Ana's second cousin's head in the living room, to get rid of the lice.

"Please," asks the aunt, "won't you give me some shampoo?"

"If you'll do it in the kitchen," says Ana. "It will make less of a mess."

The little boy begins to sing songs in Hebrew.

"Would you care for some pomegranate juice?" says Marty, adding casually, "We call it pogrom juice." Karl politely holds out his glass, although his hand is shaking. "Whoops! Careful not to spill it. It stains easily," Marty explains. "My wife had to bring several of my dinner jackets to the dry cleaners last week."

Madelyn begins to complain about the radiation—it might drive away the guests. The room is stuffy and old, with no open windows.

Karl machine guns the miniature glass kitsch, extinguishing the lights of the display case. One of the guests goes to a window, breaking it open with his shoe. He is screaming for water to be pulled up from below. The hot winds are ferocious, and he has no life rope to keep him from falling out.

Karl was already putting on his jacket.

"Doesn't your father deserve an apology?" demanded Madelyn. "What kind of a daughter leaves in the middle of Father's Day?" Ana tore a hangnail. She watched it bleed.

Marty glanced at the news, biding his time. Her mother turned to Karl. "Where are you staying in New York?" she asked conversationally.

"I have a friend named Oskar who keeps an apartment here," said Karl, "but he spends Junes on the coast of Spain." Madelyn proclaimed Spain to be a delightful country. Ana was relieved not to have to discuss Germany. Her parents drove Ana and Karl to the train station: if they hurried they could make the next train.

"You know, getting married at my parent's house won't be so bad, except for the Chuppah," Ana told Karl as they grabbed two seats in the smoking car, facing one another. "We can cash in the presents."

"Please, Ana, keep your voice down. You're embarrassing me—it's a crowded train!" protested Karl.

"It's not a train to the death camps!" said Ana, melodramatically.

"For some reason I'm not saying anything," said Karl.

"Yes, you are. You're implying something even in your silence," she asserted. "You're always directing someone or something, defining everyone's reality."

"I'm not talking any more about personal life. I talk when I work. That's it."

"When you work?" asked Ana, desperate to keep the channels of communication open.

"Well, it's better than being jobless. I believe you're jealous of me, Ana."

"Well, I can't believe we're actually going to spend the weekend in the apartment of your gay scuba diving instructor!"

"At least, we're not spending it with your mother."

They were both tired of fighting for the sake of fighting. It was a conversation that evaporated in the silent, smoky haze. Finally they arrived in Yonkers—the key was under the potted palm in the hall.

Karl wasted no time taking off his clothes as if to release himself from the constriction of having met her parents. But Ana needed to get stoned before she could think of having sex. They opened up every drawer, every door, every box. They found Oskar's checkbooks, an old passport, prophylactics, pills of every color and size, and finally, in an Indian rosewood chest brimming with theater ticket stubs, they found his dope, but no rolling papers. Enough ransacking, Karl decided. He went out to buy some.

Ana looked out the window at the kids swimming in the pool next door and rummaged through her knapsack for her bikini. She wanted to wash off the stench of the smoky train plus the musty odor of the air conditioner, which hadn't been turned on for days. She left a matchbook in the door jamb of Oskar's bachelor pad and went off to jump in the pool before the sun set.

No sooner had she started swimming her first lap than the lifeguard blew his whistle. When he asked to see her ID, she jumped out of the turquoise pool, shivering without a towel, and ran off in the direction of the apartment building. Halfway between the building and the pool, a dog came bounding towards her—half German shepherd, half Chow. He jumped up on her, marring her white torso with muddy paws and breathing dog stench into her face.

She shoved it away and pushed into the apartment, refusing to feel unnerved by a dog. Chlorine and dog drool dripped onto Oskar's carpet. She enjoyed violating it out of jealousy. She tossed her bikini in the bathroom and planted herself on his black leather couch. Late afternoon light streamed across her naked body through the blinds—she was conscious of how beautiful this would make her in Karl's eyes when he opened the door. Then she remembered the paper folded in her wallet. She quickly rolled a joint and took a deep drag of Oskar's dope. Her body was still wet from the pool, smelling of leather and chlorine as it stuck to the couch. Once stoned, she felt compelled to pull out Oskar's collection of Joan Baez. She sang "Come All Ye Fair and Tender Maidens," realizing how much of the song's unrequited love she had already lived through:

> Take warning how you court young men,
> They're like a star of a summer's morning,
> First they'll appear, and then they're gone.

She had memorized the lyrics when she was fifteen.

She changed to a faster tempo, dancing furiously to "Rake and Rambling Boy." Karl had returned with the rolling papers he had bought for them. He stood in the doorway watching her belly fly in every direction, her ovaries on fire. Between her belly dancing, in the pause before "Babe I'm Gonna Leave You," he managed to blurt out how beautiful she was.

Ana began to cry. She put on a Bob Dylan album, dragging the needle to "It's All Over Now, Baby Blue." She had memorized these lyrics, too, and now she started to sing along in a quavering voice. She was sitting in a lotus position, raising her arms in supplication to Karl, who stood half-way out the door.

"Look out, the Saints are comin' through, and it's all over now, Baby Blue!" she was singing to Karl, tearfully and off-key. Karl, who was drinking her tears like champagne. Karl, who had toasted all the times they could have shared.

He came into the room to change the record to the Rolling Stones:

You can't always get what you want,
But if you try sometimes, you just might find
You get what you need.

She closed her eyes, rocking to the beat. Karl! Kali! Karl, who had promised Ana any lifetime other than this one.

CHAPTER FIFTEEN

Inside Stories

I can no longer tell dream from reality.
Into what world shall I awake
from this bewildering dream?
— Akazome Emon (? - 1027)

Ana and Karl were each invested in analyzing the corpse of their relationship. They had gotten back together with the primary goal of investigating it, renting a small bungalow together down in Silverlake. Each had their version of love gone wrong. Ana had shrugged off martyrdom. She felt she could redeem herself and her relationship through their mutual art. As for Karl, he had long wanted to enter her creative world the way that he had first entered her body.

Karl had set up the endoscope, its long, thin metal tube capped with a miniature lens encircled by a light at the tip. He watched the monitor while Ana peered through the video camera, guiding the tube attached to its lens adaptor into her lover's mouth—a maze of white panels of teeth pushing against pulsating walls of slimy pink and purple. "How incredible!" he said, watching the image of his own mouth scrambling into a dark cave as he spoke.

"Why did you have to say anything?" she complained. They traded places, Ana spreading her legs while he turned on the camera and entered the cold steel tip of the endoscope gently into her vagina.

"Fiber optics are incredible! It's like fucking with technology," he said, pressing against the rubber eyepiece. "This is our chance to beat Emile Zola at capturing reality."

"Oh, knock it off, Karli," she said. "This is avant-garde video, not a remake of French literature."

"No, no, no. Zola wrote: 'The cunt in all its power; the cunt on an altar, with all the men offering up sacrifices to it.' What we are making is the video of the cunt, 'the cunt turning everything sour,' and I quote!"

"I'm much more interested in cinécriture," said Ana, "and l'écriture féminine." She resented him dragging her body back into the nineteenth century, especially since they were using state-of-the-art technology; no one had ever used an endoscope in experimental video or film to penetrate the human body. She was determined to match the brilliance of their technical forays with previously unimaginable metaphors. She wanted to prove that her love could withstand the strength of Karl's inspections.

"So this is the door of conception," he said in marvel. Her cervix appeared like a white moon, appearing and disappearing in a dawn of pink clouds.

"Remember, this was my idea!" said Ana, her cervix wiggling out of sight as soon as she started talking.

"I honor it," said Karli solemnly, never taking his eyes off the eyepiece. He waited patiently for the chance to refocus on her cervix. And there it appeared! "The world of video exploration has finally brought light into the dark."

"I want to see! I want to see!" crowed Ana. "Rewind the tape!"

He rewound it for her, and she took her turn, watching the cyclops eye of her cervix like a mirror.

"What about behind the cervix, where the egg and the sperm become one?" Dream on, moon child, she thought bitterly to herself. Even such a powerful, never-seen-before image wouldn't enchant her love into action on camera.

"Maybe it's better for us to meditate at the entrance," said Karl, "instead of forcing our way inside."

"*Our* way?" She pulled herself off of the endoscope and turned it off. She had wanted to make up for the pain of her loss of Andy's baby with this creative act.

"Please don't include your miscarriage." Karl felt that it would turn out to be a bad omen. It might trigger the derailment of his own tentative power of self-expression. "The fetus had nothing to do with the video that we are making now."

In post-production, Karl toyed with macrocosm and microcosm, trying to control the pattern of the stars in the sky against a background of semen while Ana kept bickering about his controlling her destiny. She grabbed the voice-over mike and crooned,

Your plane soars through my mouth
into the depths of my vagina.
I wanna take you
to the origins of my heart.
Don't leave me. Don't take it out!
Lemme be a cinéfeminist,
but just another woman, in this:
I want...to love you.
I want...to love you.

"Ah so," said Karli nervously. "You have a big...i-vagination!"

"Speak English, dammit!" she said, rushing past his joke back into the non-verbal, phallic world of cinematography:

- Zooming inside his mouth, out to his full, naked body;
- Close-ups of his penis;
- The six-pointed star of her cervix;
- Her solarized cervix: first pink, then red.

Then she would let the tip of his penis talk.

"I will use the grain of the film to symbolize my sperm," he said slowly.

"It's been done, at least ten years ago. Remember Tony Conrad and his flicker films? Every eighth frame changing till the pattern could send you into an epileptic fit? Bet you can't alter the grain patterns till they inseminate the viewer," she said, trying to deflate him. She didn't approve of his abstract point of view. She had already forgotten her part of his bargain to create dramatic conflict as they aired their differences on tape.

"If your ideas have never been executed," he retorted, "it's because no one in their right mind would represent the emotions of attempted procreation so twistedly."

"Did I hear you use the non-word, 'twistedly'?" teased Ana.

"Dammit, Ana, if you spoke my language, I could outdo you," he said, slamming a videocassette onto the editing table.

Ana stood up. "Men and women as enemies may be an intriguing concept for you to produce," she said, pointing at him, "but it is one I hope never to experience personally again!"

"Perfect!" said Karl. "Say it again for the camera, please."

But by the time he turned the lights back on, she was putting on her clothes. "I no longer have anything meaningful to say," she complained. "It's all your fault!"

"No, no, no," he said. "Say the other thing."

"What other thing? There is no other thing," she stated.

Karl was very satisfied with this. "Let's call it a wrap," he said, his arms wrapped tightly around her.

"I want disarmament in your arms," she said off-camera, and this assuaged his ego.

"I want...you, not your image," he replied. They made love for the entire week of her period without turning on the camera once.

Ana and Karl had just begun editing when the phone rang.

"Hey girl, what's happening?" crooned Andy into the pay phone. "I just got in from Memphis."

A flood of memories swept over her. "Andy! Oh, my god! Where are you?"

"At the Greyhound Bus Station in Santa Monica. Wanna pick me up?"

"The bus station? What happened to your pick-up truck?"

"Oh, baby—it got repossessed."

Andy the Space Cadet seemed to have cleaned up his act: his tall blond figure emerged out of the bus terminal minus the scraggly beard. He strode towards her, casting aside his duffel bag and bulky bass guitar case in order to embrace her.

She and Andy drove up the coast of Malibu to merge with nature. After a few tokes of Maui Wowie, they arrived on an ancient coast of Atlantis where Ana had spent a lifetime in bondage. Here he was, leading the rebellion, giving the signal to revolt! She found herself directing a boat of oarsmen, its helm red and black with a turquoise eye like CBS, encircled by monumental waves. Circles of music were rising out of the waves as their continent drowned. How could the tide roll in, roll in so fast? Only instead of the Atlantic Ocean, they were now looking out over the Pacific, which was placidly meditating on their existence. No tsunamis.

"Far out," said Andy, squeezing her tenderly.

Ana looked up at him in gratitude. She was eager to offer him a place to stay. Like the cat carrying in a dead bird, she wanted to bring in another lover. Karl should be proud of how satisfied and calm Andy's presence made her—the poise with which she could now convey her thoughts on camera.

However, Karl had already put the camera away with a mortified expression. Nobody spoke, not even a "hello". Andy brought out another joint to break the ice. He and Ana guzzled the smoke as if they were sharing a pacifier; Karl abstained. Then Andy plugged in his bass and played a soulful riff. Ana found her flute, but she hadn't practiced in years and had trouble focusing her breath long enough to get a few pure tones.

But she could always sing. "Oh, Man," she crooned, "the Om Man!" She sat cross-legged in the middle of the floor, singing out her mantra:

He was my band-aid and Mercurochrome.
He was the words that don't even need a poem.
He was the burglar when you weren't home.
He was the cotton with the chloroform.
He was the dial on the telephone.
He was the pungent aroma in the Roman bed and board.
He was the untranslatable.
He was the Tannenbaum, the atom bomb.
He was the kid who never combed or shaved or wept.
He was the Bromo Seltzer on the kitchen shelf.
He was the palindrome.
He was the foam mattress.
He was never home.
He was handsome and somatic.
He was the innate OM.

Andy and Karl looked at one another. Karl knew he would never inspire a poem like that; he was only good for conflict, the conflict they had created for themselves in front of the camera. As for Andy, he wasn't sure whom Ana was describing, but he accepted it.

Karl watched Andy and Ana improvise live jazz: Andy on his bass, with the amplifier turned down low, so as not to wake the neighbors in the early hours of the morning, and Ana on her flute that smelled like sour saliva. But the music sounded sweet, and Karl felt somewhat entertained.

"Perhaps I should beat my head against the wall as some kind of drum," said Karl.

But Andy said, "It's cool. Everything's beautiful," and it seemed convenient, somehow, for Karl to believe him.

Andy moved in with his duffel bag full of psilocybin and tears, which fell down Ana's cheeks. Ana was preoccupied sprouting whiskers and a tail. Meanwhile, Karl occupied himself with the travel arrangements for interviews with operatic divas. No one had time to log the videotapes for *Inside Stories*.

Andy couldn't cope with the cat dander inside the house. He would sit in the back yard for hours with his unplugged bass under a tree full of singing frogs who promised to give him the lyrics to pay for his third of the rent. "I'm the Frog Prince, baby," he claimed. Yet he didn't transform when Ana kissed him. He remained rather slimy.

Karli watched in disgust from the porch. Their relentless amphibian duets gave him a throbbing headache. He started to pack his suitcase with socks and underwear, but he found a cockroach in the nylon pocket of the suitcase, and he gasped.

"Insects are just another part of Karl's domestic trip," Ana said blithely. "When he lies in bed and thinks he's monogamous, he's lying. He's completely surrounded by an orgy of bedbugs."

She took Andy into the next room and disrobed him. Karl listened to her come as Andy sucked one of her earlobes like a cat nursing with sharp teeth. She came as he whispered, "your beautiful vagina" and parted her pubic hair. She came as he called her some kind of goddess, and entered her. She came repeatedly as he called her "beautiful", over and over, playing leapfrog with her clitoris, trying to help her shed her self-loathing in long, angry moans. Karl listened to Andy and Ana from the other side of the Berlin Wall and masturbated. He was beginning to ejaculate when the phone rang: the answering machine picked it up. It was Teresa, calling about another telex.

"The vibes are getting thick in here," said Andy, but Karl had left.

Andy took her to Twentynine Palms in her car, driving 90 mph through the desert.

"Let's get married," he said.

"What?" said Ana.

He grinned at her. "I'm not gonna be another broken record in your life. Let's get married," he repeated more insistently.

Ana claimed she wanted to wait. He lavished dinner, booze and drugs on her to prove that he was someone special. But he never got it up. "Don't worry, baby," he said. She wasn't worried; she missed Karl. She was already 75% faithful to Karl because of Andy's increasing impotence from the grass, the speed and the shrooms.

"Hey girl," he crooned in his womanizing voice. "None of this shit has affected my sperm."

"How do you know that?" she asked in between warm gulps of tequila, her words oozing slowly like cranberry sauce. "I wanted us to be drug-free until my pregnancy tests are positive! Yet you've been eating psilocybin all week!"

"It's cool, baby, it's cool," he was trying to say.

"If we keep on taking drugs, we're going to produce a mutant!"

They drove into Joshua Tree National Park without talking. Across the vast desert, Ana imagined a long saxophone wail like a dirge for the baby she had never had. She tried to suppress her anguish in front of Andy, who was tripping out over the phallic cacti. She would have preferred for Karl to be swimming beside her on a lake, racing above her body, splashing her with his jealous laughter. But Karl was crossing time zones. Andy touched her on the cheek. Then he promised solemnly, "I'm not gonna be a broken record in your life."

They drove back to Los Angeles in heavy traffic. Ana did the driving: she had finally remembered that Andy wasn't insured to use her car.

The key was missing from the mailbox where they had hidden it. They had to break into the little house. Ana was amazed at how adroitly Andy jimmied the lock using her credit card. He made a move to pocket it that was as subtle as glancing at a wrist watch. But his hurt, little boy look made her swing the door wide open, slam it, and fall down with him onto the futon in one mammoth movement. This time, after swigging from a bottle of tequila, she sucked at his penis, determined to keep it aloft to compensate for the uneventful desert weekend. She had just wiped the salt from her mouth and slid herself on top of him when the phone rang: it was Karl's secretary, putting his call through. Karl's ESP astounded her: this should have been the big moment with Andy.

Karl was despondent and sobbing.

"You're constantly flying from woman to woman—or from one film festival to another. What's the big deal?"

"I don't think I can go on," he sobbed. "I can't compete with your spiritual guru," he said, as her heart went out to him. "I will give up. I will stay in Europe."

"That's ridiculous," said Ana. "We're going to finish *Inside Stories* first. You can't begin to make a film and then drop it. What about your promise of a mutual work ethic?" She watched Andy's penis go limp.

"He cannot stay in the house," Karl said firmly. "It is my house, too. I signed the agreement."

"Andy wants to marry me, which you don't!" she declared. "Sometimes when we make love I have the feeling it's the last time you ever want to see me, and it makes me miserable! Can't there ever be a middle ground between feeling free and feeling wanted?"

"I will think about it," said Karl. "By the way, I have had an affair at the hotel, to balance out your infidelity."

"Infidelity?" Ana exclaimed, bursting with self-righteousness. "Fuck you! This is the New Age!" She slammed down the phone, but his words stung like tequila poured into an open wound. Who was he with?

"I'm a nervous wreck," she said, trying to meditate.

"Just relax," said Andy.

She tried to rest in the light of an indigo dawn. While her eyes were closed, he opened her wallet and pocketed her cash and credit cards.

"Everything is beautiful," crooned Andy. "Stay beautiful—forever." Then he took off for Nepal with his bass, leaving her with nothing but a half bottle of tequila.

CHAPTER SIXTEEN

Madam I'm Adam

She got a referral to a psychiatrist in Malibu from her father's West Coast associates, her father having agreed to pay the bills. Dr. Anatole Berberian prescribed a new anti-depressant that would help her stop playing the part of a serial victim.

To fill the vacuum left inside her, she had to force herself to breathe, her legs painfully tucked beneath her. Still, meditating was an attempt at spiritual awakening without drugs. She was on her fifth "Om Mani Padme Hum" when the phone rang. Hallelujah! It had to be one of the thirty companies she'd written to for a job, this time a real production job!

It was only her biological father, trying to buy her out with another material object.

"Look, I know this is awkward, honey," said Marty.

"No, really, I'm deeply moved. An Apple computer. Wow!" She knew she should be grateful. First Yale, then all these psychiatry bills, and now this. She had no right to sound dejected.

"What I mean is, I don't want you to think there are any strings attached." He cleared his throat. "It's just... Mom and I are sending you this clipping from *The New York Review of Books*," he added hurriedly. She could hear her mother's voice, prodding him to hurry. "Just read it. If you like it, respond. If you don't..."

"Wait a minute...a *personal* ad? How could you? I mean, you're a *divorce* lawyer, Dad. What good can this possibly do?"

Dear Boundless,

I liked your write-up in "The New York Review of Books," she
wrote without enthusiasm that my friends (she choked) clipped
for me the other day. We seem to have an awful lot in common.
Modern Art is right up my alley too! (As a matter of fact, I made
a film about the New York art world once.)

I'm in my late 20's (she lied: she was in her 30's), with long
black hair and brown eyes. Are you ready for commitment?
Yours truly,
Ana Fried

"Boundless" didn't answer, but she was getting the hang of it.
She turned to another message and started over.

Dear Fellow Book-Lover,

My love of literature has kept me from going out there to
hunt down men. However, if we hit it off, I promise not to spend
my entire time in bed just reading.
Sincerely,
Ana Fried

Fellow Book-Lover was probably reading a long book. She
tried the *L.A. Weekly*:

Dear Attractive, Affectionate, SJM,

I think I meet the qualifications listed in your ad. I suppose
it would be stupid NOT to call myself "bright and sophisticated,"
having graduated from Yale. I'm 5'10, have long black hair, and
most men think I'm gorgeous.

I notice that you have been divorced, and I would be curious
to know what went wrong, if it isn't too painful for you to talk
about on our first date. (My father is a divorce attorney and might
also have some good advice.) Was it infidelity, or was it merely a
statistical mishap of the 1970's to '80's?

In answer to your concern, I am quite interested in a loving, caring, committed relationship.
Yours truly,
Ana Fried

She thought of cc:ing her parents—they were the ones who wanted her committed. But there was no answer from SJM, either. So she tried a chat room, just to be a good sport:

To: *men*
From: *anagram*
Subject: *Floating in space*

Would like to achieve ecstasy in cyberspace, with nothing between what's inner and outer.

She was trying to be cool, referring to virtual reality. It was some new fad.

To: *anagram*
From: *mort.l*
Subject: *Well hello there!*

I don't ordinarily do chat room, but thought I'd give it a shot. Am looking for a writing partner, among other things. You might do, babe. What are your interests?

Ana laughed. She didn't need any more men calling her "Babe." But a writing partner?

To: *mort.l*
From: *anagram*
Subject: *Ridin' Pardners*

> Mort: What an old-fashioned name! How old are you, if
> you don't mind my asking? I'm still in my 20's (she lied again).
> Interests: Jews, computers, movies, sex.

He sent her an invitation to the movie *Shoah*—a nine-hour tribute to the Jews who had perished in the Holocaust. Nine hours next to a nice Jewish man seemed like a great way to get over Karl. Jews believed in marriage and family as primary ways of connecting to their spiritual tradition, unlike Karl. What if "mort.l" turned out not be a stereotypical nerd, but part of her destiny?

She leaped up from her Apple to put on a slinky dress. They met in front of the movie theater. "Mort.l" was Morton Joel Levin, 38, the writer, who let it drop quickly that he'd written the screenplay for "The Wonders of Adam." He was beautiful beyond comprehension or a least more handsome than the average boor. Soaring above his flannel shirt was a fiery chakra emanating diamond sparks of light, and his smile was equally brilliant.

Ana had never built a relationship slowly. She felt certain that their meeting was beyond them, beyond cyberspace even. The union of their bodies had been foretold. Mort simply said, "I'm flattered."

Midway through *Shoah's* nine hours of oral histories from those who had witnessed the death camps, Ana marveled that she and Mort Levin had been chosen to survive. She whispered her commentary in Mort's adorably large pink ears. Mort was amused by the mystical mumbo-jumbo. As a screenwriter, he dug her monologues. Ana left the movie theater with an inane smile that she couldn't erase. Would they make love at her place, or his? Did he have a box of condoms? Did they really have to use them? Should she remind him that, according to traditional Jewish law, he was prohibited from studying the Kabbalah without marriage? Or should she beat around the bush? Of course she'd never mention that she wanted to get married to make up for having been such a whore. Would her parents buy them a house in Beverly Hills? Did

Mort wash dishes? Did he want children? Did the fact that he was out of shape mean she would outlive their marriage...or was this only going to be a one-night stand?

It was an awkward moment in the parking lot between their two cars, shifting from one foot to the other. Finally, Mort spoke. "Uh, I have to drop by the Copy Center in Burbank to pick up my screenplay before it closes. Big meeting tomorrow morning."

"Oh, yeah," piped up Ana. "I almost forgot, I'm going on a retreat tomorrow. I, um, I really have to pack."

"Maybe we'll go to the Hollywood Bowl sometime. I'm a Mahler fan."

"Me, too!" said Ana, smiling inanely. She never listened to classical music.

"Great!" Mort opened up his Pinto. "Call me when you get back."

It was hard to concentrate on meditating, now that she'd met Mort. Too bad she'd signed up for a retreat. She could hardly wait for the Buddhist monk to hit the final gong, so she could go home and call Mort.

He was exactly her height, with dark wavy hair, and she could tell that his genes would be perfect for producing brilliantly musical children, as they sat in the Hollywood Bowl together.

He zipped up his rustling nylon jacket in sync to the first strains of Mahler's "Symphony Number One in D Major." She cast him a shy smile. In the middle of a delicate refrain, a glass bottle broke from somebody's picnic. She focused on Mahler and Mort. The clouds disappeared in time to the crickets—it had been raining profusely in the retreat center; but now the air was so clear that someone's perfume wafted past her like an orange grove, and she could smell it as the violas broke out of an aching silence in the middle of the last movement.

"I bet your sex is as finely tuned as a Stradivarius violin," he whispered, gently tweaking a moist lock of hair out of her eyes.

He took her to his Sunset Strip apartment after the concert. It resembled a collage of the Merz period, with its random assortment of newspaper clippings, wrinkled clothes and dustballs. She had imagined that she would begin to uncover his cabbalistic underpinnings like so many secret undergarments, but Mort was just interested in pulling off her dress.

She felt hope against hope, her eyes tightly closed, that He could be the One. When he entered her, she felt a timeless warmth, as if their physical and spiritual selves, melded together, could convey the intimacy that was lacking in their chat room conversations.

"I'd be glad to put in my diaphragm if you want me to," she said sweetly. But he only took out his penis enough to push it in even more, making her delirious with longing for a baby. She pushed his black, receding hair over his forehead, imagining a cranium like his inside of her. All other Jews on the face of the earth had been exterminated. Only Ana and Mort could save the Jewish race from extinction. When he looked into her eyes while they made love, she thought that he could see her soul.

"I want—I want..." she stuttered with joy, "I want you to come not only into my belly to impregnate me, but into every pore of my body."

Mort said, "I finally understand how women experience orgasm." Ana resented this: she was not *all* women.

But she came while he sucked her nipples, taking all of her through his mouth. She came as he rubbed his tongue against her clitoris. She came again, imagining herself as Delilah with shears, brushing her fingers through the wet, shiny curls at the nape of his neck. She moaned at his gentle affirmation of her being and lost her head completely. She came again as he held her foot, turning her into his favorite geisha from their previous lifetime. If only she could stop making love long enough for seventeen syllables, but he was pushing her against the pillow, whispering words of love.

They fucked all night in his apartment into the next day. In the morning he made her put in her diaphragm, saying there could be problems.

She was overjoyed that he could even think of pregnancy. "I'd love to have such problems," she murmured.

He seemed self-conscious about the mildewed carpet and piles of newspapers that surrounded his single bed. "Someday I'll buy you a house," he promised. "A nice house." Then he put in his circumcised penis for another go-round.

She kept coming in loud screams, worrying if the neighbors could hear her through the thin walls and if they would call the police. She came in his cocoon of blankets, tantalized by paranoia that someone might open the door. She came as she put her finger into his ear like a sea creature in search of a conch shell called home.

And when *he* came, he bellowed like a shofar calling out the New Year.

OK, so she hadn't made it as a writer or a filmmaker yet. Maybe she had to set her sights lower. The important thing was standing on her own two feet. With Dr. Berberian's help, she became more realistic about her talent and prospects, deciding that by getting jobs in cinematography, she could make ends meet. With luck, she could even start paying for her anti-depressants. She still had an eye, didn't she? After all, she had shot *The New York Art World* and her other films herself. The important thing was to look and act professional. She read whole sections of *The Professional Camera-man's Handbook* on depth of field and film stocks. She sent out dozens of resumes, and she invested in a ditty bag and a set of screwdrivers, with a leather belt to hang around her waist. Finally she snagged a job as camera assistant on a pilot.

But after staying up all night at Mort's, Ana was two hours late to Oscar Nicholls International, where she showed up tired and sore and had to be reminded more than once to keep track of the footage. She was shifting her weight from foot to foot, showing no initiative in loading the extra Panavision 35mm mags with 5247 or 5293, or even which was which: not exactly professional camera-woman material.

By now, Ana was used to being fired. No matter what happened, she was determined not to cry on the set. As a courtesy, they let her finish the day getting coffee for the rest of the Camera Department.

The Camera Operator dropped her home, asking for her number, but she slammed the door behind her. Pulling off her jeans, she wondered if Mort would mind if she called him again so soon. She thought the better of it as she washed out her diaphragm and decided to catch up on sleep. In her dream, a group of filmmakers had been rounded up and forced down a steep cliff where they were going to be executed. Ana took close-ups with her Nikon as they marched along. She began to worry about where she could hide the 35mm roll of film for posterity. Under the dead bodies?

Her mother interrupted the nightmare. "Why are you still sleeping?"

Ana groaned, pulling off the telephone cord like an umbilical cord from around her neck. "Tell me about *The New York Review of Books*. Has our ad paid off yet?"

"Mom, things are going great," she said, trying to sound enthusiastic. "I'm going out with a Jewish man. And he speaks six languages including Fortran. Can you believe it?"

"That's great. When are you two getting married?"

"Didn't you *hear* me?" She sat up, half-naked. "All I said was, I'm going out with someone!"

"Oh, well, that. Are you working, at least?"

"Um, yes. I had a job on a Hollywood project just this week—as an assistant camerawoman."

"You should be directing," said Madelyn and hung up. Her parents were never satisfied with her, she thought angrily, and they never thought about the time difference when they called from New York.

She hoped it wasn't too early: if it was 10 in New York, it was 7 AM in L.A. She threw on her see-through peasant blouse and her skimpy rayon skirt and drove over to Mort's, hungry for his affirmation after the debacle of her film job. But Mort was intent on his early morning routine of soft-boiled eggs and a trip to the Y. He was reluctant to use his guest pass, but she managed to convince him: She happened to have a bathing suit in her shoulder bag. She put it on in front of him, parading back and forth. When they got to the Y, it was agonizing to be separated from him—men to the left, women to the right—even just for a shower. She wanted to make love to him under the water, but the swimming pool had rules.

He wasn't exactly thrilled when she insisted on following him back upstairs to his apartment.

                    MORT
             (shooing her off)
        I'm a screenwriter, after all,
        with several options brewing.
        I need time alone to write.

He escorts Ana to the door, and OPENS it for her.

                  MORT (CONT'D)
        Oh, and by the way, I'm going to
        Brooklyn next week to spend Yom
        Kippur with my parents.

He CLOSES the door.

She didn't get the picture. She assumed that she'd be going with him to meet the Levins. What should she do with herself in the meantime? Ana went home and threw the I Ching. The divination said, "Do not permit thoughts to go beyond situation. Work on what has been spoiled." But she ignored it.

To celebrate their fifth month of being together, she made piroshkis, mixing the egg and ground beef together with some yogurt for the filling. Perhaps these meat-filled pastries would reach him though her offer to edit his screenplay hadn't. She wanted to impress him with her martyrdom like Tolstoy's wife, co-writing sections of his magnum opus at night after nursing eight children by day. She cut the delicate crusts with heart-shaped cookie cutters, then placed them carefully on baking sheets and painted them with a thick glaze of milk and sugar. While they were in the oven, she received the following e-mail:

To:	anagram(Ana Fried)
From:	mort.l (Mort Levin)
Subject:	Final

I don't love you. Perhaps I'm incapable.

Someone must have broken his heart along the way, poor thing! She showed up at his apartment with the hot piroshkis, determined to mend him. She should have brought along some super-glue.

"What did I do to deserve this?" he said.

"I thought of you all day," she said forlornly, and tried to embrace him. But he had a sponge in one hand and a can of Ajax in the other. She took the sponge and cleanser and was so determined to win him over that she washed out his bathtub of yellow pus left over from previous relationships.

Meanwhile Mort sat at his computer and tried to finish the first act of his screenplay. He had a vague feeling that Ana was trying to poison him and left the piroshkis half-uneaten. He was still busily writing by the time she had scrubbed all the scabs off of the shower curtain. She had hoped to take a bubble bath with Mort in the fresh, clean tub. Instead, she tiptoed out. She wanted to leave him some space for his writing.

She went home again and threw the I Ching. It said, "Molt." But she ignored it. She sat by the phone, confident that some other film company would call her with another job. Maybe it would ring when Mort finished Act One.

A month later, on impulse, she opened her computer and sent him the following e-mail:

From: anagram(Ana Fried)
To: mort.I (Mort Levin)

    Using a mouse on a digital Ouija board, I divine tides rising in your balls. Let's levitate up waterfalls!

From: mort.I (Mort Levin)
To: anagram(Ana Fried)

    If you can come up with some rhymes about the itch in my crotch or the corn on my right foot, I'll know you're really good.

But all she could think of to rhyme with *corn* and *itch* was *porn* and *kitsch*. All the I Ching had to say about Mort was "Standstill." She didn't know which was deteriorating faster: her personal life or her aesthetics.

He felt cornered the moment he opened the door. She put her arms around him, feeling his pectorals under his terrycloth bathrobe.

"Would you like to have kids with me?" she asked coyly.

"Kids make too much noise," he said, "when you're writing."

"But you haven't complained at the noise we make when we're making love," she said, pulling off his bathrobe.

"Yeah, but we never write in the middle of intercourse." He stopped talking and pulled her over to the bed.

"What if we were writing partners?" she asked. She could imagine the dialogue with pregnant pauses, then the pregnancy.

"Is this what you've been leading up to all this time?" He paused, then laughed incredulously. "You? A writing partner?"

Yet she'd done the research already: Gordon & Kanin, Parker & Campbell, Comden & Green, Ravetch & Frank...Why not Levin & Fried?

She thought to herself, "Just give him time." He threw her on the floor next to a pile of old *L.A. Weekly*'s. She fell in slow motion like a feather.

```
                                        CUT TO:
     He begins to fuck her, slamming her out
     of rage.
```

It probably wasn't personal. It was probably just rage for his unsold screenplays. She felt so sorry for him and his lack of fame—his only movie having gone straight to cable. He seemed to have more potential than any other writer who hadn't made it yet. Maybe they could do a sequel to "The Wonders of Adam," only better. Maybe they could rewrite "Geisha Girl Palace" together: He could give it some kind of structure. She could email him the pages that she hadn't shredded if he weren't too jealous of her talent. He could reassure her that he pictured her as one of those few women making a regular living as members of the Writers Guild. He was a card-carrying member, of course. But she hadn't sat down to write since her father bought her the computer. It seemed to have cooties.

"And what's your excuse for not moving forward with your life?" she asked Mort.

"I have a succubus for a girlfriend," he joked.

She offered to give him ideas for novels and screenplays: Mort merely scoffed at her mix-up of low self-esteem with self-effacement before God. He sat down at his computer desk and tuned her out.

Surely Mort didn't celebrate Channukah, because he hadn't gotten her a present. Any minute now, it would be Christmas. What was Mort going to give her?

"Merry Christmas, Tammi!" Somehow she had located her college friend's forwarding number in Toronto.

"Ana! What a surprise!"

"Brrr! What are you doing up in Canada?"

"Well, my second husband had an architecture firm up here. I figured, why should the kids and I have to move, just because I gave him up?"

Ana managed to laugh. "Gee, Tammi, that's great. I mean, my biological clock is ticking, and I... You were smart to have kids when you did." Then she started sobbing, telling her about Karl, then Mort, and her lack of employment.

"Why don't you just eradicate men from your life and get pregnant from a sperm bank?" asked Tammi.

"But I can't," she wailed. "It's not the genius sperm I want. I want Mort! I love him!"

"Well, I can't help you with that," said Tammi. "But as for the jobs, don't worry. You know how unpredictable Hollywood can be. They'll come to you—just sit close to the phone." But she couldn't sit. She paced around her little room for another month, obsessed with Mort, who still didn't call. He didn't need to marry her for a Green Card like Karl—he didn't want to marry her at all. She was ready to forgive him if she could only change his mind.

The I Ching said, "Control anger, restrain instincts." She tried. He was coming down with a cold. She restrained herself from writing and spent the afternoon making him chicken matzoh ball soup.

"Don't kizz me, I'm contagious," he said in his nasal voice, letting her into the apartment in his underwear and bathrobe.

"Poor baby!" she said.

She kissed his large, pulsating cock instead of his mouth. While she sucked it, he announced that he had found a writing partner: a staff writer on a prime-time sit-com.

The arrogant, small-minded, low-brow bastard! She stood up in disgust. He was talking about going to Hawaii with his writing partner for a weekend writers' conference. "The tropical air ought to help me recover by Monday," he said.

"OK, OK," she said. She took a deep breath. "I understand that you don't want to be screenwriting partners. What if we just get married? Next week?" Mort had a coughing fit and went searching for a box of Kleenex.

He bought her a postcard in Hawaii, writing "California Sucks" on the back. But he had developed indigestion from some sushi, and didn't make it to the post office until the following week.

Due to the severity of the situation, Ana decided she had better inform his parents:

> *Dear Dr. and Mrs. Levin,*
> *Since your son Morton doesn't have the foggiest notion of commitment* (nor did they have the foggiest notion who she was), *I'm finally moving on. I stayed with him longer than I might have, because I have loved him for almost a year.*
> *I deeply regret not having been your daughter-in-law. From his glowing descriptions, you would have made wonderful grandparents for our children.*
> *Regretfully,*
> *Ana Fried*

Then she sent the following message to the chat room where she'd first met Mort:

To: women
From: anagram
Subject: Recommendation

TO WHOM IT MAY CONCERN:

I have known the above-mentioned applicant for one year and have been faithful to him through his various arrivals and departures. Whereas Mort L. sometimes prefers to appear to be an ordinary man, with or without his clothing he has an extraordinary physique. His electric skin will make you ache with longing. He is fiery in his lovemaking, with or without foreplay. He also has an uncanny ability to make miscellaneous technical information and hard facts (such as his reluctance to be married) intimate and personable by his deep vocal inflections.

Mort L. will make an excellent husband by reason of his intelligent refusal to become a nebbish, and because he does not hit women. He comes ready to disguise as a "Nice Jewish Boy" when writing to meddlesome parents.

My only hesitation in recommending him is my jealousy to think of losing him to another woman, a characteristic I probably share with his mother.

I strongly recommend Mr. L., if you are what he says he wants more than I am.

Yours truly,
A Recent Woman in His Life

She should have gotten out of the chat room, but she waited like a fool for a message.

To: anagram
From: mort.l
Subject: Your letters

Your writing has finally achieved a level of mediocrity worthy of an Academy Award.

She took a hard look at the reality of her writing, and it glared back at her. Most of her prose was written on Prozac. Her e-mails had failed to conquer Mort's heart. God didn't dictate whatever she wrote, and Emily Dickinson she wasn't. After six more months of therapy, she wrote:

To: *mort.l*
From: *anagram*
Subject: *Happy Father's Day*

You could have changed 2,000 diapers, gone into debt to pay my maternity bills, and lost your concentration as a writer. But no, you probably had a vasectomy.

Mort's computer was infected with a virus: he never received it. Meanwhile, he had sent her an e-mail to let her know he was going to marry his agent Naomi. It caused her computer to break down.

PART FOUR

The Cyborg Goddess

I would rather be a cyborg than a goddess.
— Donna Haraway, "A Cyborg Manifesto"

CHAPTER SEVENTEEN

Anatomy of a Loser

I'd have to be some kind of natural born fool
To want to pass that way again.
— James Taylor

Tossing from another Tylenol, Ana groaned in her sleep. Her slender arm reached over the side of the canopied bed for the laptop computer on the shag rug. She had let it slip off the bed again. Her father would be mad at her: She'd promised to return his brand new PC Convertible in good condition. Not that she'd returned to New York in good condition herself. She was taking a bit of a break at her parents' after abandoning the old Apple in California.

The important thing, she felt, was to get back some of the hopeful, ambitious attitude which her old bedroom expressed, with its cheerful wallpaper in the colors of van Gogh's sunflowers. On the wall were a half-dozen high school drawings that her mother had framed, announcing her artistic worth, and in the corner was the Swiss teddy bear that she and Vickie used to throw at each other. She had seemed so sure of herself in her girlhood, a little white mutt at her feet, yapping in adoration before it got run over. If only she could extricate herself from her delusions…

She opened the word processing program and pulled up her newest proposal, impatient to make progress.

The Cyborg Goddess

Applicant: Ana Fried

Project Description:
This visual arts project uses the latest in media technology—
video (Betacam and 3/4"); film (16 and 35mm and Super 8);
and CD-ROM, etc.—to portray fascinating, beautiful, erotic and
terrifying aspects of the Goddess. The Cyborg Goddess will
explore the history and survival of Goddess-based cultures from
around the world.

Objective:
To contribute to a new world mythology, that honors the feminine
principle.

Honoring the female principle is something that Ana knew she needed in order to heal. She set about doing so in a high-pitched fervor, making up for lost time. After about a week of research, she discovered such a rich heritage of sculptured figures and painted images. But which goddesses to choose, and how to take a postmodern approach? The Mesopotamian goddesses looked like she could have baked them herself in second grade. Peter Paul Rubens' struck her as excessively cartoonish, while others stared up at Heaven from library books as if at squares of flypaper on the ceiling. Then there was the Ariadne painted by Le Sueur in colors redolent of a Lord & Taylor's spring sale.

Like a discriminating shopper, Ana decided to pick out goddesses for the qualities they represented, not just the way they looked: the powerful wisdom of Athena, the sexuality of Inanna, the nurturing of Gaia, and the intoxicating freedom of Diana. It shouldn't be hard to assemble the research. After all, it hadn't taken much soul-searching to settle on art as the preferred method of transcendence over her failure at love. Art was in the Frieds' blood. She just didn't want to be reduced to the level of her mother's watercolors.

After checking herself in the hallway mirror, adjusting her pantyhose and form-fitting sweater, she grabbed the train into Manhattan to look up one of her old roommates, Jeff Katz. He had become superbly well-connected in the world of grants. Surely she could enlist him to help with funding for *The Cyborg Goddess*. She strode across Grand Central Station and through the revolving doors of the Yale Club, carrying her knapsack full of paperwork.

They met under a cloud of cigar smoke at a long mahogany bar festooned with blue and white cocktail napkins and little plates of peanuts encircling ceramic pots of port wine cheese. Jeff had grown paunchier since her thirtieth birthday party, when he'd promised her a show in Soho. He had started wearing a yarmulke over his short black hair.

"Hi, Ana. So you finally have another project off the ground, I hear."

"It's getting off the ground," she corrected him, "and I just know you're going to help me."

"Well, I..." *He never takes me seriously.*

"We paid our dues on Avenue C, fifteen years ago," she said, in an attempt to stare him down. "We've moved beyond that, right?"

"Well, if you want to put it that way," he said laconically. He proceeded to sprinkle crumbs of cheese and crackers on his suit of houndstooth check while she rattled off a list of the top ten goddesses of the women's spirituality movement.

"Surely you've read about the Greek goddess, Gaia," she said, a bit aggressively to cover her innate defensiveness. "She's practically synonymous with Planet Earth. Then there's Isis, who preceded all the Greek goddesses. And the Indian goddesses, of course, which I actually just started researching: Lakshmi, Kali, Sarasvati—the Goddess of Wisdom. I'm sure you've heard of some of these," she added facetiously.

"Goddesses? I mean, for crying out loud!" said Jeff, spreading more cheese spread on a cracker. "You realize, of course, the very name of G-d cannot be pronounced—it's beyond human grasp, and you want to make a movie of it and feminize it, no less."

"But, Jeff. Really, I'm sick to death of Judeo-Christianity having enslaved the whole of Western Civilization."

"So that's why you're violating the Third and Fourth Commandments?"

"Namely?" She took a sip of port. "My secularism embarrasses me, under the circumstances."

"The Second Commandment says, 'You shall have no other gods beside Me. You shall not make for yourself a sculptured image.'"

"But Jeff," she interrupted. "Film is merely two-dimensional. How can that count?"

"Well, the Second Commandment is dealing with the misuse of images. I—I mean, I challenge you, Ana, to do the research carefully."

She took a cracker. "I graduated cum laude. I think I'm capable of doing the research, even without graduate school."

"It's a heart thing, Ana. It's not a matter solely of the intellect."

"Listen, Jeff, I've had enough broken hearts to know about heart things." She wasn't getting anywhere. With all the millionaires in the Yale Club, couldn't one of them have overheard their conversation by now and written her a check? "Are you going to help my goddam project or what?" she demanded.

"You realize, of course, that the Third Commandment prohibits man from using God's name wrongly or in vain," he replied smugly.

"I'm not using God's name. I'm focusing on the Goddess!" she said blindly. "You know, like Demeter, Durga, Lilith...?"

"But even the Hindu goddesses you mentioned before. They all have male counterparts. You're—you're decontextualizing them, that's what you're doing. It's wrong!"

"You mean like Shiva and Vishnu and... Zeus? That sort of thing?"

"Exactly."

"You mean the gods who specialized in appropriating the powers of female deities?"

"Rabeynu shel oylem, what oversimplification. You're dismissing the phallocentric aspects of all these different cultures." He sounded personally offended.

"Look, Jeff. I'm not rejecting phalluses per se. Just phallocentric religion. But if I address these Gods directly, then I'm blaspheming. Is that what you're telling me?"

"No, I just think your project sounds like a whim." He still sounded hurt. *He's doling out sexist put-downs in defense*, she thought. But she had to engage him.

"I'm sorry, Jeff, I really am. The Third Commandment never even entered my head. I never thought of a God leaning over me and all these books I was reading, saying 'You shall have no other gods besides Me.'"

"Well, let me be broad-minded about your proposal, for a change. I do think it's a start in terms of using your creativity to reach some kind of spiritual awareness, however half-baked it is in terms of Judaic principles. But I mean, Lilith? Come on. You used to be the Lilith of Avenue C."

"Oh come on, yourself. You male scholars have been denigrating Lilith as an orgiastic goddess of doom ever since she rejected Adam."

He blinked and took a sip of port.

Rather than continuing to argue, she contorted her mouth into a softly benign smile, hiding her desperation to make something worthy enough to redeem herself from the labels of failure and stupidity.

"Let's focus on the creativity, shall we?" said Ana, appealing to his sense of professionalism. She smoothed out her skirt and pulled the various elements for grant applications out of her knapsack: flow charts, index cards and several photographs. They worked on the layout for the proposal till the bar closed.

By then she had the basic structure down—synopsis, treatment, budget, bio—and rushed off to catch the last train to her parents', both of whom were by that time asleep, and crawled back into the womb of her canopied bed, hoping to give birth to her concept first thing in the morning.

She couldn't sleep. Maybe it was the remnant of a joint that she'd found in her sock drawer while getting ready for bed. She'd only lit up in hopes of calming down from the over-excitement of working on her project. But the specter of Jeff's taunting face gleamed down at her like Kali's male counterpart: the Hindu god Bhairava with his necklace of skulls. Each skull produced a migraine from another lifetime, clattering against the next. After a second toke, the circle of skulls was leering at her in unison, like the finger holes in a telephone dial that spins and spins but nobody answers.

Then Ana leered back. Her resolve grew stronger, and she reached over to turn on the bedside light, then the laptop. She had the educational background and the talent, certainly. More than that, she had the drive to challenge the iconographic status quo of God from an unseeable phallic presence with her Goddess project.

She had broadened her approach, amassing hundreds of photographs of statues and paintings of hundreds of goddesses from various parts of the globe as if she were one of her father's paralegals, helping him state another case. Everything was neatly alphabetized in an accordion file: Amaterasu, Brigit, Coatlicue, Diana, Ereshkigal, Freya, Gaia, Hera, Isis... all the way through Xi Wang Mu, the Goddess of the Taoists' Tree of Life, and Yemonja and Zarya—water goddesses of the Nigerians and the Slavs. And now all she had to do was slap them together by the deadline.

She hit "typeover" and got to work with wakeful determination, her body hanging over the bed, her fingers a magical whir. One copy was going to the New York Council on the Arts, and another would go to the International Art Film Association for some more seed money for another couple of grant proposals. With a look of triumph, she turned to the printer, hit one more button, and waited expectantly. Nothing happened. She frantically dialed Jeff Katz's number for help.

"Hello, Jeffrey? It's me again."

A sleepy voice answered on the eighth ring. "It's 4 AM, for fuck's sake," muttered Jeff.

"It is?" asked Ana. "I finished the project description. I finished the budget. I've only got one question."

"I'm not a night owl anymore," said Jeff.

"You promised you'd help," she pleaded.

"If you want help, call Victor Hernandez at the New York Council on the Arts. Use my name."

"Oh, OK," she faltered. "I'll do that first thing tomorrow morning. But I can't get the proposal to print out!"

"Oy Gut! Whatever happened to tech support? Hit F3," said Jeff, and hung up.

Ana hit F3. The "Help" menu appeared on the screen. She hit a few more buttons, and then, content at the quiet whirring of the printer, dropped back on the bed, exhausted. She was so tired of her many lives—not only of the lives of betrayal and abandonment through which she had suffered in countless countries across countless centuries. She was exhausted with the horror of the false half-lives which she had failed to shed in her lifetime as Ana Fried.

Once asleep, Ana morphed into the animated figure of a Vietnamese girl, blanketed by the shadows of jungle palms outside the window of her bamboo cottage. Her slender, teenage body tossed back and forth in restless sleep. Swaying in the breeze, the palms opened and closed, opened and closed like postmodern umbrellas, re-emerging into the thousandfold vision of a bee. With thunder-like crescendo, the bee was multiplying into a dark swarm. Suddenly the room exploded, throwing the pieces of the girl into the sky as thousands of ommatidia spewed countless goddesses in every direction. In the fierce wind, the fragments of the room disappeared, along with the layers of reality.

CHAPTER EIGHTEEN

National Image

A t the Bronx Botanical Gardens, a short train ride from Scarsdale, Ana opened up her notebook. The script for *The Cyborg Goddess* was almost completely revised, and she felt that she could take her time with it. Lying in the grass in the hot sun, trying to write while propped up on her elbow, made her feel faint. The lotus pond would calm her nerves and take her mind off menstrual cramps. She could vaguely remember it from when she was a little girl. Her grandmother had helped her feed the pigeons from this bench. A few of them were cooing around her feet, waiting for crumbs of stale bread. There must be some ritual involving stale bread that can honor one's ancestors to bless one's writing, she thought.

From her new perch she could observe the entire pond, with its tiny currents and big winds challenging the surface. What would a geisha writing in eleventh century Japan with a long, wet brush write about it? She poised herself for the perfect calligraphy stroke, gazing out at a perfect lotus blossom. The lotus was teaching her the purpose of each scene: to fully blossom. To achieve that perfection, great green leaves would open onto the surface of her notebook, each a distinct circle, supported only by the grammatical structure below the surface of the water to the root of emotion swollen beneath the mud. And there they were, overlapping in their phrases and various meanings—a different Goddess on the surface of each leaf! For the first time in her life, she was getting some screenwriting right.

The fire energy gave her the impetus to write. At night, the full moon would magnetize her unconscious and bring it to the page's white surface, especially now that Mort was no longer bothering her under the cool, white sheets, interrupting her vision. She could feel the waxing and the waning of her unconscious through the spectrum of earth, water, wind and fire energies, between the rising and the setting of the sun. The lotus demanded that she seize the time to write, leading her the way a conductor teaches the orchestra all of its parts, wafting its pistils like multiple batons.

I am Al-Lat, Goddess of all Creation, she wrote, disregarding screenplay format. The important thing was to tap into something universal.

I am the Goddess of Love, Art, and Healing Relations.

I am Aphrodite, I am Venus, I am Changing Woman, wrote Ana, her face upturned for further inspiration from the dull, gray skies.

I am Diana, the many-breasted Goddess.

I am Lakshmi, whose form is bliss,
whose blood made Indra King of the Gods.

I am the androgynous Mawu-Lisa; Afrekete.

I am the Black Madonna, Mother of the Son of God.

I am Isis, Mother of Horus;

I am Demeter, Mother of the Earth.

I am Kali Ma—the Creator, Preserver and the Black Destroyer.

Ana perched on the park bench in a feverish state which raindrops could barely mitigate. She called on the heavens to find her a company that could reincarnate goddesses into celluloid. She would have to rely on a company of mortals. In her pockets was a scrap of paper given to her by someone in the International Filmmakers' Alliance, who knew someone who knew someone else, on which they'd scrawled "National Image" and someone's name.

National Image was a mid-sized special effects company. The conference room doubled as a small screening room, and was badly in need of refurbishing. Len Mossbarger, the 63 year old Chairman of the Board, as well as his two backers and three investors, were waiting around the faux-oak table. Len's red plaid vest and pipe harkened back to his last Harvard reunion. He had just retired as vice president of a large accounting firm in St. Louis in favor of helping out his son-in-law in New York. His backers, Dick McIver and Sheldon Weingarten, appreciated Len's practical knowledge of books and ledgers.

Moses "MoMo" Baron, a recent black graduate of Pratt Art Institute, was a practical joker, dead serious about getting ahead and decked in a three-piece suit for the occasion. Josh, a white, cynical, 32 year old computer freak, was the right-hand man of the place. Josh leaned in the doorway in his unwashed blue jeans, his long hair in a pony-tail, above it all. The only man not present was Robert Poindexter, president of the company.

Sure enough, Robert arrived forty-five minutes late, rushing right past Josh into the room. With his tall frame, aristocratic nose, ruddy pink cheeks and carefully clipped brown hair, he looked like one of society's guardians. He opened the briefcase that he'd been carrying and pulled off his Ray-Bans, revealing large, blue eyes that blinked momentarily in the bright white light of the projector. He cast a brief smile around the table, then signaled for Len to put down his pipe and begin the presentation.

"Well, gentlemen," Len began, "considering that last year's deficit was only $46,000..."

"Something like that," agreed Sheldon. Josh sidled over to the computer and punched up a flow chart, while Len handed Robert the annual report, which he should have read the night before. The others were already examining their copies.

"Hey, nice cover," said Robert.

"Thanks," said MoMo.

Robert pulled down the screen with panache. He was a big man in stature, looming over the others seated around the table. "Sorry I'm late, folks."

There was a timid knock on the door as Josh whispered, "Talk Paintbox, you twerp."

Robert pointed to the light switch. "MoMo, can you get the..." MoMo turned out the light as Josh started up a demo film of tawdry yet dazzling special effects in abstract shapes and retro day-glo colors. No sooner had the film begun, when the door swung open, revealing Ana Fried.

Rain-soaked and bedraggled, she was still beautiful. There had been no secretary to keep her from walking right in. But flaunting her beauty wasn't her priority. It was the beauty of the Goddess she was seeking to reveal.

She pulled a little scrap of paper out of her raincoat pocket and looked about the room from man to man, the film continuing to project its abstract shapes and colors over her wet, tan raincoat until her eyes reached Robert's. She tried to ignore the instant sexual attraction. He was intently staring at her with a lopsided, goofy grin. MoMo turned off the projector.

"Uh, I guess one of you must be, uh, Robert Poindexter," she said a little nervously, her confidence wavering the more she took in this tall, middle-aged man presiding at the head of the table, exuding Old School charm. "Not of *the* Poindexters, I presume. Not that I know them either," she said, masking her flustered performance with a little laugh, "I mean, not personally."

Len was backing into the room with a plastic tray full of styrofoam cups of instant coffee. Narrowly escaping from spilling it as he bumped into her, he barked, "How did this woman get in here?" Ana hastily hung her dripping wet portfolio on the door while he brushed the rain off his shirtsleeves and faced his son-in-law. Robert leaned back in his leather chair at the end of the table, laughing a full-bellied laugh.

Len buzzed security. "I'm really sorry to bother you like this," said Ana, really sticking her foot in her mouth, "but it's a total emergency. I'm Ana Fried, and I'm applying for a New York State Council on the Arts grant—the Artist-in-Residency Program? And I'm supposed to deliver a demo of the film I've been researching for the last two months of my life to the International Art Film Association in around ten days, for, you know, seed money to prepare a National Endowment of the Arts grant application, and maybe a Rockefeller? Everybody says you're the only company that can do my special effects. I've done hundreds of drawings by hand, and I've already written the script," she continued, faltering slightly as she glanced once again at Robert. "Victor Hernandez gave me your name. Victor Hernandez of the New York Council of the Arts?" The gentlemen in the room looked at her with blank expressions. "He said you're the only people in New York who could..."

"Are you looking for an in-kind donation, or can you pay?" asked Mr. Weingarten.

"No, but I..." stammered Ana as the potential investors looked at each other.

The security guard had arrived, limping into the room as fast as he could on a bad knee.

"Monty, get this young lady out of here and dry her off," commanded Robert. "I want this door to stay closed for fifteen more minutes if you have to get a locksmith in here to do it."

"Sure thing, Mr. Poindexter," said the old man.

Ana took this to mean that she could come back in fifteen minutes. "Oh, thank you, thank you, sir!" she said, trying not to make eye contact with anything other than the computer monitor.

She picked up her portfolio and followed the security guard down the hall. But she didn't go down in the elevator. Instead, she got him to unlock the ladies' room, where she emerged from the cocoon of her wet raincoat into a well-fitting dress of dry, cream-colored linen. Good thing she had lost some weight under her mother's supervision. Her hair was almost dry, too. She took some silver bracelets and earrings out of her bag and put them on while looking in the mirror, jangling the bracelets for fun. With a touch of Chanel's newest shade of red, she seemed almost conventionally glamorous. She wiped off her portfolio with a couple of paper towels, and carefully unzipped it. She had been holding it upside down, and the photographs and drawings tumbled out: dozens of images needed sorting—from Freya to Ishtar, and Kuan Yin to Tara, as well as Isadora Duncan on the Acropolis, dancing the part of Athena.

Meanwhile, Robert was leading the men down the long hallway, giving his potential investors a complete tour of his company, optical printers clanking away over the sound of their footsteps. "We'll guarantee you the latest in business graphics, solid modeling, paint and animation…"

Ana was watching from the shadow of the ladies' room. Standing tall and proud beside the elevator doors, Mr. Poindexter apparently had made a deal. The rest of the men left in the elevator, and Robert turned to the glass door, reaching for the keys in his pocket. She slipped down the hall, carrying only the best of her drawings, lingered by the elevator, and waited.

"Victor sent you?" Robert asked, appraising her with a jangle of his keys. "What's the old buzzard up to?" She shrugged her shoulders, buying time. Robert was caught off guard by her beauty, now that she had dried off.

He touched the drawings, admiring one or two in passing. He seemed sincere enough—almost sensitive, though tired. "Let me look at those sometime later in the week," he said. "I'm around fifteen hours behind on some kung fu films for Hong Kong and then I've got to drop Dad at the airport on the way to air freight."

"You don't have to tell me all this," said Ana. He finished locking up and headed towards the elevator. Ana followed.

"Yeah, well look, I'm under a lot of pressure. What's your project?'

"*The Cyborg Goddess*," said Ana.

"The what?"

"It's a triple goddess that morphs. Creator, to Preserver, to Destroyer. Far-out for computer-generated art, huh?"

Robert took one of her pictures and looked at it with his clear blue eyes, then handed it back and hit the elevator button.

"I guess I kind of get carried away, but if we just change the way people perceive reality, the way we see ourselves—I mean, the world can be totally transformed!"

Robert suddenly wanted to impress her, too. "I suppose Hernandez already told you I work for several of the majors. Universal, Twentieth Century-Fox..."

"Look, I'm talking about making imagery that will change history, not some stereotyped, hackneyed..." she checked herself. The guy was gorgeous. Why fight?

"Only, you need access," said Robert, pulling out a cigarette as the elevator doors swung open.

"Can we talk again Friday?" Despite her meek tone of voice, he could tell that she was imploring him, even commanding him. He got on the elevator and lit his cigarette, somewhat taken aback that Ana was not going down with him. She had to retrieve her portfolio and her raincoat from the ladies' room.

"I'm working late tomorrow. Come tomorrow...around closing time," he called out as the elevator doors closed.

Ana strode exuberantly past the mid-town, rush hour crowds. Researching such powerful goddesses had buoyed her sense of confidence. With her talent and looks, it certainly should be easy enough to convince National Image to get involved in her demo in time for grant deadlines. But that was the least of it. The reflections of neon signs rippled across Madison Avenue, mixing with yellow cabs in the magical, post-rain impressionism of mid-July. To Ana, it was all a blur. Robert's technical know-how, his boyish grin, his perfect WASPiness, his marvelous, deep voice and large, commanding presence had almost swept her off her feet.

She looked over her reflection in the plate-glass window of a discount clothing store, holding her portfolio, on the verge of becoming a real artist. Despite her female id demanding that her future with Robert would be Yes! Yes! Yes!, she knew she should be asking questions about the role of Art in her life. She saw herself standing on her own two feet with fire in her eyes, compared to the faceless mannequins imprisoned behind the glass, aware perhaps for the first time in years of her erotic power. So she was in an incredibly good mood when she bumped into someone she knew on 47th Street. It was Diane Campbell, from Yale—but a profoundly more sophisticated version, in an exquisitely tailored navy blue outfit.

"Ana Fried, I know you!" exclaimed Diane.

"Diane?" said Ana, incredulously, as if Diane had just dropped from the sky. "I wrote you all those letters. I went looking for you after graduation, but... Well, you'd already left Memphis..."

"Girl, you're still crazy!" She laughed and gave Ana a brisk, thrilling hug that blasted through barriers of forgotten memories.

"You look great! I thought you were in Boston..."

"Bullshit!" said Diane. "Madison Avenue, all the way, ever since I left Prudential. How long you been back in town?"

"Well, I was travelling in Europe for awhile. I was on the West Coast..." she said vaguely.

Diane looked impressed. "Oh yeah? And just where are you residing now?"

"Well, my parents', but it's temporary," said Ana.

"If your family's still as dysfunctional as they were before you graduated from Yale, I'd say it's very temporary." She grabbed Ana's arm and pulled her towards a coffee shop. "Let's go grab a latte—or do you have a train to catch?"

"No, no. Not at all," said Ana. "And it's on me." The last thing she wanted Diane to know was that she was down to her last ten bucks.

"So, I'm celebrating my new company—Rainbow Graphics, Inc.," Diane was trying to tell her, but the busboy was clearing a booth next to theirs, clattering the dishes. All she wanted was for

Diane to commiserate with her about the white motherfuckers who had abused them long ago. But Diane went babbling on about investors and computer graphics. Ana smiled at the busboy as he rolled the cart away to pianissimo.

Diane sliced a slice of quiche in half. "So, you're still treating men like sexual objects?"

"Well, isn't that what they've been doing to women for the past five thousand years?" said Ana, defensively.

"Yes, but we need to rise above it," said Diane, looking at her friend with compassion. "We need to rise above it."

"I don't want to show Woman as an object," said Ana hopefully. "I mean, in my art, I want to show her as a universal symbol, a goddess of love, yet in control, someone with the erotic dignity of Isadora." She thought back to her dance performance in high school in tribute to the great Isadora Duncan, turning, skipping, maniacally leaping, dedicating her life to love and art.

"Look, Isadora Duncan might've been the greatest modern dancer that ever lived—to you," Diane said emphatically, "but she did not get a college degree in art history." Ana tried to interrupt, but Diane held her ground. "Number two. You cannot make any money outta Greek mythology. You gotta create a *new* mythology."

"That's just what I'm doing! See, the Greek goddesses *morph*," said Ana, with more confidence than she had ever felt as a student in the old days, when they were limited to studying the art history of the West. "I've just read Audre Lorde. Haven't you?" Diane had not. "They morph into these goddesses like Afrekete and Yemanje—or vice versa." She wanted to impress Diane with her insights into diversity. "I mean, African goddesses, Asian goddesses... it's much more universal now. Look at the Black Madonna." Diane smiled uncomfortably. "The Virgin Mary was originally black, Diane. There are hundreds of 'em, all over Europe, even."

"Oh, come on, Ana. On most of those Black Madonnas, the paint simply darkened as they aged."

"But here's the thing: She wasn't a Christian goddess at all, in the beginning. She was Isis, the African goddess in Egypt, and my project's going to show all of these changes. It all ties into the women's spirituality goddess vision—you know, Neumann and Gimbutas and the whole nine yards." She stirred her coffee, smiling at Diane, who was somewhat bemused by Ana's efforts to sail past her gaffes. "Plus, I found this guy who's going to handle all the technical mumbo jumbo, and he's got the cutest behind!"

Diane laughed and shook her head. "All those letters about Rich White Boy at Yale. Ana, what are you doing working with men? You're incapable of working with them!"

Ana was arranging sugar packets on the table top, making them look like a little white quilt against the pale green of the formica.

"I can handle it this time," said Ana.

"Sure thing. You wanna stay confident and assertive? Just don't go to bed with him. Your brain will turn to mush."

How could Diane possibly know that? She wasn't even in Memphis when Ana needed her the most.

"Look, don't expect me to be a role model," said Ana defensively. "Let's go to the movies, OK?"

"Not me. I'm on the graveyard shift again." Diane got up and put money on the table, calculating the tip in her head. Ana adjusted the skirt of her dress around her stockings and picked up her damp raincoat.

"I've got the equipment plus the deposit, but not the first and last," said Diane, who had diligently saved the majority of her earnings as Vice President of Public Relations, Prudential Insurance.

"I didn't know you were moving."

"Girl, where you been? My production company, Ana. I found a place, starting next week." Diane pulled out her Rainbow Graphics business cards and gave one to Ana.

Ana was impressed. "You mean you're in business?" They gave each other high fives. Whether or not they could personally connect, they were finally going to be friends again. Then Diane turned, jogging away with a smile. Ana watched Diane's inner self-confidence with envy as she ran down the block, stopping with perfect aplomb just in time to disappear on a bus headed uptown.

Ana wasn't really thinking of Diane on the train ride back to Scarsdale. In fact, she hadn't thought of her in years. As the train sped noisily along the tracks, she tried to lose herself in the pages of *Vogue*. Yet mixed in with the words of advice on make-up and fashion were Diane's words of advice from their brief time in college together—"Focus on your progress, not the revolution."—"Don't lose yourself in re-inventing love."—words that had gone unheeded.

She could scarcely remember a thing about her years at Yale. She pressed her cheek against the cold, steel rim of the window. The faces of a Thousand Male Leaders blurred together like fragments of faces on the train on the opposite tracks, clackety-clacking furiously past her, and then they were gone.

CHAPTER NINETEEN

Love Substitute

Unable to give love or affection, the male gives money.
It makes him feel motherly.

— Valerie Solanas

A hem of clouds fell away, revealing the naked surface of a planet. Radar-assisted and digitized, the imagery was almost as breathtaking as the Earth seen from Apollo 17. Suddenly the pale green skipped to a luminescent white. A rocket ship soared backwards along with backward swirling clouds, until all that remained in the viewfinder was a kind of green goddess dressing that was twice as pale as a prom dress.

The reflected glow of "Venus" left Robert Poindexter's face as he stood up abruptly with a haunted expression. He listened to the machines' whirring sounds mingle with approaching footsteps, running his fingers through his gray-brown cowlick. All-night shifts were getting to him. Robert was getting too old for them—arthritis in his knees sometimes acted up, leaning over the printers till dawn. He pulled and pressed various switches on one of the five optical printers, failing to turn around as MoMo and Josh walked in with a couple of bags and large coffees from McDonald's—part of the nightly routine. MoMo made room for the bags on the re-wind table. "Godzilla III's on the cabinet," added MoMo, putting the change on top of the printer.

"We're splitting," said Josh. "Twenty-two hours—I hope you're counting, man. Lining up the teeth with the skyscrapers was a mother."

Robert counted to himself as he wound the film a few frames forward, dedicated to the work at hand, oblivious.

MoMo and Josh were eager to get home. Their footsteps and voices reverberated back down the long hallway. Robert rubbed his eyes in exhaustion, then adjusted one of the dials with a coffee stirrer. He laid one of the cheeseburgers on top of the printer, pocketed the change and poured on ketchup. As the film rolled through the gate, he took off his wrinkled Brooks Brothers shirt and ambled down the hall.

Wadded up in a ball on the top shelf of the closet was his football jersey: brick red, with the number 17 on the back and a hole in one shoulder. Robert put it on and refurbished his cigarette. It was his favorite shirt—was, and always would be.

He heard a funny sound: the film must have slipped in the gate of the optical printer. He ran up the hallway, scoring a touchdown at the machine, and slammed himself into the darkroom. He had been smoking heavily: smoke hung ghostlike over the green darkroom light, over the "No Smoking" sign. He carefully peeled tape off the circumference of a large can of 35mm film, only to note a rim of light seeping through the edge of the door. Belatedly, he flipped on the red warning light, resealed the can, and opened the door.

One of the union camera operators stood in the vestibule, shaking with mirth at the film which continued to pour out of the optical printer, piling up on the floor.

"Hey, Jack! You trying to expose my film?"

"No, sir," said Jack. He stopped laughing and spit. "I'm thinking about exposing *you*, you son of a gun, with all them women."

Robert amiably put out his cigarette and flipped off the printer. He retreated into the darkroom, sealing it for any extraneous light this time with an overflow of sticky gaffer's tape—not exactly a professional procedure. Jack Stance was right to criticize his darkroom procedures: He should leave it to the union guys. Still, time was running out. He opened the 35mm magazine and reopened the can of film, then leaned over the rewinds, on the verge of hallucination.

Ana braced herself for another hellish summer in Scarsdale digging up the rhododendrons. Maybe she could get a part-time job. Would it really be so awful to type again, if it meant the deposit on an apartment? It wasn't that she was overqualified; it was the economy that was so rotten. But the regular world could shove it. Damned if she did, damned if she didn't. If only she had gone to graduate school.

Half the day was spent fighting with her mother over which bushes needed pruning. Naturally, her mother had won: the row of rhododendron bushes next to the Post Road needed to be trimmed—and don't forget the forsythias. Ana could hardly wait to get back into the city for her meeting with Robert. If she had any luck, his work would cinch her that grant; if she had any sense, she would stay in control of her feelings to make it happen. She'd cut down half of the damn bushes: now she tried to lose herself in a bubble bath, exacerbating the itch of poison ivy.

She could hear her father opening the front door. She jumped out of the bathtub in the master bathroom, peering out the window at his lithe, tennis player's body and briefcase silhouetted against a glamorous sunset. His red and white Corvette Convertible gleamed in the driveway. She hurried to dry herself off and get dressed. She could hear her parents laughing in the hallway. With any luck, her father would lend her his convertible to get down to the train station, along with another fifty dollars to get her through the rest of the month.

Robert only needed one more night to finish the last optical printing job for the week. He had braced himself with his umpteenth cup of coffee and an aspirin. He was just guzzling down a paper cup of water when Len Mossbarger handed him the phone.

"It's Suzanne," said Len, taking the pipe out of his mouth.

"Hello, sweetheart," Robert said placidly. "Yes, of course. Of course we're on speaking terms. Of course I'll pick up Conrad after pre-school." Another phone line lit up. He switched lines. "I'm sorry, but we're awfully busy at the moment. We really don't have any openings at the moment. Why don't you try the West Coast? Hello?" He switched back to the other phone. "Hello? Yes, terribly busy. You know that special due two days ago? Get Pop to send it down with a hard pillow tomorrow," he said sweetly. "Then why don't you come up to the office yourself, Suzanne? Hold on." Robert grabbed a spool of film as it came off the printer assembly. "The what?" he said, back on the phone. He grinned sheepishly at Len. "Can you believe it? I've been disconnected!"

He strode towards the darkroom with the 1000' magazine, not missing a beat. In walked Ana, eager to show Robert her story-board, all business in a gray three-piece suit. She had one week left before her New York State Council on the Arts grant deadline. Len gestured at the darkroom: its red warning lights were flashing on and off. "He's in there," said Len.

Ana walked up to the darkroom door and knocked firmly but politely.

"Just leave it over by the rewinds," called Robert, mistaking her knock for one of his employees'.

Ana was taken aback. "I can't do that!" she said to Len.

"I'll eat it later," added Robert. Then MoMo and Josh rounded the corner, whistling. Robert began to sing in three-part harmony, then broke it off. "I'm hungrier'n a pile of pirates. So what'd you bring me, mates?" he roared at them.

"The usual," said Josh. He was tired of goofing around. They deposited the food on the rewind bench and waited for Robert to open the darkroom door. Ana felt like opening the darkroom door even if it meant exposing all his film, in return for making her wait.

MoMo and Josh were eyeing her up and down and exchanging glances when Robert came out, squinting in the bright light.

"I've brought you something rather *un*usual, I think," said Ana, attempting wit to cover her bad mood and holding up her portfolio as a reminder of their meeting. Robert was intoxicated by his exhaustion. He waved at her with an awkward grimace. Len swept broken fragments of film and dust from around the optical printers, then walked slowly down the hall, turning off the lights in the conference room and the vestibule on his way out.

Robert turned to Josh and MoMo. "Whaddaya say to two all-nighters in a row, team, now that the old man has gone home?"

"You gotta be crazy," said MoMo. "It's been round the clock since Monday!"

"I think this calls for cocaine, wouldn't you say?"

"I wouldn't," said Josh.

"All right, off with their heads," shouted Robert, gesturing on a grand scale. "Walk the plank! Go!" Josh and MoMo waddled down the hall like seasick sailors, while Ana held on, hoping not to be dismissed. "Hand me that magazine," said Robert.

She hesitated for a moment. What kind of a magazine? She looked at the counter, then awkwardly handed him a heavy 1000' Mitchell magazine loaded with 35mm film. She had studied camerawork; she ought to be more dexterous. He reached over her for four more, carrying them all to the rewind table. He brushed the McDonald's fare aside.

Ana found this show of physical power both exasperating and childish. "Mr. Poindexter," she said.

Besieged by a fit of smoker's cough, Robert tore open one of the paper bags, took the lid off the cup of coffee, and gulped it. "Robert," he said, grabbing a Sharpie and starting to mark "X"'s on one frame of film on each of the magazines.

"You said this would be a good time to..."

"Later," said Robert, refusing to look up. He pulled an Exacto knife from a coffee can of assorted pens and pencils. Ana hastened to leave. "Just give me ten minutes," he said.

Ana was unsure. "Robert, I have to catch a train," she faltered.

Robert proceeded to scratch an "X" over the ink marks on each of the magazines. Then he swung around and loaded four of them on the four optical printers in the room, punctuating the phrases of his speech with assorted levers and gears. "Well, Ana, most of the optical work I do involves quite a bit of money. You're not independently wealthy, are you?

"Oh no. I'm your typical starving artist."

"I see," he said, not looking up. "Seems like everybody's got creative ideas these days. When it comes to technical expertise, they all want freebies."

"My project is pretty interesting, however." She stood her ground.

He sorted through a box of colored glass filters. Finally, he held up one yellow and one magenta, examining Ana through each of them in turn. "Did you say interesting? Or just pretty?" His smile was a Boy Scout badge of summers spent hoisting sails in Newport. "Just joking," he added as Ana blushed. "Just let me get this show on the road and I'm all yours. Lay out your storyboard here," he said, gesturing casually at the rewind table. He lifted the other McDonald's bag from the table and lay one of the cheese-burgers on top of the printer, completing the ketchup routine. Ana, meanwhile, had opened up her portfolio and carefully laid out ten drawings and photographs of the Parthenon, Isadora Duncan, and Ancient Greek goddesses. The female figures formed an animation sequence of dancing.

"I need a little optical work to rebuild the Parthenon." She was trying to sound humble.

"That's all?"

"That's the beginning. Your company does do that sort of thing, right?" Perhaps she had made a big mistake.

"I've been in this business quite a number of years, sweetheart," he said sarcastically. He left his food uneaten, deftly scanned a handful of drawings into the computer, and guided Ana over to sit in front of a monitor.

The female figures began to "dance" on screen. She tried to keep her smile demure, hiding her brewing excitement. With a little more work, Isadora Duncan would morph seamlessly into the Winged Venus and fly towards the camera.

Robert looked over her shoulder. "The trouble with these is you've only done half the work," he said.

She glanced up at him.

"No gods, just goddesses, huh?" he said, posing with a swagger.

"I'm not looking for a critique, I'm only looking for technical assistance," she said, peeved.

"It's OK, I like creative chicks...women," he said, correcting himself quickly. "You're all so adorably difficult." He cleared his throat. "Get the rest of 'em on diskette by tomorrow morning and we'll talk," adding braggadocio, "We don't like to work with paper around here."

"But I don't have a scanner."

He contemplated a French fry. "No harm in you doing it here tonight," he said, all charm, "...I guess." He popped the French fry into his mouth, strode to the optical printers and turned them into a bevy of mechanical noises, wiping his hands on his pants. Ana fingered her pearl necklace like a rosary. "Ever hear of traveling mattes? You have to mask off the background if you really want to get her moving in there," he said in a loud voice, over the clicks and grinds of the machines.

Len appeared in the hallway, his outline small and dark against the hallway lights. Robert glanced up, surprised that the old man hadn't already gone home. "You have to make silhouettes out of them," he said to Ana. "Len here'll give you the software. One matte's the male matte— that's your main image. The opposite's called the female matte."

"As in doormat?" Ana said wryly.

Robert laughed. "Effects Terminology 101. See, you put the 'Dick' matte into the 'Jane' matte, and voilà! Special effects!" But Ana didn't laugh at this. Neither did Len, who had been watching. "That's what all these optical printers do," said Robert, inanely. "See Jane run. Ha ha!" His laughter disintegrated into a fit of coughing, over the whirring and spewing of gears.

"When you going home, Rob?" asked Len, fitting his Welsh tweed hat over his white hair.

"This *is* home, Len. If you can call a submarine tank home," said Robert, gleefully.

"Go easy on the all-nighters, son. I'm locking up," said Len.

Ana remembered the software. "Um, excuse me..." she said. But Len proceeded towards the hall, walking past Ana as if she were invisible, turning the hall lights off at the end of the hall.

Robert stared at Ana's Botticelli-like beauty. "Venus on a half shell," he said softly. Intimidated by his technical prowess and bad manners, she felt vulnerable and alone.

Robert reached out and grabbed her. He wasn't about to waste any more time. "Wanna dance?" he asked. He was much taller than she was and wasn't about to be rejected. She tried pushing him away politely. "Hey, hey," he said affably. "No work without play." And he held her tighter.

"Not now, *please!*"

Robert had a one-track mind: he wanted to paw her breasts. He was like a football hero, towering over her in his red shirt that stank of his sweat, smiling as he won—all 250 lbs. of him. She was breathing hard now with fear mixed with excitement. He pushed her awkwardly against the rewind bench, pushing open her gray suit jacket and feeling her small, supple breasts, ripping open her blouse and breaking her pearl necklace almost in one fell swoop. Her pearls scattered helter-skelter on the checkerboard linoleum floor. Ana bent down to pick them up as well as some drawings which had spilled out of her portfolio. He merely looked at her ass, making her feel even more humiliated.

Ana stood up slowly, trying to regain some dignity. Plus she had learned a thing or two about the sociology of women artists back at school, hadn't she? "I really am an artist," she said slowly. "That's why I came here. Maybe I'll sue you instead, for sexual harassment."

"Sue me?" Robert snorted with laughter. "Sue *me*? I never *hired* you!"

Ana bottled up her anger in front of Robert, letting herself be swallowed by the darkness of the hall. The term "sexual harassment" had been on the radar for over a decade. She wasn't a lawyer's daughter for nothing: Sexual harassment had to be a legitimate claim, even if she was unfamiliar with the technicalities of the law. She rang for the elevator. All she had to do was ask her father: He would know. But her father would probably rather she drop dead than see her involved in a case like this. The elevator had arrived. She stared at its wide-open chasm.

Meanwhile, Robert paced the floor, at a loss, nearly tripping on some loose pearls. He grabbed a broom and began to sweep up the rest of them. Noticing Ana's portfolio, he picked up the drawings, which were scattered around the room. He brought them over to the bench and sat down, staring at one or two of them intently.

Ana came back into the room and slumped in the corner, glaring at Robert. He concentrated on her photographs and drawings out of embarrassment, running his fingers through his short, gray-brown hair. Neither of them was quite sure what to do with the other. He made up his mind to sidle over and give her a handful of pearls. Then he handed her the cold cheeseburger from the top of the printer. She mutely nibbled while he fussed with the equipment, then stopped.

"Anything else you want around here?" he asked, testing her.

"I don't want the pickles," she said, the cheeseburger sitting on her lap like a small icon while the tears welled up.

Jack had arrived for the graveyard shift and was checking his workplace ominously. But Robert was eyeing Jack's night shift "lunch". "What's in the paper bag, Jack?" he said.

"Well, it sure ain't no cat," Jack replied. Ana got up and threw her cheeseburger into the film bin, mistaking it for a garbage can. "Look, Robbie. Don't go giving any woman a man's job."

"What's for lunch? The special?"

"Pastrami," Jack said defiantly.

"Keep the pickles and give her the sandwich," said Robert. He opened his wallet, while Ana moved quickly toward the unlocked door.

"I really have to go," she said.

Robert got busy, neatly stacking the pages of her portfolio. "Wait a minute, here."

"Robert, let her go," said Jack.

"Well, I wouldn't want a lady to walk the streets at this hour," said Robert gallantly. "I mean, anything could happen." He followed Ana quickly down the dark hallway, unlocking the elevator for her, and following her into it.

As soon as the elevator doors opened on the ground floor, Ana ran out of the building. Robert followed her. It was two in the morning—except for the lingering smell of the street sweeper trucks, the streets were deserted.

"Look. Look. I'm sorry. I realize..." he struggled to keep up with her, but he was out of breath.

"Just leave me alone!" said Ana furiously. But he wouldn't let go. "You have to understand," he said. "The secretary quit a week and a half ago. I've been working 48 hours straight..." So what, thought Ana. So he's a workaholic? What right does that give him to go after me?

"I want to help you," he said.

"Fix my necklace," she said curtly, walking fiercely into Grand Central.

"No, really. I want to help you," he repeated.

"For some tits and ass?" Her voice was shrill: it reverberated through the station.

"All I did was tell you your shirt was missing a button. Maybe I touched it, to show you where it was missing." He really believed what he said.

"Give me a break," Ana said. "I'll find another company." The revolving doors were spinning: she quickly scanned the "Departures", then made a run for it. She had to make that last train to Scarsdale.

Robert stood on the platform as she jumped onto the train, admiring her talent for evasion. He grabbed her hand before she could turn the corner into the compartment.

"Come back next week and we'll do some scanning, OK?" he called out.

The train had started moving. "I mean it," he said. "Come back next week."

Len Mossbarger had just arrived with the usual Monday morning coffee, so he was surprised to encounter two cups of steaming coffee already perched precariously on the optical bench. Robert was busy showing Ana how to feed her drawings into their scanner.

"We don't have the hardware for computer animating this stuff...yet," Robert was telling her. "But we've got plenty of optical equipment you can use. It may not be state of the art exactly, but it'll save you a lot of money. Just takes a hell of a lot of time." His hand brushed gently against hers, as if by accident.

"I've got five and a half days left," she said, trying to remain calm. She was certain she could make her deadline for the New York State Council on the Arts, if she played her cards right.

Robert seemed a bit preoccupied. "How was Baltimore, Dad?"

"Rob, did you talk to your wife yet?" asked Len. Your *wife*? Ana couldn't believe that Robert was married.

"Warners sent us three shiploads of horror films," replied Robert, lighting up a cigarette.

Len just shook his head. "Always a deadline," he said. "What about your wife and the baby? Hire someone for the night shift for a change."

The night shift? So he spends his nights chasing women's tails, she thought. She stood up, squeaking her chair against the shiny linoleum floor. She looked soberly at Robert Poindexter and his father-in-law, slammed the door on them, and left her storyboard behind.

Robert smashed a cigarette into an ashtray, wanting to call it a day. He started to line up the 35mm frames for another optical, but his heart wasn't into it. He fell asleep on the subway to Canal Street, then stumbled bleary-eyed upstairs to the fifth-floor loft.

CHAPTER TWENTY

Pièce de résistance

" **J**ust tell me one thing. Are you still smoking marijuana?"
asked Madelyn. "Because if you are, I don't want you in
my house." Ana had been squiggling a picture of Robert in her
notebook until her mother walked into the kitchen. She blacked
it out with a raw squeak of charcoal and stood up, her face red,
drenched with sweat.

"Why don't you read my diary, Mama, and find out?" Ana had
been writing all night: *Oh Christ! How did it happen? Just the day
before, I was laughing. And tonight, alone, I opened up my heart and
it was full of pus.*

"Spare me the impudence," said her mother. "I want to eat my
breakfast in peace." Cups, bowls, spoons and cereal boxes were
lined up on the kitchen counter, military style. Madelyn poured a
half cup of Grape-Nuts and forged ahead to the table with cereal,
orange juice and a bottle of Xanax in hand. Ana had started to
leave. "Rake the lawn and clean the pool before lunch, do you hear
me? I'm going into the studio for an hour. The gardener's off this
week—make yourself useful."

Ana stretched out on a lawn chair in a bathing suit by the side
of the pool, trying to re-read the French poetry that had eluded
her in college. But *Une Saison en enfer* was challenging without a
dictionary. She got up and moved the lawn chair into the shade.
She didn't feel like swimming with her period, let alone tackling
Rimbaud. She was completely absorbed in a little scab on her leg

when her mother appeared on the patio, a drink in hand. Ana quickly wrapped a beach towel over herself.

"I want to hear all about what you've been doing in New York." She sounded very mellow.

"Fuck! Can't I just lie here for one hour without your bothering me? I think I'm getting a sore throat."

Her mother was oblivious, or perhaps she was getting deaf. "Did you clean the pool like I asked you to?" Ana groaned. "That's all right," said her mother. "You can do it later this afternoon."

Madelyn began to rake leaves although in the middle of summer, fallen leaves are scarce in Scarsdale. Nevertheless, a few brave souls shook themselves free, obligingly falling for Madelyn's rake. "I want this place to look perfect by the time your father comes home."

Ana dove into the pool, holding her breath under water for as long as she could. Her mother's behavior would someday cease to seem so powerful and calculating, intentional and cruel, but that would only happen after her mother's death. At the rate she was going, her mother would outlive her.

Ana spent the afternoon flipping the channel from soap operas to talk shows, convinced that her sore throat was going to kill her. Madelyn was occupied ironing sheets and shorts, occasionally checking the television screen or the stove.

"Mom, where's the Tylenol?"

"Forget the Tylenol," said Madelyn. "I'm making chicken soup. Now how do you like that?" It was probably voodoo chicken soup: its smell was turning Ana into a zombie.

"Where are the matzoh balls?"

Madelyn went back to ironing Marty's shorts with gusto. "Let me tell you what's wrong with you, Ana. You don't let yourself relax. Half the time you visit, you're sick. It's downright rude. If you weren't so stressed out all the time, you wouldn't get sick so often, now would you? Isn't that it? It's not AIDS, is it?"

"No." said Ana. "Leave me alone. I already told you. It isn't AIDS. I've been tested, OK?"

"Well, for God's sake," said Madelyn. "How should I know? All these men you run around with from one end of the country to the other."

"What do you know about it?" Ana retorted.

"That disgusting boy in Tennessee who looked like a sheep dog. Don't blame me—you sent us his photograph! All that hair! And you thought he was handsome? He certainly couldn't support you."

"I don't want to talk about it," said Ana.

"At least Timmy got married," said Madelyn. "You could have come back from—where was it? Malibu? Brentwood?—a few weeks early for his wedding. I just don't get it. You come home with nothing but A's on your report card, but you don't have any sense when it comes to men."

"How about you, Mom?"

"How about me, what?"

"Are you so perfect when it comes to men? I don't prostitute myself the way you do, to someone like Dad."

Madelyn sprayed another pair of shorts. "I don't know what you're talking about, Ana. You used to be such a charming little girl. But ever since you went to college, you've been despicable. It's hateful. It's meshugge. What got into you?"

Ana got up from the deep lap of the chair and began to pace with menstrual cramps. "I didn't need a Princess Cruise to get laid like you, Mom," she said hoarsely.

"Those were some of the happiest days in my life," Madelyn said. She grabbed the hot iron like a crucifix. "Don't you ever, ever breathe a word. I'll disown you, like that!"

Ana stared at the hot iron, sweat dripping down her face.

"Go set the table, *now!*" screamed her mother.

Madelyn Fried was better equipped to appreciate the Cinderella dream-come-true stage of her life by the time Marty pulled into the driveway in his new white convertible. She appeared at the top of the stairs fully made up in red lipstick and mascara, wearing a bright red dress that sashayed against her crimson, gold-fringed shawl as she descended the stairs.

"No more rain, thank God!" said Madelyn, striking a three-quarter profile on the landing. "What a gorgeous sunset!"

"Hi, honey," said Marty, taking out a bunch of flowers from behind his back. He followed up with a kiss, loosening his tie. But after a moment, she pulled back to examine the flowers.

"Why can't you bring me something different for a change?" she complained. "Didn't you get me tulips for Valentine's Day?"

"They match your clothes," said Ana placatingly.

"What clothes?" Madelyn retorted. She hadn't bought anything new in months.

"Honey, why don't you go in your studio for a few minutes and calm down?" His wife was trimming the tulip stems with a pair of scissors over the sink. "Paint some flowers while you're at it, any color you like," he added, under his breath.

"And ruin dinner?"

"It's OK, so we'll eat microwave," said Marty.

Madelyn threw the crimson shawl over her shoulder. The color of the shawl was resonating with the red tulips, making Ana dizzy with their menstrual madness as Madelyn slammed the screen door shut.

Ana went into the kitchen and laid the last forks and spoons on the table while her father came in to pour himself a drink. She might as well have been invisible to him. She slouched at the table in her miniskirt and fanned herself with a Japanese fan. Finally, her father joined her at the table, unfolding his newspaper as he sat down.

"Hi, honey," he said to Madelyn over the "Finance" section, some of it circled with a ballpoint pen. Ana averted her eyes, staring out the window at the fading sunset.

Her mother had come back inside and was washing her hands of turpentine-and-fuschia at the kitchen sink. "She's been lying around all day," said Madelyn over the running water. "I can't stand it."

"You never could stand me. You can't tell the truth about it, can you, Mom?"

"Listen to this! I was planning something special for dinner. Instead I've had to deal with *this* all day," she complained.

"It's OK, dear. I'll take you out for dinner."

"We're eating microwave. That's what you said on the phone, isn't it?"

"OK, OK. Whatever you want," said her husband.

Madelyn stood behind the freezer door, throwing frozen bricks of food onto the counter in an annoying series of thuds. The chicken soup was going into the freezer. She turned to Marty. "And how was *your* day?" she said, scowling at Ana to keep quiet.

"Well, one ex-wife kept me downtown for over an hour and a half, haggling over the country club memberships and a couple of summer cottages that weren't in the prenup."

"Oh, and what does *she* look like?" Madelyn demanded.

"Honey, don't start this."

"I wish *we* had a cottage like the Gottliebs' place on Nantucket," whined Madelyn. "I'd settle for something on Fire Island—just something we could get away to for a change!"

"Well, there are so many zeroes involved, maybe we can get away by Labor Day weekend," said Marty, thoughtfully. "Just let me win this one, honey, then we'll celebrate."

Madelyn prepared the microwave dinners and defrosted the blueberry pie she'd baked the previous summer. The sky was getting dark. Her husband finished the stock market report while he ate under a glaring lamp which hung over the table.

"The trouble with Ana is she was never an adolescent when she should have been an adolescent," said Madelyn, doling out the pie. "Now we have a permanent adolescent on our hands." She looked at Marty in horror. "Marty, you stupid jerk! Hold the Reddi-wip can upside down or it will ruin the table!"

Marty frowned, and passed Ana a piece of pie without whipped cream. "She's only here temporarily," he remarked.

"If only she'd go out and get a job. Do something!"

"I'm applying for grants," Ana reminded them. "I'm trying to do my art."

"There are a million artists on the streets of New York City," said Madelyn.

"That's why I wanted an MFA, remember? It would have helped me get backing much faster for this Goddess film I'm trying to put together."

"Goddesses, schmodesses," retorted her mother. "She's obsessed with making an avant-garde masterpiece that will supposedly keep the planet from exploding."

"It's a legitimate project, Mom! I've been researching the Goddess all month, remember?"

Marty couldn't really remember. The pie began to smell wonderful as it defrosted. "What is it with all the art stuff, really?"

"I like art because it's fun to create things. I'm obviously too neurotic to create a child, right?" Marty straightened his tie uncomfortably. "Art allows me to make choices. I mean, let's face it, Mom. Where'd I even get the idea of making art other than you? Mom even chose what I wore to my high school dances! While all the other girls wore stockings, *I* was wearing little white socks! My teachers chose which artists I could study—every single one of them a man. And my boyfriends chose when and where we'd make love, and for how long!" Ana was wrapped up in her histrionics. "I've earned the right to choose! Even if it's only shapes and colors to you!"

"And I suppose we're supposed to call that style," replied her mother, non-plussed. She clicked the ice against the side of her whisky glass. "All that money, down the drain. You could have paid us back for *some* of the tuition. Those quality boys you dated, that fancy school we sent you to, and you missed your chance to marry up."

"But I'm not you," said Ana.

"No, you certainly aren't," said Madelyn.

"I graduated from an Ivy League college. Cum laude. Doesn't that count?"

"Look at you *now*!" said her mother. "I was a prize-winning artist until I had *you*!"

"Oh, so now you're blaming me for being born?" shouted Ana. "Or for being such a loser?"

"Stop! Not another word," warned Marty.

"Too bad abortions were illegal in the '50's," shouted Ana, who was on a roll. "You could have aborted both your daughters!"

"I could still disown you," retorted Madelyn drily.

Ana responded with a grand operatic gesture that sent the drinks, the pie and the can of Reddi-wip crashing to the floor. The blueberry pie splattered on the white squares of linoleum and a plexiglass tumbler collided with the hanging lamp, whose swinging, bare bulb cast ominous, moving shadows around the room. "Should we have married lawyers like Dad, and done performance art on the side like *this*?"

Marty grabbed her arms. "That's enough," he said.

"I'm not doing art on the side," screamed Ana belligerently, "I'm living for my art!"

"People who take crack cocaine do things like this," Madelyn said nervously, eyeing the crack in her Tiffany lamp and the debris. "I know. I've read..."

"Enough!" cried Marty.

Ana pulled away and ran upstairs, stuffing various items of clothes into her well-worn knapsack along with her sister's knife for protection. "Don't bother calling a cab," she yelled, running downstairs with her knapsack bouncing over one shoulder, skipping steps two at a time.

"What in the hell is she doing now?" Marty asked, peering out from behind the damask curtains in the dining room.

"She's a grown woman, Marty. She knows what she's doing. She's trying to save some money by hitching a ride to the station. For Christ's sake, Marty, go get me the broom."

Half a mile down the road, a cream-colored Buick had stopped. "Need a lift?"

Ana peered into the half-open tinted window. An old, white-haired woman was seated behind the wheel, a Pomeranian on her lap. Ana shook her head yes, and got in. It was a good getaway car, getting her to the station twenty minutes before the next train.

On one end of the station platform, three teenage girls traded jokes with each other, their laughter echoing like tinkly music. Ana stood alone at the other end, serious and drained, waiting for the train to arrive. Finally they clambered aboard, Ana making her way to the back. She was taking some anti-depressants out of her knapsack when she came across Diane Campbell's business card. Not a bad destination, she thought. By the time she reached Diane Campbell's, the Prozac had kicked in.

Ana was full of bright enthusiasm at being buzzed into the building and finding Diane in her office. "Wow! What a space!" she cried, tossing her knapsack gaily to the newly shellacked floor. So far, it was a completely empty space, save for an edit bay which was only half set up. The room was exploding with funky music. "What an echo! Whoa! Whoa! Whoa! The possibilities are endless."

Diane had just finished painting one corner white. "Tell me about it," she said. "The software's going to have a palette of sixteen million colors."

"Don't make me jealous," said Ana. "What're you going to do with sixteen million colors?"

"I don't know," said Diane wryly. "I gotta finish painting the walls first." Ana grabbed a roller, eager to help. Diane held out an extra pair of painter's pants, and said, "I should be asking you to paint frescoes on the ceiling."

Ana looked up as she slipped on the oversized, splotched pants.

"How Baroque!" said Ana, trying to feel flattered. They proceeded with the base coat, painting in time to the music on the radio: Aretha Franklin, singing, "Chain, chain, chain...chain of fools!"

By nightfall, the office had been fully painted a sparkling white. Through the windows, the skyscrapers of the New York City night gleamed like a meteor shower. Diane and Ana washed their paintbrushes and scrubbed their arms at the large, industrial sink at one end of the room, talking over the din of running water.

"You found a family man, but he's already married," Diane said in disgust. "And even though he tried to rape you, you're falling for him."

"Stop simplifying!" Ana snapped angrily, taking out her little brown bottle of pills.

"Stop acting like an emotional hemophiliac," said Diane, offering her a paper cup.

"You never told me how you got over what happened to you to make you drop out of Yale," Ana countered.

"Therapy, good solid therapy."

"But what happened? I want to know!"

"I put it behind me with therapy," said Diane. "Then I went to the Wharton School of Economics. Good enough?" Ana swallowed another Prozac. Diane looked shocked. "I don't have time for idiocy," she said. "Besides, your inattention drives me nuts."

"What do you mean?" asked Ana, offended.

"Just push replay," said Diane, gesturing at the part of the computer console that was already assembled.

Ana lamely obliged, wiping her hands on her pants. She stared blankly at the monitor, tapping her finger on the keyboard like a mute secretary. Diane pulled up a chair and put on a pair of reading glasses with thick lenses. On the monitor appeared the screenplay of Ana's recent life:

```
FLASHBACK:

INT. NATIONAL IMAGE - NIGHT

Ana's drawings and pearls lie scattered over
the floor, along with Ana, who lies in a heap
like a Raggedy Ann doll, next to the optical
printer.

(COLOR, SIZE and SOUND become increasingly
distorted throughout the scene.)

                    ANA
              (sobbing)
          I understand that you didn't
          mean to hurt my feelings; however,
          when you started grabbing at me,
          what in the world could I do?


                    ROBERT
              (crooning)
          Poor baby, I'm sorr...


                    ANA
              (interrupting,
              stammering)
          I—I want to be taken seriously,
          that's why. That's why I was so
          upset.
```

Robert tries to embrace her in a fatherly manner, this time. She swipes his arms away.

ROBERT
No means no, right? Am I right?

She turns sharply in front of a large, open window.

ANA
(scornfully)
Don't even think about touching me!
Who do you think you are—Carl
André?

She spits in his face.

ANA (CONT'D)
It takes an artist to give a concept
its creative power. An individual
artist. And that's *me*! I can make
you or break you, Mr. Digital System!

ROBERT
(wiping his face)
Concepts are a dime a dozen, babe.
I can get Victor to send me another
creative chick next week like that!
(snaps his fingers)
Bet you can't raise two hundred grand
for all the ideas floating around
that lovely little brain of yours,
can you?

                    ANA

I don't need your hands all over me.
And I don't need your help. When I
get through with you in court, I'll
own your equipment.

                  ROBERT
          (dumbfounded)
What did you say?

He grabs her shoulders.

                    ANA

I know the laws about this. You
don't have to be my boss. Paid or
unpaid, I can still hold you
accountable.

                  ROBERT
          (with contempt)
You can't afford a lawyer and you
know it. There's only one company
that can give you the effects that
you need, and that's National Image.
          (whispering coarsely
          in her ear)
I can ruin your credibility if you
don't deliver this project on time.

                    ANA
          (weakening)
It's just a proposal.

ROBERT

A proposal? I'll call Victor at
the New York Council of the Arts
myself. You'll never get another
grant again. What kind of art will
you make then?

ANA
(aghast)
You bastard, what do you want me
to say?

ROBERT
(seizing the moment)
Not another word.

He pushes her up against the wall beside the
water fountain. Ana struggles to get free,
scratching, clawing and kicking. But Robert
merely holds her in her place, undoing his
pants in one swashbuckling move.

ANA
(to herself)
This isn't happening to me!

She closes her eyes tightly.

FADE OUT

When she opened them again, Ana could see her face reflected
in the monitor in Diane's freshly painted office. The double dose
of Prozac was taking a heavy hold on her. She fixed her gaze at
the screen:

—COMPLIANCE

—COMPROMISE

—RESISTANCE

Ana turned slowly to Diane. "What's this, Eat Me or Drink Me?"

"Go on," said Diane. "What are you afraid of?"

A couple of tears trickled down Ana's face. But Diane slid her chair closer to the monitor, staring at the screen through her thick glasses. Gently but firmly, she put Ana's hand on the mouse. Tremulously, Ana clicked on "RESISTANCE".

She found herself back in a new version of her past. Robert was backing her up towards the open window, getting closer and closer in the brick-red fury of his anger. But in the final instant before pushing her out—like the sculptor Carl André pushing his wife through the open window—she felt herself swiftly trading places. It was *she* who was pushing *him* out of the window—the artist Ana Mendieta killing Carl. She was sobbing both in horror and relief as she watched his body floating slowly down. She watched his body descending fourteen stories, one by one, in slow, slow motion, like a wildly gesticulating soldier thrown out of a helicopter over a rice paddy.

"Hey, Ana. You wanna push the 'delete' button now?" Diane was asking. The sun was beginning to rise over the skyscrapers, and Ana's face was reflected in the monitor, red with fever. "Look," said Diane. "There's an extra room in my apartment. My landlady's putting her kid through school by renting out part of her space. It's not exactly legal, but it's a temporary place to live, OK?" Ana nodded her head and began to cough. "Why didn't you tell me you were sick?" she added impatiently. She filled an empty Diet Coke can with water and handed it to Ana with some Tylenol.

"Thank you," murmured Ana. "Thank you for saving me."

"Hey, girl," Diane said softly, taking off her glasses and blinking once or twice. "Someday it'll be your turn to pick up the pieces, OK?" And they shared an awkward hug.

The room was tiny, but it overlooked Riverside Drive. With the ugly set of Venetian blinds rolled up out of the way, one could see a corner of the Hudson River.

"If you need anything, just knock. I'm right down the hall to your left," said Brenda O'Shanigan, the landlady. "Let me know if Brian's too noisy with his cartoons." Her seven-year-old grinned impishly and mounted his bicycle. She backed out of the way: Marty Fried was hoisting the last of his daughter's boxes through the hall, just missing the kid racing by.

"You're absolutely sure this is a safe neighborhood?" Marty was asking Diane.

"Daddy, please," said Ana, wiping her face with her shirt. There was no air conditioner. Marty's head was bathed in sweat.

"Tea?" said Diane. Ana nodded yes, Marty no. Diane hummed a tune and left the room.

"Look, I'll go ahead and give you the deposit on an East Side place if you'll land yourself a real job," said Marty.

Ana was incensed. "What do you mean, real job?" He could afford the deposit on a swank apartment, yet couldn't lend her a dime for an art film?

"You know, like *Mademoiselle*. I don't know. Do some sketches for some magazine."

"That was a summer job before college," Ana protested. "This is real life now."

Marty was taken aback. He cleared his throat and pulled a small, elegant leather briefcase out of his heavy one. It was his last stand. "I had this extra briefcase. I didn't know whether to give it to one of the secretaries," he said. "Maybe you could use it, you know, if you get serious about some new career."

Ana blew her nose. "Thank you, Daddy."

"That's my girl," said her father, mopping the bald spot on his head with his handkerchief. "See you in a few weeks, OK?" He backed out of the room, embarrassed by the possibility of emotions, apologizing profusely as he bumped into Diane.

When he was gone, Ana stared at the briefcase as if at a coiled snake. Diane poured tea.

"This is weird. I'm saving you from one of the highest-per-capita towns in the U.S. Instead, you want this?" Diane gestured at the grungy apartment.

Ana burned her lip on the tea. "I want to finish my film already. If I had to trade sex to get this damn film done, I'd do it! The deadline's in four days."

"You're in deep shit," said Diane. "You gotta get your money together. You gotta make your movies. And you gotta get laid. Just don't mix them all up."

They sipped their tea in silence, looking at the corner of the river.

"Thanks, Diane. For helping me move and all that," Ana finally said.

"Well, I don't really buy the supporting cast routine," said Diane. "I mean, what do *I* get out of all this?" Ana looked at her. "What I mean is, as soon as the carpenters are finished and the equipment gets set up in there, next week sometime, Friday at the latest, you're helping me move *my* boxes. Is it a deal? I don't trust the movers with anything that's really fragile."

She reflected on the reciprocity that Diane was asking of her. No one had needed Ana for a long time let alone trusted her. Not her mother, not her sister. Ana held onto Diane tightly in a long embrace and then they shook on it.

CHAPTER TWENTY-ONE

On Company Time

My tired, vagabond steps
erred through centuries of time.
— Sor Juana Inés de la Cruz

Robert was stirring his coffee with Creammate and listening to a baseball game, waiting for a shipment from Paramount TV.

"Aw, come on now," he said, stretching his arms out to her as Ana approached the reception area. "You don't really want to pick up that thing yet." She refused to acknowledge him as she strode past him, looking for her portfolio on a shelf full of identical or similar portfolios.

Robert put out his cigarette, came over to her, and stood behind her. She turned in fury. "How can you possibly know what I want or don't want? It's so—so presumptuous!"

He laughed, playing with her. "I know what *I* want, and I'm going to be a raving maniac until I get it..."

"Oh, please."

"I want a cup of coffee. I demand, I crave, a cup of hot, black coffee," he said, leading Ana to the coffee nook, where he proceeded to drink her very being, kissing her shoulder, her neck, her mouth...

"Not here," she said primly. She amazed herself with her own ambivalence. She'd been convinced that the only important thing in her life was the creative work at hand. All she could think of now, standing before this man, was her loneliness and sexual desire.

He grabbed her buttocks, grinding against her; without thinking twice, she seized the coffee pot and threw it at him. Most of it missed, except for a dark splotch across a freshly pressed pinstripe shirt, and his hand, which he put in his mouth. He looked at her like a forlorn puppy.

Ana stared at him, paralyzed with mixed emotions.

"I'm sorry," he said. He reached for the first-aid kit in the cabinet and put some salve on his hand.

"Look," she said slowly, "I need someone to walk me home."

"Ha! To Scarsdale?" asked Robert. "Your father'll arrest me for statutory rape."

"I'm almost thirty-four."

He looked her over. "Emotionally, you might be a minor."

"How can you say that? It's—It's so insulting!"

"I'm sorry," said Robert.

"Me, too." They could feel the silence envelope them. "Look. I live on 108th Street now."

"Riverside Drive? Of course," Robert scoffed knowingly. "There are some palaces up there."

"It's no palace."

He looked in her face. "Do you want me to build one in my imagination?" he asked.

This was too much for her. She looked away, then back at him reluctantly. "Yes," she said simply.

"You want me to walk you there?" he asked. She nodded.

They took turns arguing and holding hands as they made their way uptown, past the fountain at Columbus Circle, where they splashed each other with water in a vain attempt to lighten the mood.

"You and Suzanne have so much in common," he enthused. He was totally insensitive to her repulsion at the fact that he was married. "Two beautiful, creative babes. Ever hear of the Suzanna Moss Dancers? Suzanne believes in equality, too. She believes in…"

Ana interrupted. "Equal sex?"

"I wasn't going to say that," said Robert. He had been merely trying to con Ana into a quick affair. He started to cross the street ahead of her, walking slowly backwards. "Actually, since the birth of our son, she hasn't...I mean, her belief in birth control is more like...."—Ana had caught up with him, and held his arm for a moment, out of breath—"...no sex," but as he said the word *sex*, an electrical charge went through their bodies. They grinned sheepishly at one another as the light turned red.

"Gee, that's too bad. My boyfriend believed in free sex," said Ana softly. "You know musicians."

"On the road?" She nodded. What road where? she wondered, trying not to feel so lost.

"You travel often?" he asked.

"Not any more," she said, looking at him. They crossed the street, side by side, not speaking. Robert took her by the arm as a black stretch limousine turned the corner. Ana pulled her arm away, snapping back into reality.

"Hey, I already told you. I don't need a man to protect me," she protested.

This really exasperated him. "Why'd you want me to walk uptown with you?" he muttered.

"So you could watch me practice my jiu jitsu, and tae kwon do," said Ana. Not that she had ever studied self-defense, but it was important to put on a brave face at a time like this. "So you could put me in a kung fu movie. Take back the streets! Hi-yah!" she added, pushing him a little. But that wasn't it either. "Maybe I'm sort of horny," she admitted. "Maybe I'd—Well, maybe I'd like to jump you."

When they reached the 108th Street apartment, she slammed the door and made love to him with the urgency of combat, assaulting his erect penis with her red tongue. Then striding him in one fell swoop, she bent her knees to either side of her belly like a Neolithic goddess while raising the battle cry of her cunt. Their first orgasms splintered through the tiny room, their bodies washed by the moonlight spilling through the broken Venetian blinds.

In the next room, Brian was listening through the walls to their pants, moans and screams, blended with an occasional thud of cardboard boxes. Somewhere after their second orgasm they had turned on the radio, making a feeble attempt to drown out their love cries, which only added to the noise level. Under the influence of sleeping pills, Brenda was oblivious. Brian, however, found these noises entertaining—though sort of gross.

Brenda pushed a hand-written note under the sub-tenant's door later that morning. Brian had given her a blow-by-blow description of what he'd heard through the walls of the apartment, before going off to school. Ana was too absorbed in gazing at herself in the mirror to notice the note on the floor, letting her fingers travel absently through her matted tangles of damp, black hair. Her calm, post-coital expression floated on the surface of the small, oval mirror that Diana had given her.

She had thumbtacked a Georgia O'Keeffe poster of a giant white lily on the opposite wall. The Venetian blinds had been rolled up out of the way, and over the infamous bed hung a small gold-framed photograph of Isadora Duncan. It felt so wonderful to be settling in somewhere.

Ana turned to her cardboard boxes and unpacked her audio cassettes and the second-hand stereo that had rotted in her parents' attic. Humming nonchalantly, she found Chopin's Opus 17 No. 4. She popped in the cassette, then picked up her scissors with a flourish and began to cut some of the drawings that would be used in the mattes for her special effects. Several hours later, she had graduated to an Exacto knife, cutting dozens of "paper dolls" of Isis and the Virgin Mary. They were just beginning to sprout huge, white wings that would morph into the Victory of Samothrace, when she noticed the small, folded piece of yellow legal paper under the door.

"What's this shit?" she muttered, turning off the cassette player and sitting on the bed to read the note. How could the landlady evict her? She had just moved in!

She sat in torpor for an hour, then bitterly started repacking her tapes, her stereo, her clothes and her art work. Down came the posters and the black and white photograph of Isadora. She was just rolling up the giant lily when Diane knocked on the door. "Just a minute. Who is it, please?" she said, singsong, struggling to force a rubber band over the uncooperative, phallic shape of the rolled-up poster.

Diane strolled in, in a somber mood, and said, "You have some nerve."

"Please, Diane, let me explain," said Ana, trying to hide her embarrassment by aiming the poster like a spear into her cardboard box.

"I don't want to hear it now. I certainly didn't appreciate hearing it last night. Brenda doesn't want her kids to hear it again," said Diane, tersely, adding, "Why him?"

Ana tried bravura. "That's OK, I'm leaving. I'm—I'm considering Mexico. Of course, I've already been there once," she said. "I've been to Germany…" She faltered. "I've always wanted to see Japan. Kyoto's supposed to be beautiful…"

"There are other New York apartments," Diane said drily. "Try Brooklyn."

"It's so funny," Ana said hurriedly, turning manic as she twisted the truth. "The last time I was evicted, I was doing a documentary in Tennessee, and I invited some of my black friends over to my house for a party? Well, I think *that* landlady would've got the Ku Klux Klan to *burn* me out if I hadn't left of my own accord. Anyway, I had this grant to go to New York City! What a coincidence! I mean, I couldn't have stayed in Memphis!"

Diane pushed some packing tape at Ana. "It is one thing to be victimized, even repeatedly. It is quite another to make stupid choices. Who can you blame then?"

"Well, me," said Ana blithely. "But..."

"Well, why don't you think about your choices?" asked Diane, with all the certainty of her church-going history behind her.

"Well, I don't mean to pick such losers, necessarily. But at least I had someone to go to bed with last night."

"Ana! You're not thinking!"

"Well, who do *you* have in your life?" asked Ana.

"I have my work right now. I'm forming a solid base for my life," answered Diane. "There'll be time for me to find the perfect relationship when I'm more comfortable."

"Diane, you're scared to love. You're holding back."

"That's ridiculous," said Diane.

"You're scared of love," restated Ana. Maybe being raped had left Diane permanently scarred, thought Ana.

"Love for you is like a synthetic phenylethylamine shot directly into the brain. I need a relationship to develop more slowly, that's all," said Diane. "And I can't fall in love with a fascist. Period."

Ana stood with her boxes stacked like a pyramid behind her. "At least I'm doing the art that I set out to do," she tried to say in self-defense. But Diane had already made her exit, like Diana with her arrows and her stag.

"Coffee, boss?" asked Josh.

"Huh?"

"Coffee break?" Robert was making calculations over the film synchronizer.

"Stop interrupting me, God damn it! Every time I get it perfect, Jesus Christ."

Josh sleepwalked to the coffee nook, reentering with two cups of coffee.

"I already told you I don't want any more coffee," said Robert, angrily gnashing his teeth. Josh stood defiantly in the middle of the room. Slowly he poured Robert's cup onto the floor, creating a huge brown puddle. Then, with a smirk, he took a sip of his own cup of coffee.

"Guess I didn't hear you," said Josh.

Robert eyeballed Josh. Then he dropped his arrogance, grabbing a handful of Kem wipes from the rewind bench. "I don't know what got into me," said Robert, and fell to his knees in front of Josh, sopping up the spill. "Here, let me get this." He threw the dripping wet Kem wipes in the trash, drying his hands on his pants. "Think it's about time I headed home and caught up on sleep."

"Sleep, huh? What about that chick hanging around the office all week?" asked Josh.

"She thinks I'm helping her," said Robert with a snicker.

Josh looked at Robert skeptically and sat back down at the computer. "You won't be such an asshole in the morning," said Josh, as if to the monitor.

"You can say that again," laughed Robert. "Hey, how's—uh—Sharon?" But without waiting for a reply, Robert lifted Ana's storyboard from a pile of film cans, tucked it under his arm, and was off.

When the buzzer sounded, Ana was pulling at her hair distractedly. What an awkward time for Robert to come back. She hadn't even taken a shower, after moving all her boxes as far as the front door.

"Surprise!" Marty shouted jovially, as she opened the door, adjusting her top.

"It was marvelous," said Madelyn.

Ana eyed her parents full of tension. "What was marvelous, Mom?"

"It was the best, the *best* Broadway show I've seen all year. Spectacular."

"We were just, practically in the neighborhood," said Marty although they both knew that the theater district was sixty-five blocks south of her Riverside Drive apartment, and that parking was miserable. "So we thought..."

"Great timing, Dad," said Ana. "Maybe you can help me load up the car while you're at it."

"Why? Where are you going?" asked Madelyn suspiciously. "At this time of night?"

"She's joking," Marty said, trying to placate his wife before there were any eruptions.

"I've been evicted," said Ana. "I'm coming home, Ma."

"Evicted?" said Marty, incredulously.

"What do you mean, you've been evicted? You just got here!"

"If it's drugs, I know a lawyer who specializes..." Marty began to say, but Madelyn interrupted.

"Just tell me, was it cocaine or marijuana?"

"Stop it! It was neither one of them," said Ana.

"Well, for God's sakes, just move in with your boyfriend already."

"I can't. He's married," she blubbered incoherently.

Madelyn was taken aback. "Well, I don't know if we should let you in our house after what you did. Do you know how much a Tiffany lamp is worth these days?"

"Please, Ma. Just for a week."

"It took an entire day of my life just to fill out the insurance forms..."

"Sorry," said Ana, picking up a cardboard box.

"You think I can get rid of the blueberry stains?"

"You have to apologize," said Marty.

"Not to mention every shard of broken glass..."

"I'm sorry. I'm sorry," said Ana, playing back her broken record of apologies. Marty had already piled one box on top of another and was lifting them, while Madelyn held the door open for him.

"You'd better be. After all I..."

"Shut up!" barked Marty, as the box-laden family marched out single file into the hot, humid night of late July. Neighborhood children were playing in an open fire hydrant, the spray of water just missing the cardboard of Ana's boxes.

Ana and her father continued to load the boxes into the silver Saab, while Madelyn supervised. "Marty, you're giving yourself a hernia!"

Marty assessed the boxes in the trunk as well as those remaining on the sidewalk. He took the biggest box, the one jutting out of the trunk, and hoisted it up onto the luggage rack. Ana felt she ought to be thankful.

"So when are you going to get your shit together?" he said through gritted teeth.

"What do you mean?"

He was panting. "I mean, a regular job."

"I *do* work. I'm an artist. I do my art!"

Marty dismissed her by attacking the pile of boxes on the sidewalk. "Your mother used to paint awfully pretty pictures before she had kids," he said loudly, for Madelyn's benefit.

"Dad, that's not the kind of art I do and you know it."

"It's *underground* art, Marty," his wife tried to explain to him. "She's been in the underground for years."

But Marty still seemed confused. "Are we talking about the emperor's new clothes? We haven't seen a thing since you came back from the West Coast," he said.

"It's technical. You wouldn't understand."

"*I* would," said Madelyn. "I've seen those commercials. They're very arty."

"I haven't sold out yet, Mom," Ana said quickly.

"That's exactly my point," said Marty. "You're too old for this."

Madelyn opened the car doors while Ana and Marty used a rope to tie down the boxes on the roof of the Saab.

"These—these effects. They must be costing an arm and a leg," said Marty. "You're not charging them on my Visa, are you?"

"No, Dad," said Ana carefully. "I have a friend who's helping me."

"A friend? What kind of a friend?" They had finished tying down the boxes, and were dripping with sweat. Meanwhile, a street kid let the fire hydrant go at full throttle.

"He's doing my work on the side. At night, OK? And he's married," she said, turning to Madelyn. "I'm sure you can understand that, Mom, married to a divorce attorney and all."

Marty spoke up. "You seem to regard it as fun to fuck over marriage as an institution, don't you, Ana?"

"Watch your language!" Madelyn said to him sharply.

"Fuck you, Mom, OK? Do I get an X-rating?" said Ana. A ten-year-old turned the flow of water around, splashing Marty in the face.

"That's it," said Madelyn. "I've had it. We're going without you."

"You're not just leaving me here..." said Ana, in a daze. She felt a certain chill. "I'm..."

"Your mother's absolutely right," said Marty. "Ana, get a good shrink this time. I'll pay for it."

"Honey, let's go. I'm suffocating," said his wife from the front seat, impatient for the air conditioning to start cooling the car.

He slipped Ana two twenty dollar bills and shushed her. Ana hated her father for all his petty handouts. He jumped into the car and backed out of the spot. They rolled up the windows, driving off without their daughter. Ana crumpled up the money, preparing to throw it on the curb. Instead, she pocketed it. Then she stood for a few more moments watching the children at play, wondering what it would take for her to grow up.

Robert and Ana had just missed each other: Robert arrived at her apartment with her portfolio under his arm, only to be told that Ana wasn't living there any more. Ana rode a nearly deserted subway car to midtown, clutching her knapsack in fear, only to be told by the night shift workers at his office that Robert had gone home. They ran into one another in the hallway of his office building, each more anxiety-ridden than the other. They jumped into the elevator and waited for the doors to close to give themselves a quick chance to embrace.

"You must be a ghost," said Ana, stroking his face.

"No, I'm for real," he said.

"As in virtual reality?" she said suggestively, unable to live out the moment for its own sake. "Seriously, I need you to do this image for me," she said, as if she were capable of being serious.

"You're on," said Robert, stringing her along in his deep, assuring voice. "We'll grab a hamburger first," he added.

"As in 'do lunch'? Isn't it a little late?"

He put his hands on her waist and guided her towards the revolving doors. "Come on," he said.

They grabbed a cab and made out in the back seat as the cab sped down to Soho. In a restaurant where Robert knew all the waiters, he ordered himself a thick steak and several rounds of Scotch. Ana nibbled pasta salad, sipping her ice water through a straw.

"The Poindexters were Philadelphia Main Line. Central Avenue, Bryn Mawr," he was bragging, trying to impress her with the rotten capitalism of his childhood. "Our tree house had oak paneling. We even had an elevator in our house. It was oak-paneled, too, if you can believe it!" Ana obligingly laughed. "My mother locked me in it when I was nine for trying to drive dad's car. She called the police and had me arrested when I was seventeen."

"What for?" she asked.

"For stealing the Rolls," he answered, moving his hand possessively over hers. "I won the drag race." Ana was duly impressed. She had never met such a juvenile delinquent.

"At least your adolescence was over and done with. I had to be a perfect angel till I turned twenty," she said. "My parents threatened to disown me if I didn't graduate from college."

They started drinking competitively. "Not me. Flew a helicopter over 'Nam, instead," he said, "'til it crashed."

"Poor baby!" she cooed in a false-toned voice, as he bared his soul to her. He ordered her a double malt.

She pressed on. "What were you fighting for, anyway? Couldn't you get a medical excuse?"

Robert snorted. "Sorry excuse for an American."

Ana coughed on the burning Scotch and the acrid smoke of Robert's cigarette. "Vietnam was genocide," she blurted out, despite her best intentions of keeping politics out of the picture. "You could have been a conscientious objector!" to which Robert retorted drunkenly, "Maybe I like a little genocide now and then."

She threw the remains of her ice water at him, immediately regretting it, mopping his shirt with her paper napkin and picking up the straw from the floor. "I'm sorry! I'm sorry!"

"Gimme a war I can be proud of," Robert was saying. "If I hadn't had a family and a broken back..." he muttered, pushing her soggy napkin away. "I'm just a worthless bum. Two ex-wives can confirm that, 200%. Hardly ever see the third—trying to get a god-damned business off the ground." He burped, then studied his glass of bourbon. Only a fool would have called it half full.

"What you need is to quit smoking. All it takes is a little self-esteem," said Ana, remembering her self-help books and moving closer to him. "You can do it, Robbie."

She took his hand as the waiter arrived with the check. Ana drunkenly fumbled in her knapsack and slapped her father's credit card on the table. Robert automatically raised his soggy cigarette to his lips. Ana took the cigarette out of his mouth and put it out in the other glass of half-melted ice cubes. "It's OK," she said, mothering him. "You can do it."

She walked him slowly over to the gallery which she was using as a crash-pad for the night—an empty, echoing white hangar of a space that was in between shows. Jeff Katz greeted the drunken couple who were holding onto each other for dear life. Jeff was holding something behind his back with an indulgent smile at the lateness of the hour.

"How's that grant application going?" he asked.

"Which one?" said Ana flippantly. "I..." she faltered, realizing she'd missed the deadline for the New York State Council on the Arts application. "Thanks for your help, by the way."

"It was nothing," he said, yawning. "So did you get an artist-in-residency, or what?"

"That's funny," she said, thinking to herself how she was becoming increasingly homeless. "The residency part keeps eluding me."

"Here," he said, pulling out a small, stylish suitcase made of wicker. "Get rid of that hippie knapsack you've been carrying. This will give you a post-modern look, don't you think? Maybe it'll help."

Robert was dizzy. Ana struggled to keep her balance and support his weight as she thanked Jeff, both for the suitcase and for the crash pad.

"Yeah, well as I was saying on the phone, we're in between shows," Jeff said.

"When's mine gonna go up?"

"Just as soon as you finish your work."

"Oh sure," she smirked. "The token artist shtick you throw at all the women?"

Jeff simpered back. "We don't discriminate any more," he said. "Can you finish your work by next March? We'd have to have the showing by July at the latest. New York's dead in August."

"I'm sure I can finish by next spring! Here, look," said Ana. She opened up her knapsack and dumped assorted goddesses onto the gallery floor: Gaia, Isis, Semoulisa and Persephone—holding a pomegranate which, when animated, would roll down into a chasm of earth towards Hades.

"Where's the focus? It doesn't look like it's progressed much past that grant application you showed me, huh?" But Ana was in a daze, focusing on Robert's eyes as if they were bright blue wells of water in a desert. "Oh well, I'm sure you're working on it," he added. He gestured at Robert. "Who's this—a critic? Or a panelist?"

"Robert is helping me," she said simply.

"I see." He paused. "Robert, Ana, I've got to run."

"Thanks, Jeffrey," said Ana. She meant it.

"Sleep well. Ta-ta!" He strode off with the guard dog: half pit bull, half Rottweiler. Ana and Robert tried sleeping on the floor, an electric fan perched on top of the wicker suitcase. It was a poor substitute for air conditioning. Ana rocked Robert in her arms through another sleepless night, crooning, "Baby, baby."

Robert was hung over and taciturn when he brought Ana back up to National Image the next morning, carrying her little wicker suitcase. She tripped across the threshold to the reception area, and Robert had to hold her to keep her from falling.

"Suzanne's on her way over," Len said significantly, sitting at the typewriter, playing secretary. "Said she's bringing the cat. And Dick McGiver's on the phone."

"Tell him I'll call back in five minutes," said Robert, stretching his limbs laconically.

"He said he'd rather hold—it's important." Robert said nothing in reply. "Don't forget you have a business to tend to," he added rather sharply.

"I'll be right there," Robert said, but he didn't move, except to hold Ana closer, whispering to her, "I'm a new man."

"Please, I'm suffocating," said Ana. She appeared terribly nervous. Len stood up and gruffly suggested that she get herself some breakfast.

"There's a coffee shop downstairs, right to your left," Robert interjected, flipping through his wallet. "Um, get me two eggs over easy while you're at it, some ham, whole wheat toast, and make it a large coffee. Get yourself anything your heart desires. Dad?"

He handed Ana twenty bucks, shooing her off. Len exploded as soon as she was out of sight. "A one-night stand I can accept, but this?"

"What do you mean, Dad?" asked Robert in his deep, affable voice.

"I'm not the kind of guy who can sit back and watch while my son-in-law ruins my little girl's dreams. Dammit, Robert," he sputtered, "you have a child now! Don't you think about the little one at all? I ought to close down this company and retire for good," he said, regretting that he hadn't already done so. "If I have to tell your wife what's going on while you let your business rot, I'll do just that!"

The phone rang. "Good morning, National Image, please hold," said Robert, sounding innocent and pleasant. "I'll tell you what's going on," he said to Len, in a more authoritative voice. "I'm taking Ms. Fried with me to Silicon Valley for the Second Annual Digital Imaging Conference, so we'll know what's going on, for God's sake! She's working for me as a... as a creative consultant!" Ana had returned, balancing paper bags and Styrofoam containers of coffee and food.

"She's a tramp!" cried Len.

"Just put them down on the desk, Ana," Robert calmly said.

Ana was ashamed. Just the night before, she had held demonstrations around the stone monument of his penis. And what was he doing about it? He'd hoisted up the flag of their secret love for his entire family to salute.

She slowly put everything down and lowered herself onto the chair behind the secretary's desk. When the phone rang, neither man moved.

"Should I get it?" asked Ana. Len and Robert glared at each other. She picked up the phone. "This is National Image. How can I help you?"

"Put 'em on hold," said Len gruffly.

Ana held a pencil up in the air like a circus trainer. "Uh-huh," she said, back on the phone. She scribbled a message and smiled wanly at Len. "Certainly, right away... Thank you so much." She hung up.

She turned to Robert, sweetly. "I really appreciate your thinking of employing me as a consultant. But I really can't go to California just yet. I..."

"Shut up," said Robert. "Do you want me to drop this project of yours? It's $50,000 worth of opticals. Perhaps you have some other place in mind that's ready to help?"

"I..."

"We're going to Silicon Valley—West Coast Digital. That's where the hardware is that you need to run this crazy thing of yours." He began to pack his briefcase.

"Now just a goddamn minute," said Len.

"Creativity, technology, and business," Robert lectured him. "You lose any one of those, you're out of business. I'll be damned if I'm going out of business with a family to support. Now the creative angle, that's Ana." He turned to her briefly: "We can get the program while you're doing your job. This is not a salaried position, you understand. We're bartering here. Now, maybe you won't make your precious deadlines," he said with sarcasm, "but I'll be producing all of your goddess opticals for free."

"You're crazy!" shouted Len, slamming himself into the darkroom, flashing the red lights on and off, on and off. Ana hid her tears, angry and defiant, scarcely like a mistress or an employee. It didn't seem to matter that he was finally going to focus on her work. Robert wasn't ready to leave. He had started to calibrate some doodad on the optical printer with a screwdriver. But seeing despair in her eyes, he put it down.

"What's the matter?" he asked.

"I'm concerned for your wife."

Robert was less concerned. She walked out, smacking her hand against the elevator door. The elevator shaft had become a tunnel of molten lava. She hurried back to the coffee shop to get something for herself this time. The sun was beating on the counter. The eggs were half-uncooked, and she wouldn't eat them. Len barged in, equally desperate, searching through the red vinyl booths for his son-in-law, who seemed to have disappeared. But Len's back was turned to the counter, and hatred and fear made her silent. She toyed with a cold piece of toast, trying to stay away from her lover for another ten minutes. But the elevator sucked her back to the fourteenth floor, and they hurried off in a cab to the airport.

Ana had the window seat on the plane. She turned to the window apprehensively while Robert counted his change for two sets of headphones, then lay against the headrest and closed her eyes in exhaustion, waiting for takeoff. She was tired of running away on the treadmill called earth. Robert was giving her claustrophobia. He kept stroking the sleeve of her angora sweater, strapped in beside her. Ignoring the pressure in her ears that made her want to scream, she stared out the window as the plane gained altitude, racing along a road of dark clouds, each cloud identical to the next. *All of my lovers are cut out of one long roll of paper, like paper dolls facing a book of matches.* She thought of them vaguely as a succession of paper doll priests in some goddess' cult, one annihilating the next and taking his place. Whether they lasted seven years or only until dawn, the important thing was that they serve her like a goddess while they lasted…not that they ever had, exactly.

Exasperated with Robert, she turned her thoughts to Karl, whose name scrolled down in front of her like the opening credits of an in-flight re-run.

Then Robert broke her reverie.

"You know, the second time I crashed a helicopter, I ended up with a broken back for six months," he said. "Then the helicopter company shortchanged me on severance pay because the damn thing landed in Cambodia instead of 'nam. I couldn't even sue the bastards for breaking my back. And I used to be drinking buddies with those bastards in the Officers' Club." Ana stared at this man eating salted peanuts, headphones covering his hairy ears. He took her hand in his, and let the words come out slowly. "I'll never forgive myself for boozing it up that night while the Vietcong blew up my house. If only I'd known…"

"You had a *house*?" said Ana, stupefied. "In Vietnam?"

"A girlfriend and a house—in Saigon. Her name was Sue Hong. She was the prettiest girl you ever saw," he said, staring down at the peanuts on his plastic tray. "I'll never forgive myself! She was sleeping in my bed when that house blew up!" he exclaimed, then added in a lower voice, "I'm continually in awe that God placed me in the Officers' Club that night."

She remembered her nightmare about the exploding body of a Vietnamese girl, just before she met Robert. It felt like an omen. She pulled her hand out of his and unbuckled her seat belt. Here she was, scrunched up beside him in Coach Class, another potential victim! "You...you war criminal, bashing your way through life!" She would rather parachute out of the plane than continue to sit next to him.

"What could I have possibly done?" asked Robert.

"*I* marched on Washington," she declaimed self-righteously. "I protested the atrocities, comprende?" The more she knew about Robert Poindexter, the less she wanted to sit next to him. Under his suave exterior, his flesh seemed to ooze like the rosé wine he was drinking. His necktie was flapping like a mummy's shroud, unraveling under the relentless air stream of the overhead compartment. His chest began to cave into a dark, nicotined chasm, revealing a liver half-rotted with liquor, until all she saw before her was a series of putrid cavities filled with semen, urine and feces. But he had the aisle seat, and his body was so wide and imposing, there was no way to climb past him.

"I want you to forgive me for what happened," he said, reaching over and offering her the headphones he had bought her. But she refused to look at him any longer.

Robert admired the variety of tits and asses in the San Francisco Terminal. Ana wasn't even jealous. She narrowed her focus to finding them transportation to the Digital Imaging Conference near Fisherman's Wharf, where they were scheduled to meet the CEO of West Coast Digital.

The Super Shuttle wasted no time in getting them there. "How many people quadruple their inheritance practically overnight?" Robert said to Ana by way of introducing Tom, a short, genial man with short, light brown hair who could have been lost in the crowds. At 27, Tom Emerson, Jr. headed one of the best mid-sized special effects companies in the U.S.A., and was eager to guide Robert and Ana through the biggest FX conference the West Coast had ever seen.

"It's about time to offload those old-fashioned film techniques you're probably still using over at National Image, right, Robert?" Robert was admiring a black velvet-clad display hostess.

They journeyed through the exhibition from booth to booth. Robert spent more time ogling the hostesses than the equipment.

"Effects, man, digital effects," said Tom, snapping his fingers. "New York's ancient history. Talk about multi-mediocrity—'Lights! Camera! Giant Cockroaches!' You don't need all that!" he said. "I'm telling you, West Coast's where it's *at*!"

Robert reached into a fishbowl full of Hershey's Kisses and M&M's. "Here. Save these for the Skipper, will you?" he asked Ana. But she had no interest in holding onto a sticky collection of chocolates for his son. She popped one into her mouth, standing mesmerized in front of a bank of monitors. They displayed the latest in morph technology: computer programs explaining how to transform facial features into other facial features, animals into other animals, and ordinary men into neon Superheroes.

She was on the verge of discovering the implications of this technology for *The Cyborg Goddess* when Tom Emerson brushed against her sleeve. He handed her a green balloon, saying with a goofy grin, "Your wish is my command."

CHAPTER TWENTY-TWO

The Passion Project

*My love is a deep pool into which you
may throw yourself.*
— Murasaki Shikibu

Tom's red convertible Porsche sped across the Golden Gate Bridge, a gorgeous special effect in the death throes of a summer sun. Ana was crammed in the back seat with the balloon between her legs, unnerved by his daredevil speed and his locker room jokes. "I like my women like commercials," he was saying, "sweet 'n short, and you can turn 'em down." Robert was cracking up. He reached into the back seat to pinch her, but she gave his arm a sharp jolt, wanting to punish him for war crimes, thinking, *He's probably bombed women and children.*

"Ana, what's the matter?" he asked.

"Nothing. The wind is giving me a headache."

"We're gonna do a closefile on that headache," said Tom. He changed lanes and passed back a bottle of pills.

"No, thanks. I don't do drugs any more," said Ana, trying to convince herself. Tom shrugged and turned up the music on the stereo. "I—I like health food," said Ana.

"Try this multi-plot: seafood, organic veggies, carrot cake," Tom extemporized over the music. "On to the best motel in the Bay Area, then to Silicon Valley and the best little company on the whole fuckin' planet—West Coast Digital. Hit the programs, throw in what Ana's lookin' for, a couple of all-nighters on the computer—and you're outta here."

"That sounds good, Tom. We really appreciate it," said Ana in an unenthusiastic monotone, still obsessed by the thought of helicopters flying over burning jungles. She shifted her weight in the back of the sports car; it freed the balloon, which rose above the hills of San Francisco and disappeared into the coral sky.

That night, Ana got up on her knees on the king-sized bed of an anonymous-looking suite in the Seacrest Motel. He waited like a nuclear warhead for her to put in her diaphragm. She reached for it with trembling hands. Robert pulled her down, moaning out of love, murmuring that he loved her, needed her, calling her "baby". His flaccid muscles repulsed her—she considered hating him; but he was fucking against her clitoris, which filled her womb with desire for a baby—even *his* baby, even out of wedlock. Her womb thundered in a series of explosions; her thighs shuddered in the fallout.

He had conquered Ana out of pure, sexual greed, but now he was beginning to cough. He was rasping for water and flooded with sweat. Ana misunderstood him completely. She thought he was having a heart attack. But finally she got him a glass of water and he fell asleep, curled against her damp, virginal-looking body, looking as clean as a baby.

Her eyes refused to close, fixated on how low she'd sunk. She was aching from exhaustion, but there wasn't any marijuana in the motel. On the television set, late night commercials were in full force, and she didn't have the willpower to move Robert's elbow to find the remote that had fallen under the bed. The TV was ablaze with a sunset advertising getaways to Cancun.

It was worse than when Andy returned from jail and convinced her to run away to Mexico with him. All Andy wanted was for her to sit there stoned on the beach, listening to him and his bass. Andy kept crooning like Orpheus that he'd remake their love on

313

the big screen of the night sky when she should have been going for partner with Janyce Hardy, Inc. It could have been so easy back then. All she had to do to realize her dreams was to leave him.

Robert Poindexter propped up his big body against the headboard with the available pillows. Daggers of sunlight were stabbing the suite of the Seacrest Motel through the vinyl plastic blinds. He was smoking a cigarette with an absent look on his face, expecting his wife or business associates to call, when the telephone rang. He answered it with his most charming voice. It was only the wake-up call.

Robert put down the receiver and gave Ana's near-lifeless body a hug. "Darling, would you make me some coffee?"

"Are you kidding?" she asked.

"What's the matter?" he said, surprised.

She rolled her eyes. "I've never made coffee for a man before," she lied. "And I don't intend to start now." He waited for her. She rolled over and shoved the hot plastic cup of water and instant coffee packet on the bedstand towards him like a bucket of feces. "Here," she said.

Robert grabbed her wrists and wrestled her onto her back, saying, "Come on, what's the big deal?"

She got out of bed and stretched in front of the window, so he couldn't see the expression on her face. Then she asked in a nonchalant voice, "What would happen to my work, waiting on you hand and foot?"

"Your work? It would be your company! I could make you President!"

She laughed a bit hoarsely. "Vice President," she said.

"You're adorable," said Robert, pulling her back to the bed. She began to make love to him, somewhat reluctantly. Yet she couldn't deny the violent undertow—wanting to be taken like a slave for a ride to oblivion, chained to a shipwrecked figurehead.

In marked contrast to National Image, West Coast Digital, an oil company subsidiary in stainless steel, was state of the art in its total design. Robert was absorbed by the computer programming that could finally convince his investors of his worth. He ignored Ana completely. She paced back and forth, staring at the fog through wall-to-wall windows in her cherry-red pantsuit, reminiscent of one she'd worn at a Yale mixer.

She had been "hired" to "consult" at WC Digital. Another day without sleep, "working" on Robert's project, percolating with a nightmarish brew of emotions. Another round of disappearing into the ladies' room to break down into herself and her feelings of remorse. At the computer terminal, everyone was all smiles. Robert and Tom's assistants were too busy stabbing each other in the back to notice her. When finally she couldn't keep her eyes open any longer, the chairman of the board had pity on her. He said they could spend that night in one of his houses.

Suddenly she felt that her pale pink lipstick made it apparent to everybody that she was a whore. But Robert said he loved her ten times that night, making her come in the chairman of the board's bed. Maybe this really was love instead of overtime.

They wanted her to make omelets the next morning—the maid was off. She told them she believed in self-sufficiency and cereal. It wasn't the worst lie she'd ever told. Tom substituted a couple of beers for breakfast while Robert tried to recover from the paucity of sleep with instant coffee. Robert called her a terrible woman in front of the men, for not whipping it up for him. She ran down the hall to the marble kitchen on the pretext of finding some milk and eggs.

That afternoon, Tom wanted to show off his new house in Tiburon to a couple of executives he'd just hired. It was an imitation Frank Lloyd Wright in all natural redwood. Ana tried hard to act impressed. Tom went off with Gerry and Mike to finish the *Wall Street Journal* on the deck, while Ana dragged Robert down the ramp to the water's edge for five minutes of nature. Robert talked about money and power, adjusting his Ray-Ban glasses. He wanted a seaplane to enjoy the waves and sunsets simultaneously.

She watched the moored boats on the opposite shore shifting uneasily in the water. She had nothing left to say. He stretched and smiled, pulling his shirttails out to impress the executives twelve years younger than he—her age, exactly—and walked back up the ramp to the deck, trying to look casual and nonchalant, although the deck had begun heaving up and down in the wind.

She should have found her way to the airport. Instead, she walked down the gravel driveway, holding Tom's discarded newspaper as an umbrella in the light rain as she stumbled down the main road into the little town. She busied herself with a rack of postcards outside a coffee shop, settling on one of the Golden Gate Bridge. It was the kind of postcard she would have bought for her sister, but she bought it anyway. She scrawled on the back of it in pencil, "Hi, Diane! Thinking of escaping from the world of men..." But what good was a flimsy postcard?

She lingered in a hat shop next to the coffee shop, unable to decide between a cowboy hat the color of a fawn or a red straw one with a feather that matched the dark red peonies in the window boxes outside the shop. The fragile beauty of peonies felt ludicrous compared to the stainless steel headquarters of W.C. Digital. A cowboy hat might give her the macho courage she needed to compensate for her naiveté, but the red feather of the straw one seemed to make a statement all its own.

A few minutes after she had bought the red one, a gust of rain carried it off into the harbor. She wandered over to the dock and watched the red straw bob up and down like a blob of bloody oil. To think that since she'd left New York City, all she'd managed to accomplish was buying a hat.

She lifted the flap of her knapsack, feeling around for her sister's knife with cold, damp fingers. She'd been carrying it around with her for months, waiting to perform some kind of ritual. She trembled in the cold breeze at the end of the dock. In the distance she could hear the moan of an approaching ferry. She tossed the knife over the side of the dock—it sunk quickly. It was a small moment of absolution without any special effects.

The hulking white ferry had arrived, divesting itself of cars and people, none of them paying any attention. Other people began to herd themselves on board, most of them vacationing and happy despite the dull, lusterless sky. A small dog in a transport cage began to whimper.

She wanted so much more than the fates of these ordinary Joes. Yet she thought of joining them on their exodus—anything to get away from Robert. While she stood on the dock debating their bourgeois values, the last SUV drove up the ramp and the ferry pulled away from the shore.

Finally, she decided, "I'm not going to allow my emotional life to thwart my aspirations," repeating her empty mantra into the waves that were whipping back and forth against the dock.

She looked out over the gray-blue bay streaked with wind and rain. She struggled to picture a goddess emerging as if from a great cloud of compassion. Kuan Yin would settle her flowing robes over the white caps, replacing the turbulence of the water with tranquility. Kuan Yin would stand on an ocean of mercy, offering her a white chalice of words.

The wind tore through Ana's hair at the end of the dock, as she closed her eyes and concentrated on the healing of the universe. If she had kept them open a moment longer, she might have noticed a set of hydraulics underneath the goddess's robes. But she was too busy clutching at Kuan Yin, trying to keep herself above water.

"Ana, dear," Kuan Yin was saying, beckoning to her and sighing deeply. "I have been envisioned for over a thousand years. I am your artistic creation now." Under her sad eyes hovered a delicate smile, wet as if newly painted on porcelain. The goddess beckoned Ana to follow her over the white caps, which had become as tame as a herd of white deer. Her tiny feet barely touched their backs as they leaped across the bay towards the distant ferry. It was bobbing in the water like a rusty toy.

Ana no longer felt herself submerged in a storm of emotions. She turned from the pier and began looking for a bus that would get her back to West Coast Digital in Silicon Valley. Now that she had Kuan Yin's blessings, all she needed was Tom Emerson's help to achieve her wildest artistic dreams.

"OK, can we print it yet?" Tom sauntered around the corner, a cup of coffee in his hands. He eyed Ana.

"Couple more hours," said Robert, eyes glued to the screen.

Ana sat at a second computer terminal on a tall stool with her legs crossed. She took some scissors out of the briefcase her father had given her and began to cut paper mattes. She carefully arranged them into three piles on the desk: Creator, Preserver, Destroyer. The first set of mattes were of the ballooning figure of a goddess from 6,000 B.C., her arms held high and legs spread wide in birthing. The second set would be devoted to the goddesses of Ancient Greece, animated to Isadora Duncan-style movement. She wasn't sure where she was going with the third set, but she was cutting away furiously, oblivious of the scraps of paper beginning to take over the floor. Her mind was sinking into the deep womb of the goddess, and West Coast Digital, with all its computer-generated effects, had evaporated into an Indian jungle.

Cobras wrapped themselves around the tree trunks, and monkeys screamed from the branches. The dark, powerful goddess Durga stalked through the dense jangala, mounted on a snow white tiger. When she reached the buffalo demon, he was in a rage. Two goddesses sprang up to aid her as he charged through the trees, nostrils on fire, swearing to destroy their universe. There was no telling where Durga's arms ended and Chandi or Bhairavi's began, because in one swift propeller movement their eighteen arms chopped off his head. The demon's headless body threw the goddesses against the treetops in a thick shower of blood. Their braids were too sticky with resin, their bodies too heavy, like fruit, their fingers too brittle, like twigs, to fly out of the branches. So they morphed into a thousand ants scuttling through secret corridors under the bark, dancing around the rings of the Trees of Life, whose limbs screamed with sap.

"Hey, the cleaning lady left already," joked Tom, kicking at the shards of paper covering the floor.

Robert looked up, startled. "Huh?"

"How you can concentrate with such a gorgeous lady breathing down your neck is beyond me, Bob."

"Oh, yeah," said Robert absent-mindedly, returning to his work. "Ana, go get me a pack of cigarettes, will you, doll?"

She spun around, scissors in hand, knocking her diet soda over the edge of the desk onto the paper scraps piled at her feet.

"Look what you made me do!"

"I really don't understand this obsession with hand-made art," said Tom. "I mean, we got programs that'll do all this in minutes."

"But Robert said..."

Robert interrupted. "We got our own way of doing things, even if they are a bit old-fashioned. Right, baby?"

Ana looked at the disheveled mattes on the desk and the floor, then gave him a hard stare. The significance of the morph demonstration at the D.I.C. finally hit home. Robert Poindexter could never measure up to that technology. He wasn't "state of the art" any more, and probably hadn't been for years.

She turned to Tom Emerson, Jr., who was playing computer games with a joystick. "You saw me cutting them by hand all night," she said to Tom. "You got something better?"

"It depends," said Tom. Ana dropped the scissors with a clank. "Let me help you. You must be tired," he offered, reaching over—perhaps to pick up the scissors or maybe the soda can, perhaps to gawk at her legs.

"Stop it! Just stop it," she said.

"Tom, listen up," said Robert. "Nobody's gonna offer her anything better'n what I gave her last night." Robert turned to Ana, who was white as a ghost. "Will you get me those cigarettes now?"

Silicon Valley was a study in fog. The last thing on her mind was Robert's cigarettes. She'd wanted the reassurance of his love, thousands of miles away from any semblance of home. She hadn't slept in days. Now he seemed to be treating her like any ordinary slut.

She stumbled across the parking lot to a phone booth, where she took off her high heels and tried to massage her ankles while waiting through a series of "beeps" for some kind of resurrection. The metal floor of the booth sent a chill through her bare, blistered feet. "Thank you for choosing AT&T," said the recorded message. "Thank you. Thank you," she repeated. Just let Diane be there for her.

"Hey, Diane," she said. But Diane was busy unpacking crates of computer equipment and office furniture in New York.

"Ana? Where the fuck are you? The moving van got here three hours ago." She walked between the crates, cradling a cordless phone.

"The what?" she said.

"The moving van," repeated Diane, thoroughly pissed. "You were going to help me move. Remember, sister?"

"Move? Oh, yeah. Well, I'm in sunny California." Diane was incredulous. "Diane, can you tell me what time it is?"

"Girl, what's wrong with you? Don't tell me you ran off with that Robert character."

"Can you send me $300?" asked Ana. "Please? Western Union?"

"Oh sure, women helping women," Diane shot back sarcastically. "How am I going to get it back? Creative ideas? Decorating advice? Moving some of my boxes? I mean, God only knows I moved yours."

"I'm sorry," said Ana. It dawned on her that she had no idea what had happened to the boxes that she'd left behind in San Francisco years before, let alone these other boxes.

"Are you even listening, Ana? Every dime I have is going into this company of mine, which I started by standing on my own two feet," said Diane. "I'm not sending you airfare for another one of your so-called radical art trips. You'd fly right off the deep end!"

"But, Diane," Ana pleaded, "you don't know how it is. He...the whole time in San Francisco, in Tiburon, in Silicon Valley, Robert hasn't been letting me sleep."

"If I were only so lucky!" said Diane. The moving men signaled to her that they were finished. "Listen, Ana. I don't have time for man talk. I've got another meeting with the agency in fifteen minutes, then I'm going to an opening over at the Whitney with a friend." She paused. "Didn't a round-trip ticket come with the job description? I mean, is it really so..."

Ana interrupted, "But I want to leave *now*!"

Diane sighed. "Call me back tonight, OK?"

Ana sank to the floor of the phone booth, exhausted. She nodded her head yes, unable to hide her sobs of disappointment.

"How many times do I have to tell you?" said Diane, eager to get off the phone. "Go to the bank for money, a restaurant to be served and fed, maybe a man for sex occasionally, but don't keep going to men for *everything*! Take care of yourself, do you hear?" Ana forced her shoes back onto her blistered feet. "Next time, call me collect," Diane was saying, but Ana had already trundled off to Robert, seeking his consolation.

At the computer terminal, Robert was snorting cocaine with Tom, who had started playing baseball. "It's a 23-hour home run!" cried Tom, pitching his imaginary ball at the wall-to-wall windows. Ana was just outside, fixing her mascara in the reflection of the glass. Robert was on his second line when she walked back into the room. He paused to look her up and down. "This is the real stuff," he said, offering her some.

"No, thanks. I detoxed my senior year in college," she replied.

"Oh. Bummer!" said Tom.

"Yeah." She was relieved that they believed her.

Robert stood up and stretched. He lumbered over to Ana and gave her a hug. They leaned on each other in exhaustion. "I thought you'd forgotten me by now," he said tenderly.

She stared at him unhappily. "Could I ever?"

"And I haven't forgotten your little project. In fact, I've been telling Tom here all about it," Robert continued.

"You have?" said Ana in alarm, "What have you told him?" Tom was sitting in Robert's chair, taking his turn at the cocaine.

"It's what he's been telling *me* that's so interesting. Simulation animation, yes siree!" he said boisterously. Tom laughed evenhandedly. "When we're back in New York, get ready to upgrade."

"OK, your turn," said Robert.

Finally. She riffled through the thousands of dog-eared animation drawings and travelling mattes which she had finished cutting out before her return to New York. They'd be ready to film as soon as Jack Stance replaced the burned-out bulb in the animation stand.

"I hope the lady's got a union card on her," Jack said to Robert.

"Sure, Jack. She pinned it onto her underpants this morning, right, Ana?" He winked.

Ana sidled up to Jack, ready for a showdown in her tough-looking jeans. "Just how many 'ladies' are in your union, Jack?"

Jack slammed the door of the 35mm camera shut in reply and left. Robert walked over to the animation stand—a twenty-foot monster. He reached over Ana's shoulder for a lever, brushing his arm against her flushed cheek. "Here, little lady. Let me help you," he said, but after a few whirs and whimpers, the machine grinded to a halt.

Somehow the program wouldn't lock into place, and Ana was coming equally undone, fighting to keep the tears from falling down her cheeks. Virgin goddesses like Aphrodite-Venus were about to morph into the mother goddesses like Demeter and the Madonna, morphing again into goddesses of destruction. Robert was undaunted. "We'll just work at this baby step by step. We'll get 'er up and running in no time."

"We've got to do it tonight," she beseeched him. "How long is this going to take?" What if there was no end to this relationship?

"Could be a couple hours," he said steadily, "unless a part's broken. Then it could be a few days." He loved taunting her. "Probably not weeks," he teased.

Ana grabbed Robert. "Please, please make it work."

He reached for the telephone and dialed. "Hey, Josh, good buddy. Yup, it's the midnight maniac. Get your ass up here or you're fired!" He listened for Josh's instructions and lowered his voice. "Yeah, can do."

Robert went over to the animation stand, manipulating some knobs and buttons. "Ooh, I want to touch your buttons, girl," he said to Ana as he worked.

Ana responded like a robot, "Let's do the optical, then have sex."

He stood up and assessed her. So an animation stand without a light source was like an affair without love—was that it? "Looks like we have to wait for Josh to fix this thing. I'd say that gives us just enough time for a quickie."

"Just show me how to use the machine," she shot back.

"OK," he said, catching his breath with equanimity. He handed her a heavy, 1000' 35mm magazine. "Let's see you put this on." Ana rose to the challenge and mounted the magazine on the animation camera. She tentatively screwed it down.

"Here?" she asked.

"Good girl," he said. She looked up at him, waiting for the next step. "Now open the door and thread the camera. Just follow the line."

"Follow the yellow brick road?"

"Exactly." She opened the camera and looked at its insides— so beautiful and handsome in its niches and protrusions—and threaded it, feeling increasingly competent. Robert trusted her enough to let her finish it up on her own.

She was just closing the camera door with a big grin, when Josh arrived. He was wearing his seersucker pajama top under a leather jacket, above his perennial blue jeans. He put his motor-cycle helmet on the rewind bench.

"Hey, good buddy," drawled Robert, backing into the room with coffee. "I'm awfully sorry to drag you out of bed."

"Something's wrong with this picture," said Josh, pointing to Ana. "What's she doing on the camera?"

"The camera's broken," said Robert. "We were just pretending."

"Your wife seems to think it's for real."

"Come on," said Robert. "Fix the camera. Get outta here."

But Josh was determined to discredit Ana. "Maybe she should learn programming, too. After all, isn't she an animator?"

"Yes," said Ana. "I am an animator, Josh."

"Shouldn't animators learn programming?"

Robert took a sip of his coffee. Checkmate. "Do you have to be a mechanic to drive a car?" he finally asked. After a cursory glance at the animation stand, Josh froze into his customary pose at the computer terminal, pecking at the keyboard with two fingers, fixating on the monitor.

Robert took a sip of coffee. "How does Vice President of Computer-Systems Operations sound, if we can get this turkey rolling?" he said. Josh stood up, leaned back over the keyboard, pressed a few more keys, then shifted his activities to the camera on the animation stand.

Without losing a beat, he pushed a lever. "Looks like it was rigged," he told Robert. He zipped his jacket over his pajama top, picked up his helmet and left. There was a dumbfounded silence, and then the machines clicked into gear.

Like the laundress painted by Vermeer, Ana leaned over the animation table. She had finished shooting over a hundred goddesses, and now she was shooting her images of Isadora Duncan, one by one. Frame by frame, Isadora danced, moving almost imperceptibly between the Doric columns of an ancient Greek temple. Panning up the columns as they multiplied in a dizzying zoom, they dissolved into the skyscrapers of New York, single-framing into day, then sunset, then night. The tall, proud rectangles compressed into pillars of light, which disintegrated into the tail smoke of octagonal starships, chasing through outer space.

Robert raised his head from the eyepiece. He was a tired puppy from working without stopping. "Ana, darling." She appeared by his side. "Look at my eyes and tell me if they're alright." She looked into the blue pools of his eyes, askance. "I'm just a little dizzy," Robert said. "I feel like I'm going blind."

"I'll be your eyes, Robert!" Ana said tearfully. But he closed his eyes as he embraced her. His son Conrad's cat watched them from under the computer table while they locked themselves into the darkroom.

"God! Do you ever wash this thing?" prodded Ana, pulling off his red shirt, the number 17 half-faded like the rest of it.

He gave her a puckish grin. "But it's my favorite shirt," he said, taking the rest of it off and wadding it into a ball. He came towards her, his bare torso gleaming with sweat under the green light of the darkroom. To hell with the film. He let it run while making love under the faded Playboy calendar that was nailed to the inside of the darkroom door.

Days and nights of work without stopping was taking a toll on their nerves.

"One single cat hair," he fumed. "One single cat hair finds its way into the gate, every single frame of this film's gonna have a white stripe running down the center of it." He glared at the cat, which his son never fed.

Ana was now his eyes that saw beyond seeing. She could see Robert's fragile lover, sleeping in the cottage outside Saigon, under the silk sheets. The bamboo curtains revealed jungle palms, silhouetted by a full moon. Palm fronds opened like a broken fan, rustling ever so slightly as a Vietcong soldier threw his grenade. The young lover opened her eyes momentarily, as if startled from a dream. Then suddenly, the room rocked and exploded in every direction, Vietcong and civilians screaming in agony.

She could see Robert's helicopter, whirling between snatches of thick, Cambodian jungle, where it hit the artillery fire. She watched it crashing in slow motion.

In her film, parallel, twin spaceships now circled overhead. Gracefully, they approached a vertical position, becoming the vertical columns of the Parthenon. But Isadora Duncan was no longer dancing in Greece. The columns no longer morphed into skyscrapers.

The columns had been replaced by cold, steel legs of an animation stand. Suzanne's voice echoed on the intercom as the cat lunged out from behind the rewind table, a piece of jagged film caught in its teeth like the tail of a rat.

"Let me talk to the slut," said the voice. "Let me talk to Ana."

"I *am* Ana," said Robert. Ana appeared next to the optical printer, listening to Robert's words. Her body lined up with the lines of his body, briefly morphing into his.

"I'll ruin you," said Suzanne's voice, like a cat clawing a block of ice. "I'll ruin you, if you don't return my husband." Ana laughed— as if Robert could be sent back like a tutu which didn't fit! Or was it Robert who was laughing?

"I'm leaving you," said Suzanne. "I'm leaving for New Jersey in the morning."

"Wait," said Robert. "Let me explain."

"Let me explain," echoed Ana's voice.

"I'll sue you for every last dollar you'll ever earn," said Robert's wife, "and when I leave, I'm taking Conrad with me."

Ana had come too close to the optical printer: her hair got caught in its wheels and spokes. The machine jolted to a halt as she tried to pull away from it in agony. Robert took an Exacto knife from the rewind table and hacked off a lock of her hair, freeing her. Her scalp was still burning with pain. She only let him hold her to keep herself from falling onto the cold, linoleum floor.

CHAPTER TWENTY-THREE

The Raga and the Ragini

*A man should not abandon his work, even if he cannot achieve it
in full perfection; because in all work there may be imperfection,
even as in all fire there is smoke.*

— The *Bhagavad Gita*

Ana panted up the old, rickety stairs after Robert. He was waiting for her in the stairwell to his Soho loft, five flights above the Monday morning traffic. Under a bare light bulb, his body cast a gargantuan shadow against the wall as he unlocked the steel door. A car horn beeped loudly somewhere on the street below, causing her to jump.

"Your ghosts are haunting me," she said.

He laughed lightly and ushered her into the loft. "Relax, Ana. The family's on vacation in Jersey."

He glided her across the varnished wood floor past a rack of frilly scarves and jewelry, plywood shelves stacked with dusty sci-fi paperbacks, and a cork board tacked with pictures of the family: Robert in military uniform propped between two parents; Suzanne in a modern dance leotard, circa 1975; a framed, color portrait of the bride and groom; and Conrad's baby picture.

"Please, I'm tired," she said.

"Then I'll pour you a drink." His long arms pulled champagne glasses down from the top cabinet, and bourbon out from behind the cereal boxes. "To Dionysus?"

"To Bacchus." She sniffed her drink distastefully, swallowing half of it in one determined gulp. She put the glass down on the ironing board in the kitchen alcove, on the other end of which a dance costume was hanging. "Got some condoms?" asked Ana.

"I think we have some floating around here," said Robert. He rummaged through a storage chest behind the partition and came across some marijuana. "We're all out. I have something better," he said. Ana opened her bag and took out her diaphragm. She was rubbing jelly on its rim when Robert reappeared, a joint of marijuana between his fingers, already lit. The slippery diaphragm slid to the floor. She picked it up, but Robert stopped her at the kitchen sink, offering her a toke of grass.

"I don't want it. I've quit," she said. He blew smoke in her face. Over the sound of running water, Ana thought she could hear the echoes of Suzanne's voice over the ticking of her biological clock. She could even feel their kinship, deep in her ovaries.

"I can't control myself any longer," she said, losing her mind and her body. "You better let me put in my diaphragm the next time we make love, unless you're planning to take responsibility for a baby."

"I want you to have the baby," he said with grave sincerity. "I promise to take care of it."

She already felt the doom of confinement. She had nothing to say to a chortling infant. "That's a lot of shit. You're never home to take care of the baby you already have."

"Stop it!" said Robert. "You sound like my wife!" She turned off the faucet. Robert took a long drag of marijuana. He took her glass of bourbon off the ironing board, offering it to her. "Nightcap?" He held it like a carrot in front of a donkey, maneuvering Ana to the waterbed.

"Everything I have, I want to be yours," he said.

Ana lay on the bed, overwhelmed by liquor and emotion. "So this is your empire," she said slowly. Robert put down the joint. He took off his clothes, then Ana's. He didn't look as fit as when she'd met him. The foreplay seemed a tad mechanical; the orgasm, trite.

Afterwards, she felt a little seasick. They had nothing much to say to each other. Rather, he said that he still loved her, but his voice held no passion, while she only seemed to love him the way that metal loves acid. She wanted something more witty if not brilliant to come out of his semi-educated mouth. All he could come up with were little silvery bubbles of his wife's spirit that Ana had stolen.

"I think we've had enough," said Robert, unamused. He tried to snub out the joint, but Ana knocked the ashtray to the floor, breaking it into little silvery pieces which leaped over the floor like Suzanne's troupe of dancers.

"Enough? Enough what?" she screamed, her voice echoing. "Enough decency to prevent you from attacking me in your office in the first place? Enough honesty to tell me you had a wife who had already saved you, and that you didn't need any saving? Enough intuition to guess how much I hate you?"

He walked over to her, trying to calm her, trying to avoid the broken glass. "Enough sex," he said. She trembled, tears running down her cheeks, turning to him as if to a comforting father with a cut in need of kissing. Robert held his head above her stiffly, lost in reflection. Then he got up and turned on the computer. It was time to check his email.

Madelyn came in from a brisk morning's walk wearing her red shawl with gold fringes. She found her daughter in the kitchen, rubbing out a charcoal sketch.

"Not only are your father and I upset, but I can imagine how upset the wife of this man must feel," Madelyn stated carefully. Ana busied herself by redoing Robert's face, although the lines shook—her hands were trembling and her eyes were red. Madelyn glanced down at the nude sketch: it was not half bad, though it could use an anatomy lesson.

Ana couldn't bear to look at her mother. She picked up a piece of burnt bacon. "I've been up half the night crying, OK?"

"Well, is he getting a divorce?"

"That's only half the problem." She paused. "Mom, try to understand. If I married Robert, I'd just be exchanging places with Suzanne. I'd be sacrificing my art while he ran out on me, too." Somehow she wanted her mother to sympathize.

"I can imagine," said Madelyn drily.

"His marriage is suffocating him," said Ana. "If I really loved him, I'd be with him right now. I haven't had the courage to run off with him, other than a few days on the West Coast—and those didn't count." She put down the uneaten bacon on the charcoal smudged plate. "I mean, it's not like we've started a company together. Maybe I'm just using him to help me with my art." She faltered. "Don't you want me to make something of my life?"

Madelyn poured out the bacon fat and tossed the frying pan into the sink. "Be sure to wash and dry this when you're through," she said, and started to put away the breakfast dishes.

"Maybe he's using you, too," she said, without looking at her daughter.

Ana stood up, too agitated to sit. "I've tried to stop seeing him. But Mom, I get so addicted to these men."

I'm going to stop, she said to herself. *I've got to stop.*

"Everything will be different when I finish this film," she said, trying to convince herself as well as her mother. "I'm going to get a regular job and move out once and for all. I'm going to travel to Japan. You'll never see me again." She began to hyperventilate. "What about you, Mom? Why didn't you ever run off?"

Marty's footsteps resounded on the stairs. Madelyn took the last of the breakfast glasses and poured herself a small gin and tonic.

"Why isn't the coffee ready, dear?" he asked.

She replied placidly, "I must be getting senile or something, dear."

He grabbed the bottle of gin and emptied it down the sink. "You're damn right you're going to be senile if you keep up this drinking."

"For God's sake, Marty, I was just being sarcastic," said Madelyn. "My memory is perfect, and so's my IQ. You know damn well it's higher'n yours."

"Not again," thought Ana out loud.

"Your perfect little angel wants another hand-out," said Madelyn. "It's not enough that we gave her a happy childhood."

"Verbal abuse didn't count in those days," Ana retorted.

"Verbal, schmerbal. All the money we gave her. The finest clothes, a summer camp in France. Ooh la la! And she has the nerve to complain!" Marty started to make coffee, grinding the beans in an electric grinder on the counter. "You know what she's doing, while you're working your fingers to the bone? She's whoring instead of working." Marty stopped grinding.

"Like mother like daughter," said Ana.

Her father's elbow hit the counter, spilling a few leftover coffee beans to the floor. "Just what are you implying?" he asked, barking like a Doberman. Madelyn announced that breakfast was over, and left through the back door, carrying out the garbage with her shawl thrown dramatically over her shoulder.

Ana went for the broom and started to sweep. "Mom's right, Dad. I need to request a small loan. It'd be against an N.E.A. grant. I'm sure it's forthcoming."

"Just how much?"

"$5,000? It's for this spectacular project. I'll invite you to the opening, Dad," she begged. "I thought it would cost $50,000 at first, but it turns out I was wrong. For only $5,000 I could pay some place to finish it. I wouldn't have to get my friends to help me any more."

"Spectacular, huh? Your mother wants $6,000 to renovate the kitchen." said Marty, thinking it over. "What's the narrative? I like a good story."

"There's no story, Daddy." He was hopeless. He was going to pour out a bowl of cereal for himself. He would never commit to helping her. He was probably planning to hide behind the cereal box. He was probably still ashamed of her. Like when she asked them to pick her up from college after being sexually assaulted. Her parents didn't take care of her. All they did was fly off to the Bahamas without leaving her a single dollar.

"So what were you girls yapping about all morning? Yap, yap, yap," he complained. He was reading the back of the box of Raisin Bran.

"Nothing," Ana said sadly. A loud rattle of garbage cans emanated from outside the window.

"You don't want to hear her story. She's so obsessed with this goddess story, she could probably find a million goddesses in the bubbles of a can of soda pop," said Madelyn, reentering with the empty garbage can. "You'd think those goddesses would have elevated her to the stratosphere by now."

Marty got up to put a cover on the garbage can. "You didn't have to take it out," he said. "I was going to do it later."

"Later? How many years later?" asked Madelyn, taking off the shawl. "You know, I'm going to have a lot more time for my studio, once this kitchen gets remodeled. Isn't it just wonderful how thoughtful your father always is?"

"Can I borrow the car?" Ana asked.

Madelyn interrupted. "Lend her the convertible. So I'll drive you to the station in the morning. She needs a break." Ana looked at her mother in surprise.

Her father rummaged for the keys in his pants pocket, handing them to Ana. "What are friends for?" he asked.

She hugged him, trying to be grateful. It was the first time ever that her father had actually loaned her one of his cars. Madelyn attempted a little tenderness by placing the red shawl over her daughter's shoulders. "Here," she said, smoothing its gold fringes, "so you don't catch a cold."

Ana turned and caught her mother's eye. For an instant, each recognized the other as trapped. *After I break up with Robert*, Ana wanted to say, *I'll devote myself to saving you from your bourgeois hell.* But there was nothing Madelyn could possibly gain from divorcing a divorce attorney. Maybe after her mother's divorce, they could look back together at their years of compromises, united by celibacy and poverty. It was too much to imagine. All Ana could do was to fling her mother's red scarf over her shoulders, climb into her father's sports car, and drive off.

The dark-green Corvette convertible zipped along the New Jersey Turnpike, Ana's small wicker suitcase in the back seat. She was mercifully drowning in jazz; it was pseudo-jazz, but still soothing. Ocean winds were beginning to chase away the pollution that had choked the East Coast practically all summer. With the top down, her long hair was impossibly tangled, but the breeze felt good. Soon she would reach Philadelphia. She sighed at the low, green hills surrounding her, wondering why she hadn't thought of nature for months.

She got off the turnpike and pulled into a gas station. She was near the Bryn Mawr campus, but that wasn't where she was headed: academia was a compromise that hadn't occurred to her beyond her own botched college years. She bought a map from the man behind the counter as if she didn't know where she was going, then asked for a key to the ladies' room. Thank God it was a clean one! She had snuck in an empty glass jar to begin the ritual of her break-up with Robert. She peed into it, then fixed her hair.

With the lid screwed on tightly, she got back into her father's Corvette and took off. A few miles further, she pulled to the side and unfolded the map. It came in handier than she'd thought. Finally she reached the street where the Poindexters came from, feeling increasingly awkward about her compulsive curiosity to drive to this place in the middle of nowhere, sullenly shrouded with trees.

She looked up apprehensively, letting the uncomfortable sensation of being in an unfamiliar location submerge itself into the heat.

Ana climbed out of the convertible, looking for the Main Line mansion of Robert's boyhood. But none of the buildings were numbered. Maybe it was one of the houses being torn down to make way for a cheap development: men were digging a deep pit across the way.

Next to some two-storied plywood skeletons stood an old oak tree. Some old gray planks were propped up against it, possibly the remnants of Robert's tree house. It had probably been a tour de force, with oak paneling. Probably he had had a sign made for it, like "No Girls Allowed." Now it was nothing but a pile of rotting wood and rusty nails.

She walked up and down the block, collecting dead leaves, oblivious to the whistles and hoots of the construction workers. Then she sat down in exhaustion on a deserted bench at a bus stop, sweating under a suffocating beam of sunlight which insisted on interrogating her. She opened up the wicker suitcase. Lying on top was the cheap, spiral notebook. Its pages smelled somewhat mildewy, setting off a wave of nausea.

"I really must be pregnant," thought Ana, beginning to panic. She opened up the pillow book and found a chewed-up pencil in her bag. But after all this time, her feelings were so bottled up inside of her, they wouldn't come out. She turned the Walkman loud enough to drown out her thoughts and took out every other item the suitcase contained—a vial, a tube, a dropper, a test well, a test stand, the glass jar of urine, and instructions.

"Blue means I'm pregnant. Clear means I'm not," she muttered to herself, and took a deep breath. She wrapped the shawl around herself and conducted her pregnancy test: She would have to wait for the results. The sunlight was giving way to deeper shadows. She pulled the red shawl more tightly over her shoulders, its gold fringes falling into her lap.

She sat silently on the bench, very silently, twirling a red leaf. She raised it in front of her eyes, twirling it in front of the dying sun, counting down the seconds. The leaf kept on twirling, its veins pulsing against a bleeding sunset, dancing like the ballerina in red shoes, dancing and dancing. She had to keep dancing until she found out whether or not she was pregnant. If she was pregnant, would it be a boy, jumping out of tree houses with a wild, exuberant yell, or a girl, who'd learn to plié like Robert's wife? Or a boy who'd plié or a girl who'd yell? She twirled the leaf faster and faster. Boy, girl, boy, girl? A minute later, she put the leaf down on the bench and looked at the clear circle of the test. Negative: There was nothing in her womb but emptiness.

Well, what a relief, she told herself. She blinked at the stupefied men across the way, and rushed back into the sports car in search of the nearest phone booth.

"You've reached National Image," said the recorded announcement. "We're unable to take your call at the moment, but please leave a message at the beep. Our regular hours are Monday through Friday, 9 AM to..."

At a truck stop on the New Jersey Turnpike, Ana tried again, mooching a couple of quarters from someone at the counter. In despair at reaching nothing but an answering machine, she tried to call a friend for sympathy—any friend. She reached Tammi Bradley—no longer Bradley-Birnbaum, or any other hyphenate.

"Is this another one of your pretentious Little Prince boy-genius types?" asked Tammi, cutting off Ana's whining, blow-by-blow account. "Your 'feminism' is a joke!"

Ana was taken aback. She muttered something about wanting to move on with her life.

"I've got to get back to the lab," says Tammi. "I'm doing a glaucoma fellowship at the Eye Institute. Nice to hear from you."

Robert was working around the clock, trying to maintain normalcy while his father-in-law puttered with the inventory, covering the rewind table with heavy ledgers. Josh retreated into the darkroom. MoMo and Jack were in the corner, fighting over union rules. Nobody picked up the phone.

"I passed your fucking union test," said MoMo, who was ready to move up.

"The boys say you missed by one point," said Jack, picking up his hat to go home.

"Don't 'one point' me, Jack," MoMo said, taking a swipe at him. "Missed again."

This time, MoMo punched Jack squarely in the stomach. Jack pushed back with a vengeance, rolling them onto the floor. He was about to ram MoMo's head against the optical printer, when Len and Josh grabbed them and pried them apart.

Robert had continued working through the fight, oblivious to union rules, his eyes encircled with red bruises from constantly pressing one eye, then the other, to the eyepiece of the optical printer, obsessed with action and horror.

Greyhounds gave high-speed chase around a track, encircling it over and over; heroes on horseback bludgeoned their way in slow motion. Police cars in hot pursuit exploded; he had difficulty breathing. Ana's open sports car raced against the motorcycles of the villains: she was gaining on them, her gold-fringed red shawl flailing against the wind. Suddenly, a crash: two Greyhound buses collided behind her. They burst into flames. The camera zoomed in on her face, as the sound of a siren melted into a vampire howl. The vampire leaned forward toward the camera, teeth in position for the final bite. Robert toggled the motor forwards and backwards, dissolving the vampire's face into Ana's decapitated head. Her eyes were frozen open, staring out at him through his eyepiece. He zoomed the image out to include a red shawl, its tattered fringes tangled in the still spinning wheel of her wrecked convertible.

Robert stood up. He fingered a snake-like strand of film that had gotten caught in the printer, and rubbed his eyes as though death had appeared in a crystal ball. No more all-nighters, by golly.

"Get a good night's rest, son," said Len. He closed the books, preparing to go home. MoMo and Jack had already gone. Robert threw an empty pack of cigarettes away and staggered towards the door. His father-in-law grimly shuffled the last of the papers, locked the books in the cabinet, and followed Robert out.

Suzanne was back from New Jersey, sleeping in the loft as if nothing had ever happened. Robert had finally come in for a good night's sleep. The sound of the heavy steel door had finally woken her up. She pulled on her red velour robe and straightened some pillows under his head. He pulled an arm out from under the covers, badly in need of some warmth. But she had moved on to the kitchen alcove, in search of a glass of milk for Conrad, who had climbed out of his bunk bed to play on the computer. That was the problem with Soho lofts: no privacy.

Robert smoked a cigarette and watched his son proudly without interrupting him. That kid was already more computer-savvy than half the people in his office. Suzanne sprawled out on the waterbed and seemed to have gone back to sleep. He lit up another cigarette after his son finally climbed back up into the bunk bed and nodded off. At last, Robert, too, drifted into a deep sleep.

He dreamed that Ana was telling him to smile for a photograph. But instead, he threw a bottle of wine at the ceiling. It shattered into little pieces. Wine and blood dripped down her face. Walls and bricks crumbled as the building became a molten crater of her blood.

"Conrad!" screamed Suzanne. She sprang out of bed like a lion, her booming voice echoing into the empty sky. A fire was devouring half of the loft. She grabbed her son, who was still half-asleep, and raced to the staircase, followed by Robert, frantic to guide his family down the stairs to the street below.

When the fire truck arrived, there was some difficulty reaching the top floor of the building to put out the fire. But Robert pulled his wife close to him, trying his best to be reassuring despite the feeling of overexertion. "It's all right, dear. We're safe now."

Suzanne pulled away. "All right?" she screamed. "How dare you call this 'all right'? My whole life is going up in flames!" The costumes and sets for the Suzanna Moss Dancers had turned to ash and twirled against the billowing smoke. She looked up and sobbed.

Robert took Conrad out of her arms and climbed into the ambulance. The little boy was overcome by smoke — his breathing was wheezy and irregular. His wife got into the back of the ambulance and placed herself near Conrad's gurney. She stared out the window as the empty streets flew by, while Robert held tight to his son, as if for the very first time.

Ana lay in a shaft of light across the pink chenille bedspread, redialing Robert's number. Madelyn promptly got on the extension phone in the master bedroom. "Ana, we're in the middle of a fundraiser for Westchester Arts, so get off the phone already. It's very upsetting and embarrassing. Thanks."

Take your society balls and shove them up your ass, screamed Ana inwardly as she made her way to the bathroom and opened up the medicine cabinet. Inside was a small brown spider, intent on poisoning her life. She smashed it with a kleenex, then took out a pair of tweezers and started plucking out her eyebrows. She knew she had to stop reacting like an adolescent, but she couldn't help it. At least Robert treated her like an adult.

She would never listen to her mother again. She was plucking out most of her eyebrows. If she didn't stop it immediately, she would have almost no expression left. She stared at her face in the mirror—it was swollen and blotchy. Only Robert could save her. Hadn't he said he was going to make her the vice president of his company? Well, she should obviously reconsider that. She'd always wanted a partner. There was no way she was going to allow her mother to stop her from a fairy tale ending.

Robert stared at Conrad's toy trains on the conference table. His face was seared with soot from the fire, and glued to his body was his football jersey, the color of dried blood. Conrad's trains echoed like an optical printer, clattering around the track. MoMo and Josh arrived and began to dismantle film equipment, but Robert failed to respond. He had taken ahold of the little golden yellow film cores made of plastic that his son had liked to play with. He spun them around and around in empty circles.

MoMo was concerned, both for Robert and his own job security. "Hey man, you need an Anacin or something?" Robert had nothing to say. "Bufferin? Something a little heavier, boss?"

He proffered a joint and hinted at cocaine, but Robert was busy staring into space, praying for his son's recovery. Josh signaled MoMo to cool it. "He's a cat with nine lives," Josh whispered. "I've seen this movie before."

In the first movie, Robert Poindexter crashes an elevator. It's a double bill with his father's Rolls Royce crashing at the end of a drag race: Dad manages to pull Robert's body out of the wreck. Movie Number Three is "Boy meets girl-next-door and gets her pregnant" with a twist: He gets away. Number Four is his first wife—Debby bleeds to death, but he survives. He wants to kill his second wife, but it's only his fifth movie; they divorce amicably. Number Six is a war film in which everybody dies, including his Vietnamese mistress. Then comes the helicopter crash in the jungles of Cambodia. And now there's an eighth one starring the dancer Suzanne Moss, who demands a divorce. He has one life left.

The last thing on his mind was helping Ana.

CHAPTER TWENTY-FOUR

Sisters

A saint, if one considers only the beauty of his intentions,
a fool, if one looks at the result.

— George Sand

Diane marched a near-suicidal Ana into Robert's office. She placed herself at the other end of the conference table from Robert Poindexter, with her arm around Ana. Diane was wearing her no-nonsense tight-fitting suit.

"Look, this is an artist-in-residence with a deadline... Are you going to help with the artist part, at least?" demanded Diane.

Robert looked dazed. "I..." He looked at Ana. "We're going bankrupt. I'm sorry."

"Then why don't you give this girl back her elements? Because you have obviously failed to follow through with them!"

Ana turned to Diane like a child. "Can I have a moment with him? Please?" Diane assessed her ditzy friend, then left to make a phone call.

Ana walked hesitantly around the conference table. The car wreck had been a figment of Robert's imagination. She sat down next to him, moving the vinyl-leather chair closer to him, and opened the paper bag in her lap. She focused on pulling out the dried-out leaves which she had collected, carefully, so as not to break them.

"The old place is gone," she said sadly.

"I know," said Robert.

"I think, um, these came from your oak tree." He was confused. He twirled one of the brown leaves, then let it drop.

Ana persisted. "The one in Bryn Mawr, with the tree house. You told me all about it, remember?"

"Oh. Yes." He looked at her, yet barely saw her. "You climbed that old white elephant?"

"Oh, no. I just looked at it," Ana said. "Looked at where it used to be." He was deeply moved, and yet did not embrace her. She looked up expectantly, her hope a flickering candle, as he stood up and walked out of the room.

He opened the filing cabinet, which had already been moved toward the exit door. He pulled out the programming of her computer graphics and the filmed mattes of Isadora Duncan. This was the signal for Diane to get off the phone. She walked over to Robert and held out her hand.

"Who are you?" he asked.

"Diane," she said, shaking his hand. "Diane Campbell."

Diane and Robert began to confer while walking into the hall. Their speech was suddenly drowned out by the knocking of metal against metal, as MoMo wheeled an empty handcart out of the elevator. He stopped in his tracks, looking Diane over.

Robert cleared his throat. "Ms. Campbell, this is Moses Baron, Assistant Vice President, Creative Affairs." MoMo looked at Robert as if he had gone crazy—with National Image going bankrupt, titles were meaningless.

"Oh, here," said Diane absent-mindedly. "Let me give you my card." She opened up her Vuitton bag and pulled out a business card, handing it to MoMo as she got on the elevator. He held it in his hand like a four-leaf clover.

Robert had never planned to pull another all-nighter again, but he conceded the necessity of spending one final night working with Ana at Diane's new company, Rainbow Graphics, Inc. It was right on track for success: simple, tasteful, and well-stocked with all the hard-won equipment, supplies, and material needed for a small, commercial post-production company. Diane had also acquired a Bichon Frisé, which curled up in a little white ball on a small square of carpet. The only thing that wasn't working was the air conditioner. That put them much further on edge as they huddled over the small effects bank, stinking of sweat, racing to feed goddess images into the scanner.

"You don't know shit about Virtual Reality, let alone any other kind of reality," Diane was bragging to Robert. "A 4,000-line scanner's just the beginning."

"Oh yeah? Tell me about it," said Robert, wanting to scapegoat Diane's success.

"Someday you're going to put the monitors over your face and *feel* the movie running through your body," she said, above his jibes.

"Sure," said Robert. "I know all about that."

Ana ignored the future-speak, aware of how fast technology changes. She just wanted to finish *The Cyborg Goddess* before the normal workday began, and was glad that Diane had talked her into sticking with it. To her, the computer passes had become like telling beads, chanting a mantra over and over. She was finally feeling competent.

"Then you doubtlessly know about the Quadra 950 I just bought. With one $20,000 system, I can do more than five major studios," Diane insisted.

Robert was busy calculating in his head: prices were always coming down. She waved at him as if to wake him up. "My new company's going to have all that stuff in it and more," he said.

Diane smoothed her hands over the console. "Look at this baby. My SGI 4D/80GT."

"It'll be out of date in six months," said Robert, jealously. "I guarantee you."

Ana looked up from the keyboard. "I like this idea of fusing them all together," she said. "Here, look!"

Robert and Diane looked into the video monitor. The reflection of Ana's face had melded into Isadora's. Dancing in full, three-dimensional glory, she finally had morphed into the Winged Venus, and flew towards the camera, morphing again into the Sumerian Queen of Heaven and Earth. Out of her morning star came Lilith, her dark wings unfolding in grandeur to reveal the goddess Oshun, whose sparkling rivers returned to Gaia's womb. Each river was flowing with a myriad of goddesses—from those ancient, nameless goddesses once lost to history, to the goddess Mayahuel with her four hundred breasts.

But here the goddess imagery faltered. Each seemed phonier and more pretentious than the last. Would the goddesses have compassion for Ana's less than perfect rendering of them, or would their smiling faces leer at her like men? For truly, she had been more wrapped up in their cartoon-like, glitzy images than in the unfolding of consciousness. She cursed the charlatans who had produced so many goddesses and gods like can-can dancers and their Johns.

An extraordinary weariness set over her as she watched the goddesses of the night go by in a slow procession—Durga, mounted on her tiger, morphing into Isis, on her throne. Isis, the Great Mother, was supposed to reach out to heal all of us whose mothers enslaved us out of the emptiness of their broken hearts. Could she heal Ana's mother Madelyn from having been raped as a child? Heal Ana's great-grandmother Rosa, who'd watched her mother raped and killed by Cossacks? Heal her great-great-grandmother Deborah, thighs as heavy as the scrolls of a Torah? Heal countless ancestors she couldn't name, born into slavery in Egypt?

Crying from the lap of Isis was Horus, the baby she never was going to have, his infant cries echoing into vast chambers of heartache. She found herself tearing through countless veils of Maya, scarcely able to breathe and crying with frustration at the weight of so many illusions. Every veil she took off brought her that much closer to nakedness, in a slow motion dance of frozen tears. Hour after hour of whoredom pulled away from her consciousness. Her first hour of whoredom under Philip, another with Andy, fucking beside a river of regrets. Another hour with Karl, which felt like a hundred years. Then another, and another.

She was swinging her umbilical cord to the Goddess around the universe like a giant lasso. But none of the goddesses were going to allow her to redeem herself; instead, they were mocking her, along with her sister.

She leapt up into the arms of the Shekhina, swearing to devote the rest of her life to the visions of the soul, rather than the eye. The Shekhina enfolded Ana under her wing like a mother. Under her other wing lay Vickie, her labia open like the pages of the book she'd meant to write about her sister. *O Mother! Cover us both with your blanket of invisibility!*

Beyond the seeable lay the Divine, something way beyond digital, that Ana could never comprehend but only guess at, like a toddler encountering grown-ups in sexual union. Here was the Shekhina with God, creating galaxies, while hundreds of other goddesses stuck to her underwings like fleas. Ana realized her folly in having segregated the male and female cosmic principles, and the futility of finding images for what has no likeness.

What could goddesses possibly say to a patriarchal God? She could imagine His eye scanning the face of the earth, but it was impossible to scan the face of God. From His perspective, goddesses were merely sequins sewn to something worn once on a red carpet, or again under a street lamp. Now they were glittering on His golden robe as if He were about to go into the ring to face Satan. If thousands of goddesses were thrown into the face of God, He would possess them like hairs on His beard. And she had been trying in vain to pluck them, to eradicate the phallocentric concept of God.

If only her art could be erased, and in its place, infinity granted! In this humility lay the possibility of greatness. No longer would art issue from Ana's ego, like a geyser in a National Park drenching tourists with awe. Rather, Ana's vision seemed to have slid out of her without effort or labor. Without a single cry of protest. Her art was more like a rare flower that blooms once a year in the moonlight, when most people are asleep. But the flower was already wilting.

Here came Diane with the champagne glasses, striding across Rainbow Graphics, Inc. Ana's little project seemed complete. Robert was downloading it onto a second hard drive.

Diane grabbed a bottle of French champagne from the refrigerator, the Bichon Frisé yapping at her feet. "It's a left-over bottle from my opening—which you didn't attend," said Diane. "I forgive you," she added, twisting the cork and pouring.

Diane and Robert toasted Ana, who looked radiant, but felt shallow. "To great art," said Robert.

Great art is made with feelings, thought Ana. She had cut herself off from her feelings like a cyborg and tried to transcend them like a Goddess. Her artistry had evaporated.

"Maybe this'll be a top CD some day!" said Diane brightly, always thinking ahead to grosses and distribution. Then they clinked glasses. But the latest thing in technology was turning to ashes, even as its ghost was being readied to distribute to the next phantom culture.

For a moment, she understood what the poet Rumi meant by the "bright core of failure." It was that awesome silence that could fill one's soul when the roars and whispers of desire had faded into nothingness.

Robert gave Ana a small hug. "Friends?" he asked her. Her face was a study in mystique. "Everything's OK, honey," he said, jostling a few papers in his briefcase. "I just gotta spend some time with my kid. I'll give you a ring in a couple of weeks, as soon as everything settles down and the pressure's off." She smiled, maintaining the fiction of friendship, but she knew she would never see him again. "OK?"

Diane opened the blinds, revealing the New York City dawn. The sun was just rising over the skyscrapers. Robert looked out the window.

"Well, Robert," said Diane. She paused. "Aren't you going to wash your face?" He touched his cheek, which was still smudged with soot from the fire. He grinned like a puppy and ambled off, saying, "Going, going, gone."

Robert found himself in the morning rush hour crowd trying to enter the Port Authority Bus Terminal. He was pushing past commuters, homeless vets, winos and prostitutes, sweating in the relentless heat wave, when his beeper went off. He made his way towards a row of crowded phone booths and waited his turn.

"Hey! When are you coming out to California, you lucky dog?" Tom Emerson, Jr. was saying.

"Well, Tom..." Robert hesitated. "I don't know." An overweight businessman in his late fifties was gesturing impatiently to use the phone.

"You don't know? How about Wednesday...Like, tomorrow! You've just won yourself a small fortune, compliments of our Board of Directors, to start your long-imagined empire! Whaddaya say to that?"

"I'll be darned," said Robert, softly.

"See ya tomorrow, good buddy!" said Tom.

Robert hung up the phone and walked out of the phone booth into the bright, sunshiny day. A flock of pigeons circled overhead. He squinted at them. Then, with great determination and resolve, he tore down his own image...

...and strolls up to the reception desk of International Image, his gleaming new corporate headquarters, complete with palm trees swaying in the breeze to upbeat music. In his off-white Armani suit, ROBERT POINDEXTER looks as glamorous as a

Hollywood star. The reception desk sports a state-of-the-art PC, a laser printer, and a lavish floral arrangement. Behind the chrysanthemums CHRISTI, early 20's, the new receptionist, sits fiddling with a bottle of Wite-Out. She looks like she's headed for the pages of a *Who's Who* of blonde, ambitious females—and yet equally vulnerable. Robert gives her an incorrigibly long wink...

...FREEZE FRAME onto Diane's monitor.

She'd been watching the story all along, or perhaps she'd invented it. Diane put her computer into interactive mode, and Ana pushed the "delete" button.

"Hey, girl. You gonna fall for someone different next time, for a change?" asked Diane, folding up her eyeglasses.

Ana laughed. "I need a sabbatical from men," she said. "I can't control myself around them. I think I'd better stick with machines for awhile."

"Make 'em more human?"

Ana hugged Diane, laughing, ignoring the passing of whatever love Robert had felt towards her.

"Humanity's an awfully big word," she said.

"Something to aspire to..."

That's exactly what she needed: a new and lasting aspiration. She threw her arms around Diane again, wanting to shower her with hugs and kisses. "I feel like you're my real sister. My sister and my only real friend." She began to cry. She took out a wadded up kleenex and blew her nose. "How can I ever repay you?"

Diane put her at arm's length and picked up her dog. "Honey, that's the easy part. You've just bartered ten hours of on-line for designing Rainbow's logos and graphics: that's eighty hours of your time, minimum. You can put it all in your portfolio; then we'll move on to more commercial things. Sell out and make your parents proud."

Ana quickly started doing the math. After eighty hours, ninety tops, she could probably get at least several hours' paid work somewhere, anywhere, enough for a ticket to India, if things didn't pan out in New York.

"You can count on me from now on, Diane," said Ana. "Cross my heart and hope to die." If Diane would only give her another chance for a real job! Surely there was more to this friendship than a few measly hours of part-time work.

"Look up," said Diane.

Ana was bubbling over with hope, for the moment. "There's no glass ceiling here," she said, reaching out to give Diane a high five, her spiritual humility fading fast.

But that's not exactly what Diane had in mind. She was thinking the ceiling could probably use another coat or two of paint.

CHAPTER TWENTY-FIVE

Anagrams

…Nothing is first and nothing is last;
nothing is future and nothing is past;
nothing is old and nothing is new…
except, perhaps, the anagram itself.
— Maya Deren

It was a bright suburban Saturday. Afternoon sun bathed the hills of Westchester with golden light. Ana sped along the Taconic in the silver BMW. Speeding made her feel less trapped, if only for those few miles. She could let the golden oldies blare. Thank god the work week was over!

Now that she and Robert had finally broken up, she could go anywhere and do anything she wanted. But what was the point?

The Cyborg Goddess was an unholy piece of plastic with a hole cut in its center, scarcely the Great Round of the Great Goddess. She could smell the acrid, burning plastic as it was remaindered. She wished she could remainder the men in her life the same way.

To fill the void, Ana decided to visit the dog pound. She could have nabbed a husband if she really wanted one: she was still attractive enough, with her long black hair and long white legs. Her breasts were small but powerful, and her clitoris had turned to gold. But after going through a dozen lovers, she felt she'd be better off with a dog. She turned off the parkway and up a quaint country road, dappled in sunlight. The pound was enclosed in an anonymous complex, protected by old elms. Not a cloud in sight, except for billowing smoke from the incinerator. As she got out of the car, the pungent smell of death reminded her of the ovens of the Holocaust that she had once filmed. She tried masking her sense of moral shame in a short spurt of coughing as she made her way into the plain cement building.

At least she could pluck out one of the dogs before it was put out of its misery. The variety of dogs to choose from was staggering: Dalmations, Pomeranians, Chow-Chows or Great Danes. She couldn't leave them all here in the pound to die—surely there was one breed or one dog that was special. She glanced at their yapping, drooling faces and thought of the faces of her lovers, looking hopeful, neglected, or still panting, ready to smell her up.

She'd barked up all the wrong trees of life, howled at the wrong moons and dug up the wrong bones. All those lovers with their bribes and promises! The important thing, the shrinks had insisted, was to get past the negatives: no more love at first sight, no prisons of fidelity, and nobody abandoning her, dropping her off between the moon and the earth. She'd been orbiting ever since, waiting to land. And now she was either going to get a dog, or marry herself.

She needed to resist torturing herself with doubt again as a large black Newfoundland nuzzled the side of her hand through the chain metal fence. The smell of his cage was overwhelming: it hadn't been hosed down in ages. She wanted to belong to something — not just to any old animal or man, but to a meaningful cause, or a belief. No more spiritual gurus like Andy, with his pseudo-tantric Buddhist quotes when they got high. All those men she'd worshipped were mosaics in a church whose walls had crumbled. She didn't want to convert any more. If only she could find her way into rebirth through another spiritual realm. She just needed an opportunity to start all over, free of negative karma. Why not India?

Once she was back in the car, a dog let out a mournful howl. She could have stopped to reconsider, but instead pulled out onto the road and rolled open the windows for a breath of fresh, cool air. The wind had already blown her seven thousand miles away from the billowing smokestack of the pound.

Ana intended to research the religions of India with the same fanaticism which she could have used to research breeds of dogs, if she weren't planning to travel abroad. Her bed was a collage of crumpled job applications, pamphlets from travel agencies and guidebooks from the library, open helter-skelter to pages full of temples and mosques, Hindu deities, Jain paintings, and statues of Buddha — 34 caves full of gods and goddesses in Ellora alone, just thirty kilometers west of Aurangabad, in Maharashtra, right smack in the middle of India.

It was one thing to have sexually liberated herself in college on the Pill. But it would be a quantum leap forward to be spiritually liberated. To become spiritually liberated through sex like these Hindu gods and goddesses — what a thrill! An entire religion of lingams and yonis, honoring sexuality for time immemorial. Siva and Lakshmi's sexual postures were not only awe-inspiring, but do-able. It had been wrong to isolate the goddesses from the gods: the universe burst with cosmic activity each time they made love.

Compared with the Indian gods and goddesses, those of the West now seemed phony and pretentious. For the most part, the Greek Aphrodites looked like Playmates of the Month. On her pillow lay a heavy volume opened to a black and white photograph of Chakreshwari, whose four arms held out wisdom, compassion, fearlessness and the wheel of life.

Meditating on a smorgasbord of Indian goddesses and gods would keep her on a higher plane, she thought. However, it was more pragmatic to think in terms of a grant, if she wanted to go to India and experience them in person. And so, whipping together a proposal, *The Cyborg Goddess* was put to use as a demo reel for her International Art Film Association application, "Numinous Goddesses: Gender in the Religions of India," focusing on the ancient matriarchal goddesses of the Hindu, Jain and Buddhist religions.

The grant was only enough for some videotape and film stock. But it was so validating to find support of any kind, that she finally quit her humiliating job working for Diane. She sold most of her worldly possessions, except for her cameras.

She counted out the cash from her stereo, the last two paychecks, some second-rate jewelry from second-rate lovers, silver bracelets and the pearls. It was just enough for a round-trip discount ticket from JFK to India. The flight would go as far as Madras, on the opposite side of the subcontinent as the Great Thar Desert. Far beyond, she would reach a palace of white marble, shining like a lotus on the blue pond called Earth.

At the edge of the lawn next to the pool, Madelyn was feverishly unpotting pansies, her dyed blonde hair glowing in the sunlight. She often gardened when something upset her. She still saw herself as an Abstract Expressionist; gardening was just a hobby.

"It's ridiculous to go to India in the summer." She patted some of the flowers into the dark soil, freshly mixed with manure. "It's so hot, your clothes will cling to you."

Ana stared at her mother's Laura Ashley dress, stuck to her bra and girdle with sweat.

"Allow me my one spiritual journey," said Ana, already on the defensive.

"Spiritual? You?"

Ana chose not to fight. A hajj would allow her to get out of her parents' house for once and for all.

"Oh, come off your high horse — you've already achieved enough," said Madelyn, selecting a rake as if it were a paintbrush. "There's no need to prove yourself any more! All those documentaries: Why don't you just concentrate on losing weight for a change? A dog's a good idea — it'll force you to get some exercise." Madelyn tugged forcefully at some weeds with the rake, trying not to soil her dress in the process. She resented her daughter for not volunteering to help.

But Ana had never been the helpful type. She pushed her way past her mother and disappeared into the house. This time she was determined to meditate, if only to calm down from her mother's ridicule. Pushing the clutter of pamphlets aside, she scrunched her legs into a lotus position in the middle of her bed, closed her eyes, and took three deep breaths.

At first it was hard to focus on anything other than the pins and needles of her crossed legs. But she let herself go and slowly began to hear something reverberating in her mind. It was Sarasvati, the Goddess of Learning, soothing her with golden notes of music from the gentle movement of her fingers over an iridescent vina.

Her meditation deepening, Sarasvati's sensuous voice sang out to her with the promise of true liberation: a vast, divine liberation beyond the sexual type that Ana knew so well, and beyond the women's liberation that she had more or less ignored. One good orgasm and she'd been ready to worship at some man's altar for the rest of her life. If only she had longed for gods like Vishnu and Krishna, instead of assholes like Robert and Karl.

With thoughts like these, it was impossible to keep meditating. Ignoring the numbness in her feet, she uncrossed her legs and got up off the bed to make a list of ingredients for her escape. She'd already popped some quinine into her old knapsack, along with her 16mm Bolex and her 35mm Nikon.

She would like to have run off to India as a penitent, unburdened by material objects. But on the evening of her departure, she was carrying on her shoulders a brand-new fifty-pound Betacam package that a board member of the International Art Film Association had lent her, along with a small tripod and a sun gun. None of this camera equipment counted, compared to Ana's clay beads for chanting "Om Tare Tuttare Ture Soha" to the goddesses of India—and it all fit in the overhead compartment. The roar of

Air India's engine drowned out her chanting on the flight, sounding more and more devout the closer they came to landing.

Ana arrived in Madras like any other tourist, in awe at having finally arrived through so many time zones, but plunged into confusion by the foreign languages and accents. She was swept up by a masala of noise: the enthusiastic welcomes of tourist guides; loud hawking of brightly colored silks, fake jewels and clay vessels; desperate sounds of begging; and the honking of auto-rickshaws beyond the airport exit. The noise was giving her a headache, and she worried that she'd brought too much heavy equipment.

She thought of contacting her old college classmate, Behram Sinha, for guidance and help. Didn't he owe her a few favors? Fifteen years ago, she had left a copy of *Howl* in the back seat of Behram's Volkswagen bus. But Behram resided in an ashram now and did not wish to be disturbed. Well, boola, boola—if *he* could climb the spiritual path, so could she. She wondered whether she had really found the most direct route for her pilgrimage to Mt. Meru, the center of the universe.

She hoisted up her cameras and hurriedly claimed the rest of her baggage, rushing off in an overpriced taxi to the train station. Overflowing with people, children, mosquitoes, shapeless bags and cartons of all descriptions, steaming with the smells of humanity, the third class train wound its way across the dry, tree-covered plains of Maharashtra.

Around the curve of a river stood her first destination: Ajanta. Above her beckoned the caves, carved out of the rocky cliffs. She had read about their hidden wealth of sculptures and frescoes not only in the brochures, but in the four volumes published under the Special Authority of His Exalted Highness the Nizam. It was worth the climb up to get an establishing shot. The camera equipment was heavier than she had thought, but she managed to lug it all up the steep path to the top of the cliff. She was only overcome by the scent of jasmine flowers, sold at the mouth of the cave where the tour bus deposited the other tourists.

She fanned herself with a guidebook, impatient to get a second wind and proceed into the caves. But the statue of a king outside of Cave No. 19 looked unnervingly like Lawrence of Yale, his imperious gaze carved into cold granite. Why rehash her first college date here, when she had moved so far beyond the negatives of relationships?

She moved on to Cave No. 20. The mural on the wall of the antechamber featured one thousand Buddhas, all outlined in gold leaf. For a moment she had difficulty focusing her camera: a thousand males seemed to be glaring at her from the past.

Perhaps she should check into a hotel and get a nice cold drink and see if the water was clean enough to take a dip in the pool and wash off the sweat. But no, she'd come to India for her spiritual transformation and nothing was going to distract her. It felt to Ana as it if had been a life-long dream to come to India, to experience a Sacred Automat. She was hungry for spirituality, and here were all the delicious religions that she loved—loved because on the surface, they didn't seem half as problematic as her own. In Ellora, almost all of them would be there: Buddhism, Hinduism, and even Jainism—the religion that predated both Buddhism and Hinduism.

The caves of Ellora—and the sculptures within them—and the sculptures within *them*—were carved directly into the hills of Sahyadri Mountain, at the heart of the Deccan plateau. The sun was beating against the tour bus windows; she could hardly wait to enter the cool caves where Durga would dance right before her out of the volcanic rock. All the gods and goddesses, with their torsos, bellies and breasts, in endless stretches of erotic spirituality, greeting the tourists as they arrived. These fabulous statues had all been carved over a period of six to seven centuries by 7,000 tantric artists called Karmakara-karu, "The wretched of the earth." She could almost hear the rhythm of their 7,000 chisels forming a mighty percussive symphony in the volcanic rock as they entered the first cave.

By concentrating on the sculpture before her in the womb of Ellora, she thought she could finally worship her own body "where all the gods resided," instead of hating her wide hips, her Jewish nose, her sunburned forehead and mosquito-bitten legs. Inside her, Krishna was playing his flute: Her lungs were two caves shimmering with sculptures in the golden light of her breathing. Then gently, she broke away from her meditation to listen to the charming music of small waterfalls sprinkling over the mouth of the cave. The tour guide was hurrying them back into the bus. She tried chanting "Om Tare Tuttare Ture Soha" under her breath to steady herself. She was beginning to feel a bit dizzy. By the time the bus arrived at the Gateway of India, divesting itself of its tired, hungry passengers in front of a ferry, she couldn't remember if it was "Om Tare Tuttare Ture Soha" or "Tuttare Tare Ture Toha Soha." She disembarked on Elephanta Island, muttering mixed-up syllables and feeling lost.

She could have spent the afternoon in Mumbai sipping chai in a beachside Colaba café, or even calling Behram to see if he was back from the ashram. Instead she found herself in front of an Elephanta cave, listening to the echoes of schoolchildren and their teacher and studying the sentry figures carved in stone. One of them was missing its abdomen and legs, the other had no face. She swiveled around, steadying herself on the porch of the main shrine. She watched the sailboats calmly traverse the blue-green waters of the harbor, feeling vaguely homesick.

Finally mustering the courage to enter the rock-cut temple, she let herself be comforted by its cool darkness. Against the back wall of the main hall several schoolchildren were staring up at the gigantic three heads of Lord Siva—"five meters tall," a guide was saying, his voice echoing against the side of the cave, "and at the base, it is thought that a scroll..." though Ana had drifted off, unable to convert meters into yards, feet or inches. The triple-headed

Siva reminded her of Philip, Karl and Robert, with their pouting lips, big heads and inflated egos all rolled into one. But she must not let these annoying thoughts keep her from appreciating the Hindu god any longer. She glanced back at the mouth of the cave behind her, at the blinding sunlight with its blistering heat. The cold stone floor sent a mystical chill up her spine: a priceless scroll lay buried at the base of the statue, and she herself was that scroll, waiting to be pulled out. Once she opened it, she would understand how her life had unraveled.

Ana had kept herself from eating and drinking for a week, hoping that abstinence would guarantee these much-needed visions or cosmic union with a goddess. In a way, she wanted to get a serious disease as badly as she had formerly wanted to get pregnant. A serious disease would bring her more sympathy and attention than a suicide attempt. And if it brought her death, she reasoned, she probably didn't deserve to survive the millions of spiritual superiors surrounding her. The sooner she perished, the sooner death would purify her for her next reincarnation.

But all she got was *Plasmodium vivax*, the most mild form of malaria. She was barely beginning to sweat when she saw the peak of Mt. Abu. Her eyes became a bit unfocused in the heat. This was the mystical Mt. Meru, center of the universe. As the taxi climbed the mountain, its white marble temples gleamed like pure diamonds.

The taxi dropped her at the base of the temples. Her way up the staircase was studded to the right and left with shrines to the mother goddess: water pots with breasts of molded clay. She desperately needed the milk of compassion, or even just a drink of water. For a moment she thought of breaking her double vow of suffering and fasting. But she was in too much of a hurry to achieve Samadhi at the top of the mountain, regardless of her state of dehydration.

If she could just make it to the top of the stairs, the Goddess Lakshmi would be waiting for her — Lakshmi, with six arms outstretched to embrace her. If she could just climb up without slipping on the milky marble steps. If she could just take another step without thinking too much about her unquenchable thirst. If she could just reach the top without throwing herself down the mountain the way she had thrown away her many talents. She must not fall downstairs, so close to the very top of Mt. Abu, just because she had no sense of what to do with her life... The earth was the third eye of the universe, and Mt. Abu was its pupil, seeing Ana for the very first time, as someone who was ready to take more than a dozen baby steps into herself.

Her lungs atrophying in the thin air, she had to move carefully, step by step. The first step was truly believing in the power of creativity to bring on a change in one's life.

Step by step, one chakra at a time: tripping on the red hem of a goddess' sari while the monkeys pulled at her hair, then skidding on a handful of amber marbles, tossed by the hot wind. On the next step, a child's orange lollipop shattered under her dusty sandal along with the piercing whine of a dentist's drill—or was she still a little girl with rotten teeth, half-unconscious under laughing gas, half wanting to scream?

An old man dressed in a white dhoti beckoned her towards the entrance of the temple. He was a bit impatient; some German and Japanese tourists were already taking off their shoes and stuffing their cameras into their backpacks.

She stood there, unable to do anything but catch her breath in angry gulps. On the landing above her, a yellow-eyed cat was egging her on, smiling with certainty that she was going to fall and break her neck. Her hair matted and tangled, her body stinking with sweat, her legs petrified like stone as she pressed them forward, one by one up the last of the steps, she began to feel a wet stain growing in her blue jeans. Of all the times to get her period. At least she wasn't pregnant, she thought to herself in defiance, eager for all biological clocks to stop ticking.

Over the entrance hung a sign stating in plain English as well as Hindi: "Menstruating ladies must refrain from entering the temple on pain of severe ill fortune." She hoped that no one could smell the blood. She was barely bleeding. What did they think she was going to do, stain the marble permanently red? All of these religions were so anti-female, afraid of women's natural cycles. They'd probably come up with the idea for this sign thousands of years before the invention of tampons. It was just as off-putting as the "Photography Not Allowed" sign right next to it. But a tour was forming at the entrance of the temple. For a few rupees, she could lose herself in the anonymity of the crowd.

The floor, walls and ceiling were completely covered with shimmering white marble. It was as if she had walked into a wedding cake—each slice of it another miraculous scene through which to turn and twirl, trying to see every god, goddess and snowflake carved of marble, in every cell and on every niche of the ceiling.

"The marble was carried up the mountain on the backs of elephants," the tour guide was explaining. "It was carved by fifteen hundred stonemasons and..." But Ana was drifting into the golden heart of a lotus like a bee descending a translucent staircase of white petals. She looked down at the marble floor. A red drop of blood fell on the floor in slow motion, making its way into the stone. She quickly hid it with her sandaled foot, hoping the tour guide wouldn't notice. In Cell No. 43, the goddess Lakshmi was coming to life, reaching out with lotus blossoms in two of her four hands. She was no longer made of filigreed marble: she was blazing out of the temple's white, wintry fairyland in full color. Ana calculated quickly: This was the Goddess of Wealth, capable of bestowing millions of rupees for feature-length production, teeming with computer generated imagery.

As she took her first step towards Lakshmi, the cold marble beneath her right foot trembled, dissolving into a green lily pad, sprinkled with early morning dew. Frogs sang their ragas around her; a small herd of deer paused to listen. Her left foot was landing on a lotus in slow motion; the lotus grew larger and larger, blossoming with an infinite number of petals.

She found herself on her back, reclining on a gentle pink couch of petals. She leaned over and looked at her reflection in the cool green pond, amazed that her blue jeans had given way to a pale yellow sari. The cameras that had hung around her neck had been replaced by a strand of incomparable pearls and star sapphires. The necklace was swaying along with waist-long black hair as her tiny feet floated on the surface of the water. Terracotta lamps filled with ghee swirled gleefully around her, while half a dozen handmaidens paid homage at either side. All of them were singing in Hindi.

No longer did Ana need to film the Goddess: She *was* the Goddess. Mt. Abu was her spiritual home, center of the universe. Lakshmi née Ana found herself raising one of her four immortal arms to bestow her blessings on the world of mortals, including the busload of tourists and the tour guide. A pot of gold sat on her lap.

The tour guide was urging her to hurry before it got dark. Lakshmi turned her golden face in his direction, her eyes more glorious than a thousand suns. She held out one of her two magic lotuses over the guide, blessing him in his dull white dhoti while another hand trickled golden coins in his direction. From her veil of midnight tresses, she uncovered her vermillion mouth. "I have reached the top of the staircase to Samadhi," she sweetly informed him. "Won't you join me?"

"You are mistaken: It is well known that the Ganges is the flowing staircase to Heaven," said the tour guide. "The Ganges is 500 miles from here. You must bathe in the Ganges on Thursday! You come down from that mountain now!"

Ana was determined to stick it out. She held onto the pot of gold on her lap with all her might. But the tour guide had eradicated the divinity in her. She looked down, ashamed of her delusions. She opened her guide book and used it as a fan, surveying the panorama below.

Over the balustrade, the pale green plains of Rajasthan glimmered in the heat. A German couple gathered their backpacks from the cloakroom and surreptitiously took photos of each other in front of the sunset. She waited for the night to swallow them up, ignoring the tourists who departed on an air-conditioned bus.

She could barely see the plains any more, let alone the monkeys or mosquitoes. The dizzier she felt, the more treacherous the long climb down, but she still felt she could make it down the slippery steps without falling. It was just a matter of concentration, step by step without slipping, like the temple's artisans who had chipped away at the luminous marble for almost fifteen years, thousands of them chipping away at the marble until it was eggshell-thin, never once letting one of their hammers slip.

On the two hundred fiftieth step, she took off her sweat-soaked tee-shirt and her blood-soaked jeans like a snake shedding its skin. She had reached the dark womb of the Goddess. She looked around in terror. The Dark Goddess, Bhadrakali was riding a wild tiger, swinging her amniotic sac. Ana was trapped inside. Bhadrakali kept swinging the sac by the umbilical cord around and around like a lasso. Finally it landed on Ana's own corpse. The tiger pounced forward, its sharp claws digging into Ana's soul. She began to scream through the tunnels of her many life cycles, echoing into eternity while Bhadrakali guzzled wine and blood, kicking dead consorts left and right.

Ana still had Behram Sinha's phone number tucked away between the back pages of her passport. Someone must have called him for help: somehow they had managed to return her to Mumbai. She vaguely remembered Behram's mother's servants looking after her while she succumbed to a raging fever, though Behram himself was nowhere to be seen. Behram's father was playing the sitar — a Bhairava raga in a fourteen beat cycle — while his mother kept time with her rhythmic clapping. The god Bhairava danced up to Ana's bed besmeared with ashes, his hair a fiery spectacle of matted serpents, and wearing a necklace of skulls. He fanned her with the crescent moon, his smile ghost-white, his teeth like silver tridents, his mouth full of nectar, and his warm hands poured sunsets and sunrises onto her eyes like golden coins. Ana felt herself slipping away into ecstasy. A lion was licking her face, but it was only a washrag. Her face was like a blue cloud. She awaited death like a husband on a bridal bed, thinking of herself as finally blessed. Bhairava was a fickle lover, however. He was counting his necklace of skulls like the pearls of Chéri.

Ana wasn't capable of dying: her vision of eternity was too limited. She was destined to recover, probably completely, after a long, tedious return across time zones on the discount flight. Her knees banged against the seat in front of her every time she coughed. With her dirty knapsack full of mostly unused tape stock and cameras below the seat in front of her, there was nowhere for her to put her feet. Meanwhile, lotus blossoms were drooping out of her pineal gland.

Her father picked her up at the airport. He tried his best to start a conversation. On the Hutchinson River Parkway, they listened to Metallica and Van Halen instead.

She had wanted to find a loft-sitting gig somewhere in Soho, but a month of recurring fevers kept Ana sequestered in the split-level that stank of furniture polish and bleach. *Oh well, look at Rimbaud,* Ana wrote in her spiral-bound diary, after feelings of disgrace and spiritual failure had flitted into consciousness. Between his wild poetry, his bouts of absinthe drinking and Ethiopian gun running, he always managed to retreat to his mother's house in the South of France, when samadhi wasn't forthcoming. "My life is worn out," Rimbaud had written. "And we shall exist by amusing ourselves, by dreaming of our monstrous loves and our fantastic universes." *It's practically the same thing,* she wrote, hoping to transcend the suburbs with some haiku or other as she passed out into a dreamless sleep, her rollerball pen dropping by the side of the bed with a small clatter.

Madelyn found herself in a state of constant interruption. Whenever she so much as thought about finishing that cobalt blue painting, it was time to put another cold compress on her daughter's forehead. With one daughter home sick with malaria, the other dead, Madelyn found herself grieving for her own life as much as for her daughters'. She poured a Scotch to mask the question whether she'd ever really wanted children—or had she been forced to love them?

It would have been so difficult to forge her own way as an artist in the 1950's, when she was only expected to raise a family. As for her art, it was a helluva lot better than thousands of other wives' and mothers', painting portraits of unhappy clowns across America, lavishing hundreds of hours to get the white face make-up perfect. She'd managed to graduate from shellac-coated still lifes that embalmed the kitchen produce, to the serious abstracts that had won the top prize for two years running at the Westchester Art Show. All these housewives painted until three o'clock in the afternoon, every last one of them including Madelyn, until it was time to pick up the kids. As for her daughters, what was Vickie but a memory?...but she must not think of that. At least she had Timothy. What a consolation. She might have grandchildren yet. Here was Ana, her other grown up child, still needing mothering every hour on the hour, babbling nonsense and dribbling orange sherbet down her chin till it stained her nightgown.

As she leaned over her daughter's bed to change another compress, her hair tickled Ana's cheek. Madelyn had put her hair into a blonde page boy with a curling iron, and her hair smelled like burnt Christmas cookies. Ana moaned in feverish sleep at the sickening scent.

She remembered their cookie-making marathons at age six. It was very, very hot inside the kitchen. Mommy would have to open the window. They couldn't go near the oven. The smell of ginger-bread and sugar cookies would travel through the neighborhood.

Everyone would know they celebrated Christmas. Gingerbread men would stare at them through raisin eyes.

"Mommy, you're hurting the dough!" Ana squealed. She was six. Madelyn was branding numbers on sticky, pale yellow flesh. The girls covered the shapes she cut out with red and green sprinkles, and then their mother put them in the oven.

"I want to go buy milk," said Madelyn, zipping her London Fog over her pregnant belly. "Any minute now, it's gonna start raining cats and dogs." Vickie the toddler looked up in the sky, but nothing was barking or meowing.

"Silly! This isn't a storm with animals." Ana informed her sister. "It's a real storm." They watched out the window in identical smock dresses as their mother backed out of the driveway. The black clouds spit out candy-colored ribbons of lightning. Ana laughed at the thunder and lightning that terrified her little sister.

"You're a three year old baby, a baby, a baby!" she taunted Vickie. It was raining so hard, their dark, curly hair was getting wet. Ana struggled to close the window, but it wouldn't budge. Mommy was taking much longer than if she had just gone into her studio and closed the door on them. Ana stood on top of the piano bench on tiptoes and took down the curtains that were soaking wet. This was going to make Mommy mad for sure. Maybe she could hide them in the closet. The rug was getting wet, too, and it was probably the end of the world.

Then—*big* lightning bolt! Vickie grabbed her big sister's hand and held on tightly.

"See the lightning? Know what it means? The world is going to end," said Ana.

Vickie was screaming so hard, it frightened Ana. Then clouds of smoke came out of the oven. Ana started crying too. The house was going to catch on fire, and they were going to burn up, just like the cookies.

Ana and Vickie ran outside without bothering to put on their yellow rain ponchos, crying in the rain as their mother's car pulled into the driveway.

"What's all the fuss about?" said Madelyn. She'd taken a few extra minutes to go to the art store: they were having a sale on palette knives. She tweaked Vickie's wet curls, then held Vickie' and Ana's hands tightly as she took the girls back into the house, saying, "Someday you'll think of all this as harmless and silly."

Then Madelyn smelled the burnt cookies and saw the wet drapes. Ana tried to blame her little sister, but it didn't work. Ana was going to get a big spanking when Daddy came home, no matter what, their mother said. But whether or not she got spanked, nobody could remember, because Mommy started going into labor. Only no baby came out.

In manic rushes of fever, she emailed the cosmos for assistance.

To: Maheshvari@infinity+.com (Maheshvari)
From: Anachronic@lovemorph.com
Subject: Words are not enough

Maheshvari, Mother Goddess!
    Help me to see beyond myself. Let your Bull carry me through your cool waters into Enlightenment. Let me not gush forth like menstrual blood from the black hole in your universe. Please, give birth to me.

To: Lakshmi@infinity+.com (Lakshmi)
From: Anachronic@lovemorph.com
Subject: Grant Request

Lakshmi, Goddess of Wealth!
    Your backing is what I need. Beaucoup money for my Goddess Project. Between you and the Rockefeller Founda-

tion, I'd personally prefer your support. It's not just that I need some endorsement, it's my level of debt, far above sea level. Please have your elephant pull me out of this ocean of debt. Its backwaters are full of mosquitoes after a monsoon rain. How can you look so peaceful with your carved marble smile, holding onto your lotus, when everywhere, people are hungry? Respect all living things, even the mosquito that bit me.

The fever! Give me water. Give me medicine. Give me $250,000.

Respectfully,
Ana Fried, Director,
The Goddess Project

To:	*Vishnu@infinity+.com (Vishnu)*
cc:	*Lakshmi@infinity+.com (Lakshmi)*
From:	*Anachronic@lovemorph.com*
Subject:	*Cosmic Activity*

Creator of the Universe! I see what you and Lakshmi are doing, lying together under a parasol of cobras. You are too busy making love to her to notice me. Can't the world wait a minute?

To:	*Tara@infinity+.com (Tara)*
From:	*Anachronic@lovemorph.com*
Subject:	*Reach Me From Across the Ocean of Existence*

You see me burning with four eyes: one on each of your palms. Yet you do nothing.

To:	*Indrakshi@infinity+.com (Indrakshi)*
From:	*Anachronic@lovemorph.com*
Subject:	*See Me*

Indrakshi, Mother of the Universe!

Please don't just sit there on your lotus. Its petals are studded with eyes. Are they all blind, or what?

To:	*Vajravahari@infinity+.com (Vajravahari)*
From:	*Anachronic@lovemorph.com*
Subject:	*Seasons in Hell*

Sow-headed Goddess, dancing on your six-pointed star! Where is your wisdom in making me lie on a mattress strewn with the rotting corpses of my lovers? Take me out of your muddy trough. Let me dance with you in ecstasy, crushing delusions with our feet!

To:	*Bhadrakali@infinity+.com (Bhadrakali)*
cc:	*Vajravahari@infinity+.com (Vajravahari)*
From:	*Anachronic@lovemorph.com*
Subject:	*Severed Head*

Sister, I see you standing on a lotus blossom. You are holding the severed head of the creator of the world. Throw it to me! Please play ball!

There was a clamminess to the cold compress that Madelyn had placed on Ana's forehead before proceeding to vacuum the room. She shook her head to the side trying to shake it off, but it clung to her damp skin like a snail to an asphalt road in the summer heat.

"Mom, can I have a glass of water?"

Madelyn turned off the vacuum cleaner. "An adult child can't walk a couple of steps to the sink?"

But no, she'd have to deal with one more distraction. Madelyn made her way to the master bathroom, her pale pink terrycloth slippers plopping against the rug in the hall. She rushed back to the bed with the glass of water, and leaned over Ana, smelling like turpentine.

"Now fix your bangs," said Madelyn, looking at her daughter as if she were a model to be readjusted. She applied a fingertip of spit to the black, unwashed bangs. Ana lay in bed unable to move, thinking of shaving her head and becoming a Buddhist nun. Her mother returned to the vacuum cleaner, vacuuming Ana's room with angry jabs, pulling up Ana's identity and stripping it of every atom of dirt. She and Marty had sent that ungrateful jerk to Yale for nothing. All that hype about a thousand leaders. Ana had become a blade of grass to be trampled on, shat on by those dogs.

Ana drifted back into an uneasy sleep, interrupted now and then by the sound of the vacuum in more and more distant rooms. She dreamed that their home was not a home, but a homeless shelter. Ana was making gingerbread cookies, just like Mom's: one batch for the deep freeze, and the rest mixed with a light cord used for strangling people. She rolled out one huge cookie and wrote on the dough like a cuneiform tablet. It was fragile, and broke. Her father was picking up the pieces and trying to eat them, in between dental appointments. She thought she could hear the dentist's drill, but it was the roar of the vacuum cleaner. Madelyn was back, having forgotten to vacuum under the bed. When she opened her eyes, her mother was leaning over her again, dust and sweat mixed in with the smell of turpentine.

"You're a huge disappointment to us." Why did Madelyn always have to have the last word? "All those men you paraded in here. You had to say such nasty things to them before they even met me, didn't you? Coming in here with their sneaky expressions, not even able to look me in the eye. And you expected me to be hospitable? Always cleaning and cooking in preparation for nothing!"

But Ana was no longer listening. She was trying desperately to sleep and return to another dimension of fever.

To: *Bhairava@infinity+.com (Bhairava)*
From: *Anachronic@lovemorph.com*
Subject: *Black Fire*

I am burning in the black fire of your matted hair. I feel your lips as you raise my skull to drink my burning thoughts. Please reply quickly. Send me your chauffeured car.

To: *Shiva@infinity+.com (Shiva)*
From: *Parvati@infinity+.com (Parvati)*
Subject: *Ana Fried*

Answer me at once, or I will smear your erection with the ashes that I gather from Ana's burning flesh.

To: *Kali@infinity+.org (Kali)*
From: *Anachronic@lovemorph.com*
Subject: *Help!*

Ma! Mommy? Ma! Kali Ma!

When the fevers finally subsided, Ana decided to stay in New York for a while. Faithfully taking medication, she worked her way up from secretary to paralegal with the idea of eventually going to law school. Most of her salary went to pay for a good psychologist and group therapy, as she was determined to make some progress towards a full and normal life. She found a cute little apartment in Brooklyn, which she decorated in pastels, a far cry from the Masaccio mural of her rebellious years. Ana dates occasionally, but none of it's worth writing home about; it pales in comparison to her pillow book, which she keeps in a box on a shelf in the dark hallway, but pulls out from time to time.

AFTERWORD:

by Edwin Talbot, Jr., Ph.D., Class of '73

I saw Ana Fried at our last Yale Reunion. I remember her as being a lot of fun back in the day. Her hair was still long and black, though she'd put on a bit of weight and my wife remarked that perhaps the black was no longer her natural color. Most of our classmates have been married for quite some time by now if not yet divorced or gay; at first she stood on the outside of our conversations, looking impatient and bored by the usual chitchat. By the time the provost's reception rolled around, she'd already embarrassed quite a few of us by handing out some hand-made placards in solidarity with the Yale dining hall workers, as if that weren't embarrassing enough at our graduation. I supposed she half-expected us to hoist the signs in the air. You know the old saying, plus ça change…

At the wine tasting, she flitted from table to table and bottle to bottle, asking for the whereabouts of Tammi Bradley, the illustrious eye surgeon who unfortunately passed away last winter. (The Château Margaux was excellent, by the way.) She kept insisting—loudly—that she be added to the panel, "Global Women and Yale," to be held the following afternoon. However, the name Ana Fried was unfamiliar to our two co-moderators, the Hon. Dr. Alison Truffet of Oxford (Yale summa cum laude, 1973) and Alexandra de Hidalgo Kurzman (Yale '73, Yale Law '77), South American Executive Director of the Global Bank. We were very pleased to see Dr. Joyce Takahashi serving on the panel, however; Joyce has recently come back to us after years of tireless work with a pharmaceutical company in Africa.

Ana kept up the table-hopping at dinner, ostensibly trying to raise funds for a feminist film of some kind during the keynote speech by the Master of Calhoun. It must have been a frustrating defeat for her, but then, today's bleak economy sometimes makes one do things one later regrets, though we wish her luck. In any case, Ana was nowhere to be seen at yesterday's panels, the golf tournament, or the Yale Art Gallery, which has been holding a month-long retrospective of Yale-directed feature films from the '60s, '70s, and '80s, curated by that wonderful Academy Award-winner from our class, Nicky McDermott. She probably took an early train back to Manhattan before the fun began, or perhaps a plane to the West Coast. She didn't leave her card with any of us, and no one seems to be able to locate her on Facebook, Twitter or LinkedIn. Maybe she's changed her last name. But we all remember Ana as something of a character, an arty type with incredible determination.

CPSIA information can be obtained
at www.ICGtesting.com
Printed in the USA
FSOW03n0443161117
41054FS